THE AFFAIR

LAURA BROWN

Thank you so much for taking the time to read my work. If you enjoyed, please consider leaving me a review on Amazon or Goodreads, or telling your friends, colleagues and/or mother-in-law.

Dedication

I could make this dedication a soppy essay about my partner or family, but I'm not. This book is dedicated to me. (Well, you too, dear reader.) I've come to the conclusion recently that only I can depend on myself, only I can believe in myself fully. I am all that I need. You are all that *you* need. Once you can truly appreciate yourself for who you are, and what you can do, nothing will stand in your way.

Don't apologize for that. Trust yourself. Trust that you absolutely can make it to the places you deserve to be. Trust in the process of your unique mind and beautiful soul. You can do it, and you *will*.

Chapter One

MARIE

They say the grass is always greener on the other side, but it's all a matter of perspective, if you ask me. You'd think it *would* be greener, if you could afford the upkeep of several acres of Saint Augustine grass. The variety preferred by America's most exclusive golf courses for its jewel-toned vibrancy. It's thickly knitted, uniform texture. It's resilience.

Why on Earth would you know that, one might ask? Since I got married two years ago, I've had very few worthwhile things to occupy myself with and life consists of many hobbies. Pottery, yoga, French lessons, interior design, landscaping. There are endless hours to fill while my husband, Nicholas, is out in the wider world, busy running his empire. I'll get to that later.

I'm fortunate enough to live amongst the top one percent. Meaning: I'm never going to have to work for a living. I'm sure most women, most *people* in fact, would be thrilled at the prospect of never having to lift a finger for the rest of their lives. Their every whim catered to, never worrying about checking the price tag, because you *know* you can afford it. Having literally anything your heart desires. Let me stop you there.

Don't get me wrong, to never want for anything is great. I am lucky because being provided for gives you the type of security most people chase all their lives. But *there's* the catch. What have I got to chase now? There is no motivation to *do* anything! Us wives attend brunches that last until late afternoon, arrange fundraisers for organizations we don't even care about, marinade ourselves in peroxide and dermal filler, waiting for our husbands to come home.

We have no aspirations, no goals. We are all incurably bored.

I'd already decided long ago I wasn't going to be one of them. I was going to continue exploring avenues until I found my niche, something to *do*. And, let's just say, landscaping wasn't quite it.

The particular lawn that inspired this bit of speculation was vivid green and lush, spongy beneath my feet. As grass went, it was a pretty nice stretch.

I studied the reflection of the clouds in the surface of my tea as idle chatter swirled around me. It was one of those unusually hot, overcast days in California, where the sky is so close it could brush the top of your head, heat straining to break through the late-afternoon grayness.

I was stuck listening to a group of my husband's friend's wives discuss their latest philanthropic exploits and, if their expectant gazes were anything to go by, I was up next.

Olivia Taylor, model and star of her own reality TV show, was throwing her first baby shower that afternoon. Rich, young and pretty, she was everything a girl could aspire to be. Those same girls would sell their souls just to be photographed with her.

Olivia had personally invited me to her shower over social media private message, despite us never having met before. She wasn't being overfriendly, I knew the game by now. Having me come to her event would create a bigger media storm than she originally anticipated and *'just imagine how much a photograph of us rubbing cheeks would go for!'*

Personally, I hated this kind of attention and didn't approve of others who used this method for popularity. In fact, I hated the whole concept of popularity in the first place. The women in this 'higher bracket' of society usually only came to these kinds of events to look good in the public eye.

Maintaining their image had rules; go to the hottest parties where you don't really know anybody. Donate a quarter of a million dollars to your own charity because the *'abused animals of Los Angeles'* will benefit from the money (after the deductions and various other costs that might just make you richer). Visit the children's hospital, but make sure to only be photographed with the good-looking sick kids and take care not to get closer than five feet to an actual child, on the off chance they're infected with something deadly and contagious.

From the outside, I was one of those women; a snobbish, wealthy socialite. A member of their secretive and complex inner circle. I was in. But I was also way, way out.

The women at the baby shower, all wearing matching four-hundred-dollar silk pajamas, sat in a semi-circle around Olivia, who was beaming and holding her champagne flute of sparkling apple juice aloft as though it were an Oscar.

"I'd just like to thank all of you, my dear, *dear* friends, for being here today. I'm so grateful to be able to share this moment with you all!" *Yeah, right. You are only grateful for the opportunity to make the front page of TMZ online. And for the expensive gifts all your 'dear friends' have brought you.*

As she began opening the first overly pink and perfectly wrapped package, I stifled a yawn, my mind drifting to thoughts of the evening before.

Nic had flown us out to my favorite restaurant in New York to celebrate our second anniversary. Three years married to the love of my life. Well, the only love I've ever had in my life but that's basically the same thing, right?

He ordered a few bottles of champagne, and we drank and danced in our hotel suite. Nights like that reminded me why I had fallen in love with him. We had our share of problems, like any married couple, rumors of his infidelity being the prime concern. But we loved each other. Whatever came our way, we could work through it.

"Marie?" A hand on my arm brought my attention back to the present and to a vaguely familiar face beside me.

"Hi, how are you?" the woman continued, in a hushed tone.

"Hello, I'm fine. How are you?" We air-kissed both cheeks before drawing back to smile at each other. I took her in, elfin features, highlighted blond bob, trying to figure out how I knew her so I didn't make a complete fool of myself.

"You look absolutely gorgeous," She beamed at me, displaying two rows of teeth so perfectly white and even they couldn't be anything else but veneers.

"Thank you, you look lovely too," I replied.

"I was wondering if you would answer a few questions for me? I'm writing a few guest columns for *OK!* and I just *had* to get coverage of this event. It's all anyone's been talking about for weeks!"

Ooh, that jogged my memory! This woman was married to one of Nic's acquaintances; we met at a party last month. She crossed her legs, showing off her Chanel flats from three seasons ago and gave me a big, presumptuous smile. Those shoes would mark her down in this world. A working woman; someone to take pity on, someone to whisper about behind her back.

"Sure. Come find me after Olivia has opened the presents, okay?"

"Thank you," she released my hand. I hadn't realized she'd taken it.

I was used to people acting this way toward me and not just because I was famous. Even before I'd met Nic, people would make special allowances for me because of the way I looked. And I hated it.

My momma forced me into pageants when I was a child because, according to her, the connections it would make for me would be irreplaceable. It took me until I was eight years old to realize that was not who I wanted to be. To have people being nice to you just because you were perceived as pretty was ridiculous.

After what felt like a very lengthy, drawn-out gift unwrapping, appropriately punctuated with girlish oohs and ahhs, the reporter woman, whose name I still couldn't recall, pulled me away to a corner of the garden.

She handed me a flute of Champagne before shoving a voice recorder under my nose.

"So, Marie. How do you and Olivia know one another?"

"We actually met at Paris Fashion Week last year, front row for Karl Lagerfeld. We hit it off right away."

"What was your reaction when she told you she was pregnant?"

"I was over the moon for her. I'm so glad she and James are starting a family together. They of all people deserve happiness."

This was all crap; I'd never even met her husband. I was in the practice of doing my research before an event, just in case. It often came in useful, like right now.

"You and your husband have been married for... two years now? Are babies in the cards for you soon, too?"

"Oh, no! I mean, we both love children and want them someday, but not right now. I'm enjoying life too much," I let out a practiced, light-hearted laugh and the reporter did the same. Contrary to my reply, Nic had been asking me ever more insistently when I think I'd be ready. I was running out of ways to tell him that I didn't know.

"Do you think your high-profile status is going to have any influence on your future kids?"

"Of course. It's going to be hard for any parent to bring their children up in the spotlight. It's very difficult to find balance between living a normal life and the demanding work schedule and social scene. I guess Nic and I are lucky, we aren't as in demand as Olivia and her family. From the paparazzi to enthusiastic fans, it sounds like it can become a little too intense sometimes."

Her demeanor changed subtly, a determined look crossing her features. Why did I suddenly have a bad feeling in my gut?

"Is that why you have security with you?"

"What?" I turned and spotted a figure slouching in the shade at the back gate of the property. From a distance, it was hard to identify any of his features, but the way he held himself gave him away. That and his mop of untidy, blond hair that *he* thought made him look like the lead singer of Nickelback circa 2001, but gave off a stronger vibe of grotty cowboy wannabe slash hobo. Chuck was one of Nicholas' closest friends, and although not officially security, his purpose in life recently seemed to be to irritate me.

"I wasn't aware. That must be Nic's doing. Discretion is not something he's known for." Cue another onset of fake laughter.

"Speaking of discretion, what about those other rumors flying around?" Nic's infidelities; a topic I wished I vetoed before agreeing to this.

"Just rumors," I replied with a tight smile, although I wanted to scream to the world my accusations. There *were* stories flying around, photographs so blurry it would be hard to distinguish even the gender of the people in them. I knew Nic was being unfaithful to me, but it wasn't a full-blown affair. He wouldn't embarrass me like that. Or more importantly, himself.

The scandals never hit the papers because, of all things, Nicholas was clever. He was the founder of his own multi-billion-dollar company, he knew what these women could do to his reputation. On paper, he would appear the perfect husband. In actuality, he thought more with his dick than his brain.

He hadn't done anything unforgivable. I'd always thought of myself as a reasonable woman. Yes, it made me angry to think of him with other women. It made my blood boil. But he said he would stop. He said I was more important.

"Haven't you seen this photograph?" She handed me her large, touch-screen phone. I zoomed in on Nic and the girl. And she was a girl. She couldn't have been much older than eighteen.

I tapped the image twice to zoom in on their reflection in the mirrored wall behind them. Nic's hand was very clearly up her skirt, cupping her crotch as they both smiled dazedly for the camera.

I could feel the wedding rings heavy on my finger, the weight of diamond-encrusted band pulling me down. Tying me to him as I remembered the promises we made to each other that day, bound together by more than mere words. The words I heard echoing in my ears every time I found out he'd done it again.

Mumbling some kind of apology, I made my way in the direction of the backyard gate. I needed to get away for a bit, go somewhere quiet and collect my thoughts. And that was virtually impossible in this heat.

Out of the corner of my eye, I saw Olivia almost trip over the hem of her pajama bottoms in her effort to reach me.

"Marie! Honey, we *must* get a picture before you go!"

"I'm really sorry, Olivia. Something's come up. I'll message you, okay? Enjoy the rest of your shower," I turned before she had the chance to speak again and hurried out the gate.

Once I'd had a moment alone to breathe, it took only a few seconds for the shock to turn into searing anger.

I made my way to the car which, regrettably, I found Chuck leaning against, his ever-present smirk firmly in place.

I raised my eyebrows at him, hoping that he would get the message that I was pissed and he should leave me alone. I was really, *really*, not in the mood for this right now.

"Better watch who you're talking to there, missy."

"What?" I snapped, reaching around him for the car door handle.

"That's Diana Scott."

I blinked.

"*Gossip columnist*?" He added when I still didn't show any recognition.

Oh shit! I should have known something was up when she'd started sifting for dirt in my personal life instead of sticking to a line of questioning that was more relevant.

I pushed past Chuck, climbed into my SUV and drove. My mind reeling back to when I'd first met Nic, searching for clues to what went wrong. To why I wasn't enough for him.

The first time I saw Nicholas was in my Daddy's house. I remember thinking it was odd. Daddy never usually brought his work home with him.

The house I grew up in was a large, white-painted building with shutters and a wrap-around porch; an old-style plantation house that belonged in the pages of a romance novel. Riaton Springs, a small town in southern Missouri, right on the county line bordering Tennessee.

Nic stepped in through the wide, oak door and saw me standing at the foot of the staircase, his steel-colored eyes locking onto mine and a slow, wide satisfied grin spreading across his face. It was the first time I saw that smile and it drew me in, just as he'd intended.

"Marie, honey. This is Mr Hayes. He's here to discuss those land contracts I mentioned to you earlier."

I smiled at Daddy; he never kept me in the dark about anything.

"Nicholas, this is my daughter, Marie."

If anything, my parents raised me to be polite.

"Nice to meet you, Sir," I stepped forward and extended my hand for him to shake but Nic captured my outstretched hand and gently laid a kiss there.

"The pleasure is all mine." My heart missed a few beats. He was the most handsome man I'd ever laid eyes on. His hand engulfed mine, radiating warmth as he held on for a few seconds longer than necessary before letting go.

That very evening the telephone rang.

"Good evening, Miss. I'm calling to request your company for dinner tomorrow evening," His tone was polite and ever so slightly amused. I was picturing his mouth curved into that heart-stopping smile.

"Who is this?" I feigned confusion.

"The devilishly good-looking man you met this afternoon."

"I don't remember meeting anyone who fits *that* description."

"He remembers meeting you. Actually, he hasn't been able to stop thinking about it."

"Oh, really?"

"Really."

Right there, with the phone hanging from my ear, I blushed all the way to my toes. Naturally, I said no. I wasn't going to make it easy for him. If he wanted me, he'd have to give chase.

Little did I know, Nicholas was not the type of man you said no to. He was used to getting his own way. All that week I received all kinds of gifts delivered to my house, flowers and trinkets wrapped in sheets of tissue paper and ribboned boxes. When I finally gave in, Nic took me to the fanciest restaurant in town, first sending me a beautiful pair of shoes and a designer dress to wear that evening.

Of course, I knew this kind of attention came at a price. One I wasn't willing to pay unless I felt assured that there was some kind of future with him. Call me old-fashioned, but I wasn't selling myself out for anybody. However, not once that evening did I feel the pressure that he expected more from me than my company.

Nic was so suave, playing the part of the perfect gentleman. He was a lot older than the boys I typically dated and I was completely blown away by his charm.

I didn't know at the time that he was a high-profile business magnate and our little dinner had flown under the radar. It wasn't until our third date he told me the extent of what he did.

A month later, he asked me to marry him. Nic reserved the royal suite at the Ritz in London. A trail of rose petals and candles led the way into the vast bedroom, where he got down on one knee and offered me the biggest diamond I'd ever set eyes on, and the promise of a lifetime of happiness.

Momma had said I needed time and experience to handle a man like Nic, although she didn't approve of him in general because he was 'new money.' She had meant I needed to grow up, to be able to recover some parts of myself when we eventually fell apart because that was what a 'godless marriage' was destined for. Being young and foolish, I wanted him, and no one would've been able to tell me otherwise.

A few months after the overly extravagant wedding, I found evidence of every wife's nightmare; another woman's panties inside the pocket of his suit jacket. I went crazy, tearing our room to bits, punching every bit of him I could reach until I screamed myself hoarse.

Nicholas would tell me they were whores, that they didn't mean a thing. He would never do it again. Now, I realized we'd had that conversation one time too many. Maybe I thought he would change and we could go back to loving each other the way we used to.

I felt so weak. Even after the third time I'd caught him out, I still didn't leave.

He'd take me in his arms and slowly undress me, kissing me behind the ear in a way that he knew drove me wild, whispering how I was his girl and nothing could ever change that. Nicholas would remind me that everything I had was because of him; all our possessions, our home, our status, by buying me some extravagant gift to make up for the fact he didn't want to stick around to deal with sorting out his mess.

I felt a kind of slow-building pressure, like I was getting ready to explode. Sometimes I'd think I *could* leave him. I'd got as far as packing a bag but then where would I go? I'd dropped out of high school two semesters before graduation to marry Nic. I wouldn't be welcomed back in my mother's house, not without having to admit to her that she was right. Being subjected to daily confession and the ridicule of her church group were not activities I relished the thought of.

My life was over the top, blown out of proportion on an epic scale. I had everything I could ever want and more. It was overwhelming. I felt suffocated, drowning in our shallow materialism. Scratch that, I had everything in the world that anyone could ever possibly want. Except his word.

My phone rang, snapping me out of my dark thoughts. It was Jean, seemingly my ally in all this and most days, Nic's only voice of reason. We'd become good friends over the years, but I always had to remember to leave some kind of filter up. He was Nic's friend, too. I swiped the screen to answer the call and put it on speaker.

"Sweetheart, come home now, 'kay?" Jean spoke in the soft Cajun drawl of his home state. It was comforting to me, close as it was to my own southern roots.

"Why, Jean? Why should I have to put up with this?" My body felt completely numb, not the most desirable when driving.

"We both know he's an asshole. He's dishonest and hardheaded and proud... But he loves you. Sometimes marriage is about understanding and working out your differences."

"Staying out all night and finding used thongs in jacket pockets aren't differences! He needs to change. Or I'm gone."

"He will, sweet. Go home so you can talk this out. Avoiding your problems don't solve 'em." Wise words if I ever did hear them. Damn, why did Jean always have to talk so much sense?

"Fine," I spat out.

"Drive safe," he replied before I cut him off.

I thought of the parts of Nic I did love. Sighing, I looked again at my platinum wedding rings, the diamonds glinting even in the dull light against the ivory skin of my fingers.

Sighing again, I made a U-turn and headed back the way I came.

It was well after nightfall by the time I pulled up on the driveway. The house stood dark and uninviting, intimidatingly conspicuous against the navy velvet backdrop of heavy cloud cover. I slipped through the front door, hoping to make it to bed without running into Nic. I'd deal with him in the morning. Right now, I was too tired for one of our blowout arguments, thanks to being woken up at the crack of dawn for the flight back from New York.

No such luck. The double doors to the main lounge were thrown wide open, where I was very sure Nicholas would be waiting for me. I'd have to walk right past them if I wanted to get upstairs.

Letting out a frustrated huff of breath, I contemplated sneaking back out and entering through the back door before telling myself not to be a yellow-bellied pushover and just get it over with.

Nic was sprawled out across the expansive leather couch, sipping from a crystal glass with only a fine line of bourbon remaining. He wasn't drunk yet, but he'd had enough to stop the tremor in his hands. What do they call it? One to take the edge off?

Nicholas was accompanied by an entourage at all times; associates, he called them. He needed their advice on everything from business deals to what color tie to wear each day. That evening it was Jean Thibodeaux. I had a soft spot for Jean. He didn't seem to be operating under an ulterior motive, and he was one of the only men in Nic's circle who wasn't a sexist asshole.

Most of Nicholas' friends were like clones of each other with a different paint job. Think elitist prick. Checklist; superior attitude to women, check. Ego bigger than a house, check. Blond bobblehead of a wife, check. Forgive me if I sound rude, but I just didn't buy into the illusion that is Hollywood they way everyone else around here did.

It was a power show; who had the nicest car, the biggest bank balance, the hottest young thing on their arm. My only real friend in all this was Jean. He was one of the only ones who seemed human.

"Ma'am," he greeted me in his thick accent, tipping his trilby on his way out. That was another thing about Jean; he could judge the atmosphere of the room in an instant. His specialty was dealing with Nicholas' temperamental moods. Most importantly, he knew when it was time to leave.

Nic stayed seated on the couch, reclining back into the leather.

"You've been busy today," He didn't sound angry, more amused. I stayed standing by the doorway. I felt like a child being scolded for skipping school.

"I just went for a drive," I wasn't in the mood to argue.

"Over state lines, I hear?" His expression was hard to read, almost emotionless.

I snorted in disbelief, "From who? Do I need your permission to go out?"

"What you do is my business; you're my wife." He had an authoritative tone, like it was a matter of fact.

"Why didn't you come and get me, then?" My chin jutted out in defiance.

"I had more important things to attend to. Got a big deal going down in the next few days and I can't be running after you whenever you feel needy," He swallowed the last of his drink in one.

"Did you stop to wonder why, Nic?"

"Is this about those panties again, because I swear…"

"No," I cut across him, "It's about a picture someone showed me today."

"What picture?" he demanded, having the audacity to look confused. As if he didn't know he was in the wrong and I'd caught him out yet again. As if he didn't know that sneaking around behind my back, then *lying* about it was as demeaning as it was heartbreaking.

I dismissed him with an incredulous shake of my head.

He looked into his empty glass, contemplating something before getting up for a refill, cramming the glass full of large chunks of ice. All his drinks were served sub-arctic, cold enough to freeze his tongue and numb his brain.

"I want you around tomorrow afternoon. My brother is coming to stay with us for a while."

"The criminal?" I wrinkled my nose. I didn't want *any* stranger living in my house, let alone someone like that.

Nic swung back around, his jaw tightening, "Don't talk about him like that. Jack's a decent man."

My only reply was an insolent stare.

"And I'd like you to make an effort to make him feel welcome here."

"How long will he be staying?" I asked in feigned politeness.

"For as long as I see fit," Nicholas towered over me, backing me up against the wall. Whenever he stood so close, I was always amazed at my sudden awareness of our differences. How much taller than me he was, and twice as broad. How much more powerful in every sense of the word. He knew the effect his imposing presence had on me and he used it to his full advantage.

His physical presence was the first thing that I noticed about him. I loved how he could command a room.

Nic had a taste for Cuban cigars, fine Scottish whisky and Italian clothing, maybe in hope his exotic tastes would make him appear more cultured than he actually was. The guy was one toothpick away from a caricature of himself, but he remained a very handsome man. A head full of subtly greying, dark-blond hair (the grey part he blamed on me) and piercing, pale-blue eyes that gave the illusion he could see through anyone.

The problem was, Nicholas knew he was good-looking, but his fast-paced lifestyle was starting to show and he was the wrong side of forty to maintain it. In all honestly, he was lucky to have someone like me who'd try and deal with his shit instead of packing it in.

He leaned down toward me, his lips inches away from my ear.

"You scared me today. Don't run off again," He put his glass down on the side table and left the room. I slid down to the floor, struggling to maintain composure.

Later that night, Nicholas crossed the invisible line we normally left in the middle of the bed, wrapped his burly arms around me and kissed my neck. How many times had we gone to bed angry only to wake up in the morning like that, either him spooning tight behind me or me lying across his chest?

"I thought we were done with this, Nic?" I said in a soft voice as I stared up at the ceiling.

"Babe, I swear that photo was not what it looked like. I didn't sleep with her; she was a *kid* for crying out loud!"

"If you said that in front of a judge with *that* kind of evidence, you'd go away for a long time."

"Look, I got someone dealing with that. Come morning,

that photo will be no more. I know in the past I've been a shit but I promise, this time *nothing happened*!"

"I was seventeen when you married me."

"I remember. I was there."

"Don't get smart with me. I just need to feel like you love me, every once in a while," I was expecting him to become defensive and tell me to stop trying to tell him how to behave but his voice dropped into a growl.

"How do you propose I do that?" he purred, nipping at my ear.

"Please, I'm not in the mood tonight." Laying on my side facing away from him, tears were silently streaking down my temple into the pillow.

"Come on baby, where's my girl?" He whispered.

"I don't know! Why don't you check your phone? There is probably a missed call from her." He pulled me onto my back and rolled on top, trapping me underneath his crushing frame.

"Marie, *baby*, you're my girl." He knew how to sweet-talk me, kissing down my neck and chest.

"You know you are my one and only." I closed my eyes in defeat, quietly moaning as his fingers rubbed softly between my legs. I hated how he could do this. Make me love him again with just a few words and a caress.

"Come on, doll. I'm sorry, okay." He kissed me on the lips slowly, in the way he knew turned me on. I'd never slept with anyone else but my husband. Not even before I was married. How was that for faithful? The furthest I had gone before Nic was second base.

Nic taught me all I knew about sex, and I had to admit he was pretty good at it. I hated that I had to share that part of him with other women. Didn't he see that I could give him everything he wanted?

He tugged down the band of my sleep shorts in one fluid motion and pulled my legs up around him, slipping into my ready body so easily.

After Nic made his wordless apology, we lay together, cuddling the way we did only after a night like this.

"Nic?"

"Yeah, babe?"

"Would you do something for me?"

I could feel his eyelashes beating against my cheek, "Anything."

I had a lot of leverage in this position, right after we had made up. He was much more docile, more willing to love me in the way I needed. I could ask him to lay off the alcohol. I could ask him to stop fucking other women behind my back, but there was something else that weighed more heavily on my mind.

"Would you spend some time with your son this weekend? I think he could really benefit from some one-on-one time with you."

"Sure, doll. I can do that." And with that, he rolled over and went to sleep.

Chapter Two

JACK

The house loomed large at the end of an unnecessarily long driveway, hideously modern and angular against the backdrop of the beach and the other, more modest, homes in the surrounding area. It screamed wealth, which was fine, if you liked that sort of thing.

I rang the doorbell once, holding my finger on the button just a second longer than necessary. Standing there in the only (shabby) clothes I owned and the remaining few items I had left in a duffle bag slung over my shoulder, I already felt out of place. Not like I'd ever felt entirely comfortable around my ambitious brother. His lifestyle was a world away from our upbringing. It didn't help when the Uber, a beat-up Honda Civic, careened out of the driveway with a loud screech.

Looking up, I caught my reflection in the frosted glass of the door, unsurprised to see I looked rough. Trying to flatten my untamable mass of hair, I studied my face, marred with the wisdom that only thirty-eight years of hard living could bring, and marked with a trinity of long white scars trailing down my cheek. Scars that branded me the night I had killed.

After eight tours in the military ground combat element, I had been almost relieved to come back to North America, albeit a bit leaner and with an even worse temper than when I'd left. After a short stint trying to re-carve a life for myself in Canada, I returned home to visit the brother I hadn't seen in more than a decade. The brother who looked out for me when we were kids, saw to it I ate a couple times a day and stayed out from under the feet of our formidable, often intoxicated, father. That's when things really went south.

Shaking off that trail of thought before it could pull me any deeper, I rang the doorbell again. This was my chance at a fresh start.

I heard what sounded like sandals smacking across tiles before the front door was yanked open.

Nicholas stood an even six feet, wearing nothing but bright orange swim shorts and a pair of pool slides. Although we were half-brothers, we were almost polar opposites when it came to our looks. So different in fact that, if you didn't know, you wouldn't have been able to tell we were related. Although Nic was five years older than me, he was a few inches shorter with the burly frame of the football player he'd always aspired to be but lacked the talent to truly become. His talents lay in many other areas but never in the physical. That was my area of expertise.

"Jackie! How you doing, man?" He pulled me into a hug, smearing me with tanning oil. The rich, pungent scent of those Cuban cigars he favored hung around him and the smell hit me like an uppercut to the nose.

"I'm alright," I replied, stepping over the threshold.

"Listen. I want you to stay for as long as you need, I have enough room and I'd hate to think of you with nowhere to go. Marie will be down in a sec..."

The house was as large on the inside as its monstrous exterior suggested. Highly polished tiled floors, even higher ceilings. Double arching staircases. The hall was cavernous; I could imagine any slight noise rebounding off the walls. To testify to this, Nic's cell phone rang, the piecing noise assaulting my eardrums twice before he answered.

"Talk to me... no... how'd you fuckin' mess that order up? Son of a bitch..." He lightly hit me on the arm, mouthed 'one minute', and took off outside amidst a string of curses.

Just then, a dark-haired woman appeared at the top of the marble stairway, dressed in a low-cut bikini top and tiny shorts, her face set in an insolently beautiful frown as she descended toward me. I couldn't help but take her in. The way her body moved, curved in all the right places, increasing my pulse with every step she took.

She was very pretty but that hadn't been the reason I was so captivated by her. I'd been in the presence of desirable women before and hadn't lost my cool.

As she reached the bottom of the stairs, the rich chocolatey hue of her eyes caught my attention, almost liquid in the way they seemed to shimmer in the afternoon light coming through the open door. As those eyes met mine, I felt my entire body tense, the breath almost literally knocked out of me.

I didn't think I'd been more attracted to anyone in my life. I wanted to reach out and see if her skin, creamy white and flushed from the sun, was as smooth as it looked. I wanted to lean in and taste her lips, so plump and inviting. I wanted her in ways that were entirely inappropriate for a guy meeting his brother's wife for the first time.

Knock it off, jackass, you're only acting like this because she's the first woman you've laid eyes on in four years. But, Jesus Christ, she was perfect... until she opened her sweet little mouth.

"Jack, I presume?" She scowled and held out a delicate hand for me to shake. Her voice was all southern honey-coated venom and irritation.

"That's me, darlin'," I drawled back, feeling my lips curl up at one side in amusement. If we were going to play it that way, so be it. It had been a while since I'd had some fun.

She narrowed her eyes at me, "Don't call me *darlin'*. And don't go walking 'round here all presumptuous, leering at me like that. I am not a piece of meat!"

I snorted a half laugh, "Why don't you cover yourself up, then?" She was, like Nic, dressed more appropriately for the beach than welcoming guests.

"Your kind isn't well tolerated around here so you best be well-behaved!" Her dark eyes were intense, staring defiantly up at me, unblinking. It was hard to be intimidated by someone so small. She just about came up to my chest. A little southern spitfire.

"Don't worry about it, Kid. Your sugar daddy is the one in charge here, so I'll let him call the shots."

She looked at me in such distaste that when Nicholas re-entered, he could sense the tension immediately.

"Everything okay, doll?" He leaned in to study her expression but she pulled away, still staring at me. I saw the hint of something I didn't recognize shine in Nic's eye as he grabbed her roughly by the ass and pulled her back to him.

"We were just getting acquainted," She sniffed and looked the other way, "I'm going for a swim." She angled her face up to peck him on the cheek but Nicholas turned and captured her mouth in a passionate kiss.

Marie very distinctly avoided my gaze before turning and walking away. I watched her ass the whole time, the lower half of her butt cheeks on display, one side pink-tinged from Nic's manhandling.

"Hot little thing, isn't she?" My brother nudged me in the ribs and chuckled as I silently agreed.

"Let me tell you now, she will drive you up the fuckin' wall!"

I could already tell that this girl would infuriate me, or at best, just piss me off. Good thing she was easy on the eyes.

"I bet," I replied, smirking.

Nic gave me a quick tour - five bedrooms, four bathrooms, two lounges, a huge kitchen, study, games room and miniature state-of-the-art gym at basement level - before heading down past the pool and garden to the beach at the very back of the property.

"Nice place you got here." I wasn't one for material things but I had to admit, having this much room to stretch out in had to be nice. The abundance of outdoor space was more my thing, being able to breathe after so long in confinement.

Nic shrugged although his expression wasn't so blasé. He was very proud of his accomplishments. Very happy to rub them in people's faces. That's just the type of person he was, the type of person he always had been. No doubt he'd earned every penny through hard work, although whether that work was honest was another story. One I didn't want to go into.

We walked in companionable silence across the beach and toward the shoreline, the lack of wind really giving way to how thick and heavy the air was. Even in my limited experience, I knew the weather was unusual for California. I felt sticky even though we'd only been out of the air-conditioning for a few minutes.

"Fuck it," Nic cursed, dragging his sandal through the sand repeatedly, trying to scrape off the fresh dog shit he just stepped in, "You dump a shit-ton money on a house like this, gated community and everything, and you still can't control what happens on the other side of this *fucking wall!*"

I snorted in amusement, "Why did you buy a house here if you don't like it?"

Nic shook his head, "Fuck if I know, Marie wanted it."

"And you couldn't tell her no?"

"Okay, just wait until you're married and in that position. You can't tell her no, she's a woman."

I just shrugged.

"Like I said, you just wait," Nic shook his head.

"No, thanks. I just got my freedom back and don't intend on giving it up again."

Since joining the Marine Corps at nineteen, which felt like a lifetime ago, I'd never quite found relief from that impenetrable feeling of dread that hung over my shoulders. Even when I left nine years ago, other obligations prevented me from truly finding that sense of inner peace.

"Truer words have never been spoken, brother. There was one thing that sold me on it though," He turned me to face the vast expanse of ocean stretching out into the distance.

"What do you see?"

Was that a trick question?

"Water," I replied with a sardonic grin. The corner of Nic's lip twitched up.

"I see endless possibilities. Looking at this reminds me that nothing is finite, that there is always something over the horizon. It reminds me of where I've come from and what I've worked so hard to achieve."

I watched the water innocently lapping on the shore and thought of the shrouded power held in its depths. Two people from the same beginnings. How could we look at exactly the same thing and think two entirely different thoughts?

The pool was just as extravagant as the rest of the house; large and rectangular, tiled with tiny mosaics and seashells imprinted around the edges. Nic reclined on one of the many sun loungers and indicated for me to do the same. I would have felt a bit out of place sprawled across the lounger in jeans, so I settled on the edge instead.

Across from us, Marie was swimming laps in perfect, rhythmic breaststroke. It surprised me she would be willing to let that flawlessly coifed hair come into contact with chlorine. Wasn't that all stuck-up trophy wives cared about?

"So, man. Tell me. What's it like in the big house?" He flicked his sunglasses down, his mouth twisting into a smirk. I raised an eyebrow.

"Not much to tell, it gets pretty boring." My expression remained hard, not wanting to show him how much that ticked me off. Prison had been hell in more ways than one. Left alone with your thoughts twenty-four hours a day in suffocating confinement. Forgetting what human touch felt like. No goddamn privacy. But time away from the world had helped with my perspective on life; when you're alone you can't hurt anyone.

"Seemed to do your body good! Check out them shoulders!" Nic unintentionally broadened himself out. Being the older but slightly smaller brother was a thing he could never get over, even now we were adults.

"Well, working out becomes a way of life when you have nothing else to do all day."

"It's hard to be that dedicated when you have a sixty-billion-dollar business to run."

"Shut up, asshole," I muttered and playfully cuffed him on the arm.

Nicholas cackled, "Solid punch, bro! Think you'll ever get back in the ring?" Those days, I was a few fights away from going pro. Turns out in the world of semi-professional boxing, bowing down to authority is a big step to hitting the big time. And that was something I'd never been very good at.

"You mean getting up at four am to drink liquid egg whites before a five-mile run? Nah, that time in my life is over. And it was a *long* time ago," I reminded him.

"It doesn't have to be, you're still young enough to take 'em." A supposed movement behind me must have caught Nic's eye because he waved somebody over.

"I want you to meet someone... Jude! Come here, boy." I turned a fraction in time to see a good-natured but awkward-looking child run up to Nic, beaming, all shy and gap-toothed. Who in God's name was this kid, he surely wasn't...

"No hugging," He instructed the child, "Shake hands. Like a man." Jude shook Nic's hand and then mine, his grip firm. Nic placed a hand on the boy's shoulder, a hint of a proud smile curling his lips.

"Jack, I want you to meet your nephew, Jude." I felt my mouth hanging open wide enough to catch flies. When did the son-of-a-bitch have the time?

"Nice to meet you, Uncle Jack," He smiled at me sweetly then glanced up at his father.

"Alright, go play. Leave me and your uncle to talk," Nicholas gave his son a little shove in the direction of the pool, the boy rushing over to the pool steps where Marie waited for him in the water.

"He seems like a good kid. You and Marie must be proud, huh?"

Nic barked a laugh, "He's not *Marie's* son. I had Jude with my ex. She lives in Florida. Jude comes to stay for the summer."

Obviously, if I'd thought about it, I could have figured out that a boy of about eight years old wouldn't have a mother in her early twenties. Maybe it was the humidity turning my brain to mush.

My gaze wandered over to Marie. She was teaching Jude how to kick his legs for breaststroke, both of them holding onto the far side while he got the rhythm right. He bent closer and whispered something in her ear, making Marie laugh, the sound light and decidedly melodic.

I hated swimming, even growing up. I had no co-ordination in water and seemed to sink, rock-like to the bottom. And the chlorine would sting my eyes like hell. But the claustrophobic atmosphere made the cool water look very inviting. Especially with Marie in there.

"So, have you gotten laid yet?" I could tell by the tone of his voice that I looked at his girl a moment too long.

"I got out yesterday, Nic. What do you think?"

He held his hands up defensively and smiled wryly, "Whoa, don't bite my head off, I was just asking."

"Why? You got a nice stripper you want to introduce me to or something?"

"Don't worry. I got your back…Hey, do you wanna beer? Guess you haven't had one in while, huh?" Drinking socially had never really been that important to me but an ice-cold beer didn't sound bad right now. Before I had time to reply, Nic was up and gone.

Bringing my hand up to shield my eyes, I scanned my surroundings, squinting. Although the cloud cover was thick, the day was bright.

As soon as Nic was out of sight, I was drawn to his pretty little wife like a magnet. Her hair streamed behind her in the water as she swam beneath the surface. She lifted her face out to breathe and saw my captivated stare. Checking we were alone, Marie swam toward me and rested on the side of the pool. The kid must have gotten bored and ran off to play elsewhere.

"You just going to watch me swim all day?" I could've listened to that accent forever! Her voice had a soft drawl that put me in the mood for peach cobbler. I'd guess that voice could also be as sticky as molasses on a Mississippi summers day if she wanted something.

"That depends if you are going to be swimmin' all day, darlin'." That endearment rewarded me with what was fast becoming my favorite scowl.

"And exactly how long d'you plan on staying'?"

"As long as my brother will have me."

"Oh boy!" She rolled her eyes and looked away. Nic still hadn't returned and Marie was still situated temptingly in front of me, so I thought I'd make at least an attempt at polite conversation.

"Where'er you from?"

"Missouri," Marie replied in a far-off voice. She looked past me, fixed on something imaginary in the hedge. I could tell she was thinking about home and they didn't seem to be good thoughts. We had that in common at least.

"Ah, a mid-western girl."

"Ah'm from *South* Missouri," she pointedly enhanced her accent for effect, pouting out her bottom lip.

"Still technically mid-western," I quipped.

"And you are still technically an asshole! You have clearly never been to the South." What was it about this girl that drove me crazy? Was it that she was so easy to wind up or that I just loved her reaction?

I smirked, "I'm from Texas."

"Ah, so you are technically Mexican!"

I just cocked a brow, slightly disappointed I didn't get anything more.

"You know, Nic never did tell me about his upbringing?" Of course, Marie wouldn't have known this kind of information. Gold diggers didn't tend to know the small details.

"I bet there is a lot you don't know about him."

"You don't know squat!" Marie pushed off from the wall and swam away. She knew I had her all figured out.

I had a little chuckle to myself as Nic returned. He placed a bottle of perfectly chilled California common down in front of me, the glass frosted with condensation. Cold despite the muggy heat, no ice necessary.

"I've been thinking," he stared, reclining back on the sun lounger and flipping his mirrored shades back down, "I want you to come work for me for a bit, ease you back in. I heard it can be hard to find a job once you're back on the outside."

"I dunno, they will be keeping a pretty close eye on me. I can't afford to do anything... *dodgy* right now." If I knew my brother as well as I thought I did, he was going to ask me to do something I wasn't entirely comfortable with. The last time that happened, I ended up in jail.

Nicholas' eyes widened under his sunglasses, noticeable only by the lining of his forehead, "Nothing like that, bro! I just wanted you to do a little bit of surveillance for me."

"...go on..." I sighed, already regretting it.

"It's Marie; she's been acting up lately, running off. I don't want her to get into any trouble."

Out of the corner of my eye, I could see Marie had climbed out of the pool and was rinsing off in the outdoor shower. Nic lit a cigar, puffing in air until the end glowed orange and smoldered.

I raised my eyebrow again, "You want me to babysit your wife?"

"Not babysit, just keep her in your sight and out of harm's way. Maybe drive her around. She's a menace in that car."

"So, babysit?"

"I just don't want her to do anything she may regret later, you know?"

"Right… I'm sure that won't be an issue."

Marie faced away from us, dark hair sleek and trailing down her back. She unhooked her bikini top and it took all my self-restraint to keep my eyes trained to where I thought Nic's eyes might be under the sunglasses.

"I pay well. A thousand a week."

"She hates me." Maybe that was stretching the truth. We'd only just met. She couldn't hate me already.

"You don't have to talk to her. I'll just say you're her bodyguard."

"Can I say no?"

Nicholas shrugged, "No." He smiled his wolfish grin and clanked his glass against mine. I took a deep swig of my beer, icy-cold liquid burning down my throat. It felt good.

Marie strode off back to the house covering herself with her hands, leaving her swim top on the floor and a wet trail over the tiles behind her.

"*Fuck*, Marie! Use a *fucking* towel! This isn't Raging Waters," Nic yelled after her as she disappeared inside the house. "Last thing I fuckin' need, to slip over and do my back in again."

I did wonder why Marie thought it would be appropriate to strip off outside like that when she had company. The only logical conclusion I could come to was that she was trying to project some weird kind of feminine dominance. Mark her territory, perhaps?

Although slightly disappointed I didn't get to glimpse more, I already had enough material for later with the image of her smooth naked back, slick from the shower. I could do just fine with that and my imagination.

Jesus, fuck! I desperately needed to get laid if that was what I was resorting to. Here my brother was offering me a place to get back on my feet and I this was how I was repaying him? Wasn't it kind of an unspoken law that you didn't get off to thoughts of your sister-in-law?

As if reading my mind, Nic slapped my leg and stood, "I'll show you to your room; we have a few people coming over later."

My room was predictably huge in size and personality. Everything was mirrored; mirrored wall-to-wall wardrobes, mirrored dressers, there was even a mirror on the fucking ceiling. A gigantic suede bed stood in the middle of the room, looking rightly obnoxious but very comfortable with its many pillows. The room had an en-suite bathroom with a walk-in shower and a bathtub so big even I could spread out in it.

There were also not one but four vases of fresh, white flowers around the room, which I wasted no time in disposing of. The pollen would get up my nose if I slept with them in here all night. Plus, they stunk to high heaven.

I looked down at my tattered duffle. It was so beat-up and dirty it looked almost obscene against the white carpet. Inside the first door of the wardrobe were drawers stocked with neatly folded clothes; underpants, t-shirts, the usual. Next to this was a hanging section with sweats, jeans and pants complete with freshly ironed shirts in an assortment of colors. I threw my bag at the bottom and kicked it to the back so it would no longer offend the room.

A note sticky-taped to the inside of the door read "Jack – feel free to wear whatever you like, I bought it all for you. N." I chuckled to myself. Somehow the mental image of him arranging my new closet in color order didn't spring to mind easily.

I ran my hand over the first rail, feeling the different fabrics; what kind of man wears a pink satin shirt? Or more importantly, did Nic think I would wear clothes like this? I pulled out a t-shirt and jeans before heading for a cold shower, already knowing I would be lying to myself if I said I would not, under any circumstances, think about the infuriatingly gorgeous woman in the next room.

When Nic said 'a few people', that must have been translated using his own version of the dictionary. About thirty men turned up in various sports cars with various varieties of blond wives. Nic had his cook make all kinds of barbecued meats while everyone gathered in the large kitchen-diner area. The far wall opened out to a terrace and the pool through floor-to-ceiling bi-folding glass panels, leaving the whole side of the room open and exposed to the outside.

On a nice day, this seemed like a great idea but with the evening's unusual heat, it was just unpleasant. Fans whirred from above, just about managing to push the stifling air around, built more for appearance than functionality.

Nic introduced me to everyone. I shook a lot of hands and said, 'Alright,' so many times you would have thought the word was super-glued to my tongue. Most names I either forgot instantly or didn't happen to catch, not bothering to ask again. It wasn't like I was planning on using them.

In particular, a few people stuck out; firstly Nic's close friend Chuck, whom I met a few times before back when we'd lived in New York. We didn't get on, in part because I'd slept with his mother a few times while on leave, but mainly because he was an asshole. We grunted at each other in forced greeting.

Jean, who shook my hand firmly and made way too much eye contact, which I took as over-compensating for confidence or honesty, I couldn't decide which. I only knew I didn't trust him.

Then there was a shamelessly flirtatious blond, whose overly Botoxed face stuck with me for all the wrong reasons. She had a kind of carnal grin, like she was out for blood, her shining eyes dilated so much they looked black. She placed a clawed hand on my arm when I was introduced, probably unaware her tongue darted out to wet her lower lip. I made a mental note to scrub the area she'd touched. Vigorously.

I didn't have to make much of my own conversation; I knew the type. Self-absorbed, attention-seeking, greedy. I listened in on a few different groups but ultimately found myself standing on the far side of the room alone. I didn't have any interest in what these people had to say.

I also sensed their uneasiness around me. A lot of them couldn't meet my eye, their gaze wandering to the raised lines of badly healed skin that ran down the side of my face. It wasn't really that noticeable, especially under the scrub of facial hair, but for the people who ran in these social circles, those scars marked me as a man apart. It only further increased the divide between my reality and this world of unblemished narcissism.

Just as I was beginning to contemplate drowning my weariness in beer, Marie appeared, dressed in a simple white cotton sundress. I watched her cross the room as she took her place by Nic's side. He snaked a thick arm around her waist and kissed her hard on the mouth. It wasn't a loving gesture, more a declaration of his ownership of her. A brand.

She stayed there for a few minutes listening to whatever schmoozing Nic was doing, appropriately laughing at his jokes but adding nothing more to the conversation than as a decorative fixture.

I felt a lingering presence beside me and turned to see Botox-woman.

"Well, hey there!" she smiled at me widely. Only her mouth moved, showing off her dazzling white veneers. I gave her a small upward turn of my lip, my version of a 'get lost' greeting, and took a gulp of beer. She didn't get the message.

"How're you doing? Nic told us all about how his baby brother just finished up doing hard time." She seemed delighted; every word she said was overpronounced in her upbeat southern drawl. Much stronger than Marie's, this was more Mississippi mud pie with sugared cream on top.

Guess news traveled fast; Marie must have made sure all her little friends were well informed of my shortcomings before they arrived.

"Yeah," I replied. Why wouldn't this woman take a hint? Her eyes followed mine over to Marie and back again before I noticed and tried to feign interest in the lazy rotation of the ceiling fan.

"Pretty. Isn't she?" Botox lady said in a lowered voice. I turned to stare at her.

"Who?"

"Why, little Marie of course. You've been watchin' her

since she came in," She paused, as If waiting for my reply, "You don't need to be told you can't have that one."

"Don't know what you're talking about." Who the hell did this woman think she was! I'd been here all of five minutes and I had already decided I couldn't stand the lot of them.

"Sweet pea, I know that look. If you want some fun later, come and find me, M'kay?"

I looked at her blankly as she smiled that huge fake smile again and slunk away toward the group of girls. Jesus Christ, I bet she was a handful at home. Sneaking a peak toward the poor guy who was her husband, I could have had a pretty good guess they slept in separate bedrooms.

My eyes snapped back toward Marie again but she was not with the group. I spotted her by the pool, shuffling out of her sandals to dip her feet into the water beneath, before perching on the edge. Casually, I walked around the room and outside to join her.

"Having a good time?" I asked, standing behind her. She turned her head ever so slightly toward me.

"No. Are you?"

"Nope."

Her slender legs dangled in the pool, the underwater lighting made them glow a luminous, eerie white.

"Nicholas is talking business and the women are bitching as usual, so I thought I'd come out here and enjoy the quiet."

"Ah, I see." I took off my shoes, rolled up my jeans and sat down on the edge next to her. Maybe slightly too close for somebody who I wasn't friendly with. Then again, maybe not; I could smell the delicately sweet perfume on her skin. That smell messed with my head.

"How do you tolerate those people?"

She grimaced, "Barely. Every time I'm near them I feel like I need a detox afterwards." Her feet flicked across the surface of the water lazily.

"What were you and Cassandra talking about?"

"Is that the one with the plastic face?"

"The only woman who spoke to you, smart ass!"

I stared out across the rippling surface of the water, choosing my wording carefully.

"She asked me personal questions and offered me something inappropriate," I replied, dipping one foot into the cool water.

"Sounds about right, Cassandra is like that. Over ambitious in everything she does. If it's not a competition or challenge, she's not interested."

"I'm a challenge, am I?" I replied, trying to lighten the mood. I was feeling playful tonight.

"Judging by your lack of social etiquette, probably not."

"You think I'm easy?" I laughed.

"I don't think you're picky."

"Oh, you're so high and mighty there on your horse. Don't tell me you've never been tempted to screw anyone else besides your husband?"

"*No*... and I would *never* cheat on Nic! Can you not go two minutes without saying something completely dick-ish! Not everyone is as morally bankrupt as you!" The look on her face was priceless.

I struggled to contain my laughter.

"Dick-ish?"

"Yeah, and you know what? Quit staring at me all the time. I know you haven't seen a woman in years but that does not mean your eyes get free rein on me!"

"Free country," I shrugged.

"Egotistical pig, you've probably never been turned down in your whole life."

"What can I say, Kid. I have my ways," I took a long swig of beer, smirking.

"Don't call me Kid!" she said through clenched teeth.

"I will if you stop acting like one."

I was thoroughly enjoying watching Marie practically set herself on fire. She punched me in the shoulder with what she deemed to be a powerful throw, then swore under her breath when the punch had more impact on her knuckles than on me.

She needed to cool off! With one swipe of my leg, she was in the water. I sat, smug, on the edge while Marie swore furiously at me.

"Fucking *asshole*!" she yelled at me, climbing out at the steps. She marched toward me, the wet fabric of her dress almost see-through around her braless figure. I was so distracted I didn't see the second blow until it hit me square in the chest.

"Stupid son-of-a-bitch!" she was hitting me repeatedly, wherever she could reach.

"Hey, come now!" I grabbed her wrists, but she tried using her feet instead, kicking out, trying to make me let go.

"Right, that's it!" I gathered up her writhing body and jumped into the pool, our combined weight plunging us straight to the bottom. We fully submerged and by the time we resurfaced, Marie was motionless in my arms. I stared deep into those dark, chocolate-colored eyes for a moment too long and heard her breath hitch in her throat. My own breath apparently had been left at the bottom of the pool.

"Goddamn drama queen," I whispered. Marie drew back her fist and punched me once more, hard in the chest, then swam off back toward the house.

Chapter Three

NIC

"Right, Newt... the floor is yours."

Some greased-up weed straight outta college stood trembling in front of my desk in eight-hundred-dollar Louis Vuitton shoes his mom probably picked up for him that morning.

"Thanks, boss. I've had a look at the portfolio you allocated me over the weekend, and I think we could make a decent profit on this potential new venture."

"I've done the numbers; it's foolproof! If we merge Interlon with The Oxford Group, pump in a small investment of say, seven percent, then sell up, in six to eight months we could come away strong and see a pretty healthy return."

I gave a noncommittal grunt, if anything, just to show I was listening.

"I read this morning Macher are crying out for expansion, they'd be insane not to want a piece of the action. When we're done, they will be biting your hands off, paying well over the odds to consume them, and you'll be sitting on an island somewhere sipping Piña Coladas watching the sun go down."

"What's the capital you need?" I twisted the ring on my pinky round so the black stone faced outwards. Little fucker kept swiveling around underneath. These meetings were necessary but tedious. I'd worked too long and hard to get to where I was and I wasn't going to let anyone else make these kind of important decisions for me, despite the thumper of a headache I had.

We'd been here all of three minutes and this kid was already pissing me off with the pitchy one-liners. His voice still broke in places where he felt particularly enthusiastic. Verbally throwing the 'I-went-to-business-school' dictionary at me every chance he got, like it was impressive to know and use the words in a sentence.

And I fucking *loathed* being called boss!

"Eight hundred and twenty thousand dollars, sir."

"What the fuck, Newt? That's *seven* percent?"

"Yes, sir," The kid gulped nervously, his Adam's apple bobbing up and down in his skinny throat.

"Go back to accounts and rework the numbers. I don't want to spend more than five hundred, ya got me?"

"Five hundred dollars?"

"Five hundred thousand, you little shit. Get outta my sight!" He scampered out the door just before the heavy glass dome that served as a paperweight made a large dent in the back of it, cracking the thing into two clean pieces on the floor.

"Little cunt knows nothing about investment... cock-sucking adviser who recommended him better buck his ideas up or I'll rip his fucking balls off..."

I wrenched open a drawer under my desk and seized the box of elusive Black Dragon cigars reserved for when I was having an especially shit morning. These babies had a complex, unique flavor profile, balancing the perfect combination of sweet and sour, and a box of twenty would set you back the approximate price of a kidney on the black market. I ran the cigar under my nose and took a deep inhale, letting the aroma fill me up before cutting it, lighting the end with a match and taking a deep pull.

My brother smirked over at me from the end of the couch, looking out of place, a dark hulking mass against the stark white backdrop of my office.

"Hey *boss*, don't stress so much. All that Valium pumping through your veins will be burnt off in a few minutes at this rate."

The thick smoke slowly unfurled in my lungs, practically melting away the stress.

"What the fuck kind of name is Newt anyway? His parent's reptile enthusiasts?"

"His parents must have been lizards. That's where he inherited those bug eyes from."

I chortled a little at that. Jack had a way with words that never ceased to entertain me. Despite him being virtually extinct for the past decade, I still felt very much at ease with my brother. This was the first time I'd set eyes on him since he'd gotten out of prison and he was just as quick-witted as ever.

"Alright you son-of-a-bitch, why you here dirtying my

couch?" I poured two glasses from a rare Macallan and offered one to him. Jack waved it away and shook his head slightly.

"What's wrong with you? The Jack I know used to know drank like a fish, smoked like a chimney, and swore like a sailor."

"I saw the error of my ways."

"Fuck off! What man turns down a twelve-year-old single malt?"

"One who's been off the hard stuff for the same amount of time."

I eyed him steadily for a second, "If this whisky were a girl, I'd fuck her senseless right now."

"Too bad for you it's not then, right?"

We both laughed as I loosened my tie, "Seriously, what can I do for you, bro?"

Jack let out a breath before dropping his eyes to the rug, "I need a place to stay, if that's okay. Just 'til I can get back on my feet…"

"Say no more."

"I really wouldn't ask if I didn't have to but…" his cheeks colored ever so slightly, maybe imperceptible to someone who didn't truly know him. Now that we had a moment alone, I could see how disheveled he was. Shaggy hair, crumpled clothing, unshaven. He looked homeless. He *was* homeless, I reminded myself.

Thing was, I couldn't deny my little brother anything. He'd saved my life once, not that either of us would admit it. We were both too proud.

A deal gone sour. The wrong sort of people were riled up and I owed *a lot* of money. And when it comes to money, those sorts of people were a lot less lenient. Jack walked in the very moment I thought it was done for. Granted, he didn't need to actually kill the guy, but it did send a very powerful message.

I'd never seen something so savagely raw. As I lay there with my eyes almost swollen shut, I witnessed the cold-blooded frenzy. Overcome with rage, the guy was dead long before Jack let up.

When I later inspected the damage to my own body, I was lucky to have survived with so little physical reminders, let alone with my life. I owed Jack everything.

"I have the space. Besides, I'm sure I can think of *something* you can do to repay me."

My mobile buzzed in my pocket. I pulled it out, rolled my eyes and groaned. A vein in my temple throbbed especially hard. It was Jean.

"Fuckin' WHAT?"

"Sorry to interrupt. It's Marie."

"Oh, for fuck sake, that *woman!*" I rubbed my hot, ruddy face with the back of my hand.

"...said she found a *'used thong'* in one of your jacket

pockets?"

That was months ago, she couldn't still be upset over that, surely? Or could she? Fuck knows how that woman's mind worked.

"Where's Chuck? I told him to keep an eye on her."

"He lost track of her heading up the one-ninety."

Useless! If you wanted something done... I cut him off and downed the rest of my drink.

I knew I should've had a tracker fitted to her car! Or at least have someone a little more dependable than Chuck watching her. She hated his guts, of course she would try to give him the slip at any given opportunity.

"Look Jackie, sorry to kick you out so soon but I gotta deal with this. It's better if you come over tomorrow evening. You can grab the address from my assistant."

"Alright. I'll see you tomorrow then," Jack picked his bag up from a chair in the corner and left, carefully avoiding the large chunks of glass scattered over the marble tiles.

"Seven pm, bro," I yelled after him and he raised a hand to indicate he'd heard. I'd actually kinda missed that little shit.

With his intimidating build and messed-up face, most people would give him a wide berth. Even before the incident, there was something about the way Jack carried himself that screamed 'fuck off' to the average passerby. He looked like someone you wouldn't want to get on the wrong side of, even though anyone who knew him quickly realized he had a core of molten caramel at his center.

I sat back at my desk, rubbing my aching temple. Fuck, I needed to blow off some steam. I yanked open the drawer which contained my back pills. My back no longer bothered me, but the prescription was so good I kept it on repeat. Oxycodone.

When you were as well connected as I was, things like that were easy to obtain. Money could buy you just about anything but it was *who* you knew which was worth more than its weight in gold.

I hadn't always been as fortunate. Me and Jack were 'brought up,' in less precise terms, by our father. I hadn't seen him since we'd left all those years ago, and I was sure I had much more vivid memories of him than Jack did. And Jack's mother, Josefina.

Josefina was the only mom I ever knew, kind and soft-spoken, the complete opposite of what I was raised to know. I always wondered what she did to make him beat her the way he did. More than a few times I'd come home from school to see her crumpled and silent, maybe a nostril crusted from being hastily wiped, or a dark smudge of make-up covering any evidence.

I'd go to her open arms and she'd hug me, whispering that everything was going to be okay and I should take Jack to play outside.

One day I came home and she wasn't there anymore. Nothing had been moved from its place. Nothing had changed except for her presence. Things got worse after that; Dad was out more, coming home later and later, gradually getting more and more drunk until he would stumble through the door, his shirt stained and missing buttons, receding hair slicked over to the side. Sometimes he came home with blood on his knuckles, and shiny purpling marks on his face, sometimes without. He was in a worse mood when he came back without.

He always seemed to take it out on Jack; young and defenseless as he was, he couldn't fight back. So Jack took to hiding whenever he heard the jangle of the keychain outside the screen door.

When we finally left our father behind, we never mentioned him again.

That was when I promised myself I'd never end up like my father. I was my own man, free to choose my own path.

I'd almost single-handedly built my empire from the ground up. Granted, I'd stepped on a lot of toes to get where I was but if there was one thing I'd learned, in this industry but especially in life, it was that you had to be tough to survive. And if that meant pushing a few people out of the way, then so be it. If I had to do it all again, I would. I'd been poor and I felt no desire to ever be that way again.

My head felt like it was about to split into two, that vein pounding somewhere behind my left eye, making it feel like it was pulsating.

They say one of the biggest killers in this country is stress. So it was time to take some time out, for my health. I picked up the office phone and dialed reception.

"Jessica, baby, will you get your sexy little ass in here?"

"Right away, Mr Hayes," Her voice chimed back over the intercom.

Jessica had been my assistant for almost three months now and was shaping up to be the best I'd ever had. She looked after me, I paid her well. It was that simple. She was a stunning redhead with huge tits; it was her underwear Marie'd found in my pocket. It was a real shame I'd forgotten to stash them somewhere less incriminating. Running my fingers over the lace during the last board meeting gave me the kind of sick thrill only thoughts of Jessica's slick pussy could, especially when I reached the stiffened little patch on the crotch area.

She was also very good at her job, which was a bonus.

"Sir?" Jessica entered, shutting the door behind her. I pushed a button and blinds drew down over the windows. She smiled at me coyly and sauntered over, popping the first few buttons of her shirt open.

This only happened on occasion, when I couldn't leave the office. I had places to go in my free time, other girls on call depending on what mood I was in. They were usually blond, about five-eight. Jessica had refused to bleach her hair for me, but she was cute enough to get away with it. Plus, I couldn't wait to get my mouth on her double d's again.

My dick was so well used it felt raw, and that was the way I liked it. I always felt like shit afterward but in the moment, I could never say no.

Sure, I loved Marie. I loved everything about her. The way she rolled her eyes at me when she was annoyed; the feel of her, all soft and warm in my arms; the helpless little sighs she made when I touched her; her face when she came, her nose scrunched up.

That didn't mean I didn't notice other women. Hot women were everywhere, at the office, in the street, working in bars, cafes and restaurants. But there was a difference. These were the type of women who were only good for one thing. See, most women only wanted *you* for one thing, too, and it wasn't your skills in the sack. They wanted what they could get from you, be it money, status, tangible things. No, I didn't want that kind of bargain. I didn't mind giving, just not in return for something I should be entitled to as a man regardless.

Marie was the type of girl you made your wife. Somehow, one woman, even a world-class, drop-dead gorgeous woman like Marie, could never be enough to satisfy my needs.

From Jessica's place in my lap I could see, even through the sheer material of her bra, the fading marks I'd left on her last week, now turning an almost-healed greeny-yellow, which meant it had been far too long. I knew I hadn't been gentle - when was I ever? - but I hadn't imagined bruises like *that.* So vivid, shocking against her honey-colored skin, beautiful in their contrast. Like some kind of visceral abstract painting.

Some primal part of me liked seeing my mark on her, on all my women. So they'd think of me long after I'd touched them. The thought made my mouth water. Remembering the taste of her skin under my mouth, the shape of the delicate bud around my tongue before reminding her who I was with a sharp nip.

Truth was, I enjoyed making my women sore. I knew how

to make them come, took pride in it. They would wear my bruises like a badge of honor; every throb, every ache would remind them of me and the paradise I could transport them to. An oblivion I couldn't ever, in good conscience, completely give over to myself.

A few hours later, I was home. The meeting had gone especially well that afternoon, with us acquiring BioHault for two-thirds of the going rate, thanks to my well-respected business partner, Maxwell Lowell, smooth-talking our way in over conference call.

Despite, in the early days, taking me on as an apprentice, then protégé and practically adopting me, the son-of-a-bitch had his price; a cool thirty-five percent stake in my company.

Max was known for being ruthless, power-hungry, and unreserved in the boardroom, traits not too dissimilar from my own. At the end of the day, business was business, and the guy knew how to close, minimize cost and maximize profit margins. Although, BioHault was a company that I didn't want to be too hasty in getting rid of.

Say what you want about Max, but he knew his stuff. He knew how to get results. With almost half a century of experience in his pocket, he was an asset I just couldn't afford to let go.

Speaking of being able to afford things... over the course of the evening Jean had been wiping the floor with me. I stared down at the cards in disbelief. How could he have won again?

"You've hustled me!"

Jean snorted into his drink, "I wouldn't call it hustling if the person you're playin' with is so terrible. Easier than taking candy from a baby."

"More like taking money from your best friend."

"Pay up, ya yutz."

I threw him a bunch of balled-up fifties and lit a cigar, "How are things going with that girl from Georgia?"

"She wasn't *from* Georgia, that was her name. Anyway, I dropped her. Good while it lasted but I'm not into that homemaking shit."

"Still got her number?"

"Nic, you dog. You're married!"

I held my hands up in defense.

Jean continued, "Speaking of which, what've you done *this* time? I thought the whole 'Jessica's underwear' thing had been sorted?"

"Fuck if I know. That woman is a bigger mystery to me than the Bermuda Triangle."

"I dunno," He replied, scratching his chin, "Women are not that hard to read if you pay attention."

"She knew what she was getting when she married me."

"Just saying."

"Who are you, the marriage police? Shut your yap and deal me another round."

Jean shrugged and dealt out the cards, placing two face-down in front of me.

"My brother is coming to stay with us for a while anyway, I'm sure he can be persuaded to keep an eye on her. She won't be getting into any more trouble."

"Depending on what you call trouble."

"What's that supposed to mean?"

"She's run away again, ain't she? The only way I see this *not* happening again is you sorting something on your end."

"Let me deal with my problems my fuckin' way, alright?"

"Just remember what happened last time."

I did remember all too well what happened last time. Marie had taken a golf club to my Ferrari. In fact, you wouldn't have even been able to recognize it as a Ferrari after she was through with it.

"Didn't even know you had a brother," Jean interjected.

"There's a lot you don't know about me."

Jean just stared at me for a minute, unblinking, with a troubled expression before opening his mouth again to ask a well-thought-out question.

"Your brother, you trust him, right?"

I didn't need to hesitate but purposely left a small pause in the conversation to emphasize my point.

"With my life."

It was just like Jean to poke his nose in where it wasn't wanted. He'd always had a bit too much intuition for my liking, and not enough sense to know not to question my judgment.

Chuck, on the other hand, had always believed in me, although the bastard could be a bit dense. I guess everyone had their shortcomings.

See, what set me apart from most people is that I always had a plan. You can't get through on guesswork and luck alone. From the day I left home with my brother, I'd had my life planned out. I went to college while working two jobs, flipping burgers for just seven dollars an hour at an all-night joint in Brooklyn and hauling slabs of frozen meat from trucks at a big manufacturing plant for minimum wage during the day. I barely made enough to cover the rent and got by stealing leftovers destined for the trash. Once I'd graduated, I saved enough to buy an appropriate secondhand suit and approached the top companies in every industry until I'd landed an intern job. That's when I met Max, and the rest is ancient history.

I always knew I'd be successful because I was determined to succeed. I made things happen by doing them. And I was never content to sit around waiting. Waiting was for schmucks.

On reflection, I'd never really done anything without being driven by desire. Sexual desire aside, my business ventures have always been powered by the strong will to succeed... or was it the strong fear of failure that prevented me from dropping the ball? Without that fear, I would have nothing and *be* nothing. I certainly had no desire to go back to the kind of life I'd started out with. I'd always need to have more, push harder. My fear of failure was my safety net.

I picked up my hand. Two and a nine. Fuck... *again*? On the table, two kings and an ace. This was going to take some serious bluffing. Jean had jointly a very good poker face and a seventh sense for detecting bullshit in others. It was getting late; Marie still wasn't home, and I was fed up with losing.

"Fold," I grunted, acknowledging defeat.

"Always a pleasure doing business with you," Jean responded, scraping the pile of bills toward him.

"Yeah, yeah... go have fun losing my money in the casinos tonight."

"If I've won it, it's my money, my friend."

From beyond the hallway, I heard the tell-tale click of the front door being pushed softly closed.

"Not for long." I retorted.

"Fuck you," he smiled. "Good luck with the wife."

I was going to need it.

Chapter Four

MARIE

Dripping wet, I stormed toward the house. I was acutely aware of the silence, everyone's focus drawn away from their petty conversation to stare at the newly arrived spectacle. Crossing my arms over my chest, I realized all too late exactly why the focus was on me.

Silently cursing Jack, I felt a hot wave of humiliation flush over my face but didn't slow my stride. How dare he show me up like that? And what did he think gave him the right to touch me, let alone completely envelop me and plunge us both into the pool fully clothed?

I almost got to the stairs before Nicholas caught me.

"Your brother is a fucking asshole!" I shot at him before he grabbed my arm and pulled me back.

"Aw, come on, babe. Lighten up." Even standing on the step above him, Nic looked down on me. He'd had just enough to drink that his eyes took on a glazed quality; just beyond mellow, his manners fleeting, carnal desires taking over. He looked like he wanted to devour me.

"When is he leaving?" I yanked my arm from his grip.

"He'll be staying with us for the foreseeable future. I need his help."

"What could someone with a personal history like his

possibly help you with, Nic?"

A slow, wide smile spread over his face, "I need him to do some home surveillance for me."

"Home surveillance?" Like shit we needed home surveillance. We had a state-of-the-art camera system, linked straight to the cops.

"Certain possessions of mine keep going missing." He replied, toying with a loose strand of my sodden hair.

"You don't mean me?" I said in a lowered voice, painfully aware of how quiet it was in the hallway.

"How am I supposed to know that you're safe? That you aren't putting yourself at risk?"

"By trusting me? God. I can't believe you would do this. I'm not a child, Nic!" I whispered.

"Why don't you show me how much I mean to you, then?" His hand came up to paw at my wet breast. I tried to hit his arm away.

"Not now, we have company." I spied Jack hovering near the doorway behind Nic and narrowed my eyes at him. Nicholas was either too drunk to know his brother was watching or too drunk to care. Self-assured bastards, the pair of them.

"I'll make it quick, babe."

"You always do," I said in a low voice. He grabbed my jaw so he could stare straight into my eyes.

"We both know that's a lie. Go clean yourself up, I'll see you in ten." Nic pulled me to him and laid a surprisingly soft kiss on my lips, his hands working their way further down my back until they cupped my ass.

I could feel the heat of him bleeding through his clothes, through the wet fabric of my dress. The hardened lines of his body against mine. I shuddered with more than cold. I let out a squeak when he finally released me, almost losing my balance on the edge of the step.

"Ten minutes, doll." He slapped my ass and strode back to the kitchen.

In the shower, I was fuming. I hated the way he could make me want him so quickly. All it seemed to take was a few words, his mouth on mine, and I'd be on my knees willing to do anything to earn the kind of intimacy he offered.

I winced as I scrubbed the loofa over the back of my arm; the skin was quickly bruising with his finger marks. Nicholas wasn't a violent man. He was just a bit rough at times, not realizing his own strength. I couldn't lie and say that I didn't enjoy it, those times when he was so turned on he couldn't control himself. The feeling of his heavy body pressed up against mine as his mouth worked its way over my neck was ecstasy. It made me tremble; I became weak at the knees just thinking about it.

But sometimes it went too far, usually after he'd had a few drinks. It wasn't uncommon for things to get broken in the heat of the moment. Vases never seemed to last long in our house, likewise plates and glasses, always precariously placed to be knocked off during a heated session. It wasn't only household objects that were subject to Nic's passion. He had a thing for leaving marks, too. He liked to use his mouth, which wasn't a bad thing, but sometimes innocent licking and sucking could turn into full-on biting. I've come away before with the impression of his teeth embedded into my flesh, which quickly turned to ugly colored bruises on my pale skin. He'd even once dislocated my finger in a play-fight.

I didn't worry about his disposition to roughness; I knew he would never go as far as to hit me. Unless I deserved a good spanking, and in all honestly I didn't think I'd be opposed to that.

I quickly finished up washing and reached for a towel. My hair was still wet when Nic threw the door open. I let him pull me into him, his hands roaming over my body the way they had done so many times. Most of our intimate time together was intense, filled with his animalistic need. I was guessing tonight would be no exception.

He turned me around and pushed me down against the cold marble countertop, his large hand resting on the back of my neck. He bent down, trailing kisses up my spine.

"Baby, you drive me insane."

"So you weren't already like that before we got married?" I breathed.

He chuckled, "Your smart mouth is going to get you in trouble one of these days. It's a good thing I love it."

Nic unzipped his fly with a smooth, practiced motion and

plunged into me with a groan. I would have protested at the blunt intrusion but tonight I craved the release as much as he did. I considered this the best angle for finishing quickly; deep enough for both of us and Nic didn't have the distraction of kissing.

I arched back into his thrusts, moaning in satisfaction when he grabbed my hips and drove into me with increasing force.

He could make it so good when he wanted to. The only problem was Nic hardly ever thought about anyone else. Most of the time sex was more about his needs than mine. And tonight didn't break that rule.

With a final thrust, Nic finished with a growl of satisfaction, slumping down on top of me, panting, trying to regain his breath. Just thirty seconds longer and I would have been panting right along with him. Not that it mattered too much. It was always good, and I'd got the closeness I desired.

He rolled off, stowing his dick back in his pants. I turned around just as he shut the door, feeling cheap and used. I hated how he could do this, cheat on me then come back to show me what I was missing. It didn't help he'd been drinking or that our wild love-making was almost always preceded by an argument. I hated that I allowed myself to fall for it every single time. Let him think I could be fucked into submission.

Shaking my head to myself, I splashed my face with cold water to clear the burning feeling from my eyes. As I looked up, I caught my reflection in the mirror above the sink and wondered what happened to the head-strong young woman I used to see there. What was it he felt he didn't get with me that he needed to find elsewhere? What was it about me that wasn't good enough?

My thoughts turned back to the conversation I'd had with Cassandra and the girls earlier, before the whole pool incident.

"Who's that over there?" she nodded to where Jack stood lurking in the corner, then turned back to smile at me like she was hiding a secret she didn't want to share.

"That's Nic's brother, Jack."

"I think he likes you," She giggled like a schoolgirl. The other two women listening gave enthusiastic nods.

"Cassandra, do not start anything! You know what Nic's like."

"Just teasing you, sweet pea," she winked. Her voice took on a lower, darker tone.

"Ya'll know, I heard Nic talking earlier, about Jack. He strangled his poor wife in her sleep, bless her heart. He found out she was cheating on him... she was pregnant with another man's baby." The others gasped theatrically. If you knew Cassandra, you'd know her stories were a load of cow pie, but there was always a dash of truth mixed into the recipe.

"I don't think that's exactly right," I interrupted, "If he killed someone in cold blood, he'd be on death row, surely?"

"Not if he got away with it," Cassandra said, with a barely detectable hint of menace, "Anyway, I'm just relaying what I heard." She blinked sweetly, Bambi incognito.

I hated everything that spewed from her mouth and the way the other wives nodded along like those bobble-headed dogs in car rear windows. I hated the toxic chatter that could turn a perfectly respectable woman into a social outcast. And most of all I hated that I seemed to be one of them, too afraid to turn my back in case I was the one who got shit on next.

"I'm going to go outside," I mumbled, "Headache."

"Oh, here you go, sweetie." Cassandra fumbled in her oversized designer purse. "My doctor gives me these. Take two before you go to bed, they'll knock you out all night." She gave me a quick smile before turning back around to gossip some more.

A shrill burst of laughter from downstairs brought me back to the present. I wondered where Nic's limit would be tonight. Thank God he'd be up early for a business trip tomorrow and I wouldn't be the one to have to deal with him. Nic hung-over was definitely worse than Nic drunk.

I was still too angry to even contemplate sleep. Thinking about everything and everyone made my blood boil! I needed to calm down. I needed to go for a nice relaxing drive through town. Or maybe to the next town? I quickly dressed before silently slipping out the front door and into the night. The quiet hum of outside instantly calmed me. Although there was no breeze, out of the house there was a bit more relief than being caged inside.

My fingers had barely touched the car door handle when someone spoke, making me jump out of my skin.

"Where you going, kid?"

"None of your fucking business," I replied with my back to him, rage pulsing through my veins once again. As I yanked the car door open, a large hand came over my head and forced it shut.

"Does Nic know you're leaving?"

I wheeled around, infuriated. Jack was standing way too close to be comfortable. What was it with him and invading personal space?

"Fuck him, he can go to hell."

He wrinkled his nose slightly before making another gibe.

"You've got quite a mouth on ya, kid!" He was mocking me again, how original. However, my words seemed to genuinely bother him. I should remember to curse more often.

"Why do you care? Who the fuck do you think you are? Coming into our home, disrespecting me in front of our friends. Will. You. Let. GO! *God*!" I tugged at the door in frustration, demonstrating my point very clearly.

"Yeah, I heard. You want me gone. Nic didn't stick up for me much either." I was mortified he'd heard that whole exchange.

"You shouldn't make it your business listening in on other people's conversations. Didn't your mom ever tell you it's rude to eavesdrop?" I narrowed my eyes, hoping he'd get the message and back off. When he just stood surveying me I tried to shove him away, although it was as effective as trying to push over a brick wall.

"Just let me go, you son-of-a-bitch," I looked up into his face to fix him with a defiant stare but my expression eased when his gaze locked with mine.

"I don't want to live off of Nic's good grace for long. I'll be outta your hair as soon as possible." Disarmed by his apparent honesty, I calmed slightly, letting out a huff of breath. Only then did he back up a step so we were normal talking distance apart.

"Why aren't you at the party?" I asked in a tight voice.

"Well. I'm your personal bodyguard. Gotta make sure you don't get into trouble."

"Whoa, wait?! My bodyguard? So, you're going to be following me around watching every little thing I do and report it back to my husband?" That *asshole*! Nicholas could not simply palm me off onto his brother while he went around sticking it in anything with a pulse. Hell no! That was not the way it was going to work.

"Well, maybe if you didn't act like a toddler then it wouldn't be necessary!" he sniped.

I glared at him wishing that looks could severely injure. Or perhaps castrate.

"Look, the *only* reason I'm here, is because Nic asked me. Believe me, there are a ton of things I'd rather be doing than watching out for a little brat like you."

He continued in a much lower tone, "Do us both a favor,

Marie. Go back upstairs quietly."

"Why should I?" I shot back with the same inflection.

"Because you're Nic's wife and you should do as he says. Trust me, it's easier than the alternative." He looked subdued. I wanted to smack him. Or at least yell at him, let him know I wasn't going to make his job an easy one, but what was the point?

Rolling my eyes, I stamped back to the house. I knew what Nic was like, probably better than Jack did, but I was in no mood to argue anymore. I shrugged out of my clothes, then took some Tylenol and a bottle of whiskey to bed. The pills Cassandra had given me had probably dissolved at the bottom of the pool by now.

I didn't normally drink unless I felt tense. Although, that was becoming increasingly often. There were only a few mouthfuls left in the bottle, which I nursed and then dropped, empty, to the floor. Naked and with a severe headache, I lay on top of the bedcovers, the clammy air making my skin stick to the silk sheets. I cursed the broken air conditioning unit.

Unsettling thoughts pulled my mind to Jack, the quietly infuriating man. Something about him was mysterious, or that's what he wanted you to think through lack of speech. Brooding in a corner the whole time until somebody came to speak to him. *Asshole*!

He was particularly hard to read. I couldn't tell what he was thinking but he was obviously thinking something. His eyes were too calculating, too focused, to have a blank mind behind them. It was the most annoying thing. I was normally such a good judge of character.

I hated to admit it, but he was attractive despite his scars. Tall, well-built and good-looking in a rugged sort of way. Skin the color of caramel, darkened by the sun. Wide-set, amber-flecked green eyes that shifted in the light in a way that was almost hypnotic.

As my state of consciousness gradually dwindled, my mind drifted over the day, replaying certain parts over and over. Jack arriving. Watching me intently as I swam. Holding me in the pool, so close I could feel his breath on my skin, the proximity making the hairs on the back of my neck stand up.

I woke up in bed alone, the morning light flooding through the windows. It still wasn't sunny but it was bright. The weather in California wasn't like I'd thought it would be and certainly nothing like the deep azure skies of Mississippi where I'd spent my summers growing up. The air here was thick and hazy, brushed with grey shades that were almost blue but never quite right. Sometimes I did miss home.

Sitting at the kitchen island in my peach robe, I stared down at the half-eaten plate of rye toast before pushing my breakfast away with a sigh.

Jack slid lazily into the room half-dressed, his hair still damp from the shower. I rolled my eyes and pretended to read the open magazine on the counter next to me. I'd bought it two days ago, not realizing that pages six and seven were a double-page spread on my latest outfits. What I wore to what party slash charity event slash wherever I went. Being the wife of an extremely rich and influential billionaire had its perks, but it could be downright intrusive at times. I couldn't go out looking anything less than perfect, or I'd pay for it in the press the next day.

"What you got there, kid?" he shot in my direction without looking at me.

"Don't call me kid," I replied in the same manner.

Jack ignored me and shuffled through the cupboards looking for something decent to eat.

"Don't you have any cereal?" he asked, almost frustrated. He ran a large hand through his hair. It looked much darker when it was wet, almost the same color as mine.

"No," I replied, gazing over an article detailing Nic's latest public spat with a business rival. There was a snapshot of me in the corner looking concerned although this had been taken when I took Jude to the park the other week. He'd gone out of sight for just a second but it was long enough to make me panic. He was such a sweet little boy, he'd never run off on me like that on purpose.

Last week there was an article in the very same magazine, aptly titled 'Nicholas Hayes, forty-three, spotted in downtown LA with mysterious blond.' It detailed many events which were either factually incorrect or irrelevant to the 'story'. It mentioned he was photographed with her, inserted a hazy paparazzi shot of a man who could be Nic and then listed the scandalous affairs he was rumored to be having. Nothing had been proven, but the tabloids would use anything to fuel their growing obsession with our family.

It only got to me so much because I had a great suspicion it was true. Not all of it but I knew he didn't spend all those nights when he was 'away on business' alone.

Jack chuckled once at me.

   "Reading about your own life, could you possibly be any more self-obsessed?"

I raised my eyes to look at him steadily before flicking them back down to the magazine.

   "That's a big word for you."

   "Ha!" he exclaimed loudly and drew out a box of bran cereal from the back of a cupboard. I couldn't help myself.

   "That's perfect for you, old man! There might be some prune juice lying around somewhere if you look hard enough. You might need your glasses, though."

He poured a large bowl, grumbling something unintelligible as he splashed half a carton of almond milk on top, and took a seat on the bar stool across from me. He was dressed in grey sweatpants, displaying his well-defined torso and broad chest. Why couldn't he put on a t-shirt or something? Why should I be forced to look at this amount of…mouth-watering, rock-hard… bronzed skin? And so early in the morning?

   "Can't take your eyes off me, princess?" he mocked with a full mouth.

   "Ha! You wish!" Although I did have to admit the sight of

his semi-naked body wasn't a bad one. *There I go again…*

Jack swallowed before raising his eyebrows and shooting me a sardonic grin. That smug motherfucker! He had no problem acting like the guy who knew women would throw themselves at. Even scarred as he was, I was sure he had no problems in that department.

I just rolled my eyes again, "Get over yourself."

"Watch you don't give yourself an aneurysm with all that eye rolling." He was shoveling so much cereal in his mouth, it was a wonder he could even speak.

"I wouldn't *have* to roll my eyes if you weren't here."

"Aw, are you grouchy because Daddy has gone out again without you?"

"No. I'm pissed he left me here with a murderer," I replied, nostrils flaring. We could both hit the spot that hurt; if he was going to play dirty than so was I.

Jack had stopped eating, spoon hanging limply from one hand, "I would leave that alone if I were you." His earthy-green eyes locked onto mine, unblinking.

"No, you know what? You come into my house acting like you own the place, talking down to me. You are so disrespectful! Nic and I have taken you into our home when you have nowhere else to go, so stop acting like an asshole and show a little gratitude!" I was so angry I didn't even notice that I was now standing, yelling at him.

He got up and stepped toward me, speaking so quietly it was hard to catch his words, "This isn't your house, sweetheart. It and all of its contents belong to Nicholas. All you have do is spread your legs a few times a week. We both know why you married him and it sure as hell wasn't for love."

My mouth dropped open in shock. Infuriated, I tried to hit him as he approached, but he swatted away every attempt as if my hands were sheets of paper blowing in the wind. A sarcastic smile curled the corner of his mouth as my back hit the wall behind me. Both my wrists were somehow in one of his gigantic hands, his other against the wall, blocking any escape route.

Jack towered over me at nearly double my height, trying to intimidate me into backing down. I looked up into his smirking expression and stomped on his toe, hoping the pain would be enough of a distraction.

The dark look he gave me made me immediately still. I realized then this really *was* a dangerous man. Through my struggles, I had only succeeded in banging my head and bruising my wrists. All it took on his part was one grasp of my arms, and I was helpless.

Although he wouldn't risk hurting his brother's wife, would he? Not while he was living under his gracious care.

"Oh, Jack," I said, battering my thick, falsely extended lashes with mock confidence, "I think you are jealous because Nicholas has something you don't."

"You don't know what the hell you're talking about," he muttered under his breath.

"I think you do. I know what you did to her. Your wife. That's why you went away, wasn't it? You killed her."

"Stop!" he said more firmly, refusing to look at me.

"You are lucky you still have Nicholas because he's the only family you're ever going to have," I taunted, hearing the venom in my voice.

"SHUT UP!"

All of a sudden, he released the vice-like grip on my wrists. Before I could blink, his heavy fist collided with the wall beside my face, a few lumps of plaster falling beside his bare feet. His body was so close now, it pressed mine against the wall. I was trapped. His other hand came down and grasped my neck, lifting me inches off the floor to his eye level.

"I told you to shut your fuckin' trap!" He annunciated each word clearly and slowly, bare chest heaving.

"Let's get things straight," he hissed. "Don't ever, *ever* talk to me like that again. You don't want to be on the wrong side of me or things will start looking very bad for you. Understand?"

I couldn't breathe, more from panic than his hand tightening around my neck. His face went out of focus, blurring into dappled patches of green and caramel. The thundering rhythm of my pulse echoed around in my eardrums. My fingers scrabbled against the wall for purchase, finding none.

I jerked my leg up in the only way I could think to make him let me go. As my knee made contact with his crotch, he let out a guttural groan, automatically releasing his hold on me, and slumped over in pain.

I took the opportunity to run. I wanted to get out of there before he snapped back to reality.

I didn't stop until I reached the upstairs bathroom. With clumsy fingers, I managed to bolt the lock, sliding my back down against the door. Hot, angry tears ran in streams down my cheeks. I put my head in my hands in frustration.

This is what men were like; they hurt those weaker than them. Vicious, self-centered bastards. In a world run by them you had to be strong to survive. You had to know how to play the game with them.

Long gone was my childish pretense of glamorous Los Angeles. I now knew what the score was here, and it was pretty much the same, if not harder than it was anywhere else. If you wanted to survive, you had to fight.

It was lucky the nanny had taken Jude out for the day. Having him witness that horrific display of violence would've had a lasting impact on him, and one I'd move the Earth to protect him from. It didn't matter that he wasn't my son, I loved him as though he was.

I prayed that he wouldn't take after his father - or his uncle - that he could stay a gentle, good-natured little boy forever, a stranger to corruption. But there was a time when all little boys must grow up. I was afraid when the time came, he too, would be lost forever.

Chapter Five

JACK

I could have gone and apologized. I was way outta line, I knew that. But that's not what guys like me did. Guys like me fuck up every step of the way and, as a rule, we never apologized for anything. So, I just sat there, my pride intact, waiting until she decided she was ready to come out.

Ten minutes later, staring at the ceiling fan was getting old. Normally, I'd have been severely pissed off after an encounter like the one I'd just had with Marie. Instead, I felt strangely empty.

After being cooped up for so long, I was beginning to find an appreciation of nature I'd previously overlooked. I also found I liked to walk. The freedom of choosing where I wanted to be, and when. After every move being dictated to me my whole life, first by my father, then my coach, Captain, and then the Court Martial, I was finally allowed to be free. No schedule. No rules.

The beach stretched on for miles, strangely deserted, the waves the only sound I could hear. In his way, Nic was right about infinite possibilities. Around every turn was a new decision to make, another choice, another test of morality. I'd protected my brother and, in turn, destroyed my own life. Was that the price to pay for someone like myself? Was I destined to be lonely, cursed with self-destructive power?

I stopped to stare into the grey-blue surf. I'd been afraid of water ever since I was young. Nic pulled me out when I'd almost drowned. A chain of events all in reciprocation... were we even now? Somehow, I doubted we'd ever be even.

After a while, I thought I should go back. I *was* supposed to be watching her after all.

The bedroom door was ajar but I knocked in just case she was changing or something. With no answer, I pushed the door open and stepped inside.

Wall-to-wall white carpet, just like my room although it wasn't kept as pristine as my own. Discarded clothes littered the floor, a used towel slung onto the unmade bed. The bathroom door was open, so she wasn't in there. That left the closet.

"Marie?" I called. No reply. I cautiously approached the door, listening closely. No movement. My hand hovered over the door handle. After a few moments more of silence, I jerked the door open.

"*What*?!" she rounded on me, exasperated. She stood there half-dressed in cropped yoga pants and a very tiny matching top that seemed to struggle to hold in all of her chest at once.

"*Well*?" She pulled on a fitted sports jacket and my head cleared, although not quite enough to form words.

"Can you stop ogling my breasts every chance you get?" she snapped, pushing past me to get back into the bedroom.

I felt a little ashamed that in trying to assure myself she was okay, I'd felt compelled to barge into her closet. The place specifically where she would be changing, if I was thinking logically. I didn't want her to presume I was some kind of pervert.

"Ah'm going to tennis in ten minutes, just so you know ah haven't run off." Her accent seemed to thicken when she was being sarcastic.

"Alright. I'm ready."

"You are *not* coming with me," she looked appalled.

"I have to drive you, actually," I felt uncomfortable telling her what to do but like hell was I going to show it after all that had gone down in the last twenty-four hours. Now was not the time to back down. Especially since I was supposed to be the one in charge.

"I'm not even allowed to drive my own fucking car now?"

"Nope. Nic specifically said you were a 'menace on the road', and that I, 'have to keep you safe by whatever means necessary'."

"Well, joke's on him, isn't it? Because I'm not much safer with you," she snapped.

Judging by what happened little over an hour ago, she was right. The momentary lapse in control was something I regretted the second it registered. I needed to keep a lid on it, or I'd find myself back in the hellhole I'd just left. Her zipped jacket barely came high enough to cover the red marks on her neck. At the sight of them, a wave of shame rolled over me.

Marie, however, was still feeling defiant. I caught her eyeing up her car keys on the dresser, calculating if she could reach them before I did. Fat chance. I was there in two strides, snatching up the keys just as she lunged for them, and she let out a whine of frustration.

"I'll be waiting in the car."

Fifteen minutes later, Marie was sulking in the passenger seat of her SUV. I was driving her down to the tennis club, following the Sat Nav, so she could have a two-hour, one-on-one lesson with a private coach.

I took a deep breath, searching for the words to form some kind of apology when she slid me a side-long scowl.

"I'm not talking to you," she said curtly and resumed looking out the window. I hadn't even managed to get a single word out before she bit my head off.

"Look, I don't know where to start when it comes to this kind of thing…"

"Then save your breath."

"I didn't mean to… you know. What happened… I… but you shouldn't have wound me up like that…"

She pointedly snatched up a book tucked in the passenger door, turning her back on me to read.

"Listen, I'm only trying to pull my weight around here. If Nic tells me he wants something doing, who am I to refuse?"

"Marie?" I tried again, and when she didn't acknowledge me, I prodded her lightly in the back.

"Don't fucking *touch* me!" she spat, not turning around.

So now I was essentially her driver. Hell, she should have just sat in the back with a screen between us, it would have made things a lot easier. We traveled the rest of the way in silence.

The moment I pulled into the parking lot, Marie threw the book down and got out, slamming the door shut behind her. She stalked off ahead, leaving me to trail after her.

The weather was the same as the day before, hot and gloomy, although the sky was bright in spite of the thick blanket of cloud.

It was a real nice place; the type of fancy you felt awkward just looking at. Well-manicured plants in perfect borders, expensive-looking grass maintained by daily gardeners and hourly sprinklers. I didn't want to think about which body part you'd have to cut off and give as payment for a membership to this kind of place.

Marie's tennis coach greeted her with a hug. I immediately disliked the guy. He seemed slick, touching her inappropriately when showing her how to hold the racket for better technique. He stood way too close, pressing himself against her behind. When the lesson was finally over, he hugged her again. This time he noticed the intensity of my glare over Marie's shoulder.

She walked off without even a glance in my direction. Mr Slick came over to me before I could follow, "Excuse me, sir, can I help you?"

"Yeah, you can tell me what the hell you think you're doing touching her like that?" My voice was low, threatening. If I was going to do my job, I might as well do it properly.

"I don't know what you mean?"

"You know exactly what I mean. You seemed a bit too comfortable in her personal space over there."

He shrugged, "I have a close relationship with all my clients."

"Just don't grab her and we don't have a problem. I'm sure her husband would be very concerned if he found out you've been feeling her up."

"Who are you, if I may ask?" He smirked at me from behind his sports glasses. Who did this prick think *he* was? I grabbed him by the collar of his poncy-ass polo shirt.

"Listen here, bud. You touch her again and you'll have me to answer to. And I don't play nice." He wrenched the shirt from my grip and ran what could have been slightly trembling fingers through his rumpled hair.

I watched him slither away until he was out of my sight before getting up to look for Marie. She was in the next courtyard, drinking what looked like her second glass of champagne with a group of women. I recognized one blond from the party, Cassandra. The others had less memorable faces, but they could have been there. Drinking before noon? Marie had hardly touched her breakfast. All that alcohol on an empty stomach was not a good idea.

I kept my distance, just keeping an eye on her like Nic asked. Wishing I had a cold beer to get me through, I settled in a quiet spot to keep watch. This only lasted a short while before the girls noticed I was sitting under the shade of a tree, or what would be the shade of a tree if it were sunny enough. Marie caught my eye and gave me a death glare before realizing I wasn't going anywhere. She made her way over.

"Go home and I'll call you to pick me up, okay?"

"Can't do that, Marie."

"Look, I don't need you lurking around twenty-four-seven. Leave. Me. *Alone!*" Her voice picked up, causing a few people to look in our direction. I changed the subject quickly in case onlookers thought I was trying to kidnap her.

"Are you fucking that coach?"

"What's wrong with you?" she whispered furiously.

"You two seemed pretty friendly out on the court earlier. And you didn't seem to object when he put his hands all over you, either." I was equally annoyed and amused. No matter what the subject matter, winding up Marie was a very enjoyable activity.

"Don't be ridiculous." Her tone was dismissive, like the

idea was completely out of nowhere. Or it could have been her way of deflecting guilt?

"Not denying it though, are you?"

"I don't answer to you," she snarled. All of a sudden, she paled a little. Then her skin took on a greeny tinge. Her hand went to her stomach, eyes widening before she took off at a run toward the clubhouse, presumably to find a bathroom.

I contemplated going after her but decided against it in favor of scoping out the place. Better out here anyway, more of a vantage point. Plus, I'd rather stay out in the open any day than follow Marie into a chick's bathroom.

None of the bitches from her table bothered to get up to check on her, although they had been very interested in our little exchange. I stood with my back against the wall, arms folded.

When Marie got out, she looked slightly better, but the green tinge was replaced by a ghostly white.

"You look like shit." I knew I was being a jerk but I had no real reason to be nice, other than the fact I was going to be stuck with her for the foreseeable future. I'd have to work on that later.

"Let's just go." Without a backward glance, she set off back to the parking lot.

I caught the mouthy blonde from the table take a swig of Marie's champagne before making a loud comment, "Maybe if she sticks with it she'll lose those ten pounds just in time for swimsuit season." The table burst into cruel laughter.

That comment pissed me off, but also struck me as odd; Marie had an absolute knockout figure. She was slim but curvaceous, possessing mile-long legs and a round, tight ass that would bring men and women alike to their knees. I silently cursed; thinking about her in this way was entirely inappropriate, even if I had no plans to act on my desires. Christ, I needed to go out and find myself a woman before I went stir-crazy.

Looking up, I spotted that tight little ass twenty paces ahead of me before I remembered I was supposed to be guarding it. It took me a second too long to get over there; Mr Slick was back.

"Marie? Are you okay?" He trailed after her, looking as pathetic as he sounded.

"Thanks, Todd. I'm fine." He put his arm around her shoulders and that was enough to trigger the red haze. I threw a heavy punch to the side of his head, knocking him to the floor. The tinted glasses flew off his face and cracked.

The dick had ample warning.

"What'd I tell ya, bub? Hands off the goods," I cracked my knuckles for good measure.

"Jack!" Marie scolded. "Why on Earth did you...? Oh, Todd. Are you okay?" Slick looked up, dazed. I was surprised he wasn't out cold. He was such a wimpy-looking thing. Out of the corner of my eye, I saw a few security guards preparing to intervene, re-adjusting their hats and setting down their various methods of hastening a usually dull shift.

"Let's get you out of here." I almost manhandled Marie to the car and strapped her in.

Back on the road, Marie was quiet again, but staring straight out ahead this time.

"Why is your first reaction always violence?" Her voice was so soft I wasn't quite sure I heard correctly.

"Huh?"

She shook her head, "Let's just get home. My blood sugar is really low." Checking her hands, I could see she was right; they had a slight tremor to them even when they were resting in her lap. Up ahead was a Starbucks, I indicated off and pulled into the drive-through lane.

"What do you want?" I asked pointedly.

"I want to go home."

"Kid, look, when you start shaking like that you need something in your system quick."

She put on her sunglasses and looked the other way. I ordered her a hot chocolate and some kind of fancy pastry thing, and a black coffee for myself, paying with a tap of the credit card Nic had given me.

She took the drink and mumbled her thanks. I grimaced as I took a swig of my own, not having time to dump my usual four sugars into it.

By the time we got home, she'd finished her snack and

looked much better for it.

"Alright, what have you got planned for the rest of the day?"

"Not much," she said with a resigned sigh, rubbing her neck which had started to show a hint of color from where I grabbed her. Marie eyed me suspiciously, making me realize I'd been staring. She got out of the car, slamming the door behind her.

Over the next week while Nic was away, I took Marie to beauty appointments, public appearances and countless council meetings for a charity that Nic was apparently a huge contributor to.

I even went along with her while she helped plan a ball for the charity; driving her all over the city to pick out a location, decorations, food, music, the lot. She really was busy for somebody who didn't have an actual job.

Marie was photographed whenever she did anything, so she always made that extra effort to look good, not that she didn't naturally anyway. I must have seen her in about four outfits a day, ranging from a white suit with sleek long hair to jeans, a vest and a ponytail.

I caught her on early on Friday morning dressed in sweats and minimal make-up, loading up the car with brown paper-wrapped boxes.

"Shit! Do you have to sneak around like that? You almost gave me a heart attack!"

"What are you doing up and about so early? It's barely seven," I took a swig of coffee. The second cup of the day after my morning run, shower and breakfast. I'd always been a naturally early riser, I might as well put that time to good use.

"I just have to pop out for a couple of hours. *Alone*."

"No can-do. You know the rules."

"I don't have time to argue about this, I need to beat the traffic," she sighed.

"Hand em' over," I extended my palm.

She grumbled before dropping the keys into my waiting hand and getting into the car. Where could she be sneaking off to so early in the morning? Perplexed and more than a little intrigued, I followed her directions and pulled up in a secluded spot behind what looked to be a hospital.

She jumped down from the seat and went around to the trunk of the SUV. I got out and gave her a questioning look as she struggled to pile the boxes I'd seen earlier in her arms.

"Can't you just wait in the car?" she asked, exasperated.

"Nope."

"Fine! Just take these... and be quiet, okay?" She shoved a precariously stacked tower of boxes into my arms and grabbed a few more from the trunk before punching a hidden internal button to close it.

Once inside the building, Marie headed straight for the lift and elbowed the button to the seventh floor. A minute of silence transpired while I considered asking her what in God's name we were up to, and why we had to be so secretive about it? Before I could voice either of those questions, the elevator doors slid open, and I hesitantly followed her through a doorway on the left signposted 'Hayes Ward.'

"Can you wait here?" she whispered, indicating a seat along the opposite wall. Instead, I stood by the door as she poked her head around the first curtain on the left. A surprised, childish squeak came from behind it. Through the unintentional gap Marie had left in the hangings, I saw her hugging a small girl propped up in bed. The girl was painfully thin and frail, a brightly patterned scarf swathed around her head, features over-large in her pale, drawn face. Marie placed a wrapped box in her hands and gently helped her to open it.

So, she was sneaking into a hospital to give sick kids gifts? Surely that was something she wanted the tabloids to know about? That would get her tons of good publicity, which begged the question, why was she going about it in such an underhand way?

Marie left two hours later with a wide, genuine smile that I doubt I had seen until that moment. Tucked under her arm was a folder, filled with drawings and little notes from the kids.

When we returned home later that afternoon, she turned

to address me directly for the first time in a week.

"Okay, I think I'll accept your half-assed attempt at an apology now." Marie wasn't smiling. She wasn't saying she liked me. Or that she hated me. Just that she would tolerate my presence, which was good enough for me.

I nodded in what I hoped was a remorseful way. Her bruised neck had started to discolor a day after the incident, so much so she'd had to keep it covered all week. Now it was a green-tinted smudge.

She bit her lip before speaking again, "I'm thinking, if this is going to be a long-term thing... we should try to get on. Make it more pleasant for the both of us."

"Agreed," I replied.

"I still think you're an asshole," She gave me a small grin.

"And I still think you are a gold-digging bitch."

Just as quickly as it had appeared, the smile fell from her lips.

"Just so you know, Mr. Clarke isn't going to press any charges."

I furrowed my brow in confusion, "Who?"

"The tennis coach. With the broken nose."

"Oh... right." I didn't even want to think about that dick. As far as I was concerned, he'd gotten what he deserved, which was a hell of a lot lighter than anything Nic would have deemed a worthy punishment.

From the limited interaction I'd witnessed, I could already tell he was fiercely territorial over Marie. Any guy who so much as looked at her wrong would be in for a lot of trouble.

Of course, I was relieved the guy didn't want to press charges. Sure, babysitting Marie wasn't my idea of fun but it without doubt beat being locked up again.

We stood in the hall for a while in silence. It wasn't an awkward silence, for once, just a contemplative one.

"What did you go in for?" she asked softly.

"I...I don't want to talk about it."

"If I could just understand..."

"You can't!" I replied, voice low, heavy with warning. She held my gaze for only a second before looking away, a slight tinge of red coloring her cheeks. She knew it was none of her business. I left her standing in the hall and when I got to the top of the stairs and glanced back down, she was gone.

I locked myself in my room and slumped down on the bed fully clothed. Good God, I wished I could be the type of person who could nap. The Jack of my past would have thought now a good a time as any to have a shot or three to help suppress the urge to think. But I knew better than to try and forget.

My worst habit? Over-thinking. When I had too much time on my hands, my brain went into overdrive. Memories playing on a monotonous loop each time I closed my eyes, tormenting me.

Iraq, 2006. I disobeyed a direct order to stay put. I wasn't very popular out there, not known for taking orders well. They said I had a chip on my shoulder, one that they were determined to knock off.

Being twenty-nine, I was the oldest in my squadron. The soldiers were mostly post-pubescent boys, few old enough to shave. Fewer still old enough to buy alcohol back home. Twenty-one was no age to make that kind of decision, but apparently, it was old enough to run toward death. Youth lures you into a false sense of security. It allows you to lay trust in your invulnerability, gives you the kind of blind bravery that would get you killed.

I served for almost ten years before I decided that I wasn't actually okay with kids fighting for their country, no matter which side they were on. They could only learn through the eyes of their superiors, only believe in what they were told to believe in. There were others who deserved so much less than the reality those boys faced.

An unprecedented explosion, so large it caused the whole encampment to fall. The squadron turned their backs on the enemy, glad to see the last of them, or at least glad for a small victory. I couldn't leave them to burn.

I dragged an Iraqi kid out of the closest burning building, his legs taken off below the knees, trailing pieces of mangled flesh. His eyes were a startling bright blue underneath the grime. He looked up at me, with pain beyond words and blinked once. His thanks. He must have been all of twelve years old.

I pulled five more from that building before it collapsed. In saving them, and disobeying my sergeant, I was dismissed under bad conduct discharge. It might not have even been worth it; the medical attention available to them would have been primitive at best. The hostile environment would have seen to it they didn't survive, either through bleeding out or infection, and the US Marines would have nothing to do with helping them. There was a line and the enemy lived beneath it; beyond compassion, beyond human rights.

I was ashamed of my sentencing, yes, but I had a sense of morality that overshadowed the expectation to conform which allowed me to live with the decision I'd made.

The rest of my life decisions had been a bit more... questionable. My early boxing career had gone down the toilet over a few moments' loss of control. That same loss of control had put me in prison fifteen years later. I couldn't keep my shit together when it mattered most. It was my fault I lost the thing that should have been most precious to me. It was my fault she died.

I was left with lingering emptiness that was entirely worse than the images that slowly dissipated. The hazy hangover the morning after, profound guilt weighing me down. An aching loneliness that settled in my chest. Sometimes it was easier to drink, fuck and forget.

Although, having company wasn't always helpful. Too many women to count, all but one face forgettable. Women I'd used, more intent on my own release than their pleasure, but they were more than welcome to come along for the ride. After a while, that stopped helping as well.

I laid there for a while with my eyes closed, my bad leg

twinging with pain from a long-ago injury. That damned leg was usually half to blame for my lack of sleep.

However, I must have eventually drifted off. When my eyes snapped open again, it was evening. Long strips of sunset stretched out along the walls from the open windows, bathing the room in a golden light.

"*Shit!*" I jumped out of my fucking skin when I saw a pair of eyes trained on me from the end of the bed. Jude.

"What the hell, kid! You don't just sneak up on people while they are sleeping."

He stood up, "Marie told me to tell you dinner is ready soon."

"How'd you even get in here?" The door was locked, I'd made doubly sure.

Jude shuffled closer, "I've been practicing." His smile was mischievous.

"Picking locks? Where'd you learn how to do that?" I asked in an incredulous tone, scrubbing a hand over my face.

"Youtube," he replied, like it was obvious. His eyes were bright in a way only a kid's eyes could be, inquisitive and round with innocence. He kind of reminded me of myself when I was little.

"Look kid, it's not okay to sneak up on someone, alright?"

"Sorry, Uncle Jack."

"Just… don't do it again."

He nodded, not moving from his position two feet away from me.

"You're not supposed to wear your daytime clothes in bed."

"*What*?" I shot at him, confused.

"My mom says I have to put my pajamas on when I go to bed because my daytime clothes have germs on." I just put my face back into the pillow and groaned. I was way too tired to be dealing with this right now.

"Uncle Jack?" Jude poked me in the shoulder.

"What, Jude?" I mumbled into the pillow.

"Are you going to come down and eat dinner?"

I sighed, rolling my face to the side so he could hear me.

"If you don't leave me alone, I'll eat you instead," I replied with a growl, my intent to scare him off.

"Don't be silly, you can't eat a human," he giggled. Goddammit, what did it take for some privacy?

I dragged my body up from the bed, sitting on the edge as Jude watched with interest. Yawning, I stretched my back out and eyed him back in the same way. Time to change tactics.

"You're kinda short ain't ya?"

"I'm eight," he replied indignantly.

"I was bigger than you when I was that age."

"Well, I'm going to grow bigger soon. I just need to eat more veg-tables."

"Is that right?" I didn't have the heart to tease him anymore; clearly my attempts to make him leave me alone had only warmed him to my sunny disposition.

"Tell Marie I'll be down in twenty minutes, alright?"

I got downstairs just in time to see Nic returning home from his week-long business trip. He strode in through the front door, dropping his expensive-looking suit jacket to the ground and ripping his silk tie loose.

"God, I hate board meetings. Total waste of fuckin' time," He huffed, kicking his shoes into a corner.

Marie seemed decidedly happy to see him, running into his arms and kissing him. Maybe she realized how much she'd missed him after her eventful week with me.

"Welcome home, baby. I missed you."

"I missed you too, my sexy little vixen," Nic grabbed a handful of her ass, his other hand clutched the back of her neck as he jerked her mouth back to his in a demanding kiss.

"I see you took good care of my wife while I was away," Nic chuckled over at me, nuzzling Marie's neck, eliciting a giggle from her.

I just rolled my eyes in an amused kind of way and left them to their reunion before things got too heated.

In the garden, Jude was playing on the grass with what looked like some action figures but got up to greet Nic when he exited the house. He ran up to his father like he was going to hug him but seemed to remember himself at the last second and stopped to extend his hand.

"Hi, Dad," he smiled shyly up at Nic, slightly in awe of the man towering over him. Nic took his son's hand bemusedly then cuffed him on the shoulder, jolting the startled kid.

"Hey, Squirt. Were you well-behaved for Marie?"

"Yes. Wasn't I, Marie?"

"You're always well-behaved, my angel." She leant down and kissed him on the head on her way over to the outside table, her hands full with various fixings for dinner.

"Why don't you show your dad what you've made for him? It's on the fridge."

While Jude scampered off into the kitchen, Nic took a seat as Marie continued putting out dishes of salad, potatoes and cutlery.

"I'm going to help Hannah bring out the hot food," She kissed Nic on the temple and left just as Jude returned with a sheet of blue craft paper.

"See, it's me and Kaylee and you and Marie on the beach," He held the picture up over his head supposedly so Nic could see it without bending down, but in reality Nic wasn't that tall seated, resulting in him leaning back to focus on the quivering page.

"That's... interesting... why do I have orange hair?"

"The grey ran out."

"I see. What's that?" He pointed to a brown blob in the background.

"That's Uncle Jack."

Nic stifled a laugh, "I thought it was a gorilla!"

"No, he's just really hairy." The kid looked disheartened, Marie noticed this as she walked past with a plate of fried chicken.

"Well, I think it's the best picture I've ever seen," she interjected, putting down the plate and stroking Jude's curly hair down flat, "I'm going to put it right back on the fridge so I can look it every day."

"Then can we finally eat?" Nic relaxed back into his chair, tearing a chunk of bread from the platter in front of him.

"Your dad's just grouchy because he is hungry," I overheard Marie whisper to Jude as I passed to get to my seat, suppressing a grin which would have been a dead giveaway.

Dinner was delicious and passed uneventfully. Jude clearly felt indulged by a rare show of tolerance by sitting next to his father, talking to him about all the things he'd been doing with his nanny while Nic was away.

Being a child, he was completely unaware of all the less than honest things his dad had done, in business and his personal life. To Jude, his father was a wonderful person, someone to aspire to. He looked up to him, just like I had looked up to Nic when I was that age. The boy would one day be old enough to understand how things worked but for now, he was content believing his father was the Wall Street equivalent of Superman.

"Okay, honey. I think we should get you ready for bed now. It's getting late."

"Alright, Marie. I bet I can beat you upstairs," Jude wiped his mouth on the back of his arm and jumped from the chair, running into the house with Marie tailing close behind him. Nic watched her until she was out of sight, his gaze hidden by mirrored sunglasses.

"Damn, I wish I still had that kid's energy! D'ya want another beer?"

"No, thanks," I managed to get out through a thick mouthful of mashed potato.

Nic lit a cigar, puffing until the end glowed red.

"So, Jackie, I wanted to ask you a favor..."

I swallowed a lump of partially chewed chicken, "I wanna stop you right there, Nic. I don't want to be involved in any of your business transactions." I didn't want to be involved in anything like that ever again.

"It's a simple job; drive in, watch money trade hands, drive out. Simple."

"No."

"Please man, I really need somebody there I can trust," He put his hands together in mock prayer, the cigar smoke wafting up to the heavy sky where it disintegrated into nothing.

"I don't want a repeat of last time."

Nicholas opened his mouth to protest but I held my hand up to stop him.

"I'm sorry, it's a no."

His mouth set into a hard line.

Marie reappeared, newly refilled wine glass in hand, and slid into Nic's waiting lap.

"He said he's got it. Doesn't need my help with anything these days, it seems."

Nic flicked his sunglasses down from atop his head before a burly arm snaked its way around her, his hand resting possibly on her thigh.

The thing about mirrored sunglasses, apart from shielding the wearer's wandering eyes, is you can see your reflection echoed back on itself. I know I shouldn't have noticed how obscenely short my brother's wife's dress was, how I shouldn't be looking at her incredible legs and thinking how badly I wanted them wrapped around me as I...

Knock it off, Jack-ass! Jesus Christ, you need to get laid if you're eyeing up your sister-in-law in front of her husband. If I caught myself gawping at Marie in reflection, no telling what Nicholas saw.

First thing on the agenda, when I had some free time, was getting some pussy. I didn't realize how long it had been until I caught the faint sound of a barely contained moan through the wall later that evening on my way to bed. Except, I wanted more than a quick lay. I wanted more than just another warm body to temporarily silence the longing and the brief easing from loneliness.

Seeing them together, especially Jude and Marie, awakened some deeply suppressed feeling within me, and made me achingly aware of a yearning for the family I'd never had.

Chapter Six

JACK

I was snapped awake by the buzzing of a hushed argument taking place right outside my bedroom door. I huffed and buried my head back under the pillow, trying to squash their voices out.

"You *promised*, Nic! You promised you would spend some time with him today!"

"The kid is going to have to understand that disappointment is a part of life."

"He's eight years old! He's not going to understand that you have to take off *again."*

"He'll get over it."

A moments silence passed. And as I was beginning to hope they'd just been passing and I might be given the opportunity to go back to sleep, Marie's lowered voice carried through the door again.

"Remember, I have an appointment today. I can't miss it and I can't reschedule *again*! Who's going to look after him on such short notice?"

"Just call Katie."

"Her name is *Kaylee*, and I can't. It's her day off."

"Fuck, then call someone else. It's not a big deal."

"It's not a big deal to you, Nic! Even if we did manage to find a sitter on such short notice, we'd have to vet them. Are you happy for a stranger to be in your house, looking after your son?"

"You know what, just go. I'll sort it out."

Another silence. I could picture perfectly the way Marie would be glaring at Nic, her dark eyes narrowed and jaw set.

"Really? What kind of influence is that on Jude?"

"What do you expect me to do? We need *someone*, and he's family."

Marie huffed in a frustrated way, then her voice became fainter. I found myself holding my breath, straining my ears to listen.

"I don't have time for this. Do whatever you want. I have to go."

A few moments later there was a sharp knock on my bedroom door. I sighed, knowing exactly what was coming next.

"Jack, bud? It's Nic, can I come in?"

———————————————————————

"You wanna play ball, kid?"

Jude nodded, his eyes widening with excitement before

skittering off into the front yard.

Nic had asked, very politely for him, if I could watch Jude for a couple of hours while Marie was out. I didn't have any plans until later nor enough time to devise a convincing fictitious one, so I didn't have any other viable option than to agree. I still felt indebted to Nic for letting me stay. Besides, Jude didn't seem like he'd be a handful, and It was only a couple of hours.

"Okay, so, you have to bounce the ball like this," I demonstrated how to dribble, "You can only move if the ball is bouncing. You can't hold it and move."

I stopped and handed the ball over. Jude smacked it with the flat palm of his hand, watching it bounce once before it hit him on the chin on the way back up and rolled into the hedge. He blinked in a startled sort of way, then flashed me a small smile.

"Careful, kid. Or you'll be getting a visit from the tooth fairy sooner than you think."

"The tooth fairy isn't real," He called over his shoulder as he went after the ball.

"Who do you think puts the dollar under your pillow?"

"Dad. And he doesn't put it under my pillow, he just trades my teeth for the money."

I raised my eyebrows at that.

"How much does a molar go for these days?"

"Twenty dollars," Jude replied in an offhand way, raking

the basketball out from the back of the hedge with a wayward branch.

"Jesus, what did you buy with that?"

"Nothing yet. I'm saving for the big water gun at the toy store."

I could have explained to him that all he'd have to do is ask and Nic would probably buy him the entire isle of water pistols, but somehow the thought of Jude asking for something didn't fit. He was a quiet, shy kid, not wanting to be the center of attention or get in the way.

"Try again. Use this part of your hand," I indicated my fingertips by wiggling them at him. After a few tries, he got the hang of it.

I should have judged by his first attempt how accident-prone the kid was before trying to teach him how to dribble. He'd only manage a few steps before either losing the ball or tripping over it or his own feet. I held back a groan as the ball ricocheted off the house and flew dangerously close to the wing mirror of one of Nic's cars.

"How about we try passing instead?" Any damage to myself would be far less expensive than repairs to Nic's car, although my concern was more to save Jude's rear end from his father's temper.

"Can we stop for a drink break first?"

"Sure."

Jude flopped under the shade of a tall bush and took a few gulps from his water bottle. His cheeks were flushed with the effort he'd been putting into practicing, and I could tell he was really trying to learn fast. He looked up at me, his lips twitched into a nervous grin.

"Do you want to have a drink too? I got you a bottle," He pointed at another water bottle tucked into the base of the shrub, "I put it there to keep it cold."

"Thanks," I settled down next to him and took a swig of the water he offered me, feeling like a bit of an ass for not being a very encouraging teacher.

"Sorry you have to look after me."

"I didn't have any other plans," I shrugged.

"I'm not very good at basketball, am I?"

"No one is good at something the first time they try. You just need a bit of practice."

"That's what my mom always says."

"Then it must be true, right?"

"I suppose so."

We sat in silence for a few minutes, drinking water and, on my part, casting around for something to say. Jude was particularly interested in a ladybug that was crawling up a nearby blade of grass. He slowly touched his finger to the end of the blade, offering the creature an alternate route up his hand. The ladybug took a few hesitant scuttles onto his finger before flying off.

"Do you want to carry on practicing or do something

else?"

"What's something else?"

"What do you want it to be?"

He turned to face me then, a wide beam lighting up his face, "I have something to teach *you*."

———————————————————

Fifteen minutes later he had me standing at the kitchen counter in an apron, covered in flour.

"You have to roll it like this," He demonstrated how to roll the dough away from him, "try not to stretch it thin or the cookies won't come out right."

He had a patch of flour in the center of his forehead from where he'd pushed back his hair. Sticky, black trails of syrup covered the countertop and the smell of cinnamon was overwhelming thanks to the jar dropped at our feet. But he was having fun and that was all that mattered. I could clean up later while he was having a nap or something. Come to think of it, he could be a little old for naps.

"Do you want me to roll it? You can find the cutter."

"Uh, okay." I'd managed to stretch the dough far enough to poke holes in it again. Jude was trying to be patient but it would have made the fourth time him showing me and he claimed 'over-working the dough will make the cookies tough.' Whatever that meant.

Jude gathered up the dough and smushed it back together so he could roll it out properly while I routed around for a cookie cutter.

"What shape do we need again?"

"Well, people-shaped. They are going to be gingerbread people."

The drawer was lacking in cookie cutters of any design, let alone gingerbread people. Marie looked like she rarely stepped foot in the kitchen and I couldn't imagine Nic in the Christmas spirit enough to want to bake. We were lucky enough to find molasses in the cupboard.

Eventually, I gave up the hunt and unscrewed the lid from a peanut butter jar.

"This is the best I could find," I said, holding it out to him.

"That will be okay. They can be gingerbread circles instead."

Jude took the offered lid and imprinted the neatly rolled-out dough with it. Once done, he carefully prized them off the countertop with a butter knife and laid them on a paper-covered tray. He insisted that it was a special kind of paper that was used in the oven and didn't burn. I only fully believed him when the oven didn't catch on fire in the allotted ten-minute cooking time.

While the cookies cooled, we sat at the breakfast bar with glasses of milk. Not my refreshment of choice but I suppose beer wasn't an appropriate babysitting beverage.

"Where'd you learn how to bake?"

"Me and mom make them every Christmas. Nana calls me her star baker. She says my gingerbread people are her favorite treat."

"They smell really good. Can we have one yet?"

"No," he rolled his eyes at me in a very Marie-like way, "They have to cool down all the way and then we have to decorate them."

"What do we use to do that?"

"Icing, chocolate chips, candy. Anything."

"I didn't see anything like that in the cupboard, kid," I replied, scratching the back of my neck. I'd have another look but we might have to resort to decorating with nuts and raisins, not ideal but supposedly better than nothing.

"We still have some time left though. They've just come out of the oven."

I tapped my fingers along the counter impatiently while the sweet, spicy warmth in the air concentrated around us. I did *really* want a cookie. Jude took another sip, the milk lining his top lip when he brought the glass down.

"Dad was supposed to be here today."

"Yeah?" I didn't know what to say to that without making him upset. He was a damn sensitive kid, "We are having fun though, right?"

"Yeah," He looked a little unsure.

"And Marie will be home soon. I'm sure she'd love a cookie."

This made Jude smile, "She will, yeah...Do you want to come and play Nintendo with me? I have Mario racing."

"Err...You'll have to show me the controls," I was hopeless with any kind of technology. I'd only recently acquired a cell phone. The last time I'd had one was 1996. Now the damn things only had four buttons; one for the power, two for volume, up and down, and a mystery one in the middle that, according to Jude could do all kinds of things. Kids these days seemed to be born with the instruction manual downloaded into their brains as standard.

"It's easy." He grinned, jumping up to grab my hand and lead me away, "You can be Mario if you want?"

Chapter Seven

MARIE

"Here you are, Judes," I handed him an assortment of colorful take-out menus, "You can pick what we eat tonight." He smiled up at me, showing cheeky little dimples he must have inherited from his mom.

"Anything?" he asked.

"Anything you want, honey."

"Can we have Chinese noodles? Is that veg-it-able-arian?" He said the word with a confused look on his face.

"Sure," I laughed, "We could order Chow Mien with tofu. How does that sound?" At that moment, Jack walked past in the hallway behind us.

"Hey, Uncle Jack!" Jude shouted in a voice high-pitched with excitement, "Do you want to eat Chinese food with us?"

Jack froze in the doorway, jacket half on, keys swinging between his teeth. It was his first night off and he was dressed in what I'd imagined he'd wear out if he was trying to impress someone; dark jeans and an old leather jacket. The only smart part of his ensemble was a shirt, tucked in semi-neatly but not quite ironed enough to pass as ironed.

"Err, actually kid, I was going out..." *Called it.*

"Aww, please...?" Jude looked truly heartbroken, his puppy-dog eyes downcast. Even his bottom lip was stuck out adorably in a mock pout.

"I think Marie might prefer it if I cleared off and left the two of you to hang out alone?" he looked over to me, eyebrows raised, then winked at Jude.

"But we were going to watch movies and make our own popcorn! It would be so much funner if you were here, too." Jude jumped up onto the couch, narrowly missing a bowl of cheese puffs I rescued just in time to save the cream-colored Tibetan sheepskin rug. Nic would kill me if we stained that!

"Pleeeeaaaaasee!" The tendons in his neck stretched as he strained the word out.

Jack chuckled, "Alright kid, I'll stay for dinner."

"YAY!" Jude cheered, jumping up and down on the cushions.

"It's PJs only, so you'll have to change," I interjected, popping a cheese puff into my mouth. Jack slopped off grumbling something about not liking pajamas.

———————————————

Twenty minutes later, Jack was stretched out over the couch in sweatpants, holey socks and the t-shirt he'd arrived in. It was discolored and worn out; the collar stretched. It would have been white when he bought it but now the grayish fabric had a vaguely fluffy appearance.

Even though he had a wardrobe full of new clothes, it was understandable he'd feel more at ease in his own. It was comforting to have something of your own in a new environment. Something familiar. Like the crochet blanket my nonna had knitted for me as a baby, one of the only things I'd brought with me when I'd left home.

There was also a new addition to Jack's t-shirt; a smear of Chinese BBQ sauce down the front. He was chewing on a rib bone and raised an eyebrow when he noticed me watching him intently.

"Are you going to have some vegetables with all that red meat?" I asked.

"Meat is good for you. Protein."

"Not the way you're consuming it," I tried hard to fight off a laugh.

"Like a carnivore! Carnivore dinosaurs only eat meat," Jude chimed in.

Jack bared his teeth and let out a low growl, which made Jude giggle. Jack eyed me with an amused expression as he continued chewing, turning his attention back to the movie that was playing mainly for Jude's entertainment.

Jude poked one of his chopsticks into the takeout box in hope of spearing any remnants of battered tofu. Distracted as he was, I knew the question was going to be asked at some point.

"Marie, where's dad?"

I didn't want to make excuses for Nic's absences, but I

also didn't want to speak ill of Jude's father in front of him. It was his business what he told his son.

"He had to work, sweetie." I hated the silent disappointment he always accepted that response with. I'd been there myself as a child, and I never wanted anyone else to experience the same. The feeling of unimportance.

Despite being an only child, I'd never received my parents' full attention. I was raised by a string of nannies and our housekeeper, Betty. My father, although kind and affectionate, was hardly ever home between meetings. My mother was a different story.

That's why I tried so hard to make sure Jude wasn't left out of things. Maybe I could convince Nic to take him out for the day before he was shipped back off to his Mom.

"I wish he was here more. It would be nice if he had noodles and watched TV with us."

"It would be, yeah," I answered. I felt Jack shift uncomfortably next to me. I didn't think he knew much about what his brother had been getting up to recently. Or maybe he did and felt awkward about not being honest with me.

"Judes, do you want to show Jack a magic trick?"

"He might think magic is stupid," Jude looked down all bashful. I was fully expecting Jack to shrug or give a similar kind of noncommittal gesture that would make me want to whack him one, but he surprised me.

"Are you kidding? I *love* magic."

"You do?" Jude cried. He got up so fast he almost knocked over the food containers and ran out of the room. Jack shot me a questioning glance.

"He's gone to get his cards."

"Ah."

Jude came thundering back in holding a deck of cards and threw himself onto the couch between us. He struggled to shuffle them in his little hands before fanning them out and holding them to Jack.

"Pick a card, any card."

I put a hand on Jude's head, lovingly stroking back his baby curls. He had the most gorgeous fluffy hair, tawny in color, not that dissimilar to Jack's, I realized, once I saw them side by side. He actually looked more like Jack's son than he did Nic's.

"This one. Can I take it?"

"Yes, sir. Don't let me see it, though." My lips twitched upwards at Jude's put-on professional voice, impersonating the magician he loved to watch on TV.

"Okay, I got it."

"Please show it to the audience," Jude dramatically covered his eyes with his hand. Smiling, Jack showed me the card.

"Now put it back in the deck." Jack slipped it back into the middle of the pile.

"Okay," Jude's tongue poked out of the side of his mouth in concentration. He wiggled his fingers over the deck, then tapped it once.

"Is this your card?" He picked up the card lying on the top of the pile and showed it to Jack.

Jack stared blankly at the card for a few seconds before a thoroughly impressed smile slid across his face. For the first time it didn't come across as conceited or mocking. Actually, he looked kinda… nice.

"That was amazing, kiddo! Can you do any more?"

Jude looked delighted, reveling in the male attention he'd received little of from anywhere else.

"Yeah, I can do lots of tricks."

"A couple more," I agreed, "Then it's bedtime, you have to get up early tomorrow."

"Okay Marie, just a few. Then I will go to bed, I promise."

Half an hour later, Jude was beginning to get bleary-eyed and floppy. He rested his head on Jack's arm and yawned.

"Bedtime, I think," I stretched my arms out to lift him.

"No, I want Uncle Jack to take me. I want to show him my room." I opened my mouth to protest but Jack got there first.

"No worries, little man. Can you walk there, or do I need to carry you?"

"I can walk," Jude yawned again, sitting up and sliding his legs off the couch. He held out his hand to Jack, which he took in pleasant surprise.

I followed the two of them up to Jude's room, where he rolled into bed. His room was decorated with red and blue spacemen, his obsession the previous summer. His cot bed was shaped like a rocket ship and the lampshade beside the bed had small cut-outs and revolved slowly, throwing shadows to mimic the night sky.

"Cool room you have here."

"Yeah, it's cool... I keep the light on though because I get scared in the dark," Jude pulled the covers up to his chin and eyed a darkened corner of the room.

"That's okay, everyone gets scared sometimes."

"Not everyone. You don't get scared of anything."

"Oh? How do you know that?"

"Because you are tough. And a grown-up."

Jack barked out a laugh, "Grown-ups are scared of things too, we're just better at hiding it."

"What are you scared of?"

Jack looked thoughtful for a moment.

"When I was about your age, I went swimming with your dad and a few other boys from our neighborhood at the lake. It was huge. A flat, empty surface for as far as the eye could see. All the boys were bigger than me and I didn't want to get teased for not keeping up, so I swam out to the middle with them. I guess someone thought it would be funny to play a trick on me. One of the boys pulled me down by my leg, but it scared me so much that I opened my mouth to scream. I swallowed so much water, I felt like I couldn't breathe."

"Jack, that's enough!" I slapped him on the arm. "He won't sleep!"

"Then what happened?" Jude asked, mouth shaped into a small O, terror mounting in his eyes.

"Well, I sorta forgot to kick and kept going under. My arms and legs were real heavy, like weights. Your dad got to me just in time. Dragged me all the way back to land. I puked up a lot of water."

"Wow, that's so scary!"

"See? Now you've scared him." That was all he needed! Poor thing had enough to worry about without Jack filling his head with those images.

"No, I'm okay, Marie. Are you scared of anything?"

"Of course, lots of things. Bugs, snakes, spiders. All creepy crawlies. And needles. Big, big fear of needles... you *sure* you're okay?"

"Yeah, I'm fine. Just tired."

"Okay, well, you know where I am if you need me, alright? Just call."

Jude yawned again before nodding. I kissed him on the forehead and backed out of the room quietly. Jack shut the door behind us.

"If he has nightmares now, it's your fault!" I whispered furiously, making my way back downstairs, the plush hallway carpet soft against my bare feet.

"I'm sure he'll be alright. He's tougher than you think," He caught me by the arm, pulling me to a stop.

"You know, you're really good with him," Jack whispered, "You treat him like he's your kid."

I shrugged, "It comes naturally, I guess. I used to babysit a lot back home. I had sixteen baby cousins."

"Sixteen?"

"Yeah, my family lived on an old cotton plantation; I'm the oldest out of the lot. No southern jokes now, ya hear?" I stopped and held my finger up at Jack warningly.

"Ah wouldn't dare," Jack teased in a strong accent. I wrinkled my nose with mock annoyance and punched him in the arm.

"Let's go finish watching the movie."

Heading back downstairs with Jack moving quietly behind me, I felt at ease with the newfound companionship we'd forged. By the looks of things, Jack wasn't making any plans to head out soon, preferring to spend the rest of his night off with me. I didn't know what to make of that.

His light-hearted mood had really shown me a different

side of him, one I didn't even know existed in a man with such a hard exterior. Seeing him so tender with his nephew made me wonder where this good nature came from, and why Nicholas struggled to be that way with his own son.

What must have been a few hours later, I awoke with a start to the title screen of the movie replying over and over and a dull, low ache in my belly, maybe period pain? It must have been very early in the morning… where was Nic? Still out?

Damn, it was hot. The air-conditioning must have cut out again. I shifted the blanket I didn't remember draping across me over to the side. The movement aggravated my belly and it contracted painfully again, making me cringe.

Jack was asleep with his mouth hanging slightly open, hair disheveled and flopping over his forehead. Something uncurled in my chest. He looked so peaceful. A sleepy, contented sigh left his lips and he shifted, the blanket falling to the floor. When did he take his shirt off? My eyes glanced slowly down his exposed skin, over the multiple scars on his tanned neck, chest and rock-solid abs. His jeans unbuttoned, riding low on his hips. Enough so I could see where the trail of wiry hair from his belly button ended. And that he wasn't wearing underpants…

Stop! That's enough of that, Marie! When my thoughts slipped further down the route of dirty-minded, I took that as a sign to leave.

Quietly I disentangled myself from the blanket and stood

up. Damn, that was some bellyache. It felt like it was burning a hole right through me.

I pushed to my feet and made my way toward the kitchen, intending to search for some painkillers, when a wave of lightheadedness flushed over me. The pain intensified, a spasm of agony ripped through my stomach, bringing me to my knees. It felt like the breath was being drawn out of my lungs. I sucked in a gasp of pain.

The next second Jack was there, nostrils flaring wildly. He rolled me gently over onto my back and I grasped my belly with shaking fingers. I smelt it too, the coppery stench of blood, like a handful of dirty pennies.

After that it was all a blur, Jack talking quietly but clearly on the phone, carrying me out of the house into an ambulance, the intense heat from him feeling like the sun against my skin. His hand covering my own while I was being seen to. Comforting words murmured but quickly forgotten. Squeezing my hand before his fingers slipped from mine.

I woke up in an unfamiliar room. Pale blue walls and slowly beeping medical equipment. I had a drip in my hand which revolted me so much I couldn't look at it. Jack was sleeping in a chair in the corner, knuckles tucked under his chin to keep it from lolling. *What happened?*

I pressed a button next to the bed for a nurse. The ping awoke Jack and he blinked, trying to focus his vision as the door opened and the light flicked on.

"Mrs Hayes. It's good to see you with some color back in you. How are you feeling?" The nurse smiled at me.

"Err, fine... what happened?"

"Let me get Doctor Shah for you," Her smile dimmed as she turned from the room.

"Jack!" I felt panic wash up in me, "Jack, what happened?" Jack sat on the bed facing me. He looked like he was lost for words, not able to meet my eye. He opened his mouth and then closed it again.

"Last night... I was bleeding..."

A short, burly doctor briskly entered the room, shaking my hand in a friendly manner and reading something on his clipboard.

"Mrs Hayes, how are you?"

"Confused," I answered truthfully. I looked at Jack for reassurance, but he was staring at a spot on the floor.

"You've suffered a miscarriage. A very early one, but still a miscarriage."

Oh! Wait, what?

"I didn't know I was pregnant. I... I'm on the pill?"

"Unfortunately, there are a few things that can make it ineffective. Have you been taking it at around the same time each day?" My head was reeling, doing very quick math back through the weeks.

"Yes. Absolutely."

"Have you been taking any other medications or antibiotics?" Do you smoke or take any herbal remedies?"

"No, none of that."

"How about any sickness? Upset stomach?"

"Uhhh, yeah... a few weeks ago I think I got some bad seafood in Chinatown." The memories from that night came rushing back to me.

Nic had taken me out to dinner to make up for a particularly long trip. We'd ended up having a blazing row on the way back and it ended with rough make-up sex on the dining room table. A few hours later, I was bringing up Kung-Pao shrimp in the toilet while Nicholas slept in the other room, drugged into oblivion.

"Oral contraception may not be effective if you vomit within two hours of taking it. They don't have enough time to be absorbed by your body. If that happens again, remember to use an extra method of protection to avoid any surprises." I just nodded, slightly embarrassed. Here I was, a grown woman being lectured in sex-ed. I felt my cheeks burning.

"Now as you were only a few weeks along, you should heal up quite fast. A few days of rest and you'll be right as rain. No staining or over-exerting yourself. I'm sure your husband will look after you."

I turned to look incredulously at Jack, who was standing behind me holding my shoulder. Husband? What on earth had he told them?

"Thank you, doctor, I'll take good care of her." Dr Shah nodded and left the room, shutting the door behind him.

"Jack, you ass! What did you tell them?" I slapped his hand off.

"They wouldn't let me in otherwise. Immediate family only. I thought you would like the company?" he looked dejected and a bit hurt. *Be nice, Marie. He was just looking out for you.*

"Well, thank you. For staying with me," I offered a kind smile, hoping he'd accept that as a kind of unspoken apology.

"We should get you back home soon. I called the nanny to watch Jude but it's still early. I'm sure he won't even notice you were gone."

I chewed a bit of dead skin on my lip. If Nicholas found out about this, it would just add more flames to the baby fire. He would think that I had actually been trying and I didn't want to get his hopes up. I still couldn't believe I was actually pregnant until just a few hours ago.

"Jack, I really don't want Nicholas to know about this. Can we keep it between us? Please?"

A deep frown line appeared in his forehead, "Why wouldn't you want him to know?"

"I just don't think he should know *right now*. I will tell him, eventually. I just want to… wrap my own head around it." I felt a stab of guilt in my otherwise empty belly.

Tears welled up in my eyes as I struggled to find the words. Ever since I was a little girl, since my aunts and uncles began having their own children, I'd dreamed of one day being a mother. The feeling of utter joy as each of my nieces and nephews laughed at me for the first time made my heart swell, their dimpled smiles and tiny, upturned noses. Their scant hair, tufted up at the back from sleep, a trail of milky dribble falling down their cheeks. The happy little noises they made as they played with my fingers and made babbling non-coherent conversation with me. One day, but not now. I wasn't ready yet.

Jack put an arm around me, pulling me against his broad chest.

"Shh, shh. It's going to be okay," He smoothed my hair back with his free hand. I gave a loud sniff, wiping my eyes with the back of my hand. A black smudge was there when I brought it down again. God, I was a mess.

"Maybe it was a blessing in disguise. I'm not ready for that kind of responsibility yet."

"What do you mean? You're great with kids, and you'll have all the help you'd ever need."

"Yeah, what could *possibly* be the problem?" I scoffed, pushing him away, "I'm not ready for that, Jack. It's my choice too."

"Okay... chill out, I was just saying."

"Yeah well, don't," I huffed.

A moment of silence passed between us.

"I promise I won't tell him." I pulled back to look at him, his expression unreadable but I was becoming more accustomed to his reactions. This blankness usually seemed to translate to, 'I'm being serious.'

"Thank you."

Jack rubbed my back tenderly in reply. Through the papery gown, I felt the heat from his large, rough hand. It was reassuringly pleasant, though all too different from the touch of my husband.

Neither of us said anything more, but from that moment on the boundaries had shifted, the line drawn in the sand between us becoming less defined. The air clouded with things left unsaid, charged, like an elusive understanding had been reached. Like a flashover was imminent. Like electricity building up before a lightning strike.

Chapter Eight

MARIE

It was still early when we got home, but not quite early enough for the sun to start peeking over the horizon.

I thanked Jack, then excused myself to my room. I was exhausted and just wanted to be alone. Jack looked just about ready to pass out himself. However, once I'd had a quick dip in the bath to wash off the grubby hospital feeling, got into my pajamas and slid under the sheets, I was anything but tired. The clock read four twenty am. I lay in bed, blinking up at the shadowy ceiling for a few seconds before I remembered I hadn't checked on Jude.

Kaylee, his nanny, stayed in one of the spare rooms right next to Jude's when she babysat overnight so I knew he'd be fine, but I just wanted to reassure myself he was okay. When I peeked in, he was sleeping peacefully; on his side, blanket tucked under his chin with his toy giraffe, Mosley, for company.

Although he tried not to show it, I knew Jude was upset by his dad's absence yet again the previous day. He tried so hard to impress his father, to be accepted by him, and for all the recognition Nic showed him, it seemed Jude was fighting an uphill battle. Sometimes it seemed he was one of my only allies. I was going to miss him when the summer was over.

It was quite stuffy in his room so I crept over and opened the window a crack, then tiptoed back out. There was no sense in going back to bed with my mind racing a mile a minute, so I thought a glass of warm oat milk might help and maybe a dull book from Nic's expansive yet untouched library of classics. A lot of them were first editions; just another thing to buy when you had everything.

I used to enjoy reading when I was a child. Momma wouldn't allow television past eight o'clock in the evening, so I found other ways to entertain myself. I ended up enjoying it so much that I would continue well into the night, way past the time I'd been told to go to sleep, until I could barely keep my eyes open and the sentences started getting muddled.

Oat milk first. I padded to the kitchen barefoot, wondering if the staff had left any particularly tasty snacks in the fridge. No such luck; in fact, it looked like we could do with a trip to Whole Foods. I made a mental note to ask someone to drive to the store tomorrow and pick up some basics. We normally had a food delivery service drop off groceries on Tuesdays and Fridays, but it was about to become Monday and the fridge was looking pretty bare. There was also no milk of any kind.

Slightly disappointed, I grabbed a bottle of water and bumped the door shut. An orange-y flickering from beyond the kitchen doors caught my attention. The fire pit was lit, the dark shape of somebody slumped in the swinging chair silhouetted before it. I frowned to myself, confused. Nic was out. Jack was in bed, as was Jude, and he knew he wasn't allowed to light a fire. Anyhow, the shadowy figure was much larger than Jude's slight eight-year-old frame.

Fear tightened my chest. Who could be on our property at

this hour, and bold enough to sit out in the open with a fire lit? Should I approach? Or maybe call the cops? No, that was an overreaction. Although, the homeless situation was getting beyond the authorities' control in the surrounding areas. I'd heard in the news recently that someone had been arrested for rooting around in people's trash cans a few blocks over from here.

Okay, I couldn't just stand here until it got light... I silently slid the door open and stepped into the garden, leaving the door ajar in case I needed to run for shelter, and crept toward the fire pit. The closer I got, the more detail came into view. The man, I assumed it was a man from his proportions, had shoulder-length hair, swept back and over. He wore a thick jacket, the collar turned up again the coolness of the early morning. And when he turned his head ever so slightly to let a puff of cigarette smoke out, I let out a breath of relief. It was Jean.

Sensing my presence or hearing my sigh, he turned his head to me, collected as always, and smiled wryly.

"Bonsoir, ma petite pétale."

"Hey, Jean. Comment vas-tu?"

"Je vais bien, and you?"

"Je vais très bien, merci."

He smiled again, "Your French is getting better."

"J'ai un bon professeur."

I sat in the chair next to him, watching the cigarette smoke curling up into the dark air. The night was still heavy but a few gaps in the cloud cover allowed me, every so often, a glimpse of the bright stars they were hiding.

"Something on your mind?" I asked, noticing how worn out he looked in the soft glow of the firelight.

"Just sometimes it all gets a bit too much."

"You want to talk about it?"

Jean considered me for a second, then patted the small space beside him on the swinging couch. Just enough room for me to nestle in beside him. He drew one leg up, the other still in contact with the ground, keeping the swing in gentle motion.

He had a calm way about him that drew you in. Soft. Inviting. Maybe it was because his lilting accent was familiar. More like the voices I was used to hearing growing up. Although even now, when he was silent, the silence was comfortable.

"Do you know where I'm from?"

"Louisiana, right?"

"Right, Cajun born and bred. Third generation in fact, my great-grandmother traveled here stowed in the hold of a cargo ship. Eight months pregnant."

I smiled weakly, wondering where he was going with this, "Do you miss home?"

"Sometimes I do. I miss the smells, is that weird? Louisiana smells like no other place on Earth. And the food! Actually, it was probably the food that made it smell so good."

"Mmm," I agreed. "We had this housekeeper, Betty, she made pork chops to die for, all crispy on the edges and this amazing gravy. And biscuits. Waking up to the smell of freshly baking biscuits was the best."

"That sounds good right about now," He lifted his cigarette and tapped some ash into the fire before bringing it back to his lips.

"What else d'you miss? What about the locals? Sometimes I say things and people here look at me like I have a third eye growing out of my head."

He shook his head once, "That's the reason I had to get out of the south. Folks round them parts aren't too accommodating."

"Accommodating of what?"

"People like me."

I turned to face him, "What do you mean?"

He sighed, "It was summer 1984. The DIY perms were awful, and the neon clothing was worse. All the guys in my year were busy building the courage to ask the girls they really liked to the prom. My best friend Alex had the biggest crush on this girl, Sabrina. He'd sat behind her in homeroom every day for four years, staring at the back of her head. That was what he first noticed about her. Her hair. Dark red spirals."

I nodded in confusion, wondering how this was relevant.

"Anyway, before he got the chance to ask her out, Sabrina asked me who I was going with. I told her I didn't have a date yet. And she asked *me* out... I was so shocked I just stood there with my mouth hanging open. She must have taken that to mean yes because she turned up at my house the night of the prom in this big pink dress," He stuck the cigarette between his teeth and gestured out to the sides to demonstrate the heft of the dress.

"Don't get me wrong, she was a very attractive girl, but I wasn't thrilled to be going with her. I don't think I would have been excited for prom even if Bo Derek turned up at my door. It was Alex I wanted to go with."

"Did you tell him?"

"No. After that night he wouldn't talk to me. I understood why, it was a shitty thing to do. I could have just told the girl no and carried on with my life but the thought of Alex going to prom with someone else tore me up inside. I couldn't watch him look at her the way I'd longed for him to look at me since we met that first day of middle school. I couldn't stand by and watch as they danced together, or kissed, thinking of what they would be up to afterwards."

I was lost for words, unaware until that point that my hand was clutched to my chest. Jean regarded the flames with blank eyes, reliving the long-suppressed memory.

"The real trouble started about two weeks later. I'd been seeing Sabrina on and off since prom. She was easy to get along with and we enjoyed each other's company; we went to the movies together, milkshakes, you know?"

I nodded.

"Well, one night she asked why I hadn't kissed her yet. I didn't know how to respond. I didn't know if I could trust her with my secret. It made me feel dirty to have these thoughts about boys that I couldn't control. Back then people weren't so tolerant, homosexuals were treated like outsiders, like freaks of nature. So, you can imagine in the south..."

"Jean..." I breathed, overcome with heartache.

"It was like I was being hit with a double-ended mallet. Eventually we broke up and she started spreading horrible rumors about me, all things that were absolutely true. I don't know how but she... just figured it out."

"What did you do?"

"I moved schools. That didn't work, the rumors followed me. One day I got beat up so badly my mother was called in for a meeting with the principal. He told her I would have to move again if I didn't stop causing trouble."

"Did she know?"

Jean shook his head and tossed the end of his cigarette into the dying flames.

"Even now?"

"I never told her. I left as soon as I graduated, enrolled at a college in Nebraska. Haven't been home since."

"So what got to you tonight?" I asked, intently focused on him.

"You wouldn't believe it if I told you."

"Try me?"

"I saw Alex today. Hand in hand with his husband outside the Chinese theatre. Complete with French bulldog and six-month-old baby strapped to his chest."

I leaned in closer then, wrapping my arms around him, silently offering him comfort. He laid his cheek on top of my head and squeezed me back.

"Are you sure it was him?"

"If you had loved somebody since you were eleven, don't you think you would recognize them if they walked down the street?"

He took out another cigarette, offering me the box. I shook my head as he lit up.

"Seeing him today made me wonder what my life would be like now if I just had the courage to tell him."

I pulled away so I could face him.

"You can't live the rest of your life wondering what could have happened."

"Yeah…"

"Does anyone else know? Nic?"

He let out a light snort, "No offense, but Nic isn't the most perceptive of people."

"Don't I know it," I replied, a hint of darkness edging my voice.

"I'm sorry. I know he's shit to you."

"He's not even here half the time. He's still in New York. He hasn't called once. I had to speak with his secretary... He promised me he'd be around this weekend."

Jean pulled a face.

"I don't trust him, Jean. Not after last time."

"You're right not to. That's something he's going to have to earn back."

I looked up into his eyes, more than a little confused. "Why are you telling me this? You're supposed to be *his* friend."

"Because I can't sit by and watch him make you unhappy," He paused for a moment, "That's why you're down here?"

I looked away for a second, "I just couldn't sleep."

"Been thinking about Jack?"

I whipped back around, "How did you...?"

"I have too. Trying to figure him out has been driving me crazy."

"Ooh, Jean!" I teased, lightly nudging him in the ribs.

"No! Not like that you dirty girl, although I wouldn't turn him down..."

I let out a short, automatic laugh.

"He's unpredictable. I can't keep tabs on him as easily as I would have liked."

"Why do you need to keep tabs on him?"

"Nic seems to trust his brother, but I'm not so convinced. I didn't even know of his existence until a few weeks ago. Either Nic doesn't know the whole story or he's hiding something."

"I think Jack seems okay."

"You need to be careful, Marie! You don't know him very well at all," he warned, "From the tall stories Nic tells, he's got quite the reputation with the ladies, also."

"Nic trusts Jack with his life and if that's the case, then I trust him too."

"Just… keep it in mind, okay?" Jean stretched his long legs out before standing up to face me.

"Merci de m'avoir écouté, ma chère." He leaned down to kiss my forehead before flicking what was left of his cigarette into the glowing embers and leaving the fireside. I watched him fade into the early morning haze, assuming he was heading out the back gate toward the beach, as that was all that was in that direction.

As we had been talking, the sun had risen over the horizon, brightening and warming as it went. I was touched that Jean would share something so intimate with me. Glad for his presence in my life which until now, I hadn't appreciated.

I was wrong earlier, thinking Jude was my only friend here.
I had Jean too.

Chapter Nine

NIC

My stomach convulsed as I watched the brightly colored lights spasm on and off, watching as the frame they were attached to arched back and forth to disco music. That hot dog had seemed like a good idea at the time but even just looking at the death trap they called a ride made me want to hurl the fucking thing back up.

Some kids' abandoned ice cream cone lay splattered on the ground five feet from a trash can. A single wasp bathed lazily in its melting river, sliding toward the gap in the floorboards. Some way below that was the ocean. If the thing wasn't already dead, it would be soon.

Jude seemed content enough devouring a cloud of cotton candy, the remains of his own hot dog smeared over his cheek. He looked up at me, all big eyes, his expression unreadable. We stared at each other for a while before I spoke, "You doin' okay, there?"

He nodded.

"See? Bit of meat doesn't hurt every now and then, does it? You need protein to build up nice strong muscles."

"I don't want animals to have to die so I can eat them."

"By the time they get to you, they are already dead! Who's been filling your head with this nonsense, anyway?"

"A girl at school was telling me." *Figures.*

"Want some?" He offered me the cloud of sugar.

"Nah."

Near the top of the list of things I'd never understand is why they always put the napkin underneath the food you were trying to eat? I managed to find a relatively dry corner of hot-dog-soaked napkin to wipe the ketchup from Jude's face. He was a good kid really. No trouble, didn't talk too much or ask for things.

"Your tongue is purple."

"Is not!"

"I swear, look," I took a pinch of the multi-colored fluff and put it in my mouth. The overwhelmingly sweet taste hit my tongue and dissolved in an instant, leaving my mouth wet and my bad tooth aching.

For a few seconds of delight, it was hardly worth the payoff. No wonder it was sold by the bucket load. Kinda addictive though. Didn't I read somewhere that a sugar habit is harder to kick than coke? I stuck my tongue out at him.

"Yours is more blue," He said, with a confused frown.

"Yeah, but you ate more of the pink side, stupid."

"Oh," He cracked a wide smile and I ruffled his hair. He was a good-looking little tyke, if I did say so myself. Must have got that from his mom. Jude looked so much like Elise, from coloring right down to the mole on his left cheek. I could hardly see myself in him at all.

Elise was a girl I'd dated on and off a while back. She was gorgeous, quick-witted and one of the only women who really knew how to put me in my place. Things hadn't worked out, though. I was moving at much too fast a pace to be tied down. Elise was great fun, but I didn't love her. There was always too much temptation; I wanted to live the high life.

Then Jude came along and there were all these expectations and unspoken rules. She wanted me to commit to her, turn into the kind person I knew I could never be. Not for her.

Things turned nasty. Some shit about what she thought I owed her. So, I set her up in a little place in Florida with fifty thousand dollars a year so she could stay the fuck out of my life. Flew my son out once a year for a few weeks to keep her happy, and we both live our separate lives. Although, from time to time, I was curious how things were going her end.

"How's your mom?"

"She's okay. She has another new boyfriend." Standard Elise behavior. God, she couldn't even hold down a stable relationship for the sake of her own son.

"Oh yeah? What's he like?"

"He's not there very much," Jude said with a shrug.

"That a good thing?"

"I guess so."

Jesus Christ, getting information from Jude was like pulling teeth. He was so quiet, I found myself casting around for another topic of conversation so we didn't sit there on that un-fucking-comfortable bench all afternoon.

"Can we go on a ride now?" He asked, surprising me.

I looked up at the Ferris wheel looming in front of me. My palms were sweaty. I felt jittery, weak and strangely empty all in one go. I'd been off the sauce since the previous morning. I didn't want to be intoxicated while looking after the kid, in case anything happened.

And *technically* I did promise Marie, in a few less words, that I wouldn't drink so much. And more for myself, it was a reason to stop. Recently the hangovers had been getting much worse. A head so foggy it could have rivaled the mist that rolled in over the San Francisco Bay. Pounding temples that drove me to distraction; It was like a jackhammer going off in there.

"Please, dad?" Jude nudged my leg with his own. I looked down and found my hands clenched so tightly the nails dug into flesh, leaving mauve half-moon imprints. I could deal with the headache for a few more hours until I could get my hands on some Excedrin, for Jude's sake.

"It's okay if you're scared... I could hold your hand?"

I stretched my legs out before standing to make my way over to the ticket booth, "I'm not scared," I huffed under my breath.

A brown-eyed little thing sold us two tickets and I gave her a wink as she handed them to me. She was pretty; long, shiny hair I could just imagine twisted in my hands as I pulled her luscious mouth in for a taste. Even longer tanned legs, exposed in tight shorts, that she could wrap around me as I fucked her.

As our eyes met, I realized just how messed up those lewd thoughts had been. Hell, she was just a kid. A kid with fuck-off full, pouty lips and a rack barely contained by her tiny t-shirt. She was maybe fifteen years old? I internally swore at how very wrong those thoughts were and how very, very easily they came.

She threw me a half-interested smile before wishing us a nice ride, smacking bubblegum and all.

There was something crusty stuck all along the seat of the Ferris wheel and what looked like the remains of a pile of dried vomit in the corner. As the carriage slowly ascended, I got a better view of the park.

The inaccurately named 'Funland' was a seventies wasteland just biding its precious time until the beams it stood on were rotten enough to collapse into the murky depths below. Mechanical piles of junk and California's finest as far as the eye could see; beer-stained men in denim cut-offs, women with badly bleached hair and snotty brats hyped up on Slurpees and carnival music. It was my idea of hell.

I wished my dad cared enough to take us anywhere when me and Jack were kids. Too bad I was past caring now. The fucker could burn in hell. He'd been two of the things I hated most in the world, lazy and poor. I was a hell of a lot better off not knowing where he was, happy even, that he'd never bothered to drop by to see what became of his son. I'm sure, wherever he was, that he knew how successful I'd become. I assumed what little pride remained in him kept him far away from here. And that was completely fine by me.

The carriage stopped at the top and I peered down, then wished I hadn't.

"Don't look down, it will make it worse," Jude gave my hand a nervous pat. Maybe I was a *little* scared. The ground was a long way down and the landing didn't look like a feather bed. I looked back up and took a steadying breath.

"I'm scared of the dark if it helps you feel better?" Jude offered, "Everyone is scared of something." I looked and saw my son in a slightly different light. It was weird, he was all of eight-years-old, but his sudden and unexpected wisdom creeped me out.

"Uncle Jack is scared of water. Like *deep* water."

"How'd you know that?" The Jack *I* knew wouldn't be partial to parting with that kind of information so easily.

"He told me," Jude shrugged.

"What about Marie?" I asked, wondering if she had been a part of this conversation too.

"She doesn't like needles; she said when she was sick, they put a needle in her hand to give her some medicine. They gave her a really big band-aid for it."

"When was she sick?" I tried to keep the concerned tone out of my voice, my expression neutral. If Jude thought I was interrogating him he'd be sure to go all quiet on me again.

"The other day, when Uncle Jack took her to the hospital. I was asleep."

"What for?"

"I don't know? She said she's all better now."

So, Jack had taken Marie to the hospital and no one had mentioned it? Not one goddamn person in this family had bothered to tell me what was going on in my own home. Is that what it had come to? My wife not even telling me when something was wrong?

The carriage started to move and I felt my head start to spin again with the rocking motion. Of course, it wasn't the long drop to the ground, or the quick stop that would be my body splattered over the planked floor that really fazed me. It was the nag, nag, nagging in the periphery of my mind. A humming. A whisper. Couldn't I have just a minute without being reminded of the incessant longing for a drink?

"Can we go on the bumper cars next?"

"Sure," I replied. At least they were safely on the ground.

"Dad... do you know what happened to Uncle Jack's face?"

"Apart from being born ugly, you mean?" I laughed a little at my joke that fell on deaf ears. Jude didn't understand my humor yet.

"No, he has big scars on his face."

"I wouldn't ask him about it. That's a sure-fire way to upset him quick."

"Did he get it in a fight? He said he used to fight for a job."

"He was in the Marines, yes. But that's not how it happened."

"Do you know what happened?" Jude peered up at me, blinking innocently. He looked so small huddled in the corner.

I sighed, stuck between wanting to tell him the truth and shielding him from horrors so dark even the shadows they cast would give him nightmares.

"I can't tell you until you are older, okay? There are a lot of things that kids aren't supposed to know."

"Like where babies come from? Because Marie told me that one already."

I managed to crack a smile, "Oh, did she? And what did she tell you?"

"She said when a Mommy and Daddy love each other enough, their love can make a baby," Jude exclaimed, seemingly very proud of himself for being entrusted with this insider knowledge.

"That's a very delicate way of putting it, huh?" I chuckled.

"I guess so. She said I could figure out the rest later."

"And did you?"

"Not yet."

I chuckled again at his off-hand reply. Maybe Marie was right, I was too hard on him. At least the boy respected his father, as was expected of him. I didn't *like* my father, he was an asshole. But I'd never questioned his authority and I endured his temper until I was old enough to make my own decisions and get the hell outta there.

A moderate smack now and again wouldn't have hurt the boy, would help him learn his place. He'd do what he was told and mind his manners. No answering back. It was a hell of a lot lighter than the punishment my father doled out for much less of an offense.

One day, Jude would be old enough to understand the way I treated him helped him grow up to be a man who didn't take shit from those below him. He needed to learn to be strong. Independent. A man who'd someday take over from this father as the leader of an empire.

The carriage mercifully came to a stop and the tempting young woman unlocked the wire door of the enclosure for us to exit.

"Ya'll have a nice day," she smiled at me lazily as I passed. Damn little thing teasing me like that. If I had a daughter under the age of eighteen, I sure as shit wouldn't let her leave the house all dolled up like *that*. Plastered in a fuck-ton of make-up and clothing that could belong to her younger sister.

"Dad? I don't feel so good," Jude swayed a little, his hand clutched to his belly.

"You'll be alright in a minute; it was just the way the carriage was swinging in the wind." My head was practically pulsating, working its way up to a full roar. If I didn't get some painkillers soon, I would kneel over.

Jude nodded, his face pale and stoic. Then he leaned forward and threw up a colorful puddle of sweet-smelling vomit all over my feet.

I woke up alone. Pushing myself up onto my elbows, my head gave a sharp pang of protest and I immediately slouched back down into the pillows. The familiar pounding grew louder, offset by the morning's silence. Deep inside I felt empty, defeated. I hated feeling like this.

Being on the wagon is hard, especially when you go cold turkey instead of phasing it out. Somewhere down past the hollowness was an understanding that this couldn't go on. The hangovers were worse, the withdrawals more painful than ever before. It was either be in a constant state of intoxication or stay sober.

Marie's side of the bed was made so she was either still too pissed to sleep next to me or she slept and got up early to get away from me. She had no right to still be pissed with me, goddamn it. I had tried to spend time bonding with my son, it's not my fault he was a weed. So, I could have handled the vomiting incident better. I never claimed to be father of the year. I was trying, didn't that count for something?

"You awake?" Marie nudged her face through the door,

opening it a fraction so as not to wake anyone who might still be sleeping. I sat up again, slowly this time, and turned my head from side to side to crack my neck.

"Yeah. I feel like I've just come out of hibernation," I reached across to the nightstand where the controls for curtains were built in. One click of a button and the room slowly began to filter with light.

Marie flashed a half smile, coming over to sit on the bed. "You were so tired yesterday you practically passed out on the couch when you got home. I thought you would like to sleep in."

I gazed at her, looking so fresh and pretty, barefaced in nothing but a silk robe. Mornings like this I realized I was one goddamn lucky son-of-a-bitch.

"I got you some coffee," She indicated the tray she'd placed next to me and leaned over to help herself to a slice of toast.

"Thanks, doll. I need it," I took a gulp of coffee so hot it burned through the top layer of skin inside my mouth, although not necessarily worth it for the quick caffeine buzz.

"So, did you and Jude have a nice time at the fair yesterday?"

"Mph, he threw up all over my feet. Literally, my new sneakers are stained bright purple," I said through a mouthful of toast before swallowing.

"You shouldn't have fed him so much junk then. And you can buy more shoes, you can't buy another son."

I pulled her close to nuzzle into her neck. She smelt beautiful. "We could make one, though."

"Oh, could we?" She raised her eyebrows at my teasing but pulled away.

"What time is it, anyway?"

"It's almost eleven. You were asleep for thirteen hours. I was beginning to think something was wrong."

"Shit, I better get moving. I'm flying to New York later and I have some stuff I gotta take care of first."

"What's in New York?" she pouted.

"Just business, babe. I got a few meetings to attend to, a few places I have to show my face. I'll be gone a few days tops. And when I'm back…" I made a sudden dash toward her, scooping her into my arms and before she even knew what was happening, I had her pinned underneath me back on the bed.

I went in for a kiss but she turned her face away and my lips made contact with her ear. Not my intended target but I could work with that.

"What's the matter? You don't want a kiss from your sexy husband?"

Well, that's my question from earlier answered.

"Babe, what's wrong, huh? Are you still pissed with me?" I cupped her jaw in my hand, turning her back to face me. I took in her expression, lips pressed together, eyes burning with an almost liquid intensity, and I knew I'd be fighting a losing battle.

"No. Everything's fine," Which meant everything was most definitely *not* fine.

She pushed me away, and I allowed her to wiggle out of the small space, before leaving me, confused and horny, on the bed.

It didn't matter, not when I was going away so soon. I could take care of things in that department quite discreetly. The problem lay with understanding my wife. I could sit here for hours trying to figure out what I'd done to upset her but I didn't have the time for that. She'd either have to tell me or leave me to stew in the dark. Knowing Marie, it would be the latter.

She was the only woman I've ever loved enough to marry. I thought she could satisfy all my desires. She was perfect, so seemingly pliable and lovely. Young enough that I could mold and shape her into what I needed her to be. It turned out she would also be the biggest pain in my ass.

No matter how I looked at it, women would always be an intriguing, complex and frustrating mystery to me.

I met Max in Kasper's; a swanky, unnecessarily expensive upscale restaurant where you either brought clients to schmooze or a woman you wanted to impress. I was doing neither but Max insisted. They also had the best lobster in New York.

"Nicky! How have you been keeping?" He had one of those deep, booming voices that carried across a room, no matter how unintentionally.

"Alright. And yourself?"

"Got me an unreliable ticker these days but apart from that…"

"Sorry to hear it."

"It's just old age catching up with me. Let me tell you now, enjoy your youth because it's all downhill from forty."

"I'm forty-three, Max."

"Well, shit! I remember when you walked into my office for the first time. Cocky as anything but your head was always swimming with ideas."

I nodded and grinned. I hated going down memory lane with him, which we seemed to do each and every time we had dinner. Max was someone who liked to remind people where they came from.

Of course, we were friends. He'd been my first employer, my mentor. Now business partner. Equals. But he had some incessant need to remind me, every second I was in his company, who I used to be. Grinding me back into the dirt.

"I heard there was some trouble in the tabloids." And here we go.

"It's nothing I can't handle."

The waiter interrupted then and Max swiftly ordered a Macallan 18 on the rocks, while I went for a club soda.

"It's okay to ask for help if you need it, Nic. I want to keep the shareholders happy just as much as you do." Regrettably, Max held lucrative shares in Hayes Enterprises. Not enough to have complete control but, at just over a third, he had the second biggest influential voting rights after myself alone.

"Of course you do, you're a shareholder!" I had to try hard not to smirk nor let a Marie-influenced wave of eye-rolling from coming on. Both these conflicting resulted in a very visible face twitch.

"Excuse me for asking Nic, but what *the fuck* is wrong with you recently? Dicking around with the numbers for Interlon… You were very close to dropping the ball on this BioHault business too. Don't start getting conceited or you risk losing it all."

"That's not going to happen. Everything is going through the books, everything is insured."

"Morse have been quoted saying they're thinking about dropping out on us if things keep going the way they do. They are one of our biggest sponsors, Nic."

"I have a handle on it, alright? You can let them know they have nothing to worry about."

Like I said, we were friends. Yet the figurative hand he held looming over me would always be an indication of how much higher I had to jump. How much further I had to go to keep him satisfied. Just like Marie. The hand would always be ignored by mutual consent, of course.

Max had been as good as a father to me over the years. He believed in me when no one else would, gave me the chance to be who am I today. He taught me everything I know. I was grateful to him. But there was also a little nagging resentment there, way at the back, that I needed him in the first place.

He picked up his drink. The satisfying, melodic clink of ice against the glass, sweet music to my ears.

"Look, I've been you. I'm just trying to offer my advice. It's your choice whether or not you take it."

I looked away. I didn't need his type of advice. Chipping away, widening the black hole of self-doubt, an extensive void where pride and accomplishment went to rot. The inconsequential feeling feeding off my life force like a parasite. That shortened the margins on the need to drink, to ease that bitterness. And the feeling of *needing* a drink was a gateway to yet blacker suffering.

"It didn't escape my attention that you haven't had a drink yet either." I followed his gaze down to the guilty hand, trembling over the white tablecloth.

"The stories aren't very reassuring. The parties. The women. It's getting out of control," He paused before continuing in a softer tone.

"Like I was trying to explain earlier, image is everything. With you going and out and doing what you are doing, you inspire little faith that you can follow through."

That was enough. Who *the fuck* did he think he was?

"Look, Max. I didn't fly all the way out here to be *lectured* by you. I know what I'm doing, okay? Just because you have lost touch with the modern world, it doesn't mean we all need to be living in the dark ages."

"I didn't mean-"

I laughed sourly. Several nearby faces turned toward me, but I was past caring.

"We both know exactly what you meant! I'm trying to run this company, enjoy a healthy social life and keep my wife happy. It's impossible to do all that with you breathing down my neck!"

"Nic?" he scolded in a subdued voice, one that was filled with barely repressed accusation. I was done with this.

"If you're unhappy, you know where the door is." My tone was final.

Max came to his feet slowly, and perhaps unwillingly, shaking his head. I didn't need his disapproval, nor his sympathy or anything else for that matter. I just wanted him gone.

"Don't come back to me when you're filing for insolvency. Because I sure as hell won't be there to bail you out this time," he hissed.

I watched him leave, glaring daggers into his back, feeling like a kid who'd stupidly been caught blowing spit-wads at the teacher in class.

I understood how to run a business. I'd do what was

necessary to keep the money flowing.

My head gave an almighty thump. I could actually feel my heartbeat pulsating right up into my temple. If you were going to have a vice-gripper like this, surely you were entitled to just a few sips? For medicinal purposes.

The remains of Max's drink seemed luminescent in the dim light of the restaurant. Rich liquid, glowing gold, catching the light at just the right angle. I could almost taste it, feel its coldness burning its way down my throat. Soothing and numbing as it went. Bringing bliss. Caressing me like a lover would.

I picked up the glass and threw its contents back in one swallow.

Max thinking I didn't have a handle on any facet of my existence, that I couldn't get by without him acting as my personal life coach. My wife constantly judging me for trivial little slip-ups when all I tried to do was keep her happy. My son, wimpy and disappointing in almost every aspect. My best friends second-guess my judgment.

Why didn't anyone have any goddamn faith in me?

From the start, it had always been me and Jack against the world. We'd always had each other's backs. We had always believed in each other. If I had Jack, then I could continue conquering with him by my side. All I had to do was convince him, show him what he could achieve with me as his guide. As his mentor.

It was in that moment I decided not to take no for an answer. I never had before and, besides, I enjoyed a challenge. I signaled for the waiter to bring me another drink.

Bring it on. Bring it all on.

Chapter Ten

JACK

"Come on, you. We're going out for dinner!" I heard Marie call from somewhere behind me.

"Pass," I shot over my head, not moving from my position in front of the TV. I was very content horizontal on the couch, minding my own business and watching hockey re-runs on the huge plasma screen.

"The taxi will be here in ten minutes! *I'm* going out for dinner so, unfortunately, that means…"

I took another swig of beer and ignored her. It had been an uneventful week since 'The Incident' happened. We hadn't spoken about it after we got back from the hospital. We'd hardly spent any time in close proximity at all, apart from when I drove her places. It didn't make sense to take two cars since the whole point was that I had to follow Marie around everywhere she went. They had all been short journeys, mostly quiet and unremarkable.

"Well, I'll just go out to eat by myself then," she decided loudly. I rolled my eyes and got up, remembering my 'job'. I didn't want to go out for dinner, nor did I want to piss Nic off by deliberately not doing what he was paying me to do. Turning around, I caught the mischievous grin she quickly tried to cover.

"I'm not going to dress up," I scowled.

"No, what you are wearing will be fine!" I gave her an inquisitive look, narrowing my eyes when she didn't let up. Marie was letting me wear a T-shirt to a fancy restaurant? A restaurant *she'd* chosen? Surprising, since self-image seemed to be the only thing that mattered around here.

Marie, however, *was* dressed up. Nobody told me it was Halloween?

"What the fuck is that on your head?" Her dark hair was covered beneath a short, blond wig. She stuck her middle finger up at me in response.

I grabbed my jacket from the back of the couch and shrugged into the old, familiar leather, dreading sitting through an entire stuffy dinner with fifty or so eyes laser-cutting holes into me.

It wasn't so bad before I went in. Loads of people in prison have scars, of one kind or another. *They* mostly left you alone. It was everyone else I had to deal with. The so-called 'normal people'. The quick looks and double-takes, the not-so-silent questions unformed on their lips. *Did you see that guy?* And *I* was one of the lucky ones.

People on the outside stared. They either couldn't help it or couldn't be bothered to cover their blatant, intrusive curiosity. They wondered how you got to be so disfigured, how badly it must have hurt to leave the flesh like *that,* all puckered and shiny, as if it had been covered in shrink wrap. How they used the weapon that penetrated deep enough to leave those scars. They wondered if you deserved it, like you were some kind of villain from an old western.

Who would want to be around someone like that? What

kind of woman would be open-minded enough to look past the physical and psychological flaws, past other's judgments? Attention for all the wrong reasons. Being treated like an outcast for the rest of her life through association.

Marie's wig was starting to look very appealing. Maybe I could go out in a hockey mask?

Shit, I was really not looking forward to this. An hour, maybe two, having to sit politely beside my sister-in-law and think up appropriate conversation. Like I had the first clue what to talk to her about. I didn't have a snooty, private school education or a membership to the tennis club. I didn't do charity brunches or organized group activities or attend a bi-monthly book club. I barely even read the fucking newspaper. I was seriously out of my depth.

I couldn't just sit there and stare at her the whole evening, for crying out loud. Admittedly, that wouldn't be hard; she looked as gorgeous as always, in tight jeans and a low-cut vest that seemed to cling in all the right places. I cleared my throat and looked away when she caught me checking her out.

It was unbearably hot outside, even though it was evening, and I immediately wrenched my jacket off. The atmosphere was suffocatingly close, the air almost wet with humidity. It felt like the sky was pressing down a damp blanket over my nose and mouth. I didn't think I could stand it much longer.

In the taxi, I kept glancing at Marie out of the corner of my eye. She held her gaze firmly out the window trying to look impassive, but her twitching lip gave her away. What *was* she up to?

She finally gave in and turned to me, "So, Jack. Tell me about yourself."

"What is there to tell?"

"How old are you? What's your favorite color? How long were you in prison for?" I raised my eyebrow at her and she tried to imitate me, arching her own brow to comic effect.

"Thirty-eight. Blue. Not telling."

"Thirty-eight! You really are an old man!! Ha!"

"My turn, why are you wearing a wig?"

"So no one will recognize me, stupid. You try having most of the earth's population know who you are, trying to take photos of you doing normal stuff."

"Sorry I asked," I muttered. Most of the earth's population? How conceited could you get? My less-than-enthusiastic response to her questioning didn't deter her from her newfound game.

"What places have you lived?" she demanded.

"All over."

"What have you done for work?" she shot back immediately.

"All sorts. What is this, twenty-one questions?"

"You're no fun," She pouted at me.

I sighed, deciding it was easier to play along than have her whining at me the whole time.

"I've done many things." This, it seemed, didn't quite constitute a proper answer. She leaned forward, waiting for more.

"I served, for a while..." I started slowly before she interrupted.

"Really? Solider boy, huh? I didn't have you down as the order-taking type," she teased.

"That's part of the reason I left."

"What's the other part?"

I was contemplating whether or not to tell her when the cab pulled up outside a brightly lit restaurant in a quiet part of town. I couldn't keep the amazement out of my voice.

"Burger King? Isn't that a bit... low-class for you?" I asked in disbelief. Marie laughed at the look on my face. She was so beautiful when she smiled like that, without any pretense or inhibition.

I opened the door for her, watching in amusement as she bounded across the sidewalk, through the automatic doors, and up to the counter to place her order. This part of town was definitely 'not Marie'. There were grease patches on the dank walls, as if they bled oil. The artificial leather seats were ripped in places, the yellowed foam busting out. The whole place glowed with the indisputable aura of dead-beat youth that was all too familiar to me, or perhaps, that's just all I'd come to associate it with.

It reminded me of my teenage years, when an isolated fifteen-year-old kid had nowhere else to go, trying to stay out of the kind of trouble that seemed to follow him.

The old guy who ran a burger joint in Brownsville gave me my first job. Paid me a little over five dollars an hour to keep the floors clean on a Saturday night. And believe me, not even ten times that would not have been compensation enough to clear up all that piss and puke.

Oblivious to me, Marie seemed to order the entire menu while I found a seat. She brought a full tray over to the table. I tried to adjust my frame of mind. She was enjoying herself for once. Who was I to ruin this for her?

"Wow! Are you hungry tonight or what?!"

"I haven't been here in years. I guess you wouldn't know this, but I secretly have a thing for junk food," she smiled up at me again and started un-wrapping the greasy waxed paper before picking up her Coke.

"Nicholas doesn't like coming here. Says it's for rednecks and riff-raff," Marie took a long pull on her drink. The straw, only partially in, made a dragging sound on top of the liquid.

"He's not wrong," I tailed off. She shot me a deadpan look and took another massive slurp of cola.

"Woah, take it easy on the soda there, kid."

"What makes you think it's *just* soda?" I reached across

the table and yanked the cup from her clumsy fingers, bringing it to my nose. Christ! It was mostly whiskey. I'd not had anything stronger than beer in years. The potency of the liquor was so powerful it sent a bolt straight to my brain in what I could imagine was the drinkers' version of being electrocuted. The smell reminded me all too clearly of the wonderful, hazy fuzz the world became after a few shots of liquor.

I steadily took her in, sitting slightly lopsided on the seat with ketchup smushed in the corner of her mouth though she hadn't eaten anything yet. Odd questions that seemed to come out of nowhere, piles of junk food, Marie actually being *nice* to me. Why did I only now comprehend that it was all starting to add up?

"Marie! Have you been drinking this all evening?" Normally, I wasn't one for sticking to the rules, but it was more than my ass on the line here. Like she'd said, she had a reputation to keep intact and somehow I didn't think Nicholas would appreciate me allowing his little wifey to cut loose on the spirits. Especially if it happened to be splashed across the tabloids the following day.

"Yep! Here's to not being pregnant." I gave her a glare that from past experience would make most people cower. It only made Marie scowl at me in that endearing way I was becoming fast accustomed to.

"Aw, lighten up, soldier boy," She attempted to seize her drink back, but the resulting tipsiness of drinking on an empty stomach made her much less coordinated than usual and, instead, she smeared her hand through a large blob of ketchup.

"You can have some more. After dinner." It may have

looked like I was impassive as shit but inside I was laughing. It was almost cute seeing her this way. No air and graces. No defenses. I liked her much better in this state.

Marie grumbled until she took the first bite of her burger, her eyes rolling to the back of her head in satisfaction.

"Mmm, this is SO GOOD! Even better than I remember!" she said, licking a smudge of melted cheese from her top lip.

"You want some?" she asked through her chewing, holding the burger out to me. I shook my head and she slid the tray toward me. Grinning, I took a swig from her cup in reply.

She was quiet for all of ten seconds before a thoughtful look glazed across her face. I could tell by the set of her jaw she was going to subject me to another round of intrusive questioning. So, we were back to that again, were we?

"What's your star sign?"

Not what I was expecting. "Where did that come from?"

"I was just wondering… I'm a Leo. Nic's a Scorpio. That's why he drives me insane." The hint of a smile curled my lip. That sounded about right.

"My birthday is February third."

"Aquarius. Hmm. You an' me should get along just fine, now I don't hate your guts. Not saying I like you," She pointed a French fry at me to punctuate.

"Okay," I grinned sarcastically, rolling my eyes in a very Marie-like way which made her giggle.

"What's your favorite movie?"

"Anything with Dan Aykroyd in, I guess."

She gave me a blank look, "Who?"

"You've never heard of Dan Aykroyd? The Blue's Brothers…Ghostbusters?"

She shook her head.

Who'd never heard of Ghostbusters? I scooped up a burger with one hand and shoved it into my mouth, demolishing half of it in one bite. It had been about three hours since my last meal and I was starving.

Old habits died hard. Ever since I'd began training just shy of fifteen, my energy demand had been sufficiently higher to sustain my weight and activity level. After a couple years of hard work and discipline, at six foot three and around one-hundred-and-ninety pounds, I was eleven pounds off making the heavyweight category and made a very intimidating opponent, both in the ring and out.

That's what I told Marie anyway, when I caught her eyeing me after I stuffed the rest of the cheeseburger into my cheek.

"Is that why you pack in enough food to feed a family of four?" She asked, wiping her mouth with a napkin.

When I just shrugged she added, "Tell me more about it."

"It was a long time ago. We're talking what, twenty years? I could have been semi-professional, would have been if I was old enough."

She raised her eyebrows, "Interesting. What happened?"

"Like I said earlier, I'm not too good at following instructions," I messed up, as I did with everything good in my life.

"But what actually happened?"

I decided to confide in junk-food high, liquored-up Marie, "There was a big fight coming up. I'd been training hard, trying to keep out of trouble. Some boys from my school started messin' with me, tried to provoke me into fighting them. I'd been kicked out of that school before, for the same reason, so I was just trying to keep my head down and just get on with things."

"But you fought them?"

"Put four of them in hospital. One guy had a punctured eardrum, another a broken ribs, a fractured jaw. I'm not proud of what happened, but they never bothered me again. Of course, when my coach found out, I was banned from the sport."

"Oh... But, you were defending yourself, right? It wasn't like you went out looking for trouble?"

On that particular occasion, it *was* self-defense, but later experience proved to me that rage was always prowling a few inches below the surface of exterior calm. I'd done a lot of work to keep it contained. Manageable. It took a lot of control sometimes. I could blame it on my upbringing. I could blame it on my father. I could blame a lot of things. When it came down to it, I was the one who had to take responsibility for what I'd done.

"I was young; arrogant and impulsive. Like most kids, I believed I knew best. Like I said, it was a long, long time ago now. Let's just say I've learned my lesson."

"Don't think I'm being judgmental here because I'm not, but being young isn't an excuse."

"I know. I think some people need the life experience. Make their own mistakes."

"I guess that's true... Speaking of making my own mistakes, could I have my drink back now?"

Smirking, I handed her back the empty cup.

After dinner, Marie insisted we go to a bar for a while. If I knew her better, I could almost say she was having a good time.

As we left I hailed another cab and set off to the destination of her choosing while she pulled out her phone and started tapping away on it with her thumbs. God knows how that thing worked, I was just getting to grips with the swiping thing, let alone trying to send a message, which Jude had explained to me was done by pressing buttons on the screen rather than real buttons.

"I'm just checking in with Kaylee. Jude's fallen asleep on

the couch watching Netflix."

"Watching what?"

"Netflix," She repeated, like that would make me understand what she was talking about.

"Is that a new film I should know about?"

"…you can watch films *on* it… it's a streaming platform," She shot me a look while her thumbs continued to punch out endless words without her even looking. I reckon I could practice on the phone for years and still not able able to do that.

"A what?" Did Jude not watch films on TV anymore? And why did Marie keep looking at me like I was an alien that just crashed in her backyard?

Something clicked in my head. *Dan Aykroyd.*

"Er, Marie? Are you… are you *old* enough to drink?" I eyed her suspiciously. Reputation aside, having a glass of wine in your own house was one thing. Knowingly buying spirits for someone of indeterminate age in a bar was a whole other ball game.

"Of course I am!" She laughed and pulled out her purse. Inside were a few different licenses, with various names on them. I had a bad feeling she was underage, maybe just slightly, but the law wasn't as lenient as family might have been.

"Look, I have a few different ones for when I don't want to be recognized. It's no big deal." I still wasn't convinced.

Marie pouted in my direction, "Come on, old man. I promise I won't get carried away."

I didn't respond, continuing to stare forward in disapproving silence.

"You can even pick who ah am," she teased, waving her card holder in front of my face. I grabbed it in annoyance.

"How d'you get all these?"

She let out a snort, "How do you think I got them?"

I was pretty sure Nicholas had something to do with it. Flicking through the options, I settled on one with light hair.

"Fine, you can be... Layla Smith, twenty-five, from Washington."

"Thank you, Mr Hayes," she replied coyly, blinking up at me with those doll-like eyelashes. I had to admit, she knew how to work me. The irritated feeling melted away in mere seconds, like a popsicle left on a park bench.

"You're welcome, Mrs Hayes," I muttered back under my breath, liking the sound of the words on my lips a bit too much.

We pulled up outside a back alley downtown. Marie tipped the driver well and we made our way toward the building. I became aware, for the first time, of my hand lightly resting on the small of her back.

The building was shabby looking, the painted sign peeling so badly I couldn't make out the name. No bouncers on the door, or even another soul in sight, apart from a cat that shot out from behind a dumpster as we approached. Behind the door, there was a narrow shaft of concrete steps that led down to black abyss.

"Come on, soldier boy. I thought you liked an adventure?" She started down the steps, a little off balance. I ended up carrying her, in fear she would topple down the stairs in those murderously high shoes. At the bottom, there was another door and a single security guard. A quick flash of her ID and he let us through with a nod.

The room that lay before me was, again, something I did not expect from Marie. Apart from being so deep underground that all surrounding noise from the city was made obsolete, it was very dark. The only light seemed to be coming from sparsely placed, naked bulbs. Booths lined the otherwise bare walls, the concrete floor well worn, barely visible underneath the mass of people gathered on it.

In the corner, a live band played jazz and blues. The heavy baselines and mellow tones adding to the illusion that the room was cut off from the normal world. I guessed this was why Marie chose this place; the perception of safety in its disconnected depths.

She was undeniably the youngest person here, and the most attractive woman in any room. A lot of heads turned to look in her direction as she walked through, although she didn't seem to notice. I wondered if she was even aware that she was beautiful, or the effect she seemed to have on men and women alike. If they were anything like me, they would want to be near her, touch her. Maybe get close enough to smell her.

Marie ordered us both Amaretto Sours. I raised an eyebrow when she handed me mine, "More alcohol, is that a good idea?"

"What, you think I can't handle my drink? One gets very accustomed to spirits putting up with your brother!" She knocked her drink back in three gulps, then ordered another.

"I think we should get a table," I led her away by her drinking arm and found an unoccupied booth in the corner, welcoming the feel of the cool, upholstered seat through my t-shirt. Being small and crowded, the room was hot. And I wasn't the biggest fan of tight spaces. Luckily our table was positioned away from the throng of dancers, and we had a measure of privacy.

Marie, slightly dazed, sat a bit too close. Not that I minded one bit. I could smell her perfume; soft and delicate, just like her. A mix of light florals and a freshness that reminded me of clean bed sheets.

Her lips were bare. Took me a while to pick up on that fact. I've never really liked lipstick in general, it gets in the way, but particularly not red. I've always hated red lipstick, ever since I was young. The women my father brought home almost always had red lips. Marie's mouth was a supple, muted pink and looked very inviting…

"I was seriously thinking of leaving him, you know," her hushed voice brought me out of my internal musing.

I gave her a slight frown, "Why?"

"Despite what you think, I *do* love him. But I'm fed up of

his selfish ways, and he has all these rules. He's *completely* controlling! Then there are all the other women," Marie raised her glass again to her lips, eyes wet with tears which threatened to fall at any moment. I put my hand on her wrist and pushed it back down.

"Tell me," I whispered softly.

"You know what he's like, the gambling, the socializing. I can deal with that. I understand he has this persona to keep up, it's part of his livelihood. But there's a part of him only I see. I know what's going on. I've seen the photos. I've found things, proof he's still sleeping around."

Her voice cracked slightly and she brought her trembling fingertips to her temples. Aw shit, please don't cry. I've never known what to do when women start crying.

"Anyway, we fight, he begs me to stay with him. Begs for forgiveness. Then fucks me into submission. The next day I'll receive some lavish present, like jewelry, or a car, and the same broken promise; that he'll try to be a better husband."

"The night before you came, I was going to walk out on him. There was a photo circulating online; Nicholas in a club, his arm around a pretty young blond, they are always, *always* blond! The picture got taken down real quick, but not before someone showed it to me. The wall behind them was mirrored, his hand was up the girl's skirt. Cupping her crotch."

"Shit!" I muttered.

"It's getting out of hand now. He goes out all night, never letting me know where he is. If he's okay. He drinks, smokes, takes whatever he feels like. He just doesn't know when enough is enough. Too many times he's been dropped home so out of it that I need to shut him in a different room until he's sobered up. Too many times I'm left to pick up the pieces and try and move on like nothing's happened."

Her hand slid from underneath mine. I hadn't realized my hand was on top of hers until she lifted it to her cheek, wiping away the tears.

"Fuck me," I murmured, embarrassed that I asked her to share something so personal. It didn't sit well with me, what my brother was putting her through, but I was glad I now knew what a selfish bastard my brother really was.

Jesus Christ, I'd had it wrong the whole time. No wonder she took such a strong dislike to me; she thought I was going to be just like him.

Marie let out a feeble, awkward smile and shuffled away a little, "I'm sorry."

"Don't be," I didn't look away for a second, "I knew my brother was an ass, but I didn't know he was that bad."

"He has moments where I see why I fell in love with him. Nic can be the most charming man in the world when he wants something. When he wanted me."

"He does want you, sweetheart. He just has a funny way of showing it."

Those words jogged something in my memory. Thoughts so painful I usually preceded to shut them out... *A funny way of showing it.* All the guilt, all the grief, came flooding back.

The heavy shadow of shunned responsibility. The slow descent into a life I was being forced into. Drowning in it. I spent the nights longing for my freedom, continued living the way *I* wanted. Wishing for an easy way out.

I didn't want the obligation of a child.

And then, just as fast, the obligation was taken away.

Marie shuffled closer to me again, wide dark eyes calmly looking up into mine, "What are you thinking about?"

I let out a deep sigh, debating whether to tell her the truth, and decided I owed her back for her honesty.

"I was dating a girl, April. She had all this long auburn hair, a kindergarten teacher. We didn't have the easiest relationship, on and off for a long while," I struggled to get the words out, they felt like molasses on my tongue and sounded to my ears as brittle as dead wood.

Although she slept next to me each night, through all the nightmares, they were particularly bad back then, so vivid, she cleaned me up after every scrap I deliberately got myself into, tweezering out each shard of broken glass and scrubbing the blood out of my clothes. It was her smile that got me most, without even a trace of judgment. Like I was worth something when I wasn't even shit on the bottom of her shoe.

"What happened?"

"She died. In labor."

After being dismissed from the armed forces, it was like I'd finally accepted that darker part of myself. I didn't care about trying to do the right thing anymore. What was the point? So, I was selfish. And, for a long while, I was okay with that. Until that night April died. Since then, I hadn't even kissed another woman. Her death cured me of any urges. I'd never craved the touch of another woman. Until recently.

"Were you married?"

I shook my head once, "No. It wouldn't have been what either of us wanted."

Marie gave me a questioning look and I rubbed my chin before continuing.

"I was a shit. Literally, the worst. Torn between living freely and giving her the stability deep down I knew she deserved. Unfeeling. Unfaithful." It was hollow, fleeting pleasure. The shame came after. In turn, I'd pushed her away when she needed me most.

"I know that if things hadn't played out the way they did, she would have left me long before she realized I didn't deserve her," I probably would have been an every-other-weekend kind of dad, watching from afar as a stranger brought up my kid.

"I guess what I'm trying to say is; I know what you are going through because I've been there, just the other side. There is no excuse for Nic's behavior. If I could go back and do it all again, I would try harder. Try to make myself good enough for her and for our son, because I know what it's like to lose it all."

I showed her the photograph I kept in my wallet. April, at one of the school fetes. The sky was a wide, deep blue that day and the air was sweet with the buttery smell of popcorn. She was holding one of the kids from her class, the rest huddled around her in adoration. Her smile seemed to reach from ear to ear as she laughed at something one of the kids had said.

The photo had been slid out and looked at so often the colors had almost faded out, the edges in tatters. Marie ran her fingers over the small people, "She was so pretty."

"Yeah, she was," I seemed to stare through the picture, rather than at it, "It happened a long time ago."

"How old would your baby have been now?"

"Erm, about five, I think? Little man. I didn't find out until, you know, after." Marie reached across for my hand. It was so soft and small in mine.

"I had you completely wrong," She wiped a tear away from the corner of her eye with the sleeve of her jacket.

"Yeah. Me too, kid."

The band started playing a new song, with a different tempo from before. A low beat, electric guitar purring in the drug-hazed euphoria only a song written in the early 70's could replicate. I remembered this song playing from my mom's record player when I was very young. And I remembered how my father had smashed that very record player when she left him.

As if to purposely contradict my pet name for her, Marie pointed at my drink, taking it when I shook my head.

Before I could protest, she finished it in one long swallow then slid out of her seat, trying to pull me up with her.

The number on the floor had seemly tripled while we'd been talking. Reluctantly, I rose from my seat and followed her through the crowd to the bar, where she ordered herself yet another drink, this time a shot, before pulling me onto the dance floor.

The atmosphere was humid, devoid of air. The heat of the bodies around us pressing in. I could feel a line of perspiration running down my back, my damp t-shirt sticking to my skin.

Marie moved slowly, her hips swinging in tempo, closer and closer to me until I could feel her body on mine. I kept repeating to myself that she was married to my brother. She was married to my own *fucking* brother! At least, here, it was safe to look.

It was hard not to notice the outline of her very obviously unrestrained breasts underneath the silky fabric of her top. Heavy-lidded eyes peering up at me through those thick, dark lashes.

Jesus Christ, she must be aware of the effect she was having on me? Of course, I knew she'd had way too much to drink by this point. She didn't mean to be as flirty as she was. Good thing I was there to take care of her.

By the time the song ended, she had half-slumped into my side, only semi-conscious. I leaned down so she could hear me, my nose nudging into her hair. Inhaling the sweet scent of her.

"Come on, baby. Let's get you home."

She seemed happy enough to let me carry her up the stairs. Her cheek was touching mine, her breath hot at my ear. Hyperaware of that strange, wild energy cracking in the insignificant space between us.
I turned to look at her and before I knew what was happening her lips fell into mine in a lazy kiss.

All thoughts ceased to exist as I marveled at the sensation of her mouth against mine, the mouth I'd longed to taste. The feel of the body I'd so long desired pressed up against mine. Instinct took over as I pushed her back against the wall, hands at her waist. She half moaned into my mouth, driving me to temporary insanity. Kissing her the way she so desperately needed to be kissed. Kissing her as I had no right to.

Then I realized what I was doing. Exactly who was trapped between my needy body and this very public wall.

Shaking with desire, I pulled away. My mind racing with the dizzying apprehension of what I'd just done. I tried to tell myself this was a natural reaction to being around a beautiful woman after so long. That this could have been any woman I was having these feelings for and not the only one in the world that was unavailable to me. The only one that was off-limits!

Marie sighed in contentment, her eyes still closed as she uttered the only words that could have made me feel worse in that moment.

"Mmm, let's go home, Nic."

Chapter Eleven

NIC

"What do ya think, Chuck? Grey or blue?" I held up two fabric swatches beside my brother's face, as my tailor took his measurements. The plushly decorated lounge area of his shop was inconspicuously located on a side street just off Rodeo Drive.

Chuck took a swig of his bourbon and slumped further down in the wingback armchair, not bothering to look over, "It don't matter, he'll look like the ass end of a monkey either way."

"Your mother didn't seem to think so," Jack shot.

"Oh yeah?"

"Yeah. She wouldn't have let me get into her pants otherwise."

Funny story, Jack actually *had* slept with Chuck's mom back when we lived in New York. It wasn't as gross as it sounded; Chuck's mother was only seventeen when she had him, and was a pretty hot MILF of thirty-six when Jack seduced her. Although, being only eighteen himself at the time, maybe the correct term was convinced.

"At least my mom wanted to stick around, Hayes," Chuck replied in a dry tone. Ouch, way to hit a guy where it hurt. These two were just as bad as each other.

Jack scowled as the tailor measured around his neck.

"Not meaning to sound ungrateful Nic, but when am I ever going to need this fancy get-up?"

"I'm sure there will be an occasion. Every man needs at least one good suit at his disposal."

I currently had about six from each of the major designers, each one a slightly different cut, fabric or finish. I always believed you had to dress for the success you anticipated, so having a wide variety of the best suits available to man gave me the assurance I was still on top and, in turn, helped others put their confidence in me.

My tailor, whose goddamn name I could never remember, finished measuring Jack and slipped through a previously concealed door in the mahogany-paneled wall.

Chuck stood, and I immediately sensed danger in his self-assured posture.

"Seems like a bit of waste to me, Nic. Your boy Jack probably doesn't know how to do up the collar, let alone a tie. The only two-piece he'd be used to has an elastic waistband, no buttons and comes in luminous orange. Am I on the right track, ape-man?"

Jack started forward and I stepped in between and pushed him back, "Whoa there, big boy."

I felt the cell in my pocket vibrate, but ignored it, more concerned with preventing a fight from breaking out between my brother and one of my oldest friends. In all honesty, it would be more like preventing Jack from beating the crap out of Chuck than a fight. Jack was bigger and meaner, and didn't exactly have the best track record when it came to defining a fair fight. Fuck, I wouldn't want to come across him in a dark alleyway and he was family!

However, Chuck had been pissing me off all day, and the way he'd been digging into Jack just now, the little cocksucker deserved to be taught a lesson.

I dropped my arm as Jack relaxed back, but Chuck stepped forward, with what would have been nose to nose with my brother in a taller man but was more like nose to forehead in this instance.

"He's not got the balls to do anything that could get him in trouble, not with a room full of witnesses and a record."

"Lay off him, Chuck. You're just baiting yourself."

Chuck's lip curled, "You'd go straight back inside. You can't be as big and stupid as you look, Koko."

He glanced at me, then flicked his pale eyes back to Jack.

"Why don't you fuck off back to Mexico, huh?"

Jack surveyed Chuck for a long second, before smashing his forehead into Chuck's face. Chuck let out a howl of pain and his hand shot up to grasp his nose which was now steadily leaking blood onto his white shirt.

"Oww! I-ink you broke ma-nose!" He managed to get out from behind his hand.

Jack only snarled in response. I couldn't help but be amused. Chuck as good as asked for it. I turned back to my brother, raising my eyebrows questioningly.

"Is that how you solve all your problems?"

"Pretty much."

I smirked, turning my attention back toward the chicken-shit bleeding onto the expensive rug.

"Chuck, go get me a coffee. You know how I take it."

He gestured wildly to his face with his free hand, then at Jack and back again.

"Go clean yourself up, then get me a coffee."

"Asshole," Jack muttered as Chuck passed him. I could tell he was resisting the urge to shove the smaller man, but thankfully Chuck ignored him on his way out.

"Ah, he means no harm."

"He's damn unpleasant, like a *leach*," He made a face, somehow managing to reshape the definition of leach to mean 'wet shit.' "I don't trust him. His eyes are too far apart."

I chuckled and dropped into Chuck's vacated chair, picking up the remainder of his forgotten drink. I swirled the half-melted ice cubes around the glass. They clinked satisfyingly together, the sound greeting me like a lover's sweet whisper.

The armchair was beautiful; crafted out of a single hide of inky alligator leather, finished with solid mahogany feet and studded with bronze upholstery pins. The thing was a work of art and probably cost upwards of fifty grand. And in a single moment of greed, I wanted it. Knowing Marie would hate it, made me want it all the more.

"Little brother, let me tell you from experience; in life, it's about who you know, not what you know."

"And knowing that jack-off is beneficial how?" He interrupted.

"Let me finish," I held up a hand, "Chuck knows people. People in the right places."

Being brought up a stone's throw away from The City, in Ocean Hill, and his professional background trading blue-chips on Wall Street, Chuck was very well connected to those top one percenters who mattered, namely the ones who could be persuaded to invest in my company. This type of insider trading wasn't strictly speaking *illegal*, but it was frowned upon, which is why that information was kept hush-hush.

"I think that's all I wanna know," Jack shook his head.

"Ask me no questions…" My cell buzzed again in my pocket. Ignoring it, I dropped the glass back on the wooden side table with a clunk.

Jack stretched out on the russet-colored suede couch across from me, looking awkward and out of place. He rubbed his lip with a thumb and then slumped forward to take in our surroundings.

In all honesty, I never came to places like this, usually due to lack of time than anything else. If I needed a suit, the tailor would come to me. We were only here really so I could spend some time with my brother. Unluckily for him,

I'd had to drag Chuck along too. We had a breakfast meeting to attend after Jack's fitting and I needed him to fill me in on some details on the ride over.

I hadn't even been home to check on Marie yet, and when we'd parted, it hadn't been on the best of terms. I made a mental note to get Jessica to pick up some flowers to take home to her.

"How's my wife?"

"I dunno, man. Haven't you spoke to her?" he replied in an offhand way.

"Not since I saw her yesterday morning."

Jack nodded, more to himself than anything.

"She's pissed with me and I can't figure out why," I elaborated.

"Why don't you ask her?"

"That's not how marriages work, little brother."

"All I can tell you is what I've seen. Marie's up in this big house all day, no real friends, no one to talk to. She moved halfway across the country to be with you and you're hardly ever home. She's lonely."

I opened my mouth to protest to him sticking his nose in then closed it again. This was actually very useful insight.

"Lonely, huh?" I sat back, contemplating that thought. I could think of a few things to keep her busy... but when I wasn't there to occupy her, that was the issue.

"Do you and her ever talk?" I asked.

"About...?"

"Anything. What do you talk about?"

"I dunno, where she's going? What she's gotta do that day? Boring shit. She don't like me, remember?"

Bullshit. I knew for a fact that he had taken Marie on an unexplained late-night trip to the hospital last week... I'd get that checked out!

Jack'd been spending more time with my family than myself recently. Baking cookies with my son like some kind of nancyboy.

I opened my mouth to continue but my cell rang for the third time. Grumbling, I yanked it out of my pocket and answered.

"*Hello!?*"

"Nic, it's Jean." After Max and I butting heads at dinner, Jean was supposed to be tying up all the loose ends in New York, probably the only man I trusted to get the job done.

"Yes?" I snapped. Him calling, especially three times in rapid-fire succession was not a good sign.

"We have a problem."

Chapter Twelve

MARIE

I woke up in my own bed, feeling better than I deserved to. As I sat up, my head swirled and I ran a hand though my tangled mane of hair trying to recall the events of the night before. I remembered drinking. I remembered Burger King. I remembered telling Jack about Nicholas, and him telling me about his ex-girlfriend and then… downing more whiskey? Oh crap! I shouldn't have drunk so much. Maybe then I would have been able to think straight.

Swinging my legs out from under the sheets, I noted my half-dressed state; I was wearing only my underwear and vest from the night before. My jeans and shoes were neatly piled onto the chair in the corner. On the nightstand stood a glass of water, some painkillers and my diamond Tiffany earrings. I was sure that must have been Jack's doing because; one, I would have been in no state to prepare for the morning after if I really had drunk as much as I suspected, and two, I wasn't much of a folder.

I smiled to myself for a second, thinking how sweet Jack had turned out to be. How his brooding was just him thinking things through before he did them; he wasn't being calculating, but considerate. Underneath his harsh exterior was a caring, sensitive person who'd been through more shit than anyone should have had to deal with.

Taking the pills and downing the water, I headed for a long hot bath and braced myself for Nicholas' imminent arrival. That thought brought me out of last night's fuzzy memory cloud!

When I got out of the bath, he was, as I had expected, sitting on the bed with an overly extravagant bouquet of pale pink roses in his hands.

"Hey, babe," he said with a smirk, trying and failing to appear sincere. What was it with guilty men and their egos? Did they not know when they needed to say sorry? Or did they simply refuse out of principle?

"Hi," I replied coolly, tightening my robe and heading for the adjoining wardrobe.

"Come on, baby... talk to me," he whined, trailing me like a lost puppy dog. I couldn't stand to look at him in that moment. The anger inside began to boil up again, hot and sticky and toxic.

How dare he waltz back on in here like the past week hadn't happened? A whole week where he hadn't even called to check in on us. He was probably too preoccupied with one his side-women. We both knew why he'd really flown back to New York. It sure as hell had nothing to do with investments, unless they were of the carnal type.

"Fine. Hi. Did you have fun with your blond whore last night?" I refused to look at him as I picked out a pale blue sundress.

"How many times do I have to tell ya? Nothing happened with her!" Nicholas walked up behind and wrapped his arms around my body. I cringed in disgust. "You know you're my number one gal."

"Then why do you feel the need to sate your lust elsewhere?" He didn't reply, only slipping his hand inside my robe to cup the rounded flesh there, his teeth nipping at my ear.

"You are so beautiful. I'm so lucky to have a hot little thing like you all to myself," His wandering hand slipped lower, "Baby, you drive me fuckin' crazy."

I rolled my eyes so hard I could have given myself a migraine.

"Get off me, Nicholas," I sighed. His only reply was his hungry lips at my neck as he pulled us toward the bed, sitting down with me on his lap.

"I've been thinking, I wanna make things up to you. I know I'm always away on business."

"Is that what you call it?" I retorted, surprised he wasn't angry yet. He clearly wanted something. He pulled the material off my shoulder and ran his jaw over me, three days' worth of whiskers scratching red trails across the sensitive skin there. Coarse hair spattered with grey that he knew I hated. Presumably, the other woman – or rather, *girl* - liked it enough to request he keep it.

"I know I've not been good to you, babe. I want to leave a little piece of me with you always, so you don't miss me as much while I'm away."

I turned to him, confused, feeling my eyebrows mush together, "What are you talking about?"

He smiled widely; an expression I wasn't used to seeing. It looked alien on his face. I caught a flicker in his eyes that I interpreted as excitement, like he could finally reveal a big secret.

"I want you to have my baby."

"You are fucking kidding me, right?" My voice was low, unbelieving. It came out in a grainy whisper. Nicholas looked genuinely taken back, as if he couldn't believe I didn't think his stroke of genius was as brilliant as he did.

"No," he replied, eyes hardening a fraction, enough for me to know that I *had* succeeded in angering him now. His patience had finally worn thin enough for me to see the hairline cracks appearing in his calm exterior, barely contained.

It didn't stop me from speaking out.

"Why would that even cross your mind right now? That is probably the worst idea you've *ever* had!" I needed to talk some sense into him.

Nicholas remained inscrutable, studying me as though I were speaking Mandarin instead of a language he could comprehend. I stood up and took a few steps away from him so I could get some perspective.

"How could you think this is the right environment to raise a child in? You are hardly ever here! And I'm still much too young to be thinking about that right now."

When Nicholas had brought this up before, he had always seemed to understand that the timing wasn't right. He'd said that he wasn't getting any younger and that all of his friends had already had their babies, but he could wait a few more years. Until I was ready, too.

"It would take *complete* commitment from you; I'd need you to be around, for both of us," I paused, thinking what it would be like if things continued the way they were going. If I had a baby, I would be trapped here. Not wanting to show weakness, making sure their father's lack of attention didn't affect them, like it did the son he already had. Like it did me.

I took a deep, steadying breath, trying to end the conversation rationally.

"I don't want to be the couple that have a baby to salvage what's left of their marriage."

He stood slowly, towering menacingly over me. Filling the space with more than just his physical presence. I didn't realize I was backing away until the back of my legs hit the dresser.

"You know what? In normal circumstances, you would be right." Nicholas was so close, yet his words were barely audible.

"*But* you are forgetting whose house you are living in. *I* make the rules." Each and every hair on my body stood on end. The corners of his mouth twitched every few seconds as I studied him, wondering what had brought on this intensity.

I'd always known he had the final say on everything, but he had never taken it this far, never tried to purposely intimidate me. He chuckled slightly and I caught the faint smell of liquor on him from last night, or maybe more recently, not quite disguised beneath the scent of Listerine.

"Nic, you've been drinking, okay? Let's talk about this later," I tried to push him away but he dragged his hand up to caress my cheek.

"I can think of something to do that's much more fun than talking."

"Please?" I whispered, turning my face away. He kissed that spot behind my ear that he knew made me weak at the knees. His hand trailed down between my thighs, a confident brush of his fingers against my over-sensitive nerves, stealing my breath. A wicked smile flashed across his face.

"See, baby? You're already wet for me." I tried to protest again but all that came out was a throaty sigh as he slipped a thick finger inside me.

He used sex as a weapon, to lower my defenses. To get what he wanted. Although, when did the knowledge of what he was doing to me ever stop it from working? Accepting this dominant part of him was part of what made sex with Nic so good. Allowing him to be in control awakened something primal in me. The desire to please and be pleased. Ultimate submission.

"Turn around," He pushed my robe up, wrapping my hips in his hands, rubbing up against me from behind. The front seam of his jeans creating such satisfying friction.

Then I remembered what all this was all about. I was allowing him to do it again. He was going to get away with it. And I would let him. I tried to pull away except that only made him hold onto me tighter.

I knew any attempt of fighting him off would always be unsuccessful – he was just too strong - although that didn't stop me from trying. I struggled but he won, very quickly. Nothing got Nicholas going like a fight for dominance.

He pushed me down face-first on the bed, slamming into me in one powerful thrust that made me almost scream. He clamped a firm hand over my mouth to stifle my cries as he fucked me at an increasingly relentless pace. I could hear his ragged breath by my ear. The next second, I felt a sharp pain as his teeth embedded themselves into the sensitive skin of my neck.

It was over quickly, but not before we both cried out in unison. Then he slapped my ass and threw a, "don't wait up, doll," in my direction before leaving. I could picture the ugly, self-satisfied look on his smug face as he straightened his tie, probably one of the colorful silk ones I'd picked out in a downtown boutique back when he gave a fuck about little things like that.

Minutes later, I heard his Ferrari start up and bolt away. I let out a shaky breath I didn't know I'd been holding in. My cheeks stung slightly from drying tears. I felt dirty and cheap; the way he'd used me made me feel like one of his whores.

My thoughts ran at breakneck speed as I tried to process everything that just happened. The physical stuff didn't bother me as much as I should and it struck me how messed up it was. That kind of shit had become normal to me. No, what really scared me was the way he'd looked at me. Like he wanted to *hurt* me.

If he was really serious about having a baby, then I needed

to hide my birth control now, before he flushed them all down the toilet. Being the incredibly domineering man he was and just now discovering how finely his patience was wearing, there was no other option than to lie to my husband.

I wasn't ready to become a mother.

I knew what type of father Nicholas was firsthand; the type who had nothing to do with his child. Sure, he'd buy them expensive presents. They would have the best of everything, and they'd probably be sent off to some private school. But that was no match for a father who loved and cared for his babies. That was the distinctive difference between being a father and being a dad. I silently thanked God that Jude lived with his mom.

I checked my stash quickly, just to make sure it was still there. Twenty-four thousand in ready cash, in a fat yellow envelope tucked away in a secret compartment in the nightstand. I slid my boxes of birth control in with it and locked everything away. There was no way Nicholas would be getting his hands on them.

I hated showers, only ever taking one when I felt the need to punish myself. It was the way the droplets fell, trickling over my face and down my body, making me itch and think of ants crawling all over my skin. Since I was a child, I'd always preferred baths.

I took an unbearably hot shower, Nicholas' residual anger ghosting through me. The water cascaded over my curled-up form, cleansing not only my body but also my soul. I wanted it to hurt, I felt as though I somehow deserved to hurt. My skin raw from the abuse, my head raw from thinking.

Once I'd used up all the hot water, I pulled on an oversized sweatshirt. It didn't matter what I looked like if nobody was around to see. Would this be what it was like forever? Would I feel alone and unloved, Nicholas pushing me around for the rest of my life? A baby? *Fuck*.

Downstairs I shakily poured myself some coffee, cupping the mug to warm my fingers. Clammy, despite the heat from the shower.

"Hey kid, how you feelin'?"

I spun around so fast that the scalding contents slopped out of my mug and onto the floor, narrowly missing my naked feet.

Shit! I'd completely forgotten about Jack! It was so easy to get wrapped up in your thoughts in this huge house, lost in your own little world when no one else was around.

"Wow, you look awful! Good thing we got you home when we did..." His expression fell from amusement to concern in a heartbeat. I watched him analyze me, faint bruises already forming on my skin. Swollen eyes, all puffy from crying.

"What did he do?" Jack's eyes blackened with silent rage. His voice was low, the words almost a growl, gravelly in his throat.

"I heard him leave this morning. *What happened?*" he demanded. I couldn't meet his unblinking gaze. It seemed to pierce right through me and I stood frozen, pinned to the cool, now wet, tilled floor.

"Come with me," Jack grabbed my arm and pulled me into the garden, not slowing his pace until we reached the padded seating area at the far end of the house. He sat me in front of him as he crouched down, so we were close to eye level. Tears welled up inside me again. If they fell, all my carefully constructed composure would be lost.

"We, erm, we had... an argument." It was such a struggle to vocalize my thoughts into coherent sentences.

"What about?" His ferocious glare softened and a calloused thumb came to my cheek, wiping away the salty betrayal. It caught me off guard. The touch was so unexpected it made me freeze. For a moment everything stilled, even my racing mind.

"Well... err... he said he wanted... a baby... and I to-told him I'm n-not ready. Not *yet*."

He lowered his head slightly urging me to continue. Embarrassed, I looked away again, trying to focus on something, anything else. He tied his bootlaces in very deliberate knots, I noticed, latching onto that inconsequential detail and fixating on it. Sturdy. Practical. Just like him.

"Hey, it's okay," Jack sat on the bench next to me, tenderly pulling me into his lap. I curled into his broad chest, fingers tightly grasping his cotton t-shirt. He smelt clean and I took a deep breath of that comforting, fresh smell and held it inside me. I felt the hair being swept back from my face. He shushed me until I quietened down.

"It's okay, sweetheart," He spoke so gently his words were barely discernible, although I could feel the deep rumble of his words against me, "What did he do to you, Marie?"

I didn't want to get too deep into it. Having to admit that I had been forcibly dominated in every sense of the word was more than slightly embarrassing to admit to my brother-in-law.

"Nothing he hasn't done a hundred times before," I tried to sigh but it came out as more of a snivel. God, why did I have to be such a blotchy, snotty mess?

"You don't deserve that," Jack said in a pained voice. He delicately picked up my wrist to study the purpling blooms. In a few hours you would be able to see clearly defined finger marks. My neck was sore, too, and the ache between my thighs was growing rather than subsiding.

"It's none of my business to ask, but why do you put up with this shit?"

I started into the distance, subconsciously studying a flowering shrub at the other end of the garden; It's delicate buds had yet to blossom despite it being late in the season. Why did I put up with him? That was a good question. And one I didn't really know the answer to myself.

The principles of marriage had always been important to me, and I didn't take my vows lightly. My parents had had a long but unhappy marriage and when I was old enough to understand the concept, I wondered why they had never divorced. I'd only recently concluded that marriage didn't always start with love and, especially within the old-southern-money confines, had far more to do with power and status than individual desires.

When I left, I promised myself It wasn't going to be that way for me.

"Would you believe me if I said I still love him?"

He studied me for a second, brow furrowed.

"Plus... I would have nowhere else to go. I have no money, no qualifications. My family wouldn't even come to the wedding."

"Why?"

"They thought I was too young, that I was making a stupid mistake. My daddy came through in the end though; he signed the consent form for me. Then managed to convince my momma to do the same. The only thing she ever did for me."

"How old were you?"

"Seventeen."

Jack looked down at me with widened eyes, "Shit! How long have you been married? I mean, no offense, but Nic is old enough to be your father."

I wrinkled my forehead, thinking "We just celebrated our second anniversary. I was young and we were in love-well, I was in love. In love with Nicholas and his world. Everything seemed so glamorous and perfect."

"So, you are what? Twenty-years-old?" Jack was still

staring at me in disbelief.

I chuckled slightly, "Well, almost. Another month or so."

"Well, Christ! No wonder you don't feel ready to start a family, you are still a baby yourself. And to think I took you out drinking last night!"

"Took *me* out drinking? I had to practically drag you out the door by your ankles!" I pretended to scowl at him whilst he lightly ran a hand down my ribs, making me squirm. It tickled although he mistook my flinch for something else. Jack picked up on it immediately.

His eyes snapped up to mine, "Does that hurt?"

"No, it just feels a little weird."

As close as we were, I could see his pulse thumping ceaselessly at the base of his throat, just under the surface of his beautiful caramel-colored skin.

He skimmed his hands over my sides, applying light pressure, like he was checking for injuries, then gently prodded around my face, feeling around my neck and head. I remembered the bite mark a second too late, feeling my face flush. He stilled when his fingertips brushed over it.

I pulled away, humiliated. Oh god. He probably thought we were fighting and fucking like animals in heat. Which wasn't far from the truth. Again, not something I was tripping over myself to admit, especially not to Jack.

He cleared his throat, hand moving down to rest on my back. I could feel his heat radiating through my top, warming me.

"You gonna show me the sights, then?" I knew he wanted to take my mind off the morning's events. He was rubbing small circles on my back, still trying to soothe me.

"Sure," I gave him a small smile, grateful for somebody to confide in, "It's actually Jude's last day here so I wanted to spend some time with him before his flight home later."

"What d'you have planned?"

"Let's take him out. He's never been to Santa Barbara Zoo before."

"Neither have I," Jack smirked, flashing me the lopsided grin I'd grown quite fond of.

———————————————

Later that evening, after kissing Jude goodbye and embarrassing him at the airport, I sat with Jack in a private restaurant downtown. He wore a crisp shirt and tailored charcoal suit pants which looked totally out of character for him and quite charming with his unkempt hair.

"You'll have to trim this for the charity ball next week," I reached out to touch his beard, wondering how different he would look without it. Unlike Nic's, the hair was soft and although untidy, the fuzz suited him. I wondered if he grew it longer to disguise the scars underneath.

"It's not that I don't like it," I added quickly, "Just, you'll be in all the photographs so…"

"I'll keep that in mind."

"You'll thank me later."

After a short, awkward pause, Jack spoke again, "I didn't know I was invited?"

"Of course you are. You're family."

I lifted the glass of red wine to my nose and inhaled deeply. It was the type that would cost about a hundred dollars a bottle if you were expected to pay, which I was not. What is it about people that make them want to give you things if you were rich? It's not like we couldn't afford it. I would never get my head around how society worked.

Jack was eying the menu with an adorably puzzled expression. I didn't blame him; it was all in French.

"Steak is *bifteck,* if that's what you were wondering," I interjected through his wordless mouthing, trying not to look amused. He looked up at me, eyebrows knitted together in exasperation.

"Have I got to order it in French too?"

"No!" I laughed, "Just tell them what you want and I'm sure they can handle the rest. We're paying enough."

"Yeah, twenty dollars for beer is a fuckin' joke!"

"Just remember to thank Nic later."

It was becoming increasingly obvious that our upbringings were worlds apart. Nic had never volunteered much in the way of childhood stories, in fact, prying information out of him was pretty much like asking an elephant to jump. I had always been curious…

"Tell me about your family, Jack."

"Not much to tell. My mom took off when I was a kid, left me in the care of a violent, neglectful shit of a step-father who was never around. Nic brought me up really. Made sure I went to school and stayed outta trouble."

"Your mom left?" My heart fluttered in my chest as images of a scrawny, dirt-smudged boy filled my head; his eyes larger than saucers in the deep hollows of his face, hiding under his bed or any space small enough to crawl away from the father who terrified him.

Jack shrugged in a non-committal kind of way. The way people do when they try not to let on that they are still hurting.

"I used to think she must have died, or something. I'm sure she would have come back for us. My mom loved us, even Nic."

"What do you mean 'even Nic'?"

"Me n' Nicholas have different moms but the same dad. Didn't you ever wonder why we look so different?" I'd never given it much thought really but if you didn't know their similar expressions, you would never guess they were related.

"Oh. Was he a good brother? Or was he the type who'd tease you about girls and pull your hair?"

"Mmm, a bit of both… but he pulled through and looked after me when it mattered. We left together when I was sixteen and I haven't looked back since."

So I got the backstory, and the work history. Jack's CV was shaping up pretty nicely. His insight also helped me fill in the blanks and understand Nic slightly better too. He had to step up really young to care for his baby brother, because if he didn't do it, no one would. Nothing like me babysitting my younger cousins; their parents always came back at the end of the evening. Suddenly my privilege seemed embarrassingly stupid. Wasting twenty dollars on beer when that money could have fed two young boys for a week.

A vague thought of what Jack was saying last night came to me in a blur of fuzzy memory.

"Yesterday, you said part of the reason you left the Army was because you don't like authority. What was that other part?"

"The Marines," He corrected, "Well, I have a problem with my temper…"

"Oh really? I hadn't noticed," I teased with a lighthearted smile, which fell when Jack didn't return it.

"I mess up," he muttered flatly, "That seems to be what I'm good at. Anytime the going gets good I just fuck it up. I wasted my shot at the big time over something stupid. I ruined my chance of being a father. Top that off with a BCD and a criminal record and you got yourself a world-class screw-up!"

I opened my mouth to ask what a BCD was but before the words came out he answered.

"It stands for bad conduct discharge. I didn't leave by choice, they kicked me out," He paused, then looked away, "Don't say you're sorry. I don't want your pity."

"I wasn't going to say that. I was going to say; you get back up."

"What?" His attention snapped back to me.

"Every time you've been kicked down, what do you do? You brood about it for a bit, granted, but then you get back up. That's actually something I admire about you, Jack. Nothing stops you."

"My daddy used to tell me there is good and bad in everyone," I continued, "It's about how we find a balance that defines who we are. It doesn't matter what you have done, it's intent that matters. It's how you deal with the consequences that determine the way you view yourself. How others are going to judge you."

I expected him to be placated by my words, or at least recognize I was trying to help. Instead, his lips twisted downwards.

"You don't get it, Marie," He whispered in an annoyed tone, "It's so easy for you to spout all this poetic nonsense while you're sitting in your big, fancy house, surrounded by all your expensive things. You're used to people adoring you because you're rich and pretty and famous..."

"And I would give them all up in a heartbeat if it meant I could be happy!" I replied in an equal tone. "Being famous is more than it's cracked up to be. I never wanted to be involved in an industry where the value of your self-worth is based on your appearance. It's disgusting!"

"You seem quite content with sitting back and letting your husband provide for you?"

"Just because I haven't had your life Jack, it doesn't mean mine has been easy! I moved away from everything I knew and loved to be with Nic. I left all my friends, my family, my whole way of life, behind. For Nic, because I loved him. Because I was committed to making it work!"

I turned away, squashing down the need to cry. Is that still what he thought of me? After all we'd been through? What upset me the most was how much truth was in what I was saying. I *believed* with everything I had in me that I could make it work. Despite everything Nic did, I still loved him. And that's what got to me the most.

"Tell me, Jack. Why does he do it?"

"Do what?" He looked confused.

"Why does Nic cheat? Why is he more interested in being a playboy than a husband?"

Jack shifted back uncomfortably in his seat.

"Please just help me understand," I rubbed my temples. I'd definitely had too much wine if I was asking *Jack* for relationship advice.

He sighed deeply, "You know Nicholas. He's selfish."

"Being selfish doesn't excuse you from being a cheating asshole."

"Right. So, you can't be selfish in marriage; it's all about give and take. He buys women he can take from, who he can be a dick to without feeling guilty. He's paying these women, so he doesn't have to deal with the consequences."

"You sound as though you are speaking from experience," I took another cynical sip of my wine.

"Nic is probably using them as an escape. If he says they mean nothing, that's probably true."

I gave a disbelieving snort.

"Look, men are weak. All it takes sometimes is a bit of skin, a pretty face and a smile." At least he had the guts to look ashamed about it. "He isn't trying to hurt you," he added.

"But he is." And it was true. My insides ached just thinking about it, not just with hurt but rage. The bread I'd nibbled on as an appetizer churned in my stomach as a pang of anger radiated through me. It was so frustrating how Jack knew my own husband better than me, understood how the way he was acting was unacceptable. My marriage wasn't normal!

"In his mind, if he's not around to see it, it didn't happen. I know it's horrible but that's just how he thinks. I hate seeing the effect that has on you."

"You do?" I didn't know Jack cared enough about me to feel so strongly. I knew we'd grown closer in the time he'd been around but were we at a point now where he could feel my heartache?

"More than I have any right to."

My breath hitched in my throat and I felt the tell-tale sting behind my nose which warned me of oncoming tears.

"Would you tell me something? If you were him, what would you do?" I needed to know what was normal, how a man should react in this shit-hole situation.

His brow tensed further, knotting together in the middle as if he was concentrating, figuring out the right thing to say.

"Please, I need to hear another perspective."

He sighed, almost in defeat. The way he did before he let me in a little more.

"I'd drop everything and come home. I would tell you that you are the most important thing in the world to me. That I was sorry for being a fuck up and I would never let It happen again, because I wouldn't want to risk losing you."

I had to excuse myself from the table before I lost my composure completely. In the bathroom, I finally allowed myself to burst into tears.

Why was it only now that I was beginning to contemplate the idea that I'd made the wrong decision? One I couldn't take back very easily at all. It took three years to fully understand that I deserved more than what Nic was giving me. Jack's insight was like opening a door right into the inner workings of Nic's mind. The door that, until now had bound me, protecting me from harm.

I cried over the loss of that stupid, metaphorical door and everything it signified. Or maybe I was glad that I could now see what I should be entitled to.

Or maybe they were tears of guilt, finally catching up with me. Guilt from realizing the man I wished was in my life was so very different from the man I'd married.

Chapter Thirteen

NIC

I stared into the mirror at my reflection; the man looking back at me had puffy, sunken eyes, like he was in dire need of a good night's sleep. I hoped the stage makeup they'd smeared on would be enough to conceal it on camera. And my damn head was *pounding* again!

After the stress of the last few days winding me up tighter than a titanium spring, Chuck convinced me I needed to blow off some steam and that's how we wound up at the club. It was getting harder and harder to resist and, okay, yes, I did slip up. A few gin and tonics, maybe a whiskey or two. After all, I was only human. Wasn't I allowed to mess up from time to time?

With a shaking hand, I pulled out a few Excedrin and tossed them back with a swallow of what I wished were vodka, silently praying it would be enough to get me through the rest of the morning.

A few potent inches would help keep me sharp between the ears. Just a lick to balance me out before the interview. I had fifteen minutes for it to mellow me out, after all. I ran a hand through my hair, realizing too late I'd messed up the stylist's hard work. I tried to flatten it back down with little success.

I was trying to justify it, to convince myself I needed it. Hell, I was in pain and severely pissed off about earlier. My wife was supposed to have my best interests at heart. If I told her I want a baby, we're having a fucking baby!

Wouldn't she be happier playing house while I was gone if she had a little one to keep her busy? Keeping her satisfied was becoming the bane of my life. Damn it, how was I supposed to figure out what she wanted? Did she think I was a fucking mind reader?

I lay my pounding forehead on the dresser. I never thought I'd have to threaten her to get my point across. I didn't want to really scare her, just make sure she was aware of how important this was to me. Sure, I had Jude, but sometimes the way he acted made me wonder if he was really my son. He was so different from me in every way.

I needed a legitimate child to carry on my empire when I was gone. I needed a man I could trust, a boy who would grow up to be everything that was expected of him. Dependable.

There was a sharp knock on the door, and I heard a woman's heeled boot clack to stop before she let herself in.

"Mr Hayes, you're on in five." I raised a hand to let her know I'd heard, waiting until the click of the lock signaled her leaving. In frustration, I banged my head against the table once and then again, harder, just to make sure the thought of a drink had well and truly fucked off.

I took another few pills from the bottle and chewed them until they dissolved. The bitter taste left on my tongue felt like a reminder that life could suck no matter how much money you made. You couldn't run away from your problems. You had to either learn to live with them holding you back or fix them yourself.

I knew which option I'd pick every time.

The brightness of the studio lights set up in the penthouse suite made tiny silver stars pop behind my eyes.

"Nicholas, it's so good to see you." Ellen Dawson. The wife of one of my good friends from the poker club. She was your average-looking daytime TV personality, whose talk show had average ratings and a bit of a reputation for slander, notwithstanding. I had faith that she would take it easy on me on account of how we knew each other. I didn't normally put myself up for shit like this but I owed Matthew a favor. So, here I was.

"Thanks, Ellen. How's Matt? The kids?" I flashed her my most dazzling smile, not missing the quickly covered flash of appreciation in her returning one.

"They're great, thank you for asking. Fifi is all packed to start at Columbia in the fall and Preston just received his acceptance letter from Five Oaks Academy. It's the top-performing secondary school in the state. We're so proud!"

I nodded, without taking in any more information past the name of their first-born child, which sounded like it belonged to a cat.

"Let's get right into the questions, shall we? Since this is a taping, we can just talk normally and they can cut it all together later in editing. Is that okay with you?"

"Sure, let's get started," I smiled again. If there ever was a time to lay the charm on thick, it would be now.

"So Nic, you set up your company when you were thirty years old, a company that is now estimated to be worth over sixty billion dollars. Tell me, what it's like to achieve such success from such… humble beginnings?"

"To be honest, that's a pretty amazing achievement for anyone. I don't think I'd be here without the relentless determination to succeed. I'm a big believer in good old hard work. If you want something, you have to work for it."

Ellen batted her eyelashes at me, flicking a lock of blond hair over her shoulder. She was clearly impressed with my first answer.

"And it's certainly paid off! Have you always been so motivated?" she asked.

"More so when I was younger. I had a fearlessness in me that kinda got dulled with age. Now I'm more aware of the risks." Pause for endearing smile.

"Age isn't the only thing you've had to contend with though, is it?"

Hmm. How did one respond to that?

"In what regard?" I rubbed my jaw, looking thoughtful.

"Well, a powerful man like yourself must have other *issues* to deal with?"

What the fuck kind of question was that? Why did she emphasize that particular word? I smiled again, settling back into my chair.

"Sure. There are many things I have to take into consideration. Reputation is everything in this industry, not that I'd do anything to tarnish it, but you have to be quite careful about what you say and who you keep close."

"Speaking of reputation, the rumors have been flying around about what you get up to in your spare time."

A laugh escaped my lips, "What I do in my spare time is probably of little interest to most people. Trust me, my life is pretty normal. I spend time with my family, I hang out with friends. I do very little apart from work. I'm pretty boring."

"What about that photo in the press the other week...?"

"Just propaganda. Next question, please," I cut her off. Stupid bitch didn't know what she was talking about.

"It was quite a rather... *explicit* photograph." There she goes again with the emphasis!

"Which has absolutely nothing to do with this interview. Next question?"

She was treading into dangerous territory, but it was nothing I couldn't handle. Her lips pursed into that tight smile women try on when they are damning you to hell, her eyes shining with malicious intent. I'd angered her. Good. Might put her in her place.

"How is married life treating you? People were beginning to wonder if you'd ever settle down."

"It's fantastic; it is such a comfort to know I have Marie

waiting at home for me after a long day at the office. She's been my absolute rock ever since we met."

"Is the age difference ever a point of tension in your relationship? She's quite a bit younger than you, isn't she?"

"Let's just say she keeps me on my toes," I winked at Ellen, more to keep her going on this line of questioning than flirt, but I would take it where it came. I had a job to do, which was to get through this interview coming out on top and I would do my damn hardest to achieve that.

"Should we be expecting the pitter-patter of tiny feet anytime soon?"

"Oh, for sure. You never know what's around the corner," I replied. I damn well hoped so.

"Wonderful!" She smiled at me again. A wide, PR smile that was engineered specifically for TV and the stay-at-home moms who would eat this shit up.

"So, back to business. How are you finding the challenges of investing in a new field? You've never been involved with in pharmaceuticals before, especially something on so grand a scale as BioHault!"

"It's exciting. I typically stick to what I know but I'm a big advocate of medical advancement and I'm learning new things every day. Yeah, it's a fast-evolving industry, it *burns* through money and I don't understand half the things the scientists are looking into, but I believe these people are our future. It's a rapidly growing, ever-changing field and I can't wait to be a part of that." Nailed it. I tried not to let any hint of smugness show through.

"What are you working on at the moment?"

"Well, many things, but I'm most interested in this cancer drug we're working on. I couldn't tell you how it works, but the formulas being tested have actually managed to shrink stage four malignant cells in mice by up to seventy-eight percent, *and* sustain it, which is insane!"

"I see. How would you respond to recent claims that BioHault have been using the unregulated formulas in human trials?"

"Excuse me?" Where the fuck did that come from? I had to work quickly to come up with an answer, "The drug in question isn't in the stages of human trial yet. There hasn't been sufficient evidence..."

"We have an inside source claiming test subjects are suffering horrible side effects due to a large increase of genetically modified hormones being secreted into the blood," Ellen cut in. It took me a second to process what she was saying.

"Those claims are bullshit. I wouldn't subject anyone to unethical testing or allow shareholders to be in the firing line for wild, unprecedented accusations like that." How fucking *dare she*!

"But a few years ago, there was that scandal regarding the shutdown of your weapons manufacturing plant in Missouri? Isn't that how you met your wife?"

"It was a mechanical engineering plant, that was in fact, not making weapons, but state-of-the-art aircraft radio equipment and if I'm just here to defend myself against an onslaught of ill-advised allegations then this interview is *over*!" I tore the mic from my collar with such force that the material ripped and stormed out of the room.

That was the last time I would subject myself to the travesty of an unsolicited interview. I wouldn't allow myself to be at the mercy of any woman, let alone a bottom feeder like her, making a living off combing through the lives of successful people, scavenging for shreds of information, bulking them out with lies, just to get her ratings up. *Pathetic*!

So, some of what she said might have some basis in fact. I *had* met Marie while down south buying land to build another manufacturing plant; her father was the intermediary for the people who owned the land. The factory *did* fabricate airplane equipment, among other less ethically sound things, but that was by no means advertised to anybody but a select few.

The pharmaceutical company I had acquired was, in want of a better term, experimental, sure. But implying it was illegal was a damn lie! My lawyers had advised me it was risky, nevertheless, the odds were on my side.

And that stupid, *fucking* photograph would haunt me until the day I died! It was a constant reminder of the biggest mistake I'd ever made. In my defense, she did say she was nineteen. And she was very convincing.

But to top it all off; *me*. Why couldn't *I* keep my shit together?

It wasn't how that stupid bitch managed to cut so close to the bone, or the way she was twisting things to show me up on national television. No, I was annoyed how I'd fucking *dealt with it*. My (over) reaction spoke volumes about me. I should have finished the interview. I should have fixed it.

And right now, a drink had never sounded so *fucking* good!

I yanked my cell out of my jacket pocket and hit the first number on speed dial. It rang twice before he picked up.

"*Jean*, tell me what the FUCK is going on!"

"What are you talking about?"

"I was just in an interview with Ellen-*fucking*-Dawson, and she was blabbering on about the human trials like it was everyone's business. Get my publicity team on this. *Right now!* Sue the show if you have to, just cover this shit up. I wanna know who said what and I want them gone. *Today!*"

That bitch had really gotten under my skin. Without a second thought, I hurled my cell toward the paved sidewalk below me with such force it shattered the screen and busted open the corner enough to expose the battery. The impact made a satisfying crunch, although it wasn't quite satisfying enough to release the steadily building rage I was all too used to hiding. I *needed* that release!

Until I realized I didn't have a ride. *Fuck*. I'd picked up Chuck on the way and he'd taken my Ferrari back to the office. I would have to pay through the nose to get an Uber in midday traffic and I wasn't sure I could take *that* journey sober. That was if by some kind of miracle my cell still worked.

Matthew was going to get one hell of a laying into when I next saw him. It was clear that friendship was over. It was a shame, I'd been growing quite fond of him, but the man had gone seriously down in my estimation if he couldn't keep a handle on his woman.

Tiny fragments of glass from my smashed cellphone glittered on the asphalt.

Okay, I just needed to breathe. I'd lost my temper, something I'd been making every effort to control, not too badly but badly enough to do something stupid. *Fucking hell!*

My painkiller buzz was wearing off and the ever-present humming at the back of my mind seemed to intensify with every passing minute. I knew how to silence it. A decision would have to be made to save at least a portion of my sanity today. At least just enough to help me think.

It was just past eleven o'clock on a Thursday morning. The only place open was a grim old Irish bar a few blocks away on the wrong side of town. Strangely, I didn't mind it so much. It was badly lit and smoky enough to conceal my identity from any patrons whose idea of light entertainment would be watching a guy drink himself into a stupor before lunchtime.

I wasn't in the mood to talk to anyone so I indicated to the bartender to leave the bottle and threw him a few fifties. I didn't know what I was going to do; I didn't want to go home just yet and have Marie question me about my morning. I was still too worked up.

Always with the questions. *Yap, yap, yap*, like an annoying little pup you wanted to throttle just to shut it up. *Where have you been? Who were you with?* Questions dripping from her like a leaky tap, never-ending nagging. Constantly on my back about *something*!

She was probably going in on Jack too, although I'd bet my right arm he wouldn't just sit there and take her shit, like the whipped little bitch I was becoming.

The first gulp of whisky burned all the way down, infiltrating my empty stomach like wildfire. It felt *good*.

I wanted to go back to the studio and grab that cunt Ellen by her scrawny, chicken-y neck until I could feel her pulse racing against my fingers and see the light of pure terror shining in her eyes. I could make her life a living hell. I'd have her helpless, on her knees begging me for forgiveness. I'd show her that nobody messes with Nicolas Hayes and lives to gloat about it.

It was dark by the time I'd finished the bottle and I'd calmed slightly. It didn't get much busier in the bar, so there was no indication that time was actually passing. The uninterrupted hours alone allowed me to figure out why I drank.

As soon as the biting liquor touched my tongue, I started to feel better. A few more pulls later and I didn't quite hate myself so much. Booze was like an eraser for my mind, scrubbing it clear of conscious thought. As long as it was in my system, I felt good. Ready to take on the world.

But the pencil that engraved my memories was too sharp, the paper beneath indented with pain. Enough to still be visible after the eraser had worked its charlatan magic. Listen to me making up all this analogy shit. *Stupid, drunken logic!*

Like I said before, I know I should lay off the stuff. I knew it wasn't good for me. It's just too damn hard! *I tried.*

My eyes resisted focusing on the small TV at the darkened end of the room where everything was bleary. I blinked slowly, trying to figure out where the indoor fog had come from.

My name, spoken from the screen, dragged on my attention, "'Earlier this year, the accuracy of Hayes Enterprises bookkeeping came under question again after a tip drew attention to payments made to director Chuck Blake amounting to just under ten million dollars. These were later attributed as finder's fees for recent acquisitions.

This comes after news that General Counsel Jean Thibodeaux is under investigation for tax evasion after failing to pay sales tax on a foreign import vehicle purchased using company funds..." I lost interest.

The media, lowlifes just like Ellen *fucking* Dawson, were forever on the prowl, looking for ways to bring me down. Just like my dear wife. When would I catch a break? Was I such a bad guy? Trying to carve out a decent life for myself in this cruel world; Didn't I deserve acquittal on those grounds?

I was just starting to contemplate the meaning of life when a familiar female voice brought me back.

"Nic, *thank God* I've found you!" A sheet of dark red hair came into focus before her face, a concerned look washed over her features as she studied me.

"You're looking a bit worse for wear, aren't you? Let's get you to a hotel room so you can sleep it off before the flight."

"Flight?" I mumbled into my arm as Jessica tried to drag me off the stool.

"You're going to New York again this evening? Early morning investors meeting with SkyeTron."

I managed to drag my head up, groaning as the room slid to the left and I slumped back down onto the bar.

"Fuck sake! Cancel it!"

"Can't do that, you told me not to let you. It's really important. Nic, If you don't sleep, you're going to feel awful later," She dragged me up again by the arm before placing hers around me so I could steady myself.

"I feel awful right now," I grumbled.

We walked slowly out of the bar, Jessica's close proximity overwhelming as the liberal application of perfume that I usually loved made my stomach turn over. I paused to throw up on the sidewalk while she routed around in her purse for a tissue and bottle of water.

"You're too good to me, you know that?" I asked her, taking a swig from the bottle and wiping my mouth hard with the tissue.

"It was in the job description, honey." She helped me into the car before getting into the driver's seat and pulling out onto the road smoothly. The late-day traffic was moving steadily through the darkening streets, the car lights blurring into one long streak of color.

"How did you know where I was?"

"Jean," she replied.

"How did *he* know where I was?"

"He sent me the last tracked location from your phone, so I googled bars within a five-mile radius. It was the seventh one I checked."

I placed my hand on the inside of her smooth stocking-covered thigh, "How did you know I'd be at a bar?"

She snorted softly, "Tough day, no car. *Please*, I know you."

"Do you now?" My hand slid up a little further.

"Yes, and I know that you need to sober up in three hours if you want to make this flight," She reached between her legs and removed my hand, "I have to concentrate on driving, you know."

"Also, I found your cell," She indicated a shiny, non-broken cellphone lying on the dash.

"You fixed it?"

"Ha! No, that thing was beyond help. I rescued the SIM card and put it in a backup. Like I said, I know you. First thing, you need a shower. There's a toothbrush and a spare set of clothes in your flight bag. I'll order you room service then you need to nap until it's time to leave. Trust me, you'll feel so much better after."

God, what would I do without her?

A quick nap and a shower later, I was feeling more like my usual self. I came out of the bathroom wrapped in a towel. The suite had a full wall of floor-to-ceiling plate glass window on one side, displaying the twinkling lights of the city just the way they were intended to be seen.

I spied Jessica's reflection behind me, tucked away in a corner with her face illuminated by her laptop.

"I didn't know you wore glasses?"

"Only when I'm looking at a screen for a long time. I get headaches," she replied without looking up.

I walked up behind her on the pretense of having a nosey at what she was doing.

"Why don't you just take a break?" Christ, she smelt good.

"I could but I have a lot to do today."

"What time is the flight?"

She barely turned away from the screen, "Eleven."

"Well, I think you've earned a little relaxation time," I leaned down and gently moved her hair off her neck, allowing my fingertips to trail over the soft skin there. Her fingers stilled over the keyboard.

"You should really be getting ready to leave."

"I got time," I laid a trail of wet kisses down her neck, making her breathing hitch in pleasure. "I have to say, those glasses do something to me. You should wear them more often."

"How would you ever get any work done?"

"I'd manage."

She turned to face me, her lips inches from mine. I usually didn't kiss anyone on the lips but my wife, but I was feeling particularly indulgent tonight. Her mouth was hot and tasted subtly of chocolate peppermints.

"Maybe I can spare ten minutes?" She breathed as I caught her lip between my teeth.

"Call it twenty and I'll make it worth your while."

"That assistant of yours is something, huh?" Chuck eyed Jessica in appreciation through the cabin window as she walked back into the airport hanger, ass swaying in her tight little skirt.

"Yeah, and you're going to keep your dirty paws off her, understand?"

"You don't need to act all territorial, boss. Just a bit of harmless admiration."

I ignored the 'boss' quip. He was just trying to get a rise out of me. He was always up for stirring a bit of trouble, was our Chuck.

"I remember what happened last time you 'admired' one of my employees." We'd almost had a lawsuit on our hands. Harassment. He didn't seem to understand the word 'no'.

He held his hands up in mock surrender, attempting (and failing) to keep the smirk from his face. See what I meant about stirring up trouble?

My back was starting to play up again and I'd left my pain meds at home, only realizing I needed something stronger than over-the-counter as we pulled onto the tarmac.

I tossed back my drink in one, struggling to undo the seatbelt with my free hand. Being clamped down in this restricted position was only making it worse.

"Fuck, what is the point of these things anyway? Like this piece of shit is going to help me if we go down," I managed to un-click it just as the head stewardess came back into the cabin.

"Sir, you need to keep your seatbelt fastened for take-off."

"Look, I don't wanna make your job harder but..."

"The captain has switched on the fasten seatbelt sign!"

"Do I really need to...?"

"It's only for takeoff, Sir, just please sit back and…" She leaned in, shoving me back into the seat and reaching for the buckle.

"*ALRIGHT*, Jesus!" I gave up struggling and let her strap me back in.

"Thank you." She walked away fighting the pink flush that was rising in her cheeks.

"Fuck, get me another drink," I called to the other hostess standing near the back of the cabin. "If you can't do whatever the hell you want when you charter your own private fuckin' jet, when can you?"

"Everything alright?" Chuck asked, handing me what was left of his own drink.

"I just got a lot to deal with at the moment," I replied, massaging my temple with the cold bottom of the glass.

"Anything I can help with?"

I sighed, wondering where to begin.

"You know a way to convince my wife to have a baby?"

"She don't need *convincing*. All she has to do is lay there while you give it to her, lounge around for nine months, and then pop it out."

I pointed a finger at him, "Careful!"

"Look, what I'm trying to say is she knew the deal when she married you, right?"

"Well it's not like she's contractually obligated, but yeah, I told her." I'm pretty sure I told her.

"And you ain't young anymore, man."

"This isn't making me feel better, Chuck," I unfastened my seatbelt again and arched my back. Fuck, I needed my pain meds.

"The way I see it, she should do whatever the hell you tell her to. The only reason she wouldn't want one would be…"

"Go on?" I raised my eyebrows slightly.

"Okay, say *theoretically* she was seeing someone on the side. Wouldn't she be worried about that kind of thing? What if the kid came out… black or something?"

"Are you suggesting I don't satisfy my wife? I fuck her very well, thank you very much."

"I'm not questioning your skills in the sack. I just can't think of any other reason."

I started out the window seeing nothing but dark wisps of cloud beyond the taxiway lights. A while back, I thought I should take matters into my own hands.

See, even the most reputable of people can be corrupted. Businessmen, lawyers, even doctors. And owning a large-scale pharmaceutical company allowed me access to things even a doctor can't prescribe. A bit of a selfish investment, but worth it all the same.

Owning a very large stake in said company gets me in

close with the people who matter. People who conduct their own trials into drug effectiveness. Say one of those trials was testing the effectiveness of a new contraception, they would need a control group to take their new drug, another group to take something else, and a third to take a placebo. There is no telling which group you were in; all the drug packets are identical, for the purpose of the trial.

"Boss, I'd put your seatbelt back on. Toots is coming back this way," Chuck smiled at her all too widely as she sauntered past him trying to remain professional. He swiveled in his seat to leer at her as she continued walking away.

"Where the fuck is my drink?" I wondered out loud.

"What's wrong with mine?"

"It's Vermouth."

"...So?"

"Jesus Christ, I'll get it myself!" I stood up to make my way to the end of the plane just as it lurched forward to begin taxing down the runway. I stumbled over backward onto my ass, looking like more of a drunken fool than I was.

"*FUCK IT*," I managed to roar, before smacking my head against the trolley and passing out cold.

Chapter Fourteen

JACK

Gently, I lifted Marie from the back seat of the cab. Her cheeks had a slight pink flush, a halo of hair curling up around her pretty face. I could tell she'd been crying in the bathroom but I didn't mention it. She probably felt vulnerable enough without me making her self-conscious.

She looked so peaceful in my arms, like she belonged there. I shook the idea out of my head, trying to stop thinking of her like that. Like someone who made me feel calm and normal and *right*. Those were dangerous thoughts to be having.

I carried her up to her room and laid her down in the bed, taking her shoes off before tucking her into the soft sheets.

"Mm, Jack?" Her voice came out in a throaty whisper that did things to me. Things that I wouldn't let myself think about until I was alone and well out of ear shot.

"Yeah, sweetheart?" I replied as quietly as I could, trying not to let my voice break.

"Comm'ear..." Marie stretched her arms upwards, eyes still closed. I felt a fuzzy warmth spread over me as I leant down to hug her. Her movements were almost childlike, very deliberate and methodical despite her sleepiness.

"Thank you for today. It meant a lot to me." I could feel her warm breath at my ear as she pulled me close. So close I could smell the faint sweet scent of her skin; a mix of talcum powder, lightly floral and purely Marie. A comforting smell that lazily pulled me in to relax into her embrace, like the surf on the sand. Before I knew what was happening, the softest of lips touched my disfigured cheek.

"Would you stay with me?" Internally, I was torn. If my brother came home early and caught me in bed with his wife, innocent or otherwise, he would castrate me with a blunt knife and probably beat the shit outta her.

Anyway, I had no goddamn business thinking of her in that way. She was off limits! Looking down at the young woman in my arms, I told myself I felt nothing more than friendly affection for her. She just needed me to watch out for her. Marie's eyes were closed; in no less than a minute would she be out cold.

But when I tried to pull away, one of her hands drifted up to my neck and she breathed the one word that could weaken my resolve, "*Please?*"

Mentally chastising myself, I slipped from her arms to lock the bedroom door. Just in case. I unlaced my boots and climbed in behind her, inhaling the scent of her hair in sweet agony. Marie smelt like heaven.

Wrapping my arms around her, a comfort I told myself she needed, I watched the steady rise and fall of her chest. She made a contented purring noise on each exhale. I slowly distanced my mind, concentrating on Marie's warmth and gentle breathing. I promised myself I'd slip out before she woke up. I didn't think I'd get much sleep anyway, but maybe her presence would ward off the nightmares if I did happen to doze.

This time, with her in my arms, I felt light like the softest sunrise fill me inside and drifted off with blissful awareness that Marie wouldn't only be in my dreams tonight.

An intense orange glow glowed from behind the curtains, making me feel like I'd awoken in the middle of the sun. A stream came in through a gap, falling right on my face, bringing me out of a deep sleep. The room was almost unbearably hot.

Strangely, the first thought I had was I had never slept that well in living memory.

And I knew, without a doubt, that next to me the bed was empty.

I should have left immediately, but I couldn't bring myself to shatter the illusion. I didn't want to move, not yet. Instead, I clutched onto the bleary semi-awareness a person experiences upon first waking. The heavenly sense of insignificance.

Rolling over, I buried my nose in the pillow. It still smelled of her. Still carried a hint of her residual warmth.

I kept my eyes closed for a moment longer. Breathed in the scent of her all around me, and told myself all the sensible things I knew I needed to hear. Things I'd told myself a thousand times. All the things I was starting to doubt.

"Morning!" Shit, she caught me off guard!

Wet hair hung in tendrils down her back. She had wrapped a towel tightly around her lithe figure, her features illuminated in the morning light.

"Mornin'," I replied, managing to crack a lazy smile.

"You've been very smiley lately, Mr Grumpy."

I immediately dropped my brow into an animated scowl.

"Oh, that's more like it!" She giggled and flopped onto the bed. I shuffled the creased bedcovers around me, trying to hide my growing erection. That small towel was the only thing separating me from all that damp, naked skin and my body seemed to be well aware of that fact.

I must have discarded more than my boots last night; miscellaneous items of clothing were in a crumpled heap at the bottom of the bed. I could feel her examining me from my rough, stubbly jaw down to my stomach.

All of a sudden, the light from outside dimmed, as if the sun had become obscured by a heavy cloud. Marie's eyebrows furrowed together as she reached out her hand to touch a silvery-white jagged mark on the upper portion of my chest; the grizzly reminder of a near miss with death.

"Was this from the night you saved Nicholas?" Her voice was low.

"No, Iraq. A few inches lower and it would have killed me."

"What about this one?" Her dainty hand kept its place

on one particularly thick scar on my neck, a straight diagonal line. The type made by a slashing knife. I shrugged, not wanting to get into it.

"It's hard to remember." I tried to keep out of trouble but it always managed to find me.

I put my hand over hers, covering it completely. I could feel her shaking.

"It's okay," I spoke softly. It almost sounded like an invitation. Her face was so close to mine. Without makeup she seemed younger but so much more beautiful. My free hand came up to trace the contour of her cheekbone as she leaned into the caress. Her skin felt silken, so fragile under my calloused fingertips.

Her eyelids fluttered closed as she relaxed into the gentle touch. Her lips parted slightly when I ran a thumb across them, then down her neck. A sigh escaped her as outside, a deep rumble of thunder growled its way across the sky.

Our faces were now inches from each other. I could feel her desire pulling me closer and closer until I gently molded my lips over hers. The sensation was like touching a live wire. Every one of my demanding breaths drawn from hers, every heartbeat reverberating in my ears.

She pulled back slightly.

"It's okay," I reassured her, moving in closer to run my hands over her arms, silently urging her to relax before coaxing the towel from her body. At first glance, I took in her wonderful curves from the hollow of her neck to the fullness of her breasts. Natural and pretty, pink nipples hardening on contact with my thumb.

Then I saw fading bruises in places that couldn't come from an accidental knock or bump. Long streaks in a pattern of four on her hip, like they could be finger marks. A purplish-green smudge on the back of her arm like she'd been grabbed. Were they teeth marks on the underside of her breast? I traced over a particularly nasty one on her side. She jumped and tried to cover herself, as if suddenly remembering she carried tell-tale marks all over her. Marks that show she has been claimed by a very dominant male.

"Was this him?" I stared at her, hard. Marie tried to avoid my disgusted gaze as tears streaked wordlessly down her cheeks. I sat up and pulled her into my lap, kissing the top of her head and then her cheeks, tasting the saltiness on my lips. Moving lower I captured her mouth in a slow, deep kiss.

I wanted her to feel love like I knew she wouldn't have experienced with him. I wanted her to feel safe wrapped in my arms. Most importantly, I wanted to be the one to make her happy.

Tender fingers stroked away her tears. A hopeless attempt to not let on that I needed her as much as I had irrefutable belief that she needed me.

Outside, the wind grew louder, light rain starting to spatter against the window. Through the shadowy light that managed to filter in through the rain, I could make out the way she was looking at me. It was all-consuming, fierce. Fully zeroed in on me. *Fuck*!

The realization shot a surge of dark heat spiraling through my belly. Then her mouth was on me.

"I want you!" she moaned into my ear, her heartbeat quickening against my own chest. How could I deny her what I'd been fantasizing about the moment I'd laid eyes on her?

Something, way in the far back of my mind, was screaming that this was wrong, except it was so insignificant in the chaos of my overwhelmed senses that it was drowned out.

Trying to form anything that resembled conscious thought right now was next to impossible.

I rolled on top of Marie, my groin pushing hard against her, my underpants the only thing between our bodies. Marie's kisses were more urgent now, hushed moans escaping between her erratic breaths. It was driving me insane. Her nails raked over whatever skin she could reach, then an urgent tugging at the waistband of my pants.

Chuckling slightly, I moved up so she could pull them down off my hips. As soon as I sprang free, Marie took me in her hand, pulling hard in desperation.

I raised an eyebrow but her tortured expression made me give in far too quickly and I slipped in slowly, pushing all the way inside her beautiful slickness. A low groan came from the back of her throat. She was tight, almost painfully so, which did nothing to help tamp down on the small measure of control I managed to hold onto. It was the first time I'd been with a woman in years and I didn't want to blow it all before it even started.

I stilled, letting us both get accustomed to the bliss of being so deeply connected. I flexed my hips and she arched into me, eyes closed in ecstasy. She was so responsive. Much more so than I fantasized. This was far *more* than any fantasy I could have thought up.

That was all I needed to start a steady pace. The noises she was making were going to drive me over the edge sooner rather than later. I sped up but still held back just a little, until the only sounds she could make were soft, helpless pants of pleasure.

I felt her heels digging into my ass, her thighs clenched so tightly around my waist.

Marie bit my ear, urging me, begging me to go harder. She didn't have to tell me twice! I pounded into her so hard, so erratically, I was afraid I was hurting her.

Her cries quickened, expression altering between bliss and twinges of something more complex that I couldn't name. She was so close.

"Come on, baby," I growled, reaching down to stimulate her with my thumb which had the desired effect almost instantly. Watching her shuddering beneath me pushed me over the edge too.

My release was so powerful I swear it blinded me for a few seconds. I collapsed on top of her, panting heavily, taking care not to crush her under my weight.

I leaned down to kiss her forehead, those delicate lilac petals of eyelids, and then every mark on her body, trying to kiss away the pain my brother had brought upon her. I couldn't even think his name let alone begin to comprehend what he must be doing to her when doors were closed.

When she finally opened her eyes, there were tears and the glimmer of something else I couldn't quite work out.

"Please, get off of me," she whispered.

Puzzled, I moved so she could wriggle from the bed. She rushed to the bathroom and locked the door. There was a rust-colored stain on the bed where she had just been.

I couldn't seem to get my head around what had just happened. What I had done to her. She didn't say no, in fact, she had encouraged me. I kept telling myself it was justified because I cared about her. But that didn't make it right.

I should have shut my mouth and walked away!

I swung my legs out of the bed, my feet coming into contact with Marie's discarded towel, now cold and damp on the floor. I slung it over the end of the bed before starting to look for my clothes, only just realizing the heat of the last few weeks had finally broken.

Through the gap in the curtains, rain came down in torrents washing away the stickiness, purging the atmosphere of the sweltering tension that had hung in it.

Pulling on my pants, I tried to think of something to say to her. It would be wrong to just up and leave. I so badly felt like taking the cowards' way out and disappearing for a few days. I knew I had to at least try to make this right. Not an apology exactly but something.

Finding the bathroom door locked was no surprise. I'd expected it to be. After knocking, with no answer, and waiting a full minute, I *needed* to check on her. After all, the lock was only a single flimsy piece of metal between us.

I shouldered the door, once, hard, and went crashing into the bathroom. Marie blinked, hardly acknowledging my appearance, like men came hurtling in on her unannounced on a regular basis. She was looking out the window on the front yard and driveway, sitting curled up in a plush chair. The other side of the room, the slowly filling bath was letting off a thick steam which was starting to fog the tiles and mirrors. I averted my gaze so she didn't think I was there to leer at her.

Then her eyes flicked to mine, impassive. "I locked that door."

I came to kneel in front of her, so we could be at eye level. Also, so I didn't have the temptation to stare at her body.

"I know," I bent forward, so close our foreheads almost touched, "I wanted to make sure you were okay?"

"What happened in there, can't happen again. You need to leave, Jack."

"I know, but I can't."

Marie laid back, not looking at me.

"Did I hurt you?" She continued to ignore me.

"Marie, baby, please? Did I hurt you?"

"Does it matter?" Her tone was dismissive. If I didn't know her better I would say she didn't care but I knew this was a defense mechanism—a way of dealing with shit she didn't want to address.

"Of course it matters," I was a big guy and she was so… well, *little*!

"No, okay? It was… it was amazing, but a serious lapse of judgment on my part." Hearing that stung. It hurt a lot to know she already regretted what we had done. It felt like a kick in the gut.

"He's my husband and your brother. And now *this* has happened," she closed her eyes again.

"He's vile and manipulative. He does unspeakable things to you and I have to protect you from that!" I felt like I was begging her not to toss me to the gutter like the trash I was.

I didn't even know where I stood on being good enough for her but it sure as hell had to be better than a man who treated her like she was his favourite plaything. Surely I was better than that?

She jumped to her feet.

"He trusts you! Trusts us. We're his family! All he wants is love and respect from us and look how we've repaid him." Her sturdy resolve broke right at the end.

It didn't escape my notice that neither of us could say his name.

I was falling hard; becoming dangerously obsessed with

something that was not mine to have. Now I'd had a taste, it was one I wouldn't easily forget. I'd crave her. I'd need Marie like she was oxygen. And now she was pushing me away.

Although I couldn't fully justify it, I needed her again despite her telling me no. My self-restraint was slipping. I needed to show her how much I cared as much as show her what she had been missing.

My mouth came crashing down on hers. Somewhere far away I could hear her making weak protesting noises as I backed her into the wall. My hand came up to caress her breast, feeling her plush skin against my fingertips.

She emitted a hushed moan before pushing my hand away.

"Please, stop."

I bent my head lower so I could kiss the flushed planes of her neck before whispering in her ear, "Do you really want me to stop?" I caught her earlobe between my teeth as my hands themselves wrapped around her hips.

"No," she breathed. In her lust-hazed state, I doubt she could have given more than the one-word answer I needed.

I knelt before her, not breaking eye contact as I brought my mouth to the soft flesh of her stomach, trailing kisses down past her belly button and lower until I reached the most sensitive spot between her legs.

She let out a whimper and arched into me, eyes rolling back as she was lost in sensation.

"You are still on the pill, right?" Marie didn't reply. That was definitely something I should have asked the first time.

Struggling with one hand, I managed to pull my pants down far enough to reach inside, not wanting to let her go even for a second. She started to protest again, more vehemently this time, until she felt the tip of my cock brush against her, making her involuntarily still.

"Let me go!"

"Baby, I won't let you go until you are screaming my name."

Hoisting her up, I pushed in inch by inch, slowly and carefully. Her face shone with a mix of heavenly gratification and shame. The expression was beautiful. I wanted this to be good for her, for her to know that I was much better at this than him. I needed to make her understand that I was the better man.

"You're an asshole," she breathed.

"Get out." Marie wasn't looking at me again. She hadn't screamed my name but did finish loudly. I wasn't sure how, but we'd both ended up in the bath together. I just sat in my end, my wet clothes on the floor beside the tub.

"Fine," Marie got out quickly and sat on the toilet to pee. She wiped then grabbed a towel from the rack and walked toward the door.

"You didn't flush," I called over, trying to lighten the mood.

"Bite me!" she spat and held up her middle finger, continuing toward the door.

"Don't take it out on me, kid."

She stopped and turned to look at me.

"Don't call me kid."

"Why?"

"Because we've fucked!"

"Hey, watch your mouth!" I felt like I was scolding a child but I was genuinely annoyed. Swear words just didn't look as though they should come out of her delicate little mouth. And fucked was completely the wrong word for what just happened!

"No, fuck you, you bastard! You are just as bad as him!" She stormed out, leaving the door swinging open on its hinges.

I didn't know how I felt about that, only that I should have at least tried to go after her. Although, I knew she wouldn't listen to me, especially after what had just happened... again.

It dawned on me that the concept of the 'friendly affection' I was deluding myself with was something way deeper. I cared a great deal more than I should for my brother's wife. Probably more than we both even realized. My attraction to her was intensifying to an uncontrollable, almost frightening level.

I couldn't tell her any of this; it was as if I needed some kind of affirmation first, like her rejection would break me otherwise. I couldn't go through that kind of pain again. A man's resilience can only be tested so much. And how in the hell was I supposed to explain to her that I had feelings that were so much more than just about getting my dick wet?

I wanted to hold her again, kiss her with the tenderness she deserved. Tell her things that I desperately wished I had the right to; that I'd be there, no matter what. That she belonged to me.

That I loved her.

Chapter Fifteen

NIC

As it turned out, I wasn't destined for New York. I couldn't even charter another flight. The asswipe of a pilot had made sure I was barred from airline travel for the next forty-eight hours 'for my own safety.' Like fuck I wasn't sober enough to fly!

So, with no feasible way to get to the SkyeTron meeting, I missed it. Luckily Jean was there to hold down the fort. I'd get the run-down from him later.

After a few lengthy, unnecessary hours in police custody, I found myself stuck in the car with a thumping headache and Chuck, cruising toward downtown Los Angeles. While he yammered on about the incompetence of the LAPD, I scrolled through my phone checking messages. Nothing yet from Jean, the person I really wanted to hear from. One from Marie, asking if I'd landed safely, which I skipped over. I wasn't ready to explain that one yet. One from Jude's mom, which I didn't even trouble myself to open.

I was still waiting for a reply from Jack. I knew he was shit with his phone, but this was taking it to a new level. As soon as I'd been let out that morning, I'd sent him the address and the time to meet me, offering no explanation. I didn't want to ruin the surprise, after all.

I'd at least expected a thumbs up or something to show he read the text. Maybe that was being too optimistic, but the bonehead could at least type, right? Although maybe he didn't bother replying, me being an arrogant jerk summoning him like I did. He'd been around long enough to know that was just part of the package, and he would just have to deal with it like everyone else. Either way, it wasn't my fault if he was basically illiterate.

However, when we pulled up in front of the high-rise, Jack was there waiting, hood drawn against the drizzle. With his face obscured and large, hunched frame, he looked almost menacing and I thought again that I wouldn't want to cross someone like him on a dark night.

"Everything okay?" he asked as soon as I stepped out of the car.

"Yeah… why wouldn't it be?" I replied in a leading tone. He just shrugged, then flicked his eyes up in time to see Chuck get out of the driver's side.

"Whatd'ya bring that dick for?"

"Don't get your panties in a twist, shovel-face," Chuck sneered. "We're not staying long."

I'd deliberately not told Chuck we were meeting with my brother because I didn't want him chewing my ear off over it the whole way here.

"Listen, can we take this inside? As much as I love listening to the two of you have at it on street corners, I'd rather be dry." I shot Chuck a glance, noting his aggressive stance and tendency to get under my brother's skin, and decided it would probably be better if he didn't come in with us.

"On second thoughts, Chuck. Stay with the car."

He opened his mouth to protest but I shot him a look that very clearly said 'don't fuck with me right now' and he shut it again. He settled for leaning back against the car with crossed arms, looking mutinous but otherwise obedient. I didn't miss Jack flip him off behind my back either. Children, the pair of them.

Once inside the dry lobby, the concierge greeted me politely and handed me a set of keys, then I motioned for my brother to follow me to the lift where I inserted the smallest key and punched the button for the penthouse. We stood in silence as the lift rose the thirty-five floors to the top, Jack shifting awkwardly, me trying to keep the grin from cracking over my face and giving me away.

The lift doors slid open to reveal the minimally furnished but stylish loft. Floor-to-ceiling plate glass windows offered the best view of downtown money could buy, the rooftops of other similar buildings, and the Hollywood hills beyond.

"Well, what do ya think?" I asked, finally dropping my aloof manner, and grinning broadly.

"Huh?" he replied, distracted, his gaze focused out the huge windows.

"What do you think of your new place, bro?"

His eyes snapped back to mine. He suddenly looked uncomfortable, "Nic, you didn't..."

"Shut up, I wanted to," I interrupted him. Then when his expression didn't change, I elaborated.

"I'm not kicking you out, man. Far from it. You're welcome back whenever you want to come. But this place is for you, for you know, when you wanna be *alone*." I raised my eyebrows suggestively.

"What about Marie?"

"What about her?" I replied, feeling a light cloud of suspicion beginning to form.

"Well, I was supposed to be watching her, right? Am I off the hook?"

Oh. The cloud dissipated in an instant. Of course that's what he meant. What Chuck had said must have had more impact on me than I'd initially thought. And in any case, this was Jack! He and Marie hated each other. If he knew what she was up to, and if she *was* up to anything, I'd doubt he'd cover for her. His loyalty was to me. Although the aforementioned hospital incident still hung over me like poisonous smog.

Naturally, I'd found out what happened using my sources. The little snake thought she could keep it from me. Information that as her husband I had every right in knowing. Especially since my signature had somehow found its way onto the release forms despite me being the other side of the country. That was a conversation I needed to have with Marie though, not my brother.

"Job's finished," I punched him lightly on the arm, "This is my way of saying thank you. I don't know what I would have done without you, bro."

"I'll probably still be around. It's nice to have the company."

"Thought the two of you didn't get along?"

"She's not so bad," he said after a pause, "And if you're going to be home, maybe we can hang out?"

"For sure. I know if been busy recently, but we'll definitely find some time to do that. Speaking of."

I strode over to the kitchen area and pulled two chilled beers from the ready-stocked fridge, handing one to Jack.

"It's ten in the morning…"

"Time doesn't come into consideration when you have something to toast, little brother," I responded, cracking the top off my beer.

Jack smirked and followed suit, "Is this another piece of advice from Nic's little black book of bullshit?"

"Yup! Cheers," I responded, clunking the top of my bottle down on the neck of his, causing a geyser of foam to spurt out all over his hand and the highly polished wooden floor.

"Dick," he shot, shaking the remaining froth off of his hand. I just laughed and took a deep gulp of my beer.

On the way back down, I stopped at the fifteenth floor, knocking on the door at the very end of the hallway.

"Nic? What are you doing here?" Her long auburn hair was all mussed up and she was wearing a very tiny, very sexy camisole set that barely covered anything at all. If I didn't know her better, I would have sworn I'd pulled her away from her lover lazily dozing on a Saturday morning. Except, I did know her better, and she was wearing those black Prada glasses that happened to remind me of my favorite 'naughty schoolboy' scenario.

"Thought I would drop in for a cup of coffee," I gave Jessica my most dashing grin.

"What if I have company?"

"You don't have company," I replied with a confident smirk.

"No. I don't." She countered with a coy smile, stepping back to let me enter.

I felt sure she already knew about the events that transpired at the airport and was rescheduling my introductory meeting with SkyeTron. I had good faith that Jean had adequately covered for me, but the service Jessica provided was on another level. And in more than the professional sense of the word. Part of my rewarding her hard work was this apartment, paid for outright by me so she could live comfortably without worrying about renting a place near the office in this extortionate part of town. This was mostly the reason; I liked to have her close in the week in case I needed her. I also, however, took pleasure in knowing where she would be when she wasn't at work. For moments such as these, where I could drop in unexpectedly.

See, Marie could bitch about what she thought I owed her, but some men needed a particularly long leash. I couldn't stay chained to her when there was so much I would be missing out on. I had to do what was in my best interest.

I'd always assumed, and quite rightly so, that my partners got what they desired whilst I was satisfying my own needs. I knew that pissed my wife off, but it was also what drew her to me in the first place. That integral cocksure attitude; it was just in my nature to be that way. I radiated power, and women sensed that, wanted a little piece of it for their own. Wanted to relinquish to that wild, male strength. It was instinctive. They gave themselves over to me not in spite of that, but *because* of it.

And who was I to stop the force of nature, its calling. No matter how selfish it made me sound, that's how I was going to justify it.

Chapter Sixteen

MARIE

It had gone too far. It had gone too far the second I let him touch me.

The past two days, I'd been trying to avoid him. Avoiding his intense gaze and caressing hands. Prowling the halls for me like a lion sniffing out its next meal.

After the first encounter, I stripped the bed right down to the mattress and burnt the contaminated sheets in the fire pit at the bottom of the garden. As if to erase the evidence that I was a guilty, cheating wife.

What made it worse was how often I found myself thinking of him, for some reason, particularly in the shower. I'd be washing my hair thinking of how much I hated that water thrumming over my skin when my fingers would find their own way down between my legs as I remembered how good he felt. How gently he'd caressed my skin. How attentive he was to my needs, putting my satisfaction first.

Afterward, I sat under the stream of water until it ran cold, hugging my knees to my chest, sobbing noiselessly. I was so fucking mad at him for letting this happen, for what we had done. For the insatiable desire he'd stirred in me.

Over the next few days, he lost no time reminding me of what I was missing while Nic was around. Most of the time he was topless, tending to the garden or in the gym. I couldn't help but check him out. The chiseled contours of his tanned back, working when he clipped the hedge or the way his biceps bulged when he picked up the weights. The way each hardened line formed on his body had me practically melting on the spot. And he knew it.

As soon as Nic was out of the house, Jack began his hunt for me. I could feel my self-control waning too, feeling a magnetic force pulling me into his orbit. I saw it in the way he looked at me. Hungry, for more than the small taste he'd had.

I heard him leaving around eight in the morning and decided it was safe to venture out of my room. He eventually cornered me a few hours later, strutting into the basement gym just as I finished up working out. His bronzed, naked chest glistening with sweat as he licked a line of perspiration from his top lip. He knew exactly what he was doing.

"I need to talk to you."

"We don't have anything to talk about." I tried to push past him, but he blocked me with a hefty arm.

"You still want me."

I shook my head as he leaned down to kiss me sweetly on the lips. Damn, why did he have to make it so good?

His lips came to mine again in a hungry, open mouth kiss. I bit down on his bottom lip causing him to break away, cursing. I took the opportunity to rush to the bottom of the stairs, but he got there first, blocking my escape.

He wiped the drop of blood from his mouth with the back of his hand and stared at me with darkened carnal desire, drinking in my body. It was a mistake to wear only a sports bra and yoga pants. I could feel him starting to pull the pants down. My hand found the door handle and we fell backward out of the room, Jack landing heavily on top of me.

"What the fuck is wrong with you!? He could be home any minute!" I whispered furiously, struggling against his solid hold. He was caressing every inch of skin he could get his hands on, his mouth on my neck while he worked over the front zipper of my sports bra.

"Get your hands off me!" I tried to hit him, push him off but I was encased in his vice-like grip. He ground his hips into my core, making me involuntarily still. He took the opportunity to grab both my hands in one of his, holding them above my head. Proof again that I was at his mercy.

Then he bent his head and circled an aching nipple with his tongue before drawing it into his mouth.

"Please, *please*," I begged in anguish. I wasn't even sure what I was asking for any more.

"Look me in the eye and tell me you don't want this. Then I'll leave you alone." I stared up at him in silence as my exposed chest heaved. He waited a moment before nudging my legs apart and pulling down his own sweatpants.

I cried out as he entered me, forgetting all about keeping quiet. The abrupt intrusion sent convulsions through my whole body. He made a growling sound that I felt unfurl deep within his chest. I shuddered, my legs involuntarily tightening around him, and he groaned then thrust again, suddenly hard and primal. And fuck, it felt good!

He bared his teeth and started pushing in and out with slow, powerful strokes I was not accustomed to. I struggled not to moan, not wanting to give him the satisfaction. It would be a lie if I said I'd experienced this level of pleasure before.

He let go of my hands to steady himself as he picked up the tempo as I pushed against his thick forearms for some leverage. I ran my hands over his glorious body, feeling the muscles bunch and tense, the sheer, raw power in them, trembling with restraint.

"Tell me how much you want me, baby."

"Fuck you," I hissed in his face. He just smirked and sped up to a frenzied pace. I couldn't keep quiet anymore. It felt so good it was almost painful. My butt was sliding on the polished wooden floor. He grabbed my hips, arching me up into him, changing the angle and…

I finished, shamefully loud. Jack wasn't far behind. I thought he would at least have the decency to pull out, but no.

He gripped me so hard it hurt as he came with a strangled yell and collapsed on top of me, panting. I was just as much out of breath. I closed my eyes, shaking my head in disbelief at what I'd let happen again. *Why*? Why couldn't I just stop?

I looked up into his green eyes, wild and shifting in the sunlight, as he faintly traced my cheekbones with his fingertips, leaving a tingling trail of awareness in their wake.

I hated how much I wanted him. He knew that I couldn't really resist, even if I wanted to. Whatever this was, he was a man and he was going to use it to his advantage. This couldn't happen again. If I couldn't refrain, I had to remove the temptation.

"Move out. I'm not asking."

"Finally, just you and me," Nic breathed into my ear, as we waved Jack off. I smiled at Nicholas trying to fight off my bad conscience. He'd slept with plenty of women behind my back so this was no big deal, right? Of course, I wasn't going to bring it up. He returned the smile but it didn't reach his cool, grey eyes.

"I really missed you, doll." He leaned in to kiss me slowly, the way he used to when we were first dating, almost like he needed my permission first.

"I missed you too." And I did miss the version of him that was this tender. Maybe he'd already taken his Valium today? Or he felt guilty? Or was that me?

"Let's get to work on making that baby then, eh?" he whispered, kissing me again before grabbing my denim-clad butt and leading me upstairs. I was still taking my birth control, like hell was I coming off it with what was going on. That was a situation I *really* didn't want to think about.

Later that evening, somber piano music floated in from the rarely used dining room. Nic didn't play so it must have been someone who was visiting. Curiosity got the better of me and I went to go and see.

As it turned out, Jean had another secret. I watched for a few minutes, intrigued by the way his long fingers seemed to glide over the keys so freely. He made it look effortless. I'd had lessons as a girl, but I didn't pick it up easily, and eventually, other 'hobbies' took precedence. Basically anything momma thought fit.

He must have sensed somebody watching as he cocked his head slightly in my direction.

"I didn't know you played?" I said in a low voice, approaching.

"Only when I'm sad, chéri." There was a stout glass of bourbon sitting atop the piano lid. He kept playing.

"I guess that makes two of us." I sat down next to him on the wide bench. There was just enough room for us both to squeeze on.

"Pretty lady like you has no business being sad. Want to talk about it? I have an ear to lend and a shoulder to cry on."

"No," I mused, "But thanks. What's the matter with you?"

He paused, fingers hovering over the keys before answering, "I lost a lot of money tonight."

"Oh."

"Oh indeed." He started playing another song in a minor key, the music penetrating in its intensity. I'd never heard something so beautiful, yet so heartbreaking.

I leaned my cheek on his shoulder as he carried on playing. I tried not to let any tears fall but gave myself away with a hearty sniff. Jean didn't ask, just lifted a hand away from the piano and wrapped his arm around me. Not having to talk was nice sometimes. Sometimes all you needed was silent comfort.

"I'm so glad you're here, Jean. You're my only friend."

"Non? I know that's not true. You seemed very keen on Jack last time we spoke."

"I don't want to talk about *him!*"

Nic burst into the room at that moment, making us both jump out of our skins.

"YOU!" He pointed to Jean. "*OUT!*"

"...And that's my cue to leave."

Jean slid out of the room, collecting his jacket and hat from the top of the sofa on the way out. Nic barely looked at him as he left, his jaw clenched, gaze trained intently on me.

"That was a bit uncalled for, Nic!"

"You wanna tell me what the fuck is going on?" Nicholas asked almost too causally, a complete three-sixty from his dramatic entrance. I flushed cold. This didn't sound good.

He looked pissed off but also, his eyes had a slight glaze to them like he was struggling to focus. It scared me.

"Are you fucked up right now?"

"Answer the question." He settled on the edge of the solid wood dining table across from where I was still seated.

"What do you mean?" I swallowed back my fear, trying not to eye the nearest exits.

He dropped a beige-colored manila file at my feet and raised his eyebrows expectantly. The file had, 'Hayes, Marie' written in neat script on the tab and then, 'Medical history.' I felt a small wave of relief wash over me. It wasn't as bad as I thought.

"H…how did you…?" How the hell had he got his hands on that? Health records were only accessible to doctors and to give up that information would be a major breach of confidentiality. In fact, it was illegal. Deep down I knew I wouldn't have been able to keep it a secret for long, it was just the timing was never right. He'd become increasingly harder to talk to.

"Guess what else I happened to find?" He reached into his jacket pocket and threw a handful of little foil-covered packets in my direction. It was my birth control. *Shit*, this was bad! I tried not to look as guilty as I was.

"I can overlook the money you were squirreling away. I get it. You need to feel secure. If that's the way you want to do it, then fine. But this…" he indicated the pills, "I won't tolerate being *lied* to in my own house!" How was he so calm right now? My belly flipped, slick and oily with anxiety. That me more uneasy than the screaming matches we were always on the verge of.

I took a deep breath, calling on some deep reserve of mental energy I didn't know I possessed, "I told you, I'm not ready!"

"AND I TOLD YOU..." he roared, surging toward me. Spit flew from the corners of his mouth, veins erupting in his forehead, purple and throbbing. Jean's abandoned drink was launched from the top of the piano and smashed against the wall, glass and bourbon everywhere.

There was the overdramatic husband I knew. Too bad it wasn't going to put up with it anymore. I stood up to look him directly in the eye.

"Save it, Nic. I'm not in the mood for your bullshit." Nicholas stared at me a long second, with that look that scared me a little before. Then raised a large hand and smacked me around the face. The force of the blow caught me off balance and I stumbled back.

We both stood in shocked silence for a moment, me staring at him in disbelief. He'd *never* hit me before.

He grabbed me and leaned forward to say something else but before he could, I spat in his face. It rolled down his cheek and he let go in outrage, his whole body visibly trembling.

I took the opportunity to break free of his grasp and run up the stairs to the bedroom, locking the heavy door behind me. By that point, Nicholas had caught up and was hammering on the other side.

"MARIE!! You better open this FUCKIN' door *RIGHT NOW!!*" I looked around for an escape route. I was angry as well, but I didn't want to face him like this. He was too dangerous right now.

"LEAVE ME ALONE!" I yelled, hoping he didn't hear how badly I was shaking from my voice. The banging on the door subsided and I heard what I imagined to be his forehead make contact with the wood instead.

"Come on, babe. Let me in and we can talk, okay?" he replied with forced calm.

"Go fuck yourself!!" I grabbed my largest Prada purse from the closet and stuffed things in as quickly as I could.

"WHO THE FUCK do you think you are talking to? When I get in there, I'll show you how to FUCKIN' RESPECT YOUR HUSBAND..." his voice faded as I climbed out of the window onto the porch roof. The brick beneath me was rough so I managed to scramble down to the floor, scuffing my manicure and knees on the way down.

I stormed from the house and into the car, texting Jack en route to meet me then deleted the message, throwing my phone into the bushes at the bottom of the driveway.

I was furious and horny and so *confused*. I fought with Nic and my first thought was I couldn't wait to jump another man? Cheating on Nicholas was not something I wanted to persist with but sometimes he was *so hard* to love. And even the thought of Jack's rock-hard body turned me on. No one had *ever* made me feel what he did.

I was mad with him too, for being such an idiot! He should have known better. He should have thought of the consequences before starting this.

He was already in the room when I arrived at the shabby motel across town. I knocked with force and he answered the door, naked. He started to say a probably well thought out, smart-assed comment but I pushed past him.

"Shut it," I shot, stripping down and almost tackling him under me on the bed, my legs wrapping around his waist, kissing him roughly. He responded just as fast, reaching up and massaging my breasts. I grabbed hold and thrust him inside me, letting out a sharp cry at the bliss being filled so completely.

"This what you wanted, huh?" I rolled my hips, dominating him like I'd never done before. Rapidly establishing a merciless pace, the one that usually got me off the quickest.

Jack didn't do so well when he wasn't in charge. He inspected me with a confused look on his face, stilling my movements by taking gentle hold of my forearms.

I realized I was doing what Nicholas did to me. I was just using him to get to my end.

He sat up and hugged my body to his before rolling me underneath him. He started to move his hips in long lulling strokes which had me whining in seconds.

"Do you love me?" he growled into my neck. It rumbled from someplace deep within him.

"*No*," I moaned in ecstasy.

Jack just shook his head, deepening his thrusts to the

point where illusion and logical thought blurred into one indistinguishable, heavenly blob.

I couldn't tell what he was thinking, yet I had the suspicion he wanted me to have fallen for him. He wanted me to leave my husband.

Minutes later, we lay side by side, not touching, staring up at the mold-speckled ceiling. He reached over to graze my cheek, colored already from where Nicholas struck me earlier. I rolled off the bed away from him.

"Baby, talk to me?"

"Why? There is nothing to talk about." I pulled on his large t-shirt. The fluffy, discolored one I loved so much.

"Tell me what's wrong?" he frowned at me.

"Let's see; My husband is off fucking whores behind my back, my family practically disowned me, I've moved across the country from everyone and everything I know. Oh, and my brother-in-law is trying to seduce me every chance he gets. Anything else?" There were actually many more things wrong, but I'd run out of energy to voice them.

"What the fuck, Marie? You came to me!"

"I'm not leaving my husband for you."

"I didn't ask you to." He looked bewildered.

"And you are happy fucking your brother's wife?"

His eyes narrowed, "You're a big girl, Marie. I didn't force you."

"Yes, but you took advantage of a situation that you knew you shouldn't have! Is it me you want, or the convenience?"

He stood up, coming to stand directly in front of me so I had to bend my neck up at an odd angle to look at him.

"If I'm so terrible, why don't you stop?"

I looked away because he would see the answer in my eyes. I didn't want to stop.

I couldn't tell him that having sex with him was the highlight of my day. I couldn't admit, even to myself, how much I ached for him to hold and touch me in a way Nicholas wouldn't. I couldn't say that maybe I had started to fall for him. Because where would that leave me?

"Oh please. You know that after what I've just dealt with, anything you say will make me beg you to stay."

I showered in the crappy motel bathroom, trying to wash away the near-constant dirty feeling I'd had since this had started. The cubical was tiny and rimmed with the filth of countless other bodies before me. There was a weird brown stain on the plastic base and a sickening clump of hair that reminded me of a dead rat caught in the drain, which I tried to avoid touching with my toes.

I heard Jack enter. Locking the door would've been useless; he would just break it down anyway. I had paid for the room with the little cash I had on me and I sure as hell didn't want to cover any damages on my credit card.

He pulled back the yellowed curtain, eyeing me wearily. No point sending him out, he wouldn't listen. This game was getting old and I was fed up with arguing.

"Come on, you're letting the cold in."

He stepped in, taking up nearly all the space. He gathered me in his arms, and I rested my head against him, trying to keep the sobs at bay.

"I'm sorry," I mumbled into his chest. Most people struggle to say those two little words, swallow their pride, and let go. But when I know I'm in the wrong, I apologize. Sometimes it's just easier than continuing to battle it out.

Jack stroked back my hair.

"It's okay, kid." His hands skimmed my body as he started washing me. Ever since he'd first touched me, I'd been fascinated by his hands. The sheer size of them, how those massive things, so gnarled and rough, could be so gentle when he needed them to be.

"He *hit* me." My voice broke.

"Yeah, I thought that's what that was." His fingertip traced the mark on my cheek.

"He knows about the miscarriage. He knows I'm still taking the pill."

He paused, "Does he know about us?"

"No. I don't think so." We were quiet for a long time. And he just held me, the water cascading over our bodies, the splashing echoing off the tiles in tinny repetition. Despite the water, despite everything that was happening, I felt safe.

"Jack?" It came out as a croak.

"Yeah?"

"I don't want to have his baby."

He gently kissed the top of my head, rubbing his hands over my back, massaging away all the tension. It felt amazing. Then he lifted my chin so I'd look at him before he spoke.

"Even if it's just one time, I want to feel that you need me just as much I as need you. Please give that to me?"

It was hard to tell but the streams of water coming down his face could have been mixed with tears. I stood on my toes so I could kiss him fully on the mouth, pulling him down by his shaggy wet hair.

"Okay," I whispered, because I wanted that too. This time I could pretend it was real. My own tears were forgivingly masked by the shower spray as well. Real fairytale love didn't exist; this was the closest I would ever get to a happily ever after.

Jack lifted me, pressing my body between his and the wall, both his hands on my butt. I moaned into his mouth as he entered me again. As he started moving inside me, my back slid down the wet tiles only to be pushed back up by the next thrust.

My hand flew out to grip something for stability, but he grabbed my hand back, linking his fingers with mine as he leaned in to capture my mouth in a deep kiss. This time felt less like going at it like wild animals. This time felt like making love.

"I need you, Marie." My fingernails raked up and down his strong back, leaving raw trails behind.

The most I could manage as a reply was a breathless whisper, "I'm so *close!*"

I could sense the desperation driving him on with some kind of urgent demand. A single word repeated itself, although I knew it was just my imagination. I could practically hear it with each thrust, in possessive rhythm; *mine, mine, mine, mine.*

We climaxed together in a strained silence before Jack lightly set me on my feet. He knelt down, hugging his face to my belly so tightly I couldn't see his expression.

"I can't share you with him anymore," he moaned against my skin, his voice broken.

I knew what he meant. I couldn't take that risk. I couldn't say yes and face an unknown future. There was a good chance that we were both just using each other for comfort. That what we had didn't stretch far beyond the physical.

"I know." I stroked his wet hair out of his pained eyes.

How much longer could we really continue like this? Deceit and pain and unspoken words. Lingering on feelings that weren't real. He didn't love me. He wanted me, sure. But that wasn't enough.

He told me before that he wanted desperately to be free. To not be tied down. That meant not shacking up with his brother's wife, at least not for long, because I would want more than he would be willing to give.

If I did decide to leave Nic, I would be alone. And that thought terrified me.

A molten wave of guilt crashed over me. Bleak, scalding guilt, because I was abandoning him. Although I had no right. It wasn't my place. It was going to be so difficult to say because I really didn't want to.

It was time to let go.

"That's why this can't happen anymore, okay? We need to stop and walk away now."

"But..."

"Please. Don't make this harder than it already is."

Jack nodded, solemn lipped, understanding. My eyes blurred with tears, all I saw was the dejected, forgotten little boy from southern Texas staring up at me, silently asking me why.

Chapter Seventeen

MARIE

I gazed into the lovely brown eyes before me. They twinkled, as though a dark secret was concealed within.

The long mirrors in the closet were ornate, held within gilded frames. Inside her reflective cage, a young woman stared back at me in unabashed silence. She had my face but there was something unfamiliar about her, something off about the set of her mouth. A ruby smile two sizes too small.

The dress, a custom Versace, was conservative in structure but somewhat revealing in design. Intricately beaded overlays covered only that which needed concealing for modesty while the rest of the dress was constructed from sheer panels of lace. Needless to say, it couldn't be worn with underwear.

And through all the glamour, behind the façade, I still saw the secret.

The faint imprint of shadowy circles under my eyes were a new addition, heaped with makeup to conceal them. Just add sinful insomniac to the list of the many things I was. The mirror may have shown a pretty, confident young woman, but all I saw reflected back at me was my own inadequacy.

"Ready to go, boys?" I called from the top of the stairs. Both Jack and Nicholas were waiting for me, looking every bit the brothers they were in twin black tuxes. I felt the heavy beading on the dress swing around my ankles with every step I took. Both men were gawping up at me as I smiled and made my way down the marble staircase.

Jack looked very handsome; his usually untamable mane of hair had been smoothed back. He'd given his beard a trim as well, although badly. Some parts were longer than others.

Nicholas looked as he normally did; smug. His gaze actually made me feel uncomfortable, like he could see me stripped bare. He'd obviously seen me naked a hundred times, however, the way he was studying me couldn't be described as merely lecherous. It was domineering.

Approaching, I gave Nic a chaste kiss on the cheek and ignored Jack. I hadn't forgotten yesterday's argument I'd had with Nic. Luckily my cheekbone hadn't bruised too badly; the makeup artist managed to cover it up.

I've always thought of myself as a patient woman. I tried very hard to understand Nic, everything he stood for, the way his mind worked. I got that he had a lot of responsibility. I accepted that he needed to find ways to blow off steam. There was only so much I could take, though.

And I definitely wouldn't stand for being hit.

We hadn't had a chance alone to talk it through. That would have to wait until later but for now, it would have to be all smiles and small talk, for everyone else's sake.

Before I could speak to Nic, he turned and walked out the front door. Jack came up close behind me as we followed. I could still feel his gaze burning a hole through me, intense and piercing. I wish I had a bit more time to gauge his mood before the party; I needed to know where his head was at, if he was going to make some stupid mistake and give us away. I didn't have him down as the tantrum-throwing type, but Nicholas definitely was and Jack took after him in more ways than one.

"I like you in that dress." His voice was low, hot breath by my ear.

"It's not for your benefit," I hissed back. He pushed into me from behind and I felt just how much he liked me in the dress through the crisp fabric of his suit. He tried to grab my hips but I pushed him off, throwing an incredulous look over my shoulder.

Jack just smirked at me and walked ahead to the waiting limo. Glad to see his ego hasn't taken a hit. What the fuck kind of game did he think he was playing? Had yesterday's conversation just bounced right off that thick head of his?

The journey there was nauseating. It was weird, I didn't normally get this nervous before an event. I blamed it on Jack's presence, persistent green eyes roaming over me like I was something good to eat. I glared across at him while Nic checked his phone.

I managed two glasses of Prosecco before we got there. It helped settle my nerves, put me more at ease.

The second we arrived, the paparazzi noticed. They clawed at the tinted windows with their talons. As soon as the door opened, they'd swarm the car. Craning to get the first shots, hoping to catch the last few private moments before the performance began.

That was the scary part. Right before the adrenaline kicked in. Listen to me, I made it sound like an extreme sport. It had taken a lot of deep-breathing practice and self-belief mantras to get to this point.

It was kind of like being sucked down a black hole. Deep and unknown and suffocating. Offering yourself up for sacrifice. You're being subjected to all that scrutiny, and the pressure to look absolutely perfect. Because really, what did it all mean?

Still, I didn't sit in three hours of hair and makeup to chicken out in the car. It was like armor, expertly crafted to perform a specific function.

Once out, the game was simple. Smile and play for the camera.

I took a deep breath, and concentrated on embodying confidence. Realigning my focus with the Manipura chakra or whatever hippy bullshit people in la la land seemed to take as legitimate truth. I didn't believe in all that nonsense, but I do think there is something to be said about self-empowerment.

I had this. I was ready. It was show time.

I held Nic's arm for balance as he helped me from the car. People called our names from every angle and we stopped to pose for them every few steps. Cameras flashing, blinding, dazzling white. The golden couple.

I let Nic walk up ahead to greet a friend and turned back

to find Jack standing, apprehensive, by the car. Nobody was interested in photographing him, and why would they be? To them, he was nobody.

As we made our way inside the building, the interior took my breath away. The ballroom was vast and high-ceilinged. Chandeliers sparkled from above, their multi-faceted crystal droplets casting rainbows around the room. Everything was decorated in black and gold. There were fluffy cream feathers and velvet chairs. A live band in the center of the room played smooth jazz and swing music.

"Good job, doll," Nicholas whispered in my ear. He pressed an inattentive kiss against my temple before dashing off again to speak to someone else.

The room was permeated with the glittering array of society; film stars and celebrities, adorned with pearls and diamonds. Rolex's strapped onto every man's wrist. The net worth of the room must have been staggering, without doubt enough to fulfill the charity's needs this year. I invited those in that elite division of the bourgeois because I knew they would give lavishly at such an event. Only because it was expected of them, of course. I don't think half of them were acquainted with the cause.

I sat down at one of the tables. Immediately, a waitress appeared to offer me a glass of pink champagne. Jack took the seat next to me, facing away so he could watch the crowd.

"Do you know everyone here?"

"No," I answered hesitantly. "I know *of* everybody here but I've not met them all."

"Hmm." Jack mused, his forearm wound around my waist from behind.

"Knock it off." I swatted at him, attempting annoyance but I couldn't help the smile that lifted the corners of my lips.

"I can't help it, baby."

"Well cut it out or someone might see us!"

"Meet me somewhere private later?" His voice was low and serious. I turned to look at him, speechless. That was *not* the agreement we came to! I opened my mouth to tell him off but was cut short by Nic's reappearance.

Jack managed to pull his hands away just in time. Nic sat in the chair next to me and, for a minute or two, was silent, surveying the room with approval.

"So, Jackie." Nic turned to speak to Jack. "Whadya' think?"

"What do I think of what?" He hadn't touched his drink.

"*This*!" He gestured grandly to the room. "All *this*!"

"Yeah, it's nice, if you like that kind of thing."

It was true. I couldn't imagine Jack coming to an event like this of his own free will. He'd be much more at home, well, at home. I could imagine him stretched across the couch, beer in hand, wearing his favorite t-shirt and pair of faded old jeans, just like that night he'd sat with me and Jude. Dressed up in his suit, he looked stiff and uncomfortable, as though he'd been starched right along with his shirt.

Someone else caught Nic's eye and he stood up.

"Baby?" I reached out for his wrist, not wanting him to leave me. I was slightly overwhelmed with how unexpectedly out of my depth I felt. As Jack had brought to my attention, I didn't really know anyone. I wasn't as fearless a host as Nic.

"Would you dance with me?"

"Not now, doll. I've got some more schmoozing to do." He leaned down and grabbed my face roughly, planting a wet kiss on my cheek. I craned my neck to see who Nic was going off to talk to although I couldn't see over the heads of the nearest table.

"Why don't you talk to whoever it is later. You have all evening to network."

"Don't insert yourself into the situation, baby. I'm here for fund-raising, not keeping you company all night." He chuckled darkly, "I'm *sure* you can keep yourself entertained."

My cheeks flamed but I kept my mouth shut. Of course, he was still hacked off about last night. He was going to enjoy showing me up with the least amount of prodding. If that was how he was going to play it, then whatever! I wasn't going to waste my evening pandering to his idiotic pride.

"Don't worry then! I'm *sure* Jack won't mind 'keeping me company' while you work out your priorities!"

I left Nic standing there fuming as I pulled Jack up by the

arm and toward the cleared area that served as the dance floor.

"He's being an asshole!" I muttered under my breath.

He checked over my shoulder to see where Nic was before replying.

"That's him on a good day, ain't it?"

I just rolled my eyes in response. He chuckled, pulling me closer to him. A bit too close to for present company. His lips rested an intimate distance from my ear as he faintly hummed along with the music, low but surprisingly in-key.

I drew back to look up at him. At this proximity, I could really take in the depth of his eyes. All the tonal variation, the most predominant olive-green in them warm and inviting, sweeping me in. It was too much. I was starting to believe in things that weren't real.

"Please, stop looking at me like that," I whispered.

"Why?" he replied softly.

"Because it's making me uncomfortable."

"What's making you uncomfortable, Darlin'?"

I looked up into his eyes once more, feeling my resolve melt like ice cream under the blazing sun.

When he looked at me, it felt as though he knew me the way I knew myself. Saw who I truly was. He made me feel like I was the most important person in the world. In that moment, I realized I wanted to feel that way forever. I wanted to stay in his arms where I felt protected. Loved.

But I couldn't tell him how much I wanted that. How much I wanted him to hold me, touch me in a way that showed me he cared more than words ever could.

Less than twenty-four hours ago, I'd made the decision to stop. I promised myself I wouldn't be sucked into feeling this way again. My mental state fractured into little fragments of thought that made no sense on their own, my nerves in tatters.

I ached to feel him again. The solid weight of him over me. The stretch and wonderful burn as his thickness filled me, and that blissful feeling coiling tighter and tighter as he teased and caressed and rutted until I came apart in his arms. Feeling his body tighten and shudder as he spent himself inside me, following me there. The languid satisfaction that came after, the closeness leaving me defenseless. A closeness that I doubt either of us had ever shared with another. I craved that. I craved *him*.

I was *so* tired of fighting it. Tired of feeling responsible, and confused and guilty, no matter how much I knew I should.

I wanted him, no matter how wrong that was.

Then all the doubt brought me crashing back down. Was what he was offering enough? Every time he touched me, every time he opened his mouth and said exactly what I needed to hear, all the sense I possessed went flying out the window.

I used to think the only person that you could trust was yourself, and now I wasn't even sure I could do that. I had so many unanswered questions even I wasn't certain where *I* stood anymore. I couldn't even claim moral high ground over Nic, because what I'd done was just as bad, if not worse! Because my heart was involved.

My head swam, my vision going cloudy as I fought off the vague feeling of unawareness that came before a panic attack.

"I can't breathe! I... I c-can't. Can't. B-b-breath."

I felt more than saw Jack pull me from the room into a dark hallway. He used a napkin to gently wipe my tears away then the scarlet lipstick.

"You are so beautiful; you don't need all this crap."

I realized the hallway was actually another room, smaller than the ballroom, but just as grand. Ghostly outlines lingered in places. It took me a while in the dark to identify them as sheets draped over large, weirdly shaped objects. It must have been a storage room.

"Please don't cry," Jack murmured.

"We said... You said we would *stop*!"

"I can't stay away from you." Then his hands were on me, stroking down my arms, his hot mouth at my neck.

"I know how much you want me, baby. Tell me you need this." Jack slowly unzipped my dress and it pooled around my feet, leaving me bared and at his mercy.

I moaned, surrendering so willingly into his tight embrace, my skin prickling all over. His hands went down my back, pushing me flat against him. I reached down to feel him, solid and ready, squeezing as I bit my lip in anticipation. This is what made it so hard to resist. It was *so* good.

His fingers splayed out as they sunk lower, brushing over my skin, warm and possessive.

My legs were hoisted up and wrapped around his waist. His mouth turned its attention to the sensitive spot just behind my earlobe, making all apprehension cease to exist. Then he pressed two fingers inside me and all at once, I was completely lost.

I tried to find the strength to breathe even a few words, form a coherent thought, but couldn't. Not while he was stroking me like that. I could feel it surging up inside me like a tidal wave. All the emotion. Feeling without thinking. Pure bliss.

I felt myself building up and up before powerfully tumbling back down. And I couldn't help it, all that pent-up energy coursing through my veins. I let out a loud, wet sob.

He held me close to his chest; one hand stroked my hair down and the other held me tight to him. All I could think was that this wasn't right. It was too much.

"It's okay. Shhh, it's okay." And I no longer cared whether it was. His concentrated scent filled me and I breathed deep, greedy lungfuls. I didn't want to let go but I couldn't keep living a lie.

"It's not okay. I can't do this anymore."

I pulled my dress back on quickly, trying to cover myself. I knew what he was thinking; the same *any* man would be with naked breasts in front of him.

"I can't keep doing this with you and lying to him. It's *killing* me inside." I couldn't even think his name. The guilt was consuming me whole.

"Baby, I care about you." I could not hear that right now. Not in this situation when he would say anything to keep me, anything to stop me from pushing him away.

"He does the same to you. Why is it any different?"

"Because I *do* care about you, Jack, but I also care about Nic and I …" I couldn't continue because it hurt so much. It felt like my insides were being ripped out.

"You still love him? After everything he's put you through?" Jack stared at me for a minute, his eyes cold. I wilted in his steely gaze.

"Are you still sleeping with him?"

"He's my husband," I said in a small voice.

Jack nodded to himself and looked down.

"What about me? Was I just some sort of pawn in your twisted plan for revenge? Was I just a way to make yourself feel better about your 'situation'?"

"You know that's not what it was like."

"What *is* it like then, huh? You too good for me now? Did you figure out fucking me wouldn't keep you in a nice house with all your fancy clothes and expensive things?" I tried to get around him; I was cornered to the wall.

"No, don't fuckin' run away from me." His arms came up into a muscled cage, blocking my way out of his personal space. Why was he being so unreasonable? I was shaking now too, unable to control myself.

"Why do you do this, Jack? What do you want from me? I can't leave him!"

"Why not? What does he offer you that I can't?"

"You know what he offers me!"

"*Money!*" He spat, looking disgusted.

"It's not about that! You know it's not about that! It's about the promise I made to Nic. Marriage means you don't give up when the going gets tough. He may seem like he doesn't give a shit but I know deep down..."

"Deep down he's a slimy, no good..."

"Remember what you said the other night? Men are weak, right? They use women as an escape. All it takes is some skin and a smile. You know just the right words to say to bend me to your will. It's so easy for you, isn't it?"

"And what's that?"

"You're *using* me!"

"Whoa, back up? I'm using you? Says the woman who comes running to her husband's brother when he doesn't satisfy her. For all I know, you're just one of many bored housewives out looking for a bit of fun."

My cheeks flamed, "This goes both ways, Jack. Don't be so childish."

"ME! Childish?"

I stared at him for a second, thinking he was just the same as Nic. What were these twisted mind games they played? This was just entertainment to him, a stupid, carnival-style game where I was the prize. He'd play until he got bored and decided he needed a new challenge. A new victim to hunt down and pounce upon.

"You have nothing to lose, so why are you hell-bent on destroying my life?"

"I've got nothing to lose? I'm risking losing the only member of my family I have left." He paused for a second, taking a breath. "You know, the thought of him touching you makes me sick! Putting his vile hands on you, hurting you! This is what I don't understand Marie, the guy is an asshole!"

I could tell this was his one last attempt at keeping me. I knew what I had to do.

"But he's the asshole I fell in love with. Stop interfering with my marriage and *leave me alone*! Whatever this was, it's over."

"*Fine!*" he growled, pulling away from me so fast it was disconcerting. I watched him cross the room in long strides, before sliding through the door and yanking it closed behind him, leaving me in darkness. I crumpled against the wall in a heap, exhausted. This was the right decision, so why did it hurt so much?

Granted, he didn't have a very good argument, but his harsh words must've been coming from a place so raw they came out unfiltered. I'd hurt him. But he started this, not me. And he didn't deny *anything* I accused him of.

Every time he opened his mouth, I wound up more and more confused. Every conversation we had never seemed to end up making sense. One minute he was backing Nic up and the next he was verbally tearing him to shreds. He let me in just enough so I thought that I stood a chance of understanding him, only to withdraw back into himself.

He was so stubborn and unreadable and chaotic, it made me dizzy.

I cleaned up my makeup in a nearby bathroom before heading over to the bar and swallowing a few Valium with a shot of whisky, then made a poor attempt at looking for Nic, knowing I probably didn't want to find him. We were still furious with each other.

I'd had more than enough of tonight, so I pulled out my cell and texted Jean to come and take me home. He hadn't come with us tonight. After the way Nic had yelled at him, I didn't blame him.

Another glass of champagne later and the walls started to spin, though the dull aching inside was more manageable. Stupid, *stupid* Marie! Where did I think this was going? Obviously, he was using me. I was so alone and defenseless and *available* to him. I showed him I was weak by letting him in.

Just then, from across the room my eyes connected with a stunning auburn-haired, doe-eyed woman. She was statuesque, dressed elegantly in a simple black shift that accentuated her lithe figure. And I knew from the single look she shot me that she was sleeping with my husband, who was currently standing right next to her, his arm snaked around her waist.

Until now, these women had all been faceless. I'd always *suspected* him of cheating but never had any concrete evidence, never caught him at it. Until now!

I stalked over to them, intent on making a scene. How *dare* he embarrass me like that! Parading her in front of all these people. If he expected me to just stand there and take it, he was wrong!

"*Nic*, Where have you been? I've been looking *everywhere* for you!"

Nicholas excused himself from the group of people he was talking to and pulled me, disobliging, to the quiet entrance hall and fixed me with a cold stare.

"I asked Jack to keep an eye on you. Where is the bastard?"

"How should I know? Probably off with one of your whores." His eyes flashed dangerously but I was too drunk to care.

"Oh please, I've seen her running after you with her little tail wagging! Tell me, is she your full-time mistress or does that privilege belong to someone else?"

"Marie, keep your voice down!"

"No, Nicholas. I'm fed up of the way you treat me, you should have some respect..." the rest of my words were cut off as a burly arm thrust me back. My head collided with the wall with a painful clunk, my vision actually dimming for a few seconds.

"Who do you think you are talking to, you little slut?" He hissed in my face.

The next second, I was shoved aside as Jack smashed his brother into the wall, pinning him up, forearm to throat.

His unwavering gaze bored into Nic. If I didn't know better, I would have said he looked unstable. Untamed fury and hatred mounting, barely concealed by a man trying so hard to hold onto the last shreds of control. I finally saw the man who could have committed murder.

"You don't have the right to touch her like that," he growled, "No one does."

Nicholas' tongue darted out to flick over his lower lip before they twisted into a baiting sneer. Even cornered and struggling for breath, he looked conceited. Like he still held the upper hand.

"She's my wife; I'll talk to her, and I'll *touch* her however I please."

Jack's eyebrows knitted together, but his glaring eyes remained inscrutably hard.

"Do you think I don't see you lusting after her?" Nic taunted. "I see the way you look at her. What man wouldn't want my girl in their bed?"

My face heated. Is that how he considered me? Some kind of trophy that came with bragging rights?

"*Jack*!" I shrieked from the floor.

"Jack what?" He didn't turn away from Nic for a second.

"Let him go!"

"Why should I? Give me a reason," Jack snarled into Nicholas' face, standing half a foot taller.

"Because he's the only family you've got left!" It was then I noticed that the steady buzz of background noise from the party had died down. I felt the glare of their scrutiny as they watched like my unfolding nightmare was reality TV. Like our lives were nothing more than a performance for their entertainment.

"*Please*," I murmured.

Jack's resolve weakened, and he let out a huff of breath before jerking his arm away.

Nicholas, probably in sheer relief, emitted a soft laugh.

The quick sound was all Jack needed to shove the little self-control he still held onto aside.

He snapped back around with surprising speed for such a heavyset man and landed a solid punch to Nic's face. His fist made a dull thud as it slammed into flesh and bone, sending Nic sprawling to the floor. The blow seemed to resonate in the silence, the sound having more finality to it than the action itself.

Jack didn't look back as he brushed past me and into the night.

I felt lean arms reach around me, helping me gently to my feet. Fresh tears masked my vision. And the room was spinning again.

"Come on, sweetheart. Let's get you home."

Jean helped me into the back of the car, sliding in after me.

"I know what's been going on, Marie. I've known for a while."

I shook my head defiantly. There was no way he could have known what was going on. I wasn't altogether sure myself.

"I don't know what you're talking about." I tried to rein it in. Tried to rebuild the impenetrable barricade I usually had up to keep everyone out.

"Shh, baby girl. Don't cry." Jean pulled me closer, hugging me to his chest as I broke down, clutching at him with frantic fingers. Is this what he meant when he said he'd been keeping tabs? He'd been watching us?

"P...please. *Please* d...don't tell him," I stammered, shuddering through my sobs.

"You think I have a death wish?"

"I...it's *over!*"

"I know. Je suis désolé." Jean held me to him as I cried.

Nic wouldn't be home tonight. He'd continue drinking,

trying to bury his embarrassment with stupid male bravado. His mistress would probably fawn over him, and Nic would lap up the attention, telling everyone that it had been a big misunderstanding, working his superficial charm until the damage had been covered up.

He wouldn't face me until he had his shit back together. By then, I'd need to be ready.

Chapter Eighteen

NIC

I drank so much I could only remember patches of the evening before. And when I woke up, murky-headed, in a bush downtown, soundless noise like TV static surrounded me. If there was one day I didn't want to be woken by the fucking sun it was today. I checked my phone, which had also seen better mornings, peering at the time through the cracked screen. Five thirty-two am.

I rolled over to throw up but nothing came, other than an awful retching sound from the pit of my empty stomach.

God only knows why I'd decided the parking lot of a 7-eleven was a good place to sleep it off. And where the fuck was I?

Yeah, I know what you're thinking. Pathetic. Crawling around in the dirt like some kind of animal.

I blinked, trying to dislodge the crud gumming up my eyelids. I was sure my aching head had less to do with being hungover than Jack's solid right hook, one moment from last night I remembered vividly. Mostly because of the blinding pain every time I touched my nose. I was lucky to still have all my teeth in place. Either way, it felt like a socket wrench was being screwed through my eye. And my mouth tasted like shit.

Peering around in the bleak morning light, I assessed the situation. Damaged phone, luckily still functional. One shoe missing, I didn't have a clue. Fuck it, what was the point? All these things were replaceable.

Only when the rain began, did I drag myself up. Unsteadily at first. Then picking up on things previously unnoticed: my palms scraped up. Shirt ripped, missing buttons. I don't even remember how that happened.

I don't remember much past the party; everyone conspiring against me. My own brother humiliating me. Jean taking my wife away into the night, tucking her snuggly under his arm like he was *entitled* to her.

It could have been either one of them, the slippery bastards. Of the two, I suspected Jack the least, mainly because he was my brother, and I was almost certain Marie still despised him, and she seemed pretty keen to get shot of him the other day.

Whereas she had this special sort of smile for Jean, like they shared something no one else knew about. Had an understanding. Heads together, whispering in conspiratorial tones. They definitely held an obvious overfamiliarity, any halfwit could see.

All the signs were there.

He was always skulking around where he wasn't needed. Poking his nose into things that didn't concern him.

And the envelope of cash I'd found. Surely that was proof she was planning to leave me? Why else would she need that much lying around? Jean always did have a bad habit of losing money. What if that was a ruse? What if they were just combining their resources?

I wasn't the world's most clean-cut guy, point taken. Yeah,

I slept around. However, your wife having a *relationship* behind your back was entirely different. That was a whole other ball game.

No one made a fool of Nicholas Hayes and got away with it!

I had tracking software installed on her phone so I knew her location at all times. Ever since she pulled that stunt climbing out the bedroom window, I'd thought it necessary.

There was every possibility that she would try to pull her disappearing act on me again, and if that was the case, I'd hunt her down and really smack some sense into her this time. Woman or not, I didn't have a problem with disciplining people who clearly needed it. I wasn't the type to be telling people *three times* what they were supposed to do! Those expectations should have been obvious by now.

I wanted to block the thoughts out. Shove them away somewhere so deep and forget about them. Like loose change that vanished between couch cushions.

How much of my doubt was fabricated? It was hard to say. I was so messed up right now I didn't even know what day of the week it was, let alone what direction to start walking in. The lines between truth and make-believe were blurring into an undefined smudge.

How much of this was in my head? All I had was a bunch of suspicions and an uneasy feeling of paranoia looming over me. I felt fragmented. How damaged must I be not to see where I ended and everything else began? *God*, I was becoming unhinged.

I know, I fucked up. I know I did. She'd given me more chances than I deserved. But only now did I understand what it was like.

It wasn't just the physical evidence. It was the not knowing. All that time spent wondering. I'd been living my life, expecting to come home to the same Marie I'd left. However, life continued even when you weren't there to see it.

For the first time in my entire life, I didn't know what to do.

I could've called her. Apologized. I could have done that. But I knew I wouldn't have been able to go through with it. I *couldn't*. Because I couldn't bear the thought that she might not listen. That the small flicker of belief she still held for me had been extinguished.

Across the street, a quite clearly homeless woman shambled by clutching a piece of cardboard with words colored in magic marker. It read, '*faith does not make things easy, it makes them possible.*' Smug bitch.

I couldn't decide if it was a sign. I mean, *obviously*, it *was* a fucking sign. But aimed directly at me? It was the first thing I'd seen all morning besides the floor. Did it actually *mean* anything? Maybe? Or not. It was probably irrelevant.

I pulled my jacket over my head as the rain started to fall more heavily, creating vast puddles of grey against grey. As I walked, the buildings grew steadily taller. Cars started appearing more frequently, rushing past, their tires kicking up dark water. Not caring about who they drowned in their hurry to bag a twenty-dollar bagel and artisanal latte on their way to the office. Fucking stuck-up part of the city.

At least I started to recognize my surroundings. Mustn't have wandered too far last night.

Then something caught my eye. Something usually overlooked.

A phone booth. Grimy. The yellow light flickering. I stopped, staring at it like I'd never seen one before. I doubt it even still worked. Did they even keep these things running anymore? Was there any point?

People stepped around me, some hardly noticing, faces glued to screens, others muttering to themselves, cursing layabouts like me who were a drain on taxpayer's resources. Filthy scavengers.

I could just call. At least try. She'd have to believe me this time. I'd make her.

But I continued staring until the patterns in the black filth that stuck to it grew indistinct, and the lost, empty feeling inside me made its way up into my throat.

She'd *have* to forgive me. I needed one more chance. Just *one*.

"That's a fuckin' big shiner you got, boss."

Chuck pulled up alongside the curb, not long after I'd called the office, grinning like some cunt who found my misery amusing.

"Yeah well, what do you expect? He knows how to throw a punch," I replied sourly, climbing in the passenger side.

"Looks like you spent the night in a gutter."

I reached into the glove box and grabbed the container of Excedrin, shaking out a handful of little white pills, the rattle they made music to my ears. Throwing them back dry, I crunched them up and welcomed the bitter taste on my tongue like an old friend.

"Where to?"

"Work," I grumbled into my hand.

"Don't you want to go home and er… clean up?"

"I'll shower at the office. Have you seen Jean?"

He paused a few seconds, "Not recently, no."

That wasn't what I needed to hear. The little rat was going to need more than an alibi and a lawyer when I got hold of him. Some answers would have to be given if he was going to stand a chance of coming out of this.

After a shower, a change of clothes, and some food, I was feeling a little more human. I'd just managed to slump at my desk when Jessica poked her head around the door.

"I've got Max on hold, line one," She didn't give me a chance to tell her I'd call him back later. I was in no mood to be yelled at but the little red light was already flashing. Hanging up now would be like trying to smother a grenade; the explosion inevitable. I braced myself before I picked up the receiver.

"NIC! What the FUCK do you think you're playing at?"

"Hi to you too, Max."

"Don't take that sarcastic tone with me, boy. Haven't you heard what's been going on this morning? Or have you been too busy feeling sorry for your own miserable ass?"

"What the hell are you talking about?"

"THE INVESTORS! SkyeTron! They've just held an emergency meeting. Unanimous vote. They're out."

"What?" I replied, struggling to get my head around his words.

"Your antics last night. Don't tell me you don't know what I'm talking about. It's splashed all over the tabloids this morning."

Oh, *fuck*!

"I told you to be careful and what do you do? Create some massive fucking public scene?"

"Listen, I'm not capable of having this conversation right now. Can we-"

"I don't give A SHIT!" he exploded, "This is *exactly* the kind of bullshit I've come to expect from you. You've let your ego get the better of you and that's not happening on my time."

"I'm going to help you out because *my* reputation is on the line," he continued, not letting me get a word in, "I'm not letting this company go bankrupt with the percentage of shares I own. So you just continue living your privileged, deluded existence while I try and salvage something from this wreck!" I heard something heavy the other end hit the ground with a crash before the line went dead.

I couldn't believe the day I was already having, and it wasn't even past nine yet. Max could take his disapproval and his *fucking* shares and stick them straight up his pompous, overbearing, elitist ass.

What did I need *him* for anyway? Or the investors for that matter? The company was doing just fine without outsiders sticking their Hasidic noses in. I didn't need fucking *help*, I was one of the richest men in America, for crying out loud. I'd basically built this company from the ground up all on my own sorry-ass. It was Max's fault if he was too visually impaired to see what a great job I'd been doing rocketing our profits into the exosphere!

All I needed was some goddamned appreciation. A little love from time to time. Be praised like the good little puppy I was. And a beautiful woman with my dick shoved down her throat sounded like a good way to be appreciated.

I made a beeline for Jessica's desk, working up my most charming smile deep where it wallowed somewhere south of my balls. She didn't even look up from her screen.

"What do you want, Nic?"

Christ, not her too!

"You've got to be fucking kidding me?"

I grasped hold of her elbow and pulled her out of her chair and into a nearby meeting room.

"What have I done wrong *now*?"

She raised her perfectly shaped eyebrows in a parody of disbelief.

"Oh, you don't remember palming me off in favor of that blond slut last night? How convenient."

What the fuck was she talking about, I'd been with her most of the evening? Unless one of those lost periods of time had been spent with *another* woman, which knowing myself wasn't too far of a stretch. But I was careful enough to keep all facets of my life separate, there wasn't any cross-over. Usually.

The only explanation; the trauma of last night made me mess up my timings, and I'd accidentally chased my back meds down with whisky. Fuck it, it would have been on purpose. Damn internal crisis was making me sloppy.

But I'd already decided this thing I had with Jessica had gone too far if she thought she had any right to call me out on it. It was time to just rip the band-aid of deceit off in one clean swipe and get it over with.

"Jesus *Christ*. Did you think you were the only one? Did you think you were special?"

"I can see very clearly now that I'm not!"

"Where did you think this was going, Jessica? I'm married."

"You don't give a shit about that. You use people to get what you want and when you get bored, you leave."

I rolled my eyes, "I don't want to deal with this right now."

"You are going to listen to what I have to say." She jabbed me in the chest with a manicured fingernail.

"No, *you* listen to me! You mean nothing to me. NOTHING, get it? You are a secretary! You asked me what I want? What do I want? I want a little respect. I want you to know your place. I am paying you, Jessica!"

Her beautiful eyes narrowed into a death glare; a look I was all too used to seeing on Marie's face.

"Don't you *dare* talk to me like that! After *everything* I've done for you. I've been there to pick up the pieces too many times to count."

"It's your job," I snarled back, "Now you can continue doing your job like a good little girl, or you can pack your things and find someone who *will* deal with your lack of subordination."

She opened and closed her mouth stupidly, like a fish.

"You are out of your *mind* if you think I'm staying!" She moved to leave, one hand resting on the door handle, before turning back. "You think you hold all the cards, don't you? The press would have a field day if they got wind of half the information I know about you!"

"Is that a threat?" I lashed out, jerking her back and kicking the door shut. She thought she was so clever, using her position of trust as leverage. I was the one who gave her this power and I could take it away just as fast.

"Don't forget who you're talking to. I could make sure you'd never work in this city again. You want to stay on my good side!"

Then I remembered how much I enjoyed her sweet little pussy, and the thought of never being able to taste it again was heartbreaking. So maybe I'd have one last-ditch attempt to keep her. After all, she was *very* good at her job.

"Do you know how you can *stay* on my good side?"

"Fuck you!" She spat.

Well, it was safe to say I'd misjudged that one. She drove a well-aimed knee right in my balls and the earlier urge to throw up came surging back. I let out a noise not dissimilar to a bawling heifer, before slumping sideways into the wall.

Jessica pointed a finger at me, "You need help!" She hissed through clenched teeth, before stalking out.

Okay, fair game. I was pushing my luck a bit far on a day when I didn't seem to have any. It would be a shame to let her go without one final roll in the sack. Replacing her particular skill set was going to be a challenge, and not one I was inclined to tackle today.

Her comment bothered me though. I needed help? *Me?* Dumb bitch!

Fuck, would this hellish day never end? I was seriously contemplating going back to my office and locking myself in until I either died and was reincarnated as an animal with a lower level of consciousness or transcended into nothingness. Or just be put into a state where I no longer needed to think. Honestly, I was driving myself crazy. I needed *something* to get me through the rest of the day. I could work on fixing the rest tomorrow.

I needed help! The idea was so bizarre to me, it was almost comical. No one had helped me since I was in Goodwill jeans, and that was a long fucking time ago. I didn't accept help. I wouldn't. I couldn't think of anything more demeaning than having to admit your weaknesses to a group of strangers. Or worse, people I already knew. How would that make me look?

I could get through this myself. Besides, I didn't have a '*problem*.' I could stop if I really *wanted* to. It's just I didn't really want to right now, that was all.

The rest of the afternoon was spent in an Ambien-induced sleep on the couch in my office, with all the blinds shut and a sign taped to the door telling anyone interfering to fuck right off.

After possibly the worst twenty-four hours in living memory, Chuck thought I needed to socialize. If my recent track record was anything to go by, I should have known it was going to be a shit show.

Once we'd been hassled by the paps, struggled to get in anywhere, and had no luck with the ladies, I knew it was time to call it a night.

I was seriously off my game today. Was this karma coming back round to bite me in the ass? If a stupid thing like that even existed?

By the time I got home, it was early morning. I crept up the stairs, planning on slipping between the sheets next to my wife and hoping she'd think I'd been there most of the night. I really needed to just make up with her and forget about this whole business. But I should have known there was no such thing as luck anymore.

Marie was curled up in the armchair with a book resting on her lap, the table lamp casting a dim halo light around her. She looked up when I shut the door.

"You're not asleep?" I asked, surprised.

"It's kinda hard to sleep when I'm all wound up. I don't know how many times I tried calling you."

I swayed a little before sinking down on the edge of the bed across from her, trying to kick off my shoes before I realized that was a stupid idea. They were triple-knotted onto my feet. I suppressed to urge to laugh.

"How much have you had to drink?"

Perfect! Just what I needed to hear.

"Oh, can't you lay off for five minutes, Marie? I've had a hard day."

"And staying out till God knows what time in the morning is going to help with that?"

For some reason, her comment struck me as funny. Yes, in

fact, I did think staying out all night was a fine way to let off some steam. It beat staying home like a pussy-whipped mutt and being lectured on the 'importance of family' and 'how my actions made her feel.'

"I don't know how to deal with you anymore. Your rapid-fire mood swings are giving me whiplash. And I definitely won't stand for being hit, Nic. If you ever raise a hand to me again, I'm gone."

I just managed to blink, "Deal with me?"

She shot me an incredulous look, "Is that seriously all you picked up from that?"

I leant down to try and untie my shoes and ended up face down in the carpet. "*Mmphh*." Might just stay here a while.

"I'm not going to talk to you when you're in this state. Go and sleep somewhere else and we'll talk when you've sobered up."

That time I did laugh. The whole situation was funny if you stopped for a second and thought about it. I managed to draw myself up and finally get a good look at her. Pretty, like always. But underneath she was just as rotten as the rest of us. A deceitful, conniving little snake.

"I know what you've been up to."

She blinked up at me.

"Don't give me that innocent face." I leaned into her, boxing her into the chair, my face only inches from hers. Her eyes avoided mine.

"Women's minds are intricate little devices, aren't they? All those cunning, manipulative thoughts brewing in there, thinking of the next way to bring me down. You're always twisting my vision, trying to change me into the man you think I should be. Like I'm not good enough for you."

"That's not true and you know it."

My hand shot out and seized the back of her head, anchoring my fingers in her thick hair.

"Mummy and Daddy never approved. No one is good enough for our little girl, they thought. No man who hasn't gone to college could ever be good enough. All this affirmation and praise was slowly absorbed, inflating your self-importance. Your presumption that you are *better* than everybody else."

"Most people wouldn't see it. You think I don't see it because it's all hidden behind this beautiful little face. Butter wouldn't melt, would it? But I see right through you, right past that delicate exterior."

She let out a whimper and tried to loosen my grip on her hair but I had her right where I wanted her. There was no way she was going to slide out of this one.

"The way you skulk around here, turning your nose up at me. Thinking you're always right. Do you know how *hard* it is to keep you happy?"

"I want to hear you say it. I want you to look me in the eye and tell me. Who have you been fucking behind my back?" I shook her to make sure my words were being absorbed.

She still wouldn't look at me. Her reaction and lack of denial were all the proof I needed. Like I said, I could always see right through her. I took a step back and she took advantage of the momentary freedom by trying to escape. However, I was still close enough to block her only way out.

"I ask nothing of you! Not to work, not to lift one fuckin' finger. Your *only* job is to please me!"

My words seemed to spark a reaction in her, giving her a burst of courage.

"Is this what this is all about? My reluctance to bear you a child at the snap of your fingers? I'm not your servant, Nic. I'm your wife!"

"It's hard to tell when you are acting like a whore."

The next second her fist collided with the side of my head. Luckily for me, it was the opposite side to the one Jack hit but it would still bruise. It was a good hit!

I didn't miss the spark of panic in her eyes, or the rapid rise and fall of her chest, barely covered by her loosened robe and God, I'd never seen anything sexier.

"I'm leaving you!" she screamed.

"*Are* you?" I shoved her up against the nearby dressing table, forcing myself in between her legs so she could feel how much I desired her. She tried to wriggle out of my grasp but I had her exactly where I wanted her. Her breath came in short, sharp little pants, the pitch sending the blood pooling straight to my groin.

"Where are you going to run to this time? Because that's what you do when you feel hard done by, isn't it? You ran away from home to marry me because you thought I was the easy way out. You run away from me when you don't want to talk. Go on, leave if you want to. You'll soon come back when you realize how hard life is without *me* providing for you!"

I'd show her what she'd be missing. No one could attend to her needs quite like I could. I'd taught her to crave the dirty, untamed sex we had when she wound me up and I had a week's worth of pent-up sexual aggression ready to take out on her.

"I know you can't live without my cock either," I breathed, forcing my hand between her legs before my lips crashed down on hers with hungry ferocity.

She struggled only until I managed to slip a couple of fingers into her, gasping into my open mouth. She was already wet and ready for me.

I flipped her over, practically tearing the robe from her body before I tugged my own pants down and drove into her with a groan. Fuck, she was always so tight from this angle. Almost painfully so.

She cried out with every thrust, already trembling with need beneath me as I increased to a brutal pace. There would be no mercy. I'd fuck the thought of any other man right out of her head. Nobody would *ever* be able to give it to her as good as me!

I wound my hand back through her hair, pulling her up so she could see the look of pure euphoria reflected back at her.

"See that? Does that look like a woman who wants to leave?"

A few more slams and she was as good as done, and I wasn't far behind, digging my fingers into her hips so I could finish deep inside her, where I belonged.

As soon as I let her go, she slumped downwards, sniveling on the floor like some kind of wounded prey. She enjoyed herself so what was she blubbering about?

I wasn't going to stick around to find out. As far I was concerned, we were done here. I'd done my part, the rest she'd have to figure out for herself, and we both knew she had no better choice than to stay.

Content in the knowledge of a job well done, I stowed myself back in my pants before heading toward the bathroom.

"You *promised* me you'd stop drinking," she sobbed.

Well, well. Was that how it was going to be?

"And you promised me a kid but look where we are; my slut of a wife still taking her fuckin' birth control."

"I *never* promised you that."

I turned to study her, balled up pathetically in the corner. If it were any other situation I would feel differently. If she wanted to be treated like a whore, then I would gladly let her have what was coming to her.

She was my wife, goddammit. Not some woman of the

night prowling the streets for her next encounter.

"You promised me everything the moment you said 'I do'."

Chapter Nineteen

JACK

I'd shoved her out of the way to get to Nic, and she'd fallen to the ground as inconsequential and unsubstantial as a discarded piece of paper.

I was disgusted with them, all of them. Marie, Nic, the crowd of passive onlookers. And once I'd calmed down enough to try and convince myself I didn't care, I'd smashed my own brother's face in. I couldn't stand to be around them for another second. I had to leave.

And she'd just laid at my feet, crying. It wasn't my place to comfort her any more, no matter how much I wanted to scoop her up in my arms and make it better. Kiss away her tears. But I couldn't.

I wouldn't even allow myself a final glance as I left, because I didn't want the last image I had of her to be her broken, on the floor.

I knew I was better than this. Better than *him*. So why was I acting like I didn't give a fuck?

I'd used this time to psychoanalyze everything. Every word... every touch... Why wouldn't she leave him for me? Why wouldn't she leave him for *herself*? I'd look after her the way he didn't, treat her right. I'd make sure she was loved. It was true, I'd never thought about the future but I knew she would have to be with me.

The TV hung limply off the wall, carpet gleaming with glass shards. Moonlight filtered in through the ripped drapes at the window. All anger had gone; nothing left to break, but there was still restlessness inside me. I laid on the bed, naked and wet, staring up at the ceiling, studying patterns in the shadows.

Why did she doubt my intentions? Did I do something to make her think she wasn't the only woman in my life? I'd never given her any indication I was seeing anyone else. Hell, when would I have ever had the chance?

The only thing keeping me away was that she didn't want me. She chose *him*.

A distant rumble of thunder sounded, a few spots of water hit the window. I had always liked the rain but from now on it would always remind me of what I'd lost.

Across the room, I let my cell ring until it fell off the dresser. Probably Nic again. I was in no mood to talk to him.

Slowly sitting up, I stumbled my way to the window. The street below was devoid of life despite the persistent and blinding lights on in all the buildings.

I hated this apartment right in the middle of the city; loud, over-populated, snobby neighbors. And a constant feeling of being watched. Perhaps it was all the glass?

I could leave again. Disappear and start over. But what had that gotten me last time? Crushing grief, remorse, and a shedload full of new terrors to haunt me. How many times would I get a do-over? I couldn't be trusted not to screw it up! I didn't deserve another chance, but also, where would I even go?

I was twenty-two miles from Santa Monica. From her. I could have driven over to check on her. She wouldn't have even seen me; it would just be me making sure she was okay. Before I even had pause to talk myself out of it, I'd pulled on jeans, a t-shirt and boots, not even bothering with underpants.

Down in the apartment's parking lot, I found my scraped-up Mercedes GLS (yet another over-extravagant gift from Nic) with the keys still in the ignition, door hanging ajar. Whatever happened, I didn't care. My memory from the party until now was like one continuous motion blur.

I turned the key. It wouldn't start. *Fuck!!* The battery was dead. My fist collided with the door in blind rage, and when that wasn't satisfying enough I resorted to attacking the rest of the car. Why was nothing I did ever enough?

Exhausted, I slumped to the floor, forehead falling onto bleeding knuckles, finally surrendering to defeat.

I'd stopped keeping track of time but I knew it was late afternoon. I could tell by the orangey shadows that stretched out long on the walls. She hadn't called. Nicholas, on the other hand, had been calling non-stop for weeks, asking if we could put *it* behind us, and most recently asking where the fuck I was. I hadn't spoken to him, just letting it go to voice mail. Eventually, on the fourth call of the day, I picked up.

"Jack! The *fuck* is wrong with you?" He asked in an

exasperated tone.

"Hey, Nic. I'm good thanks, how are you?" I countered with dripping sarcasm.

"Quit it bro, you ok?"

I sighed, "I'm fine, why wouldn't I be?"

"Marie said you had some business to take care of but I haven't heard from you? You tied everything up?"

That was, at least, one thing I could still bring myself to respect about Nic. He didn't pry.

"Yeah."

"Listen man, I need to see you. There are a few things we need to discuss."

Talking to me normally, like the last time we were in the same room I hadn't punched his face in.

"Look, Nic... I'm not..."

"I *really* need to see you, it's important... about Marie..."

I took a deep breath and sighed, like he was inconveniencing me, "Alright." I rubbed my neck, hoping I didn't sound too concerned.

"Nine o'clock, Bar 12. I'll set us up."

"Fine." I hung up without hearing what else he had to say. I knew what setting us up meant and I was definitely *not* in the mood for that.

Bar 12 turned out to be a fancy bar in downtown LA, big surprise there! Out back there was a seedy strip club where inevitably Nicholas would end up later that night.

"You look like shit, dude."

"Thanks," I mumbled. "What's so important?"

"What's up with you? And where have you been for the last three weeks? You had me thinking you'd died, or something."

Was he seriously asking for an explanation why I didn't want to see him? As if my right cross was open to interpretation.

"I was just lying low for a bit, tryin' to get back on my own two feet."

Nicholas nodded, seeming satisfied with that answer.

"Why'd you call?" I asked again. He took a large swallow of straight vodka and grimaced.

"It's Marie… I think she's been cheating on me?" He was glaring at me, or into me, more like. "She won't admit to anything but all the signs are there."

"What d'ya mean?"

"Well, don't say I told ya but she won't come off birth control. I mean we've been married two years, what other reason would there be? She doesn't want to risk getting knocked up by another guy."

"...I think there might be other reasons you're overlooking?"

"I wanna know where she has been sneaking off to..." he paused, leaving me hanging for what felt like an indefinite amount of time, "Tell me, when you were watching her, did you see anyone who she could have been fooling around with?"

I kept my expression blank.

"For a second there Nic, I thought you were going to accuse me!"

"Ha! I know what I said at the party, but no. I trust you. I know men are going to look at her, she's a fuckin' gorgeous piece of ass. I was drunk and I'd had a few... ya know," He swiped the bottom of his nose with the pad of a finger.

"I thought you were going to stop all that?"

"Christ, you sound like my wife! Look man, we good?"

I contemplated him for a second.

No. We wouldn't ever be 'good' again; the shit had the woman I loved, tormenting her, forcing himself on her. What sick fuck *bit* the woman he had in his bed, no less his own wife? She wasn't some skank he met at a bar. She deserved so much more than what she had settled for.

There was a time I would have felt remorseful for what I'd done, the guilt of a less-than-clean conscience weighing me down. All I felt was bitterness. I couldn't forgive him! He wasn't happy unless he had his thumb firmly pressed down over our heads, ruling over us with tyrannical force, his money, his influence. But mostly, I couldn't forgive his sadistic tendencies toward Marie.

He wasn't worthy of her love, and on those grounds, my respect. He was beyond redemption.

The most recent events that transpired only reaffirmed to me what I had suspected for a long while, as far back as that niggling suspicion I'd had that night Marie had opened up to me; that he was toxic!

"Yeah, we're good," I answered.

Nic curled a crisp hundred-dollar bill into the sparkling panties of a perky blond.

"Come on, sweetheart. What have you got for me?" He flashed a toothy grin, reminding me of a wolf who'd set eyes on his prey. The girl, apparently named Amber, straddled his lap and laid an indulgent kiss on his neck.

"Another few hundred and I'm yours for the night." Amber purred, giggling in a way I found highly irritating when Nic rammed his face into her huge fake tits, tucking a few more bills into the front of her underwear.

"Call me old-fashioned Nic, but doesn't being married mean you're done with this kind of bullshit?"

"Only for the wife, little brother! Stop being a tight-assed motherfucker and let loose a little."

While she took him out back, I sat by myself in the secluded VIP lounge, nursing my drink. It was the same brand of whisky she preferred. Isn't it strange how now it was my preferred poison? I pushed away the undrunk glass, watching the ice cubes clatter together.

A girl with long, brunette hair came over to me, dressed head to toe in tight leather lingerie. Classy.

"You not havin' any fun, sugar?"

"I'm doing just fine, thanks."

"You don't look 'just fine'; in fact, you look a little lonely." She even had a southern accent, coated with golden, dripping honey. The girl was very alluring, small-framed with a sweet face and couldn't have been much older than eighteen. Jailbait, if I ever saw it.

"What's your name, Darlin'?"

"Whatever you want it to be." She straddled my lap and wiggled into a position that pressed right into my groin. There would have been a time when I would have been very attracted to this girl but I couldn't even think like that anymore. There was only one woman I desired, and she didn't want me.

Taking pity on the girl, I gave her a quick smile from the corner of my mouth.

"Tell me your name." My hands slid up her back to hold her steady. Delicious little jailbait, small and warm in my hands. The management here sure knew how to attract customers.

"Elaine."

"And how'd a nice girl like you end up here, Elaine?"

"What you talkin' about?" she pouted.

"Baby, I been to a ton of places like this and I can tell you don't belong here. You must be what, seventeen years old?"

She leaned in and kissed me softly on the lips, "I could do things to you, you couldn't even imagine."

"I'm sure you could but..." I took out a fifty-dollar bill and slipped it into her hand. "I want you to leave here and get something to eat, then..." I proffered another fifty dollars, "You'll get a bus back home, okay?"

She stared at me with wide, doleful eyes then kissed me again, her sweet lips this time pressing to my unshaven cheek.

"Why you bein' so nice to me?"

"Because you are too young and beautiful to be out here. I'm sure your parents would want you home safe, not being leered at by a bunch of old perverts."

She slid off my lap and took the seat beside me.

"You've got a girl at home?" I could see the shy, innocent thing she once was.

I sighed, "No. She wasn't my girl." I left out the emphasis, "She wouldn't have wanted that. I mean she couldn't have, look at me."

"I'm lookin'."

I shook my head, "She's perfect, you know. And here I am, all the mistakes I've made. Damaged goods. What would a sweet, kind, funny, loving woman want with me?"

"I think you're being too hard on yourself. If she's as perfect as you say, she'd be able to see past your flaws." Wise words from such a young girl.

I shook my head again, "It ain't always that simple, kiddo."

"See these scars." I pointed to my face. "They remind me every time I look in the mirror exactly what I'm entitled to. And it's nothing."

"I'm sure there's more to the story than that."

Despite myself, the corner of my mouth turned up, "How so?"

"Well, I don't think we would be having this conversation for starters."

I reckon her experience of men had been tainted by the hoards of animals that made it through that club. Maybe I was the first one since she dropped out of high school who was actually sober enough to string more than three words together. Or it could have been that I didn't want to fuck her. She seemed to think that made me a good person.

I waited for her to get her coat and bag and watched her leave through the front door. She turned to me and raised her hand in goodbye before walking off into the night. I knew she'd be back, strippers could make hundreds of dollars a night, especially pretty ones like her. I could delude myself into believing that the money she made would be going toward improving her future, and hopefully, that future would come with health insurance that would cover a shrink.

Nicholas came back drunk and high out of his mind. Security escorting him forcibly, ignoring his less than half-assed attempt to swat them off. I made out the slurred words *"Bitch thinks she can talk to ME like that!"*

Amber came to the door of the back room, her cheek smarting bright pink. I would have to take him home. Maybe I should stay the night, just to make sure he didn't try anything.

He was out cold by the time we got in, drooling slightly, and I could tell it wasn't just the after-effects of alcohol he was suffering from. I thought it would be safer if I shut him in a room the opposite end of the house.

As soon as the door was locked, animalistic need hit me, the immediate want for my girl pulling me now I was close. Soundlessly creeping down the hall, my heart pounding against my ribcage so hard and fast I thought I'd die before I saw her. The door handle wouldn't budge, she must have locked herself inside, knowing what intoxicated state her husband would come home in. Clever girl!

I knocked, scabbed knuckles rapping on the newly whitewashed wood. Shuffling from inside, another door opening. Not my door! A retching noise echoing off the tilled wall then taps being turned on. The sound of running water and lack of response was a combination that made me feel uneasy. Impatiently, I knocked again, harder. A moment later she opened the door, peering up and down the hallway.

Relief washed over me, seeing she was safe. I wanted to pull her in my arms, kiss her all over. Tell her it was okay now because I was here to protect her.

"Where is he?" she questioned in a small voice.

"Passed out in the spare room," The dim glow from a bedside lamp cast dark shadows across Marie's face. She didn't seem to be hurt but there were brownish smudges below her eyes and she was missing at least twenty pounds from her already slender frame, her complexion as pale as porcelain.

"Baby, are you okay?" My face twisted with due concern. This was no doubt caused by Nicholas' reign of terror. I pushed my way into the room, making her back up.

"What happened? What did he do to you?" I wondered for a moment if I was talking about myself or her husband.

"I'm fine, just a little sick." She looked exhausted, her shoulders hunched in on themselves with the effort of holding her up. Picking up her frail form, I carried her to the bed, tucking her quivering body into the sheets.

"I'm going to get you something to eat, okay?" I kissed the top of her head, feeling the clammy skin of her forehead beneath my lips.

I returned in no less than four minutes, the time it took for me to find and heat some soup in the microwave. She seemed so fragile, struggling to pull herself up in bed, swallowing slow mouthfuls of soup, smiling up at me gratefully as each hot spoonful touched her lips.

She barely managed half the bowl before bringing it all back up. "I think we should get you to a hospital."

"No hospital! I just need some sleep!" She was huddled in the corner of the bathroom by the toilet.

"How long have you been like this?" She was so thin; her limbs poked out at odd angles, cheeks hollowed. I could even see the bones in her chest starting to protrude. My voice was barely containing the rage I felt. I was so angry with Nicholas. I couldn't believe he'd just left her to fend for herself when she was this ill.

"Just a few days. I'm fine."

This was not what 'a few days' of sickness did to a person. She couldn't even hold down water, which probably meant she was severely dehydrated and needed urgent intervention. I didn't even want to think about what would happen if she didn't get help.

"I'm taking you to the hospital." I crossed the room and pulled a large designer holdall from the wardrobe where I assumed it was kept and started packing a few things she would need. Warm pajamas, fluffy socks, toothbrush. Marie just sat on the bathroom floor, her back propped against the ornate tub, too tired to argue.

There was vomit on the oversized t-shirt that served as her nightgown; I recognized the shirt as my own, the one I came in. Faded cotton, large and softened with much wear. The fibers visibly sticking out giving it a fluffy appearance. It reached the waistband of my jeans when I wore it but it was only an inch or two above her knees.

"Here, let me help you." I gently helped her to her feet and pulled the dirty t-shirt off. Beautiful creamy white skin, unblemished and perfect. Delicate networks of green and purple veins visible underneath like a road map.

Although her figure was slight, her breasts were voluptuously full. I hungrily took in the body I had obsessed over for weeks, stoking every inch of exposed skin. My hands glazed over her chest and she winced, as if still bruised. And in between her prominent hip bones was a slight swell, hardly noticeable to someone who hadn't seen it before. A gradual curve from her lower belly to mid abdomen. My hands went down to cup the almost imperceptible bump, not caressing but just holding.

"Why didn't you tell me?" The words came out much harsher than I intended. Marie couldn't meet my eye. "You could have called and told me!"

"And say what?" she whispered back, the words barely slipping from her crusted lips. "Guess what, I'm pregnant and it might be yours?"

"Well, Yeah!" It bothered me I didn't know until this moment. I had a right to! It took all I had to keep calm and quiet. "There is a good possibility that this baby is mine."

"And if it is?" Marie was trembling but I wasn't sure if it was because she was physically drained or emotionally fragile. I looked her steadily in the eyes, staring deep into the soft brown abyss.

"Then me and you are going to get out of here."

Marie was whimpering. Her next words were barely audible.

"And if it's not." She closed her eyes as if waiting to be ripped apart by the beast she thought I was.

I belatedly stepped toward her then, bringing my hands up to cup her cheeks, hating the flinch and sharp inhale of air that movement caused.

"Then I'm going to be there for you! Why would you think I wouldn't be?" I whispered, voice thrumming with quiet intensity.

"Because this wasn't what you wanted." She choked out a loud, wet sob. Something about her broken reply stirred inside me. The last thing she needed right now was me yelling at her.

"Baby, why would you even think that? I want you however you come and of course, I want you even more with our child growing inside you."

"It might not be yours!"

"You know what! I don't care. I'm fed up of sharing you with Nicholas like you are some toy. I can't stand it!"

A moment of deafening silence passed before I spoke again, "Does he know?"

She shook her head once, looking down at her bare feet.

"I see how he treats Jude. I see the way that little boy pines for his approval and I don't what that for my baby," She sniffed and wiped her running nose on the back of her hand.

"I was going to get rid of it…"

"No… *no*.." I whispered unable to comprehend what she was saying. I couldn't lose another child, not again. Just like I couldn't lose Marie; she had become my whole reason for existence. The only light in a world of shadows.

"Look, I don't want to ask you to make promises you can't keep… but *please*. Take me away from here. I can't stay here with *him* any longer!" Tears streamed down her face, held between my large hands, her eyes downcast, unable to face me more than unwilling.

But she had to know what she was getting herself into.

"You have to understand, before you make this decision, what you are asking. Your life is going to be completely different." Like I'd kept repeating, I was nothing like Nic. I had no means to support us, nowhere to take her. But I'd manage. For her, I'd manage. I didn't want to be separated another second.

I stroked her cheeks with calloused thumbs, wiping away her tears for what I hoped would be the last time.

"I already thought about it." She responded quickly. "It's all I've been thinking about for weeks. Ever since I found out."

"I can't stay here and I *know* I can't do this by myself. So I'm begging you, please. *Please*, take me away from him."

I didn't want to be the only other option. I wanted to be the one she chose because she cared for me, not needed my support but if that was all I got, then that was fine by me. It stung that I couldn't be good enough to choose outright although what had I expected? I was partly, if not completely to blame for this whole situation.

Raising a kid wasn't how I pictured this turning out, especially when she seemed so reluctant to open her heart to me. What we had couldn't even be defined as a relationship, not really. It had taken until this point for me to realize what lengths I'd go to to keep her in my life, bringing up her child. Our child, even if it wasn't.

The possessiveness of it all sent a shudder through me. Maybe I'd been alone for too long to pass up the opportunity. Or maybe I was more like my brother than I thought. Both concepts, although stark in their contrast, frightened me.

I held Marie to my chest, trying to ease the tight pain that had been growing steadily for weeks. And somehow we were on the floor again. I clutched her even closer to me, exhaustion making her limp. I held her selfishly to comfort myself more than her, breathing in the scent of her hair, filling myself with my favorite smell in the world.

I wasn't going to fuck up this time. Marie was the only thing I had worth living for, her and our unborn child. I didn't want to let her go. I wouldn't *ever* let them go!

Chapter Twenty

MARIE

My head was reeling. I was so weak, emaciated to the point where I struggled to even stand by myself. Every smell, no matter how mild, overwhelmed my senses and turned my stomach inside out. And I'd just made arrangements to run away with my brother-in-law.

I closed my eyes what felt like for a few seconds. When I opened them again we were on the freeway.

The next time I managed to open my eyes, I was lying on an unfamiliar couch. Heavy drapes were drawn over the windows so I couldn't figure out where I was or the time of day. I could just about make out low conversation from the other room, the deep rumble of Jack's voice recognizable and comforting even from a distance.

I went to sit up but the motion instantly made me nauseous again. A thin tube protruding from the inside of my arm caught my attention. Following the tubing, I saw it connected to a bag of clear fluid suspended from a coat hanger. Narrowing my eyes in the dim light, I struggled to make out what it was. The text was too small to read from here and my eyesight seemed to be blurry.

The sound of carpet muffled footsteps approaching caught my attention and Jack appeared from an archway that I guess divided this room from another, possibly a kitchen.

"How are you feeling, baby?" He knelt down and smoothed my hair back, which I was sure was slick with grease and possibly had dried vomit in it.

"Awful." I managed to swallow around a dry throat. "Where are we?"

A kind-looking stranger in a wrinkled shirt and wire-rimmed glasses laid a hand on Jack's shoulder, before lowering himself to my level. I surveyed him warily.

"Marie, this is a friend of mine, Doctor Reyansh Sharma. He's going to help."

"Try to help, Jack. Remember, I'm a pediatrician, not an OBYN." He chided before turning to me, "Nice to meet you, Marie. Call me Rey."

"Hi," I replied, smiling a little awkwardly and offering him my free hand which he shook.

"What's that?" I motioned to the bag of liquid hooked over the lampshade.

"It's just a saline solution, to help bring up your fluid and salt levels. It should help you feel better. Marie, do you mind if I examine you? Just have a feel of your stomach?"

"Err, sure."

"You've taken a pregnancy test?" He urged me to shuffle down flat and hitch up my pajama shirt. Jack moved around the couch to allow the doctor easier access to me.

"Yes, two weeks ago. It was positive."

"I assume your period is late?"

"That's when I took the test." I flushed, nodding.

"Tell me if anything feels uncomfortable, okay."

After Rey examined me and took note of my height and weight, I settled back on the couch for him to take my blood pressure.

"Your blood pressure is a little high?"

"Sorry, I'm a bit nervous. You don't want to take any blood, do you?"

"No, that's okay. Even if it were necessary, I wouldn't be able to get the samples to the lab. I'm not practicing anymore."

"Oh?" I replied.

He eyed Jack over my head.

"No... I was disbarred. That is, in truth, how me and Jack know each other. Just try to relax. I'm not going to do anything invasive. Promise."

"So you lost your license?" I asked, closing my eyes.

"I was working in a low-income area. Writing prescriptions off the record for families who couldn't afford food, let alone medication. Some of the stuff was critical too. I don't regret what I did, it's just unfortunate that someone sold me out for trying to help people."

Jack squeezed my shoulder reassuringly and I took a

deep, steadying breath.

"That's better," Rey nodded, noting down the reading. "You will need to visit a midwife sometime soon though. There are some important things I can't test for here."

"Alright," I gave him as big a smile as I could muster, which probably wasn't very convincing.

Jack stroked my temple with a tender finger, "Marie, d'you want to try eating somethin'? I got supplies in the truck."

"Sure." I nodded.

As he headed out, I got a glimpse of outside and decided it was just before dawn. It was still just dark enough to distinguish the porch lamp on in the house across the road. That same house had bars on the windows and a heavy-duty security door.

"Jack helped me out of a few scrapes when I needed him. Always hoped I could repay the favor one day. He's a good guy. Dependable. You're in the best hands."

I nodded, tears filling my eyes.

"I'm sorry. It's just the situation is really complicated."

"Yeah. I recognized you as soon as he brought you in. If it makes you feel any better, I think your husband's a shit."

I let out a weird tearful, snotty laugh, "Thanks." Despite my initial hesitation, I quite liked Doctor Rey.

He offered me a glass of water, which I gladly accepted

and actually managed to sip without it coming back up. When Jack reappeared a minute later, I nibbled on a few Trisects too.

"Just eating small, frequent snacks to keep the nausea and vomiting at bay. You should start to feel better soon. If it gets unbearable, you'll have to get a prescription for Zofran, but like I said, I can't write you one. You'll have to go to a clinic."

"Thanks, Doc," Jack lifted me from the couch, "We need to get back on the road."

"Jack! I can walk," I protested.

"Nope, not risking it."

Rolling my eyes, I waved to Rey over Jack's shoulder, "Thank you for your help."

"Anytime."

Our vehicle was a kind of grayish, brown pickup. Very indistinct. And judging from the other cars that drove by, very common. As we passed similar bar-windowed houses, then streets in the neighborhood, we lapsed into a comfortable silence. The steady cadence of tires on asphalt lulling me into a peaceful, heavy-lidded state.

But despite the cushioning silence and aura of safety that Jack cast, I still felt the considerable shadow of what we'd left behind looming over me.

"Where are we going?" I mumbled, eyes practically

rolling into the back of my head.

"Someplace safe. Away from Nic," his deep voice replied, "Try and get some sleep, it's going to be a long drive."

I took his words as permission to submit to the lure of sleep, and the promise it brought of not having to think, at least for the next few hours. He was going to watch over me. I trusted him. That was all that mattered.

My eyes blinked open as we drove past a flickering motel sign. I sighed and rolled over to face Jack. He sat hunched at the wheel, very alert. There were two Styrofoam containers in the cup holder, black coffee by the smell; one was empty the other was almost the same. I watched tiny numbers on the dash click through zero to nine every minute or so, the neon yellow glowing luminously. Everything else was dark.

It was warm in the cab and I had Jack's jacket over me as a blanket. My eyelids drooped as merciful black, dreamless sleep swam up around me again.

When I finally awoke, the terrain was very different. The last time I was lucid enough to take in the surroundings was somewhere just north of Seattle, where I had a vague recollection of the border crossing. Now we were driving along a dirt road lined with steadily darkening trees. Through the partially cracked window, the air felt cooler. Fresh. It was a nice change.

"Where are we?" I muttered, shuffling around in my seat and shrugging into my borrowed jacket.

"Canada," Jack grunted, "We're almost there."

That was welcome news. My butt cheeks felt like they had fallen asleep when I did, and it seemed I'd slept through a few much-needed toilet breaks.

Through very sparse gaps in the thick trees, I saw what looked like a forest stretching out below, and possibly a small town, from the few steady lights in the far distance.

Jack pulled off of what could have loosely been called a road, onto an uneven muddy track. The evening, completely devoid of moonlight, was inky black. I could just make out an emerging shape coming into view up ahead. The headlights eventually revealed a small log cabin nestled into a clearing. Off to the right was the largest open stretch of sky I'd ever seen, so engulfing in its vastness I felt a little frightened and more than insignificant. Below this, a dark lake stretched out as far as the eye could see, stoic and eerily still.

Jack carried me to the door of a wooden cabin and set me down on the porch bench while he fished a key out from underneath a withered pot plant and unlocked the door.

I'd left my wedding rings, purse, phone and a letter for Nicholas back at the house. I'm pretty sure it wouldn't have made much sense in the state I was in but it didn't mention Jack or the baby. Some things he didn't have to know. The only things I'd brought with me from my old life were a few clothes, basic toiletries and my IDs. I thought they would come in useful. As if he'd read my mind, Jack spoke.

"It's a rental, taken out under a false name."

I didn't reply. He was acting very strangely. His manner had changed since I was last awake. He picked me up again and carried me inside, straight past the simply decorated open-plan living area and into the bedroom, passing one other closed door I assumed was a bathroom.

Jack set me down on the bed, which was plush and very inviting despite the many hours of sleep I assumed I'd had on the journey over here. He reached over and flicked the bedside lamp on, throwing the room into softly lit relief.

"It's the best I could do at such short notice," The terse air he gave off was starting to unsettle me. I wondered if I'd done something wrong.

"It's nice. Cozy," I countered honestly.

I could imagine us living here very easily, at least for the foreseeable future. The rooms were small but functional. And most importantly, we'd be saved the trouble of being disturbed. The cabin seemed to be the only one around in the immediate area.

"I've managed to get a job with an old friend. I start there as soon as you are feeling better."

"Oh, okay," I replied in a small voice. I'd be home alone all day, secluded in this little shack.

I gazed down at my pale hands in my lap and fixated on a loose thread on an over-long sleeve of the borrowed jacket, winding it around my little finger. Doing anything to avoid getting entangled in what was sure to be a scrutinizing look from Jack.

He softened then and pulled me into his lap, wrapping his arms around me. Although I had just left everything I knew and I was in unfamiliar surroundings, I felt safe here in his arms. It was still hard to hold back the tears. I was starting to feel lost. I'd never been north of Sacramento before. The numbing cold was a big change for me.

"It's not easy to come by a job when you have a history like mine."

I nodded. Of course, we needed money. That was something I never had to think about before. I'd always had someone providing everything for me.

Jack was uncharacteristically tense, and It worried me. He was normally so strong. He reached across to the bag he'd thrown at the foot of the bed and placed something heavy and cold into my hand. Without looking, I knew what it was.

"It's loaded but the safety is on."

"Jack, I..." my voice fizzled out.

"Please. It's for my peace of mind as well as yours."

"Do you really think he'll find us here?"

He shrugged, "Have you ever known him to give up so easily."

He had a very valid point. My heart sank like it had been

filled with lead.

"I will keep you safe!" he said, the finality in his tone loosening only a minor fragment of the oppressive weight that had settled over my chest.

That's when the nightmares started. Those horribly realistic ones where you can't run fast enough, the panic building up inside you until you jolt awake and realize you've been holding your breath. Falling, falling down into suffocating darkness where you can't even hear yourself scream, or see your own hand in front of your face.

My stomach swirled with unease, round and round until I woke up, disorientated and terrified. I was worried I was going to throw up in the bed, even though I didn't have much to bring back up in the early days. Jack seemed to know because he was right there, rubbing my belly in slow circles. His whiskered cheek rough on my neck but still comforting, nuzzling with his nose and steady breath at my ear.

"It's okay. I'm here," He paused, rubbing a calloused hand over my arm. "Try go back to sleep, baby." He mumbled groggily.

I must have managed it because the next lucid thought I had was being chased and I couldn't get away because my legs were getting slower, heavier. I felt long-fingered hands reach and wrap around my throat from behind, crushing. I opened my mouth to gasp for a breath, to maybe cry out for help, and it filled with water so cold it was like swallowing ice.

That time I really did scream. I screamed until my voice gave out on me. Every inch of my body ached, my mind driving me insane with instant playbacks. Then I broke down, the tension of the last few days finally peaking and flooding through. Jack pulled me into his lap and held me tight. He didn't let go.

"He's co-ming for m-e." I got out through convulsive sobs, "I k-know it."

His arms tightened around me, "I won't let him anywhere near you. I promise."

A week later, Jack started working at a lumber yard thirty miles away from the secluded cabin we now called home. He had to get there for sunrise to make the most of the shortening daytime hours, so he didn't say goodbye when he left.

When I finally woke up, the sun had already been up for a while. Daylight reflected off the snow banks, dazzling me into awareness, pouring into the bedroom, and bathing the bed under the window in pure, brilliant light. It was beautiful but nothing like a Southern morning. I'd almost forgotten what they felt like; hot and thick like sweet cream.

The house was dead quiet even when Jack was home. The silence pressed on my ears like I was ten feet underwater, almost obtrusive in its volume. I think that's what being at the center of the earth would feel like. Muffled.

Although we were alone, I still felt that we were being closed in on. I keep looking out the back door window and expecting a hooded stranger to be staring in. A bubble of anxiety grew ever larger in my stomach, inflating like a balloon the longer the day stretched until Jack came home. Even then, it never went away entirely.

As soon as I was able, I'd see if there was a job I could pick up in the nearest town. Anything to get me out of the house and the suffocating isolation.

I just sat in the middle of the bed, in the narrow shaft of sunlight and tried to concentrate on what I could hear. I missed the sound of wildlife and cars outside and the noises you can't name but are always there, letting you know you aren't alone. We should get a clock, I think. One that ticks.

———————————————————

The following Saturday, we took a trip down to the nearest town of Bertrner, the one I saw over the lake the night we arrived. It wasn't much; Main Street's commercial buildings comprised of a store, library, church, a single diner and a doctors clinic held in the church hall. Not even a surgery or practice. The clinic was open a few mornings every week, however we were assured by the reverend whom we got the details from, that the doctor did live locally if an emergency arose.

In all, it was much better than staying by myself all day in the cabin. And it was the first morning where the urge to throw up my breakfast was no longer top of the list, which I counted as a triumph. I'd take them where they came right now.

I scanned the stack of outdated magazines piled neatly on the table while Jack was giving over our details to the receptionist. My eyes rested on the spine of September's edition of OK, the most recent copy I could see, and I slid it out from the middle of the stack.

There was a picture of me plastered over the cover, the way I used to look all glammed up for an event. I was smiling cheek to cheek with Nicholas. In big white letters it read, "Where's our Sweetheart?"

Glancing over at Jack to check he wasn't paying attention, I flipped to the double-page spread.

"Marie Hayes, 20, has still yet to be spotted in public, following the well-documented family spat at a charity ball last month. Even her social media pages, which were constantly updated with private photos and stunning selfies, have been shut down, leaving fans wondering what's happened to her."

"Husband, Business mogul Nicholas Hayes, has yet to make comment. The 44-year-old has been laying low of late also, rarely being photographed in public, although most recent pictures show him pale and ill-looking."

There was a small photo of Nicholas looking worse for wear in the corner and about six of me at different events and a selfie captioned 'Teenage beauty, Marie Hayes, photographed July.'

"Hayes, who has been in the press recently for having links to suspicious trading activity, regarding his acquisition business Hayes Enterprises, has also had his active social life splashed across the tabloids in recent years. The staggering twenty-three-year age gap between Hayes and the young southern belle, Marie, has had critics questioning if this union was destined for failure from the start. It turns out we will just have to wait and see."

The article, if three boxes of text were sufficient as an article, was obviously complete nonsense, but the wording annoyed me so much my hands started to shake. Why did they have to point out the age gap so blatantly, and the part about our marriage being 'destined for failure' had me seething. Like I couldn't meet his needs.

One moment I was accused of being a slut for wearing a low-cut dress and the next I was an inexperienced little virgin girl. I hated the tabloids, absolutely hated them and the way they twisted everything up into a ball of lies.

"Well, they are mostly correct," Jack muttered into my ear, making me jump out of my skin. I hadn't noticed he'd walked up behind me and was reading over my shoulder.

"Christ, Jack! Do you have to do that?!" I threw the magazine down so he couldn't read anymore.

"Sorry, baby," He chuckled, kissing me lightly on the neck, "Why do you read that crap anyway?"

I shrugged, "What do you mean, 'they are mostly correct?'" I felt a flush starting, thinking about the 'destined for failure' quote at the bottom. Surely he hadn't been behind me that long?

"You haven't been out public since the party..." He moved to pick up the magazine and pointed at the part about my age. "But, you didn't tell me it was your birthday?"

"I guess I forgot."

He eyed me suspiciously but before he could reply, an older female doctor opened the closest door and beckoned us inside the examination room. She introduced herself as Doctor Berry, and after a quick examination where she performed the same basic tests Doctor Rey did, she pulled out an ancient-looking monitor with an attached overly-completed keyboard from a cupboard.

"Let's have a quick look at baby then."

"Wha- A look?"

"This is an ultrasound machine. It's going to show you a scan of your baby."

She instructed me to lay back and expose my lower belly to the air, which I did while eyeing the machine. She then pulled out what looked like a checkout scanner from the grocery store, dropped a blob of lube on my stomach and smushed the scanner into it.

"This just helps the wand glide over more smoothly."

Doctor Berry spent a good few minutes probing around with pressure harder than I thought necessary for a belly that housed a growing fetus, but eventually turned to me and smiled.

"Here baby is." she turned the screen, keeping her wand hand still, and on what looked like footage from the surface of Mars she pointed to the quickly pulsating bean in the center.

"That's…" The ability to vocalize evaded me. There. That tiny, rapidly flickering kidney bean-shaped thing on the screen was my baby. So small that I couldn't even feel him yet. So new that he didn't even exist a few weeks ago.

"Wow," I managed to get out.

When the Doctor eventually turned the machine off and wheeled it back away, she informed me she needed some samples, which of course turned out to be blood. Up until this point Jack had sat impassively beside me, and now he held out his hand for me to squeeze.

"Everything looks fine for now. Try and keep your stress levels low, stay moderately active and eat well."

"What do you mean 'for now?" Jack asked.

"As you were previously advised, Marie's blood pressure is a bit on the higher end of the scale. In medical terms, we'd call this 'mild hypertension'."

"Which means?" He pressed.

"Nothing in these early stages of pregnancy. I'll like to see you regularly though, Marie, just to make sure you are keeping yourself well."

"What if it doesn't go away?"

"Well, hypertension and protein in the urine are indicators of a rare condition called preeclampsia developing. Your hands, feet and legs could swell too, and you may see flashing lights. However, it's much too early to test for that now, it would normally start to show itself around the twenty-week mark."

Jack's hand tightened over my own, I felt his whole body stiffen beside me.

"Just make sure you can get to me every four weeks, and we'll keep an eye on you, okay? Being such a small town, we're not prepared for things such as c-sections so I would recommend going to the city hospital when the time comes for delivery. But we can talk about that nearer the time."

I surveyed a shelf stocked with pre-natal supplements. There were so many brands to choose from, all offering something slightly different. I wrinkled my nose reading the back of a packet, trying to figure out if I needed more zinc than magnesium. Didn't I read somewhere that too much vitamin A was toxic?

"Get this one and this..." Jack handed me the boxes. "You'll need to keep your iron levels up."

I raised my eyebrow at him in the manner he normally would. This only got me a slight smile in response, the corner of his lip twitching up before falling back into his usual scowl.

"Is everything alright?"

His expression shifted, and then his gaze dropped to the floor. When he spoke, his voice was quiet. "I've been through this bit before. It's..." He paused, "...bringing back some old memories."

I reached up to stroke his cheek, trying to catch his eye as he avoided mine. I wished he would let me in enough so at least I could get an idea as to what he was thinking. But I knew this angle would get me nowhere. I'd have to wait until he was ready to tell me.

It was frustrating though. He should've been comforting me, not the other way around. I leaned in and planted a kiss on his chest before heading over the the check-out.

"Find everything you needed?" The girl behind the desk asked, her long blond dreadlocks swinging with the momentum of her hips as she moved to a song playing on the stereo behind her.

"I think so. Thanks."

"Not seen you around before?" Despite the cold outside she wore a cropped band t-shirt and sported heavy winged eyeliner, which made her deep green eyes pop.

"No, we just moved here."

"Ah. It's a small town. You'll get to know everyone pretty soon. I'm Lisa," She beamed, showing off twin dimples.

I'd already decided I was going to utilize my old fake ID to avoid recognition.

"Layla," I smiled back as she packed my items in a paper bag. She looked maybe only a couple years younger than me, but by comparison, I felt at least a decade older.

"I was wondering if you knew of any jobs going around

here?"

"Nothing major really. I know Dina is looking for someone to help around the diner," She motioned out the window to a building across the street, "Just her and her old man, Sid, although he's not up to much nowadays. Arthritis."

I felt the cool prickle on the back of my neck which usually warned I was being watched. I looked around for Jack and saw the top of his head over an aisle. Guess I was just being paranoid. Those dreams were coming back to haunt me.

I turned back to Lisa, "That's a shame."

"Yeah, really nice guy he is too."

"Well, maybe I'll give her a call."

She nodded, "That's twenty-two-fifty, Hon."

I turned to see where Jack had got to and found him at my side, causing me to jump for the second time that day.

"Don't do that!" I swatted at him, "Do you want me to have a heart attack?"

"Sorry, baby," He handed the money over to Lisa with a wry grin.

Outside, the weather was taking a turn for the worse. The wind was picking up and the sky, so clear when we left that morning, was filled with heavy, ominous clouds.

The truck was parked a bit further up the road, where the

clinic was held and we crossed over on our way toward it. The open sign for Dina's diner swung and clattered in the stirring wind as we passed. I noticed the piece of paper blue-tacked to the inside of the glass advertising for help.

"One sec," I stopped, rummaging around in my purse for something to write with.

"Marie, there's a storm coming," Jack growled.

"I just have to take this number down," I found a pen stashed at the bottom but nothing to write on, so I made do with what I had, scrawling the number down on the back of my hand.

"Okay, let's go."

We made it to the truck just in time. Rain pelted down over the windows, so violently it blurred everything outside into obscurity.

"Might as well wait until the road is visible again. I wouldn't exactly call the way back home safe," Jack grumbled.

"Might as well put this time to good use then," I replied pointedly, "Tell me what's been bothering you. You've been quiet since the check-up. Actually no, you've hardly spoken to me since we got here," I slid in closer to him and lay my hand over his where it rested on the gear shift.

He stared into the rain-washed windscreen as if not really seeing it. Then he shook his head.

"It's nothing," He stated, sliding his hand from under mine and starting up the truck. We sat for a few minutes until the downpour eased off, tension bristling between us.

He was silent for most of the way home. And I sat there on the brink of tears, feeling like I'd done some unknown thing to anger him. The less he said, the more annoyed I became. He could be so stubborn at times!

At the back of my mind, old insecurities bubbled up to the surface. His and mine both. Maybe I wasn't enough for him after all? He didn't want this life of domesticity, I knew that already. And I'd forced him into taking me with him because I was terrified of being alone. Of having to raise a baby by myself.

He wouldn't give up on me, even though he wanted to. He had something to prove to *himself*. It had little to do with me and the child growing inside me. So he'd stay. Not because he loved me, but because his inbuilt sense of duty told him to. He'd stay by my side even though every part of him longed to run.

"Why'd you take that number down?" He suddenly burst out.

"The girl in the store said the owner was looking for some part-time help."

"And you think you're a suitable candidate?"

"Um, yeah! Why couldn't I do it? I've been feeling loads better recently and I think it would do me good to get out of the house," Maybe that was a slight overstatement; I'd only been feeling *marginally* better this morning.

"Because you're pregnant? Because you've never worked a job in your life? You want me to list them all?"

His sudden hissy fit took me off guard because it came seemingly from nowhere. "That's really shitty of you, Jack..."

"Look, you're not exactly hireable material. Say they are interested; you have no experience, no references, and no permit to work in this country."

Shit, I forgot we weren't in America anymore.

"Is this why you're angry with me? I thought you would like some help paying the rent?"

"We can do just fine on what I earn, thanks."

"What about food, things for the baby?"

"Marie, I will not have you exposing yourself to any necessary dangers!"

"It's going to be a couple of hours a day waiting tables and refilling sugar shakers. Are you seriously going to sit there and tell me I'm allowed and not allowed to do?"

He pulled in at the top of the long, dirt track that constituted our driveway.

"No... I'm just... concerned, okay?"

"Why? You don't think I can handle it? I'm not some kind of helpless damsel in need of rescuing."

"I know you're not."

"So shut up and quit telling me what to do!" I grabbed

the bag of supplements and slid out of the truck.

"Marie, where the hell are you going?"

"I'll walk the rest by myself," I slammed the door and stormed off through the mud toward to house. Jack followed at a crawl a few meters behind the whole way.

By the time I reached the front door, I realized Jack had the keys, and I had to wait for him to fetch the rest of the groceries before coming over. He stood surveying me as he fumbled for the key in his pocket.

"Look, I didn't mean it like that... I just want you to stay safe."

"I'd feel a lot safer if I were around people more often. Living here I feel so cut off from the rest of the world. If something were to happen, wouldn't you prefer that, too?"

"Yeah, babe. I would."

"See, maybe I'm not so 'unsuitable' after all, huh?"

He rolled his eyes in impression of me before I smacked him in the shoulder, "Now let me in. I need to pee."

"One second, I have something more important to do first," He set the grocery bag down on the porch and leaned down to capture my lips in the first kiss I'd received in weeks. My knees weakened as I surrendered into it, feeling his lean hands working up and down my back and then into my hair.

When he eventually broke away, I was almost trembling with need.

"Does that make up for my shitty-ness?"

"Almost. A round in the bedroom wouldn't hurt your chances either."

"I'll see what I can do." He replied, pulling me closer again to continue what he started.

Chapter Twenty-One

JACK

There are a lot of things you don't know about someone until you live with them. Like Marie didn't know how to pick up after herself or cook anything that wasn't toast or clean the goddamn bathroom. She left blobs of toothpaste in the sink, and crumbs in the bed and things all over the floor.

One Sunday morning, she thought she'd surprise me with breakfast, which was a nice gesture until the smell of burning set the smoke alarm off.

"And this is?" I asked, forking through the mixture that had the aroma and appearance of burnt rubber.

"Scrambled eggs."

"How did you get them that color?" I chuckled.

"I cooked it in the same pan as the bacon," She indicated a small stack of charcoal on a side plate.

"Thank God they weren't hiring for a chef!"

She stuck her tongue out at that before pouring us both a bowl of cereal.

She probably didn't know I was a neat freak. In Afghanistan, the dust had a way of working itself into every fold of clothing, sticking to every part of your body. It was one of the little things I still remember about it. I guess that had an effect on me.

I liked the shoes to be lined up neatly by the door and not haphazardly all over the house. I liked the bed sheets tucked in hospital corners and pulled tight enough to bounce a quarter on. She used my razor. Wore my clothes. Left hair *everywhere*, especially in the shower plug hole.

All these things I could deal with. It wasn't like I was asking her to clean up after me, on the contrary, I was more than happy keeping house. It was nice coming home to a place that actually felt like home. Warm. Lived-in. My girl waiting for me.

Marie was learning things about me too, more important things. Like when I was quiet it wasn't because I was annoyed or upset with her, but that I was trying to sort something out in my head. Formulate my thoughts before forcing them out in a way that probably wouldn't make sense. It would've probably helped if I were more consistent with my mood or vocalized it once in a while, but it was a lot easier said than done. I wasn't used to having someone to share that kind of stuff with.

Every so often a memory from my life before would slip into view, taunting me. Maybe I shouldn't have come back to southwest Alberta. Maybe we should have been closer to the hospital or at least civilization.

It wasn't like I had much choice. The timing hadn't exactly been right, the cabin was the first thing I found suitable at such short notice. It was secluded, but on high ground so any snow that fell wouldn't block us in. There was an emergency generator and two fireplaces that would see us through until spring. Then we could move somewhere else in time for the baby.

The nights had been especially hard for her. Whereas I was normally one for nightmares, they were kept at bay due to lack of sleep. I'd felt her struggle all night, tossing and turning in the sheets. When I'd wrapped her in my arms, she'd felt hot but clammy, a fine sheen of sweat over her skin, silent sobs wracking her whole body until she managed to drift off again for a few hours.

I was worried about her. She spoke with Dina, the woman who owned the diner in town, and aced the interview. The job was helping out around the restaurant, waiting tables, making coffee, the usual. Very luckily, Dina didn't want references or experience, just a friendly manner and willingness to get the job done. She also paid cash weekly.

I knew it was nothing Marie couldn't handle; I'd seen her deal with Nic, for Christ's sake. It was she'd be on her feet for close to nine hours, surviving on very little sleep. Her blood pressure was already high and worse, she would be an hour's drive away if she did need me. The only consolation was Doctor Berry lived in town, although I prayed we wouldn't have to have need of her services. And, the thought made my blood run cold, if something went majorly wrong, even she wouldn't be able to help.

Work at the lumber yard was hard but satisfying, and nothing I wasn't used to. I always preferred manual labor to being cooped up inside all day, the smell of the fresh-cut pine carrying in the wind. The other men mostly kept to themselves and that suited me just fine. The cold was a bit of a shock though; it had been a while and I had forgotten how much the temperature dropped once you got this far north.

"Oi Hayes, we need this done by lunch," The foreman shouted over.

After weeks of sleepless nights and the constant worrying about Marie, I didn't have as tight a hold on my temper as I would have liked. I'd had much more control over it recently as the reality of what was at stake weighed heavily on my weary mind.

I turned to the guy and snapped, probably with more malice than intended, "It'll be done."

"It better be."

Me and the foreman hadn't seen eye to eye from day one. Not that I harbored any ill feeling toward him, but the guy irritated me. Constantly lurking, watching me as if waiting for me to slip up. Like he knew.

I'd been close to snapping the other day when the shop boy told me the price of gas had gone up by fifty cents. And the twat who tried to blame me for scraping up against his car in the parking lot of the mini-mart. Like I'd give a shit if I had, his car was just as much a pile of junk as mine.

Some primal, deep-seated part of me welcomed these confrontations, silently begging for release from the suppressed guilt and anger that still simmered within me. Perhaps if I'd gotten things in check a long time ago things would have been different. People wouldn't have been hurt.

There was still a fear, one I didn't want to acknowledge,

that I wouldn't be able to hold it all in. I saw only the parts of myself that were broken. The shame and resentment and burning pain. I was terrified Marie would wake up one day and see that, and discover she'd made the biggest mistake of her life.

I knew if I had to do it all again I'd make the same decisions. I couldn't have left her. Maybe it had nothing to do with doing what was right, and everything to do with what I wanted. Selfishly grasping hold of anything to numb the agony of the past. I just hoped I could do enough for her, be enough. I knew I didn't deserve her.

But Marie was worth fighting for; having her was worth whatever price I had to pay.

Three month's worth of sleepless nights was becoming too much to handle, even for a professional insomniac like myself. Marie had managed to cocoon herself in the entire bedsheet, so her legs were bound together, one arm stuck across her chest, the elbow from the other periodically poking me in the ribs as she jerked, lost within a vivid nightmare.

I sighed, scrubbing a hand over my face before giving up on the idea of sleep and flicking the lamp on.

Marie awoke with a sharp intake of breath, her eyes popping open, wide but disorientated. It took her a few seconds of blinking until the tears started.

I held my arms out to her as she disentangled herself and crawled into my lap, curling her face into the warm crook of my neck.

"They won't stop," She shuddered.

My hands moved easily along her bare arms, trying to rub away the stubborn goose pimples that refused to go down.

"I know."

I lay a kiss on her damp forehead so she knew I wasn't angry with her. I did know from painful first-hand experience what it was like to have both your waking and night-time hours plagued with horrors from your own mind. Twisting scenarios round again and again until they are a side-show on repeat, and suffering the crippling anxiety that they left in their wake.

"Tell me what they are about?"

More tears leaked from the corners of her eyes as she pulled back to look at me before shaking her head.

"I'm just...so *scared*."

"Babe, I promise you. He will not find us here."

"It's not that..." she looked at me almost reproachfully, her eyebrows knitting together.

All of a sudden, I knew exactly what she was thinking.

This must have been either her previous relationship experience or her fears over mine coming to light. Granted, I'd not been the most faithful companion in the past. Hell as a person, I was as shitty as they came but it had taken me almost four years alone time to work out that wasn't who I was going to be anymore. I was not going to be my father and I sure as hell wasn't going to turn into my brother.

"I'm not going anywhere," I rested a hand on her belly, still small but unmistakably pregnant.

She blinked up at me, all wet lashes, moving slowly forward until her lips brushed over mine. She kissed me lightly and again harder when I let her, clutching herself tightly to me. Searching for something I reckon neither of us could name but that she needed desperately. Something she knew I would give her.

"Baby, hold on..."

She shook her head against mine, her fingers twined into my hair to prevent me from moving away. She saw an opportunity in my open mouth, kissing me deeper.

I managed to pull back enough to look her in the eye. There was a desperate need there, raw and animalistic. It reminded me of someone I didn't want to think about. It was a mirror image of the way he would have looked at her. Was there a chance she missed him and his abusive nature? Or was she just reacting in the way *he* would have expected her to?

"Please, *please!*" She begged. I had to let her have this, just once more so she could feel some measure of control over these feelings. But I was going to show her that it could be done nicely. She didn't need him to push her to her limit.

I shifted her off my lap so I could lay her down, kissing her neck as I slowly undid the buttons of her nightshirt. Her figure had started to round considerably in the last few weeks and I stared almost proudly as I caressed the swell. She shifted, looking uncomfortable before I smiled at her. *See look, I'm different. I'm never going to hurt you.*

I was going to show her that being made love to gently was better than a rough fuck, show her how tender a man could be. Sure there were times where the animal in me just wanted to go crazy but that time in my life would have to be over now. I would never let that feeling get away with me again. And especially when she was carrying such precious cargo.

"Touch me," she whined.

"I don't want to hurt you."

"I hurt when you don't touch me," Her hands ran over my sides.

"Take this off," she whispered into my neck. I sat back on my haunches to obey, then leaned down to lay a soft kiss on her lips. I took my time caressing and nipping her skin, finally settling between her legs. She shuddered and let out a small whimper as I licked up her entire length. Her fingers reached down to tangle in my hair. Only when my fingers joined in a steady rhythm did her breathing start to become erratic. Fresh tears prickling in her eyes as she begged me not to stop.

"Look at me, baby. Look so you can see it's not the same," But still she didn't. "Do you love me?"

"*Yes,*" she cried in ecstasy.

"Tell me."

"I love you so much."

With a muted groan pushed the last of my apprehension away, letting it fall back to where the darker part of myself dwelled and pulled her underneath me. I would hold it back. Not just for her, but to prove to myself that it could be done. That I could be a better man.

Because this is what she needed. Stability. Tenderness. Someone to call home. Because she'd just confirmed that in which I needed to hear. The reason why she had thrown it all away. I wasn't the only other option. I wasn't her get-out clause. It was more than I deserved, more than I could have hoped for. She loved me back.

Between lumbering all the daylight hours, working around Marie's shifts and her erratic new sleeping patterns, we'd hardly spent any real time together in months, despite the hour commute to and from Bertrner. During those journeys, it was either before sunrise or after the end of a long day, and Marie would take the extra hour to catch up on sleep. Jointly we made enough to cover rent and food, and even had enough left over to start buying some second-hand baby things.

After a laid-back Sunday afternoon, where we'd picked up a stroller from a store in the next town over, Marie was adamant she was making dinner. I was pleasantly surprised when, an hour and a half later, she proudly slid a plate of steak and potatoes under my nose.

"What d'you think?"

"That looks delicious!" I replied with a grin, taking a forkful. The potatoes were just over and the steak just under, but I'd always liked my meat on the rarer side anyway.

"I think you should cook yours a little more, just to be safe. But well done! How'd you make these potatoes?" I asked, forking another mouthful in.

"The guy at work is showing me things here and there, when it's quiet."

"You should be proud. These are good."

She slid onto the couch next to me and I put an arm around her.

"I'll get there. I'm not one to give up on something."

"Don't I know it," I pulled her closer and kissed her temple before digging back into my plate.

"Aren't you eating?" I asked around a mouthful of steak.

"Maybe a bit later. It's hard to fit a meal in around this baby. He's starting to take up a lot of room in there."

"Him?"

She shrugged, "I've actually been thinking of names."

"Enlighten me."

"I always liked the name Noah. When I was a kid I went

to Sunday School. My favorite story was always Noah and the Ark. I liked the message. I kinda feel like this baby is saving us in a way, bringing us to new lands to start over."

"It's nice, but what if it's a girl? You have a fifty-fifty chance, ya know," I teased.

"I just kind of have a feeling it will be a boy."

"Well, you can't call a girl that." I snorted.

She looked indignant. "Why not?"

"If your little boy wanted to dress up in a princess dress and heels, would you let him?"

"Yes. I would," She retorted. "He could be anything he wanted to be. And if your daughter wants to rock climb and cut her hair short she can!"

She had a very good point. I wouldn't deny my baby girl anything, and not just because I'd be having to face the wrath of her mother.

"You're amazing, you know that?"

"I know," She quipped. "Since I cooked, you can do the dishes. I'm going to have a bath," She pecked me on the cheek before heading off for the bathroom. I tried to enjoy the rest of my dinner instead of thinking about my fate, which undoubtedly would be a very large mess to clear up in the kitchen.

Marie had been sleeping on and off for the past few weeks. Except when she slept, I didn't. I awoke most times with a yell that woke her up too, but not tonight. My leg ached something fierce and *fuck* the room was hot. So I went into the kitchen to get a cold glass of water.

There were no clean glasses and more than a day's worth of dirty dishes stacked in the sink, so I had to maneuver that morning's coffee mug at an angle under the faucet, which only allowed it to be half-filled. Cursing, I unpiled the sink and washed a few bits. I was partly to blame for the mess as well, we'd both been too busy to deal with things as mundane as chores.

I splashed my face then filled the cup to bring back for Marie. On the way back to the bedroom, I had to side-step the vacuum cleaner, then back-tracked to make sure the cable was coiled in. That would be a disaster just waiting to happen. By the time I'd got back into bed, my late-night antics had woken her.

"Thanks," She sniffed and took the mug with shaking hands, drinking half of it in one, "What time is it?"

"Little past four am."

She lay back down and I spooned her from behind, squeezing her tight to me. It must have been a bad one. I could still feel her trembling against me.

My hand gently rubbed over her breast as I tried to soothe her back to sleep. It wasn't working in the same way for me. As her stomach had grown, they had swollen too, making them much rounder and firmer, and no doubt much more sensitive. I tried to angle my hips further back but I was caught out. She twisted around and placed her lips against mine.

When I didn't reciprocate, she moved up to my ear, lavishing it with attention. Only when I felt a sharp nip, hard enough to draw blood, was I aware of a shift in her desire.

"Hang on a sec, I think we need to talk," I grasped hold of her shoulders and lowered her off of me.

"Sorry, I didn't mean to…"

"Just take it easy, okay."

"I'm not made of china, Jack. You can be a little rough with me."

Her words reconfirmed my suspicions. Did she not understand how twisted it was, that she would deliberately press all the wrong buttons? Start a fight just because she was feeling frisky and craving the brutal sex *he* doled out best when fueled by his rage.

"Why do you want me to be?" I wanted her to say it. To tell me why she wanted me to treat her exactly the way he did.

She only looked at me, her expression unreadable in the semi-darkness. I sighed and reached over to turn the lamp on.

"Listen, I think you've come to expect sex to be a certain way, either as a reward or a punishment… And I think I know why…"

"Hold up? Who do you think you are lecturing me like

this?"

"What do you mean? It's affecting our relationship! Can you really not see where this is coming from? What he was like?"

"Oh, Bullshit!" She spat.

"Marie!"

"What?"

"You know what! I don't want our kid to come out knowing every swear word in the English-speaking language."

"You think I *liked* the way he treated me?" She snapped. "You think I *chose* that? I didn't enjoy being hurt by him, Jack. I didn't have a choice how it was done. I didn't have a say in *anything*!"

I grabbed her knees and pulled her down the bed so we were almost nose to nose.

"Do you want to be afraid of me? Is that how you get off? Knowing I can hurt you? I'm *nothing* like him. I won't give in to you, and I'm certainly not going to lay a finger on you when you're pregnant."

She slapped me hard across the cheek; I bared my teeth but didn't move off her.

"Fuck me!"

"No!" I snarled.

"Jack, I swear to God, telling a horny, pregnant woman you won't touch her is a bad thing to do!"

"Touch yourself then! Maybe a little fantasy session is what you need right now."

This was getting fucking out of hand. It was four in the morning, we both had to be up for work in less than two hours.

"Where are you going?" She asked, suddenly apprehensive.

"To get some sleep!" I yanked my solitary pillow out of the tangled bedsheets, and Marie's many strategically placed pillows, and left the room, closing the door behind me.

I lay on the couch, feet and at least half of my calves hanging off the end. Luckily the embers from that evening's fire were still smoldering in the grate and the room was warm not, thankfully, sweltering like the bedroom.

Despite the milder temperature and peace, I still couldn't sleep. Now I felt guilty, like *I'd* instigated the argument. I knew I could have handled it better. I'd left before things got too heated, before I allowed myself to do something I would later regret. Maybe that was the issue. There was no resolution.

I tossed around on the couch, leather squeaking beneath me until I found a semi-comfortable position a few minutes later. Still not comfortable enough to sleep. I was contemplating whether or not to finish the dishes when I heard the bedroom door open and bare footsteps padding across the wood.

"Please, I don't want to fight. We're both just tired okay." She lay her head over my stomach.

I rubbed her head, curling my fingers through her hair, "I'm sorry."

"Me too, I didn't mean what I said," She paused, "But I think you're right, we do need to talk. I need you to tell me when something is bothering you so we can work it out together. Recently, I've been wondering if… you've been having second thoughts?"

My reply was immediate and steadfast, "No, not at all."

"It's just now that we're here and you have me, maybe you don't want me anymore. Where is the thrill of chasing after me? I want passion like before. I want to feel like I'm still worth something."

"Passion doesn't have to equal rough-housing. What Nic did to you…" even the thought of it made me shudder.

"I'll admit sex was a little dysfunctional between us. Whenever we had an issue, we'd use sex to keep us from actually having to talk or deal with any of our problems. I don't want us to be like that. It's not healthy."

"Listen, Marie. I want you," In fact I *needed* her but I couldn't find a way to put that into words that wouldn't sound so desperate. Since the moment we met, I wanted her. In my arms, in my bed, right by my side. Only now I'd had a taste, I couldn't go back to solely wanting her ever again. Without her, I'd thought I'd fall back apart. Back into the dark void so deeply there would be no redemption.

I tried again, "The way I am... it's just in my nature. I'm supposed'ta take care of you because that's what I'm hardwired to do. I'm bigger and stronger because I need to be able to provide for you, protect what's mine, and give you stability and comfort, when you need it..." I trailed off again, fearing I was becoming too mushy.

She squeezed me tighter in understanding, "That's a nice sentiment, but I can take care of myself."

"But I don't want you to have to. I wanna show you how much you mean to me," I pulled her chin up to look at me, "Baby, it's like I've won the jackpot."

"But look at me, I'm all fat now." She pouted, presumably putting it on a bit now she had me.

I chuckled, "You're not fat, you're pregnant. And besides, I love it."

She rolled her eyes, but there was a very pretty flush underpinning that nonchalant action.

"I swear you're the best decision I've ever made."

"You're mine too," She whispered back.

Chapter Twenty-Two

NIC

It had been four months since she'd left. Four months of steadily drinking myself into oblivion. Two-thousand six hundred and sixteen hours spent alternating between lethargic nothingness and smashing everything in sight. Sure, I was drunk as fuck, but I could still read the time. I was burnt out, semi-delirious and losing touch with my existence but at least I'd managed to take the edge off.

Empty bottles littered the floor. Not a drop left. I dragged myself to the bathroom and threw up in the shower. In normal circumstances, I held my liquor much better.

Not bothering to undress, I turned on the shower and slumped under the cold spray. I didn't feel it. I couldn't feel anything.

Without her, my life was falling apart. Slowly unraveling.

At first, I thought she'd just gone on another one of her drives, getting the angst out of her system. When she didn't answer her phone after the hundredth time of calling, I started to suspect something was up. I'd finally found her cell crammed into the back of the nightstand drawer, complete with the medical files and birth control pills, but missing the fat envelope of cash I'd stupidly let her keep.

When I realized she wasn't coming back, I called Jack. His cell was switched off. The first thing that sprang to mind was 'mother-fucking technophobe.' I got in the car and sped toward the condo I'd bought him downtown. I used my key, obviously I had a copy just in case, expecting to find him in bed, asleep or otherwise engaged. The place was deserted.

Only then did I put it all together like some sick, twisted puzzle. The fucker had run off *with* my wife.

Fast-forward a few more weeks and Jean was nowhere to be found. Neither was Chuck. Then my own company unanimously voted me off the board. Said I wasn't making '*smart decisions*', throwing around words like '*commitment*' and '*professionalism*' like they were some kind of holy fucking authority on righteousness.

Even the house staff deserted me after I yelled at the cleaner for getting under my feet. Stupid bitch.

So now, I was functioning on a few hours of spotty sleep a night, holed up in this shitpit of a house while I slowly lost my grip on reality.

Eventually, I knew I had to get out of the shower. I dumped my wet clothes on top of the accumulated mound of dirty laundry and used towels in the corner and fell back into bed, naked and wet. It didn't matter anyway; who was around to judge me?

I had a new dilemma now; I was out of booze. Which meant I either had to give it up or actually get dressed and leave the house to get some more. Staying in bed was the easiest option but the longer I laid there thinking about it, the more sober I would become. And that was dangerous. I couldn't decide which was worse; being left alone with my thoughts or not being able to think at all.

Even for my standards, I'd admit It had gotten bad. A few days ago I had stumbled over the edge of the rug and smashed my head against the dresser. I must have passed out because when I opened my eyes again, I was lying on carpet sticky with half-dried blood. It looked as though there had been a lot. The stain was still there, covered with whatever debris I'd thrown/ dropped over it.

The scrapes and bumps concerned me, especially when I couldn't remember how they'd happened. But that wasn't the scariest part. No… What frightened me the most was there were whole periods of time I couldn't account for. Black holes in my memory. The darkness took up most of my waking hours until I could sleep, and finally get a few hours freedom from unobliging, conscious thought.

The fresh food had run out weeks ago, so I was left with whatever was crammed in the back of the cupboards, and even that supply was starting to run low. I found a lonely tin of tuna and the remnants of a stale box of Raisin Bran lying around. I'd given up on formalities such as plates and cutlery a long time ago, and so I cracked open the tin of fish and picked out the flakes with my fingers.

The nails had a layer of filth collecting under them, craggy and blackened. I'd have to give them a trim later. If I could find some tool to do it with and if I could be bothered. I'd at least skewer the dirt from underneath before I ventured out. I wasn't homeless, and I sure as hell wouldn't be caught dead with fingernails that would rival a bag lady.

One quick hack job later, courtesy of the kitchen scissors,

and after finding a set of relatively clean clothing, I finally opened the back door and stepped out into the grey morning, or was it afternoon, heading down the garden path to the gate and the beach.

Outside, people still had their Christmas lights up, which was ridiculous as we were well into January. I walked along the sand, wishing I'd thought to grab a jacket on my way out. The actual temperature wasn't too cold, but the wind coming in from the ocean was picking up fast, whipping through my shirt and jeans.

I grit my teeth and kept walking. Waves roared in the distance, the only noise to be heard for miles. It helped to clear my head some. It was undoubtedly better than the resounding silence I'd gotten all too used to. The fresh air might have had more of an impact; it was the first time I'd left the house in... God, I don't even remember when! Days? Weeks?

The walk to the store wasn't long, the route familiar and strangely devoid of passers-by. Once closer, the smell of coffee carried on the air from the Starbucks across the street. I could see figures inside, people sitting with steaming mugs in hand, lining up to collect their over-priced lattes to go, baristas taking orders and payment with smiles on their faces. *Smiles*. In *January!* You wouldn't get that in the city!

I turned my back and carried on to the liquor store.

A sign in the window reminded me to '*Have a Happy Holiday*' with an intermittent flicker that did strange things to my vision. My own face, reflected back at me in the glass, lit up a sickly green then a vivid, angry red, and I saw I looked just as bad as I felt. Jessica's final words to me came back in a nauseous swell of comprehension. I *did* need help. As much as I could get.

Because clearly, my approach hadn't been working.

But where would I even start?

I'd fucking destroyed the name I'd worked so hard to make for myself. Lost even my closest friends. Driven my wife into the arms of my brother, the only family I had left, both of them deserting me. I could moan about it like a little bitch... I *could*... but it's my fault. Nothing in this world worth having came easy. I would find her and bring her back home if it was the last thing I did. I had to make this right.

The urge to drink was strong, sucking me in, until the blackness begins to pull at the edges of my consciousness.

The liquor lined up behind the counter shone in the yellowed light of the old fluorescent lamps. If I hadn't known better I could have sworn a few of the bottles on the top shelf winked at me as I shook my head. I simultaneously made awkward eye contact with the checkout clerk through the window. He half-raised a hand to me in mute greeting, the corner of his Fu Manchu mustachioed mouth turned up in that knowing way that really pissed me off!

That was the deal breaker. I would *not* choose him and the fleeting solace he offered over the life I'd struggled to carve out for myself from nothing. Over the respect of my colleagues and friends. Over the love of my wife.

I picked up a cup of black coffee from next door before

heading back to the vast, empty shell that used to be my home.

I decided I needed to *do* something! I'd start from the top of the house and work downwards. Beginning with the bedroom, I shifted piles of clothes until the carpet was visible again. Once the rug was rolled away, I started on vacuuming, really getting in the corners and under the heavy wooden dresser.

It was only once I'd made my way out into the hall that I remembered the blood stain, jarringly absent from the cream-colored carpets and that heavy feeling of terror rose back over me, threatening to swallow me whole.

I paid the girl what I owed her, although four hundred dollars was a little pricey, in my opinion. She was slender and dark-haired but without Marie's curves. Bright blue eyes. I kept her face turned away so my imagination would have an easier time.

I never thought I'd pay for something I could quite easily have for free. However, nowadays I wasn't exactly looking for the same thing. I used to enjoy the prowl; always keeping an eye open, chasing down the girls I wanted in my bed. Now, I only wanted the one I couldn't have.

The hotel room, shabby by my standards and probably even by the Polack hookers, was situated across town in an area I wouldn't be caught dead in. That was how I wanted it. I never brought them into my house. Even with Marie gone, I couldn't stomach the thought. It brought the phrase 'don't shit where you eat' into a whole new light.

The door had barely swung shut behind us before I

grabbed her and buried my face in her dark hair, just the right shade, my hands roaming up and down her body. She smelt wrong, like hairspray and cheap perfume. I heard her stutter something under her breath as I yanked her panties off from under her skirt and undid my jeans before shoving her toward the bed.

She stumbled awkwardly onto her hands and knees, offering her bare pussy in a way that wasn't exactly convincing me she didn't do this often enough. I didn't like the fact I had to share her with every other man on the western seaboard and fuck knew how many others before them.

Russian was my next best guess, not being acquainted with many Eastern Europeans. Their accents all blended together into one indistinguishable category: *foreign*. I found Eastern Europeans also had a distinctive smell about them. Maybe from a diet rich in olive loaf and 'wodka', or maybe there was just something different in the water. Of course, that was dependent on how often they bathed.

Regardless, I was determined to plant the flag of our great nation into questionable Soviet territory once more. I gave myself a few vigorous strokes before lining up to her entrance, squeezing my eyes shut. I threw my head back, almost growling at the feel of her impaled on my cock. It had been too long.

But I couldn't pretend she was Marie. Too much was off about it. I tried my best to imagine. The little noises she made; whimpers, sighs. The feel of her under my hands. All the inconsequential things that could pull me deeper into that beautiful, infinite oblivion.

I grabbed a fistful of her hair, thinner than Marie's but still the right color. I opened my eyes to watch it run through my fingers, but she turned her head at just the wrong moment, nearly ruining my fantasy. I shoved her face back down and fucked her harder.

Close, *so close*. The sounds she made were wrong. Not breathy sighs but throaty grunts as I pushed into her.

She's not Marie.

Like I gave a fuck. I just wanted — *needed*. I yanked her up by her hips, thrusting deeper, faster. Losing control. Need her to - *just a bit harder* - so *fucking* close!

Her struggling would have made the friction better. Why did she have to be so goddamn compliant?

She's not Marie! **Shut up shut up shut up!**

I let out a roar, grabbed her by the arm and flung her halfway across the room. The girl crashed into the door, hitting her head on the way down. She blinked the tears out of her eyes and focused her gaze back on me. Blue eyes. Not my Marie.

"LEAVE!" I roared, "NOW!"

Not-Marie didn't have to be told twice. She gathered up her clothes and purse and ran out of the room, leaving behind a lone shoe.

I collapsed back onto the bed, panting. *Stupid bitch!*

What had I done to deserve this? Reduced to sleeping with a call girl in some hovel of a motel room while my wife was somewhere out there fucking my brother!

You know what? I could forgive her. I knew I'd messed up. I'd practically driven her into his arms with the shit that I'd pulled. Because I was a terrible, fucking sick bad, *bad* guy! It had taken me until now to appreciate the extent of what I'd put her through.

If anyone was to blame, it was Jack. Not my wife. Not the Marie-substitute I'd used to try to lessen the pain of losing her. I was starting to feel remorse over the way I'd treated the girl. I didn't need to be so rough with her or throw her into the wall like that. At least she was smart enough to ask for the cash upfront.

I huffed a listless sigh and stood to pull my jeans back on. I felt sorry for her, actually. Young little thing in the city by herself. Until I realized she'd stolen my wallet on her way out. For *fuck's sake*!

It wouldn't have been such a big deal before, but since I'd been away from work, things had been going steadily downhill, and more than just where my mental state was concerned. My personal accounts had been blocked because of 'suspicious activity.' The only thing suspicious is that they hadn't been used in months! My corporate card had, of course, been confiscated and there was no way in hell I was going to call Max on that one. Almost every line of credit available to me was gone.

The only capital I now had was a moderately sized parcel of cash taped to the underside of my bed, alongside a loaded nine-millimeter Smith and Wesson. I grew up in a rough enough area to know that home security should be a priority and strictly enforced when necessary.

Looking back, I should have paid quite a bit more attention to security. If I'd only known she had it in her to pull a stunt like this… I hadn't seen it coming. I still couldn't comprehend what she'd done to me. Not just that she left me, but the deceit. The lies. Stabbing me in the back repeatedly, over and over again until all that was left were lacerated memories and a gaping, soulless existence.

All at once I felt defeated. Fractured.

I'd been completely sober for twenty-four hours now. No drink, no meds. Not even Excedrin. And it felt fucking terrible. My mind was playing things over on loop, like that ridiculous fairground thing Jude made me ride. Mental images of them together, what they were doing, raising questions that gnawed away at me like acid. How long had it been going on for? Had it happened right under my nose? Under my roof? In my own fucking *bed*?

I had half a mind to file a missing person's report for her, but somehow I knew getting the cops involved was not the best way to go about it. She'd chosen to go with him. That wasn't going to stand in court.

I had to track her down on my own accord. Carry out justice myself. I had a connection who'd been able to trace Marie's passport and found out she'd crossed the border into British Columbia. From there it was anyone's guess where she might have gone, although I was very sure Jack was still with her.

She wouldn't be able to support herself for long on the money she'd stolen from me, especially no longer being in the States *and* without a visa. I also knew Jack had citizenship as he'd lived there for a stint after leaving the armed forces. Another indicator they'd both fucked me over. Plotting, scheming, conniving against me.

I understood now the way I'd acted was wrong. But I no longer felt like shit. Because what she'd done was worse, far, *far* worse than meaningless sex with strangers.

I could forgive her, but not him! I wouldn't ever be able to forgive Jack for what he'd done to me. When I finally found them, I'd bring her home. And I'd kill him!

Chapter Twenty-Three

JACK

"Son-of-a-fucking-bitch!" I yanked my hand out from under the sink where I'd been tightening the waste back up.

"Careful Jack, I don't want our kid to come out knowing all the swear words in the English language," Marie chided, returning to the kitchen with an empty washing basket, ready for refilling.

"Smart ass! I just cut my finger," Blood ran over my palm from a diagonal gash in my forefinger and dropped onto the floor, painting the tiles with crimson spots.

"Oh baby, that looks deep," She pulled me up and ran my hand under the cold water before retrieving the first aid kit out of a nearby drawer, bandaging the finger up and laying a kiss on it.

"All better," she said in a soft voice that did all kinds of things to me.

"Talk about a stellar bedside manner!" I teased, brushing her cheek lightly with the newly trussed-up finger.

"Bet you don't get that kind of medical attention at work, mister." She winked and went back to sorting laundry in the bedroom. "We need to leave soon so finish up!" She called behind her.

We'd taken the morning off work for Marie's twenty-week scan, which she told me we could find out the sex of the baby. She was adamant she knew it was a boy and didn't need confirmation of that fact, but we could find out if I really wanted to. I said It didn't matter either way.

I had a kind of fluttery feeling in my stomach the whole drive over into town, which did nothing to taint the contentment I felt with Marie by my side and a fresh, bright winter morning sparkling outside the truck's window.

Although, by the time we'd parked up, the butterflies had turned into full-blown jitters.

Inside the clinic, Doctor Berry carried out all the routine checks and ensured us the baby was growing normally. Although once Marie mentioned she'd been getting headaches often, the doctors' tone quickly turned from jovial to concerned. She questioned Marie about light-headedness, blurred vision and seeing flashing lights, which she couldn't deny she might have seen.

"Now you're a bit further along, the warning signs will start to show more frequently. You'll need to keep of record of everything unusual you may feel, however trivial you may think it. Preeclampsia can be very dangerous if it's not caught early enough."

"How do you treat it?" Marie asked, her eyebrows knitting together in apprehension.

"There isn't a cure except to give birth. I'll put you down for more regular visits just so we can keep an eye on you. But try not to worry, stress can exacerbate the condition."

Marie just nodded, thanked the doctor, and collected her things to go. I followed as if on auto-pilot back to the truck.

All these weeks and she hadn't even mentioned it. A leaden weight settled in my stomach, heavy and very much virulent. It was happening all over again. The nightmare that plagued both my waking and nighttime hours. I was faced with the very real possibility that I could lose her. And again, it would be my fault!

I could feel my expression hardening, feel the emotion burying itself deeper inside me. Hiding the fear, and the anxiety. Throwing my guard up on reflex. My muscles twitching, burning to run instead of facing it.

I couldn't tell her! Couldn't say the past had finally caught back up with me. That I didn't deserve shit. Because the truth would terrify her. And I didn't want that on my conscience on top of it all.

All too quickly, we were pulling up onto the drive, and I cut the engine.

"Jack," she asked in a tentative voice, "Are you okay?"

"I'm fine." I muttered, my mouth dry.

Sensing her eyes on me I got out of the truck, collected the bags from the backseat and made my way inside the house.

"Hey!" She yelled after me, slamming the car door. I didn't have the courage to face her yet. I needed some time to work out how I was going to tell her.

I deposited the groceries on the counter and turned to head into the bathroom, but Marie blocked my way, eyebrows raised expectantly.

"I need to shower," I said in reply, and stepped around her into the bathroom, closing the door with a soft click. I'd taken the lock off when we'd moved in as a safety precaution; the damn thing had a habit of sticking and it would be just my luck that Marie would get locked in when I wasn't around.

I ran the water to heat, stripped off and stood under the blessedly hot spray. Steam had already started to fill the tiny windowless bathroom when I heard another door thud shut.

"Would ya' give me five minutes!" I practically growled.

Without responding, she removed her layers of clothes, many coming off together, and yanked the shower door open.

"Let me in." She snapped, pushing her way into the small cubical, forcing me up against the wall in doing so. There was barely enough room for the three of us in there, me, her and the baby.

The bare skin of her back was pressed up against my stomach, all soft and wet, and I relished in the feel of it. It took a lot of self-control to keep my hands by my sides. She turned her head to eye me through the shower spray, then turned back around to wash.

It was becoming increasingly hard to ignore her soaped-up body rubbing against my over-sensitized flesh. She must have known the effect she was having on me?

Only when she bent forwards on the pretense of picking up a shampoo bottle and ground her ass into me did I get what she was trying to do. Angry and horny were not a good combination for a pregnant woman, especially when those two were becoming synonymous of each other.

"Marie…" I rumbled warningly.

"I thought you didn't want to talk?" She shot over her shoulder.

"This is hardly the place,"

She turned on me, "I agree, I think the most appropriate time would have been directly after it happened but since you didn't give me that option…"

"I don't wanna talk about it."

"I don't accept that. We're apart all day, and I look forward to when we can come home and be together. But you're distant all the time and pissed off and you won't tell me why. And you've hardly touched me in weeks!" There was a note of steadily rising defiance in her voice.

"Don't push me…" I wasn't ready to talk. It would only come out wrong.

"What, I'm not scared of you. You're being an asshole!"

"*Marie*…" It was a warning that had a little edge to it. She was pushing me dangerously close to snapping point.

"Whatever," She dismissed me and turned around to wash her hair.

She was right; we hadn't been intimate in weeks, mainly due to lack of time more than anything else. Nevertheless, my experience with pregnant women was that as time wore on they became less frisky and needed extra rest. Clearly, Marie was the exception to that rule.

She'd been on my case every waking second of the day, wordlessly urging me to fulfill her dark desires, when I had quite plainly told her no. Suppressing that part of myself had become necessary to protect her, something I found neither natural nor easy. Hell, if she knew what I was capable of, what I *could* do to a woman. Perhaps she did know; I wouldn't have described our previous encounters as tame. Maybe she thought I'd been holding out on her, which she would have been correct to assume.

The water cascaded over her naked form, her full hips, swollen breasts and caressing her wonderfully rounded stomach, heavy with child that suited her so well. And flaunting all that in front of a man who was trying so desperately hard to resist temptation was paramount to insanity.

All of a sudden, I couldn't restrain myself any longer. I was so hard it hurt.

I pushed her closer to the wall, perhaps rougher than I'd intended to, hands roaming over her beautiful curves. She pushed back, seemingly denying my touch but the sharp intake of breath and low wanting moan gave her away, her body slumping into mine as I bit her neck.

I aligned myself best I could before I took her from behind, her on tiptoe to try to balance out the height difference. She all but screamed at the abrupt, passionate intrusion she'd yearned for.

The strokes were powerful, the pace brutal, and I knew I wouldn't last long.

Her cries morphed, alternating between pain and pleasure, rising in quick crescendo with her impending climax, echoing off the walls in the confined space. A few more seconds torturous bliss were enough to send me over the edge and I came deep within her, my large hands wrapped firmly around her bucking hips.

My forehead came to rest between her trembling shoulder blades for a second while I caught my breath. Then I was out of the shower with a towel wrapped around my waist, closing the bathroom door behind me.

What *was* that? That was the first time I'd allowed myself to slip back into my old ways; using a woman's body solely for my pleasure and gratification instead of finding solace as one. The idea sickened me, but what sickened me more was that I'd actually *enjoyed* it. I enjoyed taking some of the frustration out on her. I'd enjoyed release from the confines of the very small box I'd placed myself in.

I didn't miss the swirl of blood make its way to the drain either, spiraling around the plug before sinking into the void.

I made sure there was a fresh towel neatly folded outside the bathroom door for her, then sank down onto the couch, head in my hands.

A few moments later, Marie joined me, albeit tentatively and on the other end of the couch. I hated the idea that she was too scared to come closer. I probably repulsed her.

"I'm sorry..." I muttered from between my fingers. I'd hurt her, I knew I had. I couldn't bring myself to look at her. See the betrayal in her eyes. It felt too raw, like an exposed nerve.

"Jack, you are scaring me." When I didn't reply she shuffled closer, placing a cautious hand on my naked leg.

"*Why* are you pushing me away?" I met her soft, dark eyes which were wary and full of hurt.

"Come here, baby," I patted my lap and she slid over onto my legs, curling up into my warmth, her spill of wet hair slowly dripping over her back and the arm I had wrapped tightly around her.

I pulled the comforter from the back of the couch and draped it over her shoulders for an added layer of warmth.

"I need to understand... Please?" She whispered.

"Back then, before I went away..." I started without a clear destination to where I was headed, looking out of the window behind her and not seeing anything but distorted memories.

"April, she had preeclampsia. I didn't realize how severe it was until it was too late. Her water broke on the bathroom floor. She screamed as she pushed... but there was so much *blood*. I called 911 but they couldn't make it up in time. Her cries grew weaker and she stopped pushing... her breathing slowly... fading away." I felt the hot tears streaming down my face.

"She was in so much pain and I couldn't do anything but hold her and watch. I buried her with our unborn son still inside…" That was all I could manage. My throat felt like it was closing up.

Marie was crying too, her hand pressed over my heart. Tears dropped from the end of my nose into her towel and we just sat there, huddled together while I confessed my biggest secret. The one I swore to myself I'd take to the grave.

"I learnt a long time ago that you don't get to live a bad life and have good things happen to you… I *drove* her to that. What I did, how I treated her *caused* that. You have no idea…" the guilt ate away at me, still gnawing through me, flesh, bone and soul.

Of course, I'd never laid a finger on her, but the emotional torment I'd put her through was paramount to murder. All the nights I'd left her wondering where I was, what I was doing and with whom, and when I finally did make it home, in just about one piece and smelling like a brewery, we hardly spoke at all. Sometimes I would have been gone for days at a time, desperately trying to lose track of reality, anything to keep me from facing up to the consequences of my actions. My responsibility.

"Everyone around me just seems to… and it makes me so fuckin' *scared*."

She reached for my hand and placed it on her stomach.

"It's not about what you've done before, it's about what you do now. Me and this baby, we need you! Right from the start you've been there for me, looking out for me. You gave up everything to make sure I was okay. You're the best man I've ever known! Even if you don't..." she broke off suddenly.

"Don't what?"

"I... I don't need you to love me. You being here... your support is enough."

"You think that?" And suddenly a lot of things started to make sense. Her near-constant fear I was going to desert her. Her need to be independent, to earn money of her own. Her reluctance to open her heart to me.

She worried her mouth as she looked at me before dropping her gaze to the floor.

"Baby, you're my whole world."

She shook her head and shifted uncomfortably, but I turned her around and pressed her against me before kissing her hungrily and whispering, "I want this...I want you to have my baby, Marie..."

"I just thought... you never said..."

"I love you so fuckin' much!"

With the admission, she planted herself over me in a swift motion and dropped her mouth to mine in a touching but desperate embrace. I didn't fight it this time, I relinquished to the sweet taste of her mouth. The towel and blanket fell away as she pressed herself against me, grinding her hips down on my own in wild attempt to chase her release.

"Baby, you still wanna..."

"*Yes!*" She all but screamed, "You're not the only one who has needs, ya know!"

With a dark chuckle I surrendered to her will, not that it was a hard feat on my part, and helped guide her toward her goal. She moaned something unintelligible into my throat as she sunk down, taking a few thrusts to full seat herself. *Fuck!*

At this newfound angle, she was impossibly tight and I was utterly at her disposal. I grit my teeth as she slid up painfully slowly and sunk back down, rocking her hips into me to deepen the thrust.

"Are you…"

"Shhh!" She chided, slapping a small hand over my mouth. After a few more moments of stillness, she let out a frustrated sigh.

In anticipation of being hit again, I moved to roll her over onto her back, which she resisted at first but allowed me to do once I'd buried my face in her neck. I made my way down her body, pausing at certain points to enjoy her squirm, coming to rest with my head between her legs.

Being with Marie, someone who was so free and intimately acquainted with their own body, had its advantages. I knew what positions she preferred, what rhythms got her off the quickest. I knew how she liked to come; wholly filled so she had something to clamp down on, but she came hardest when there was a lot of pressure on the soft little spot of engorged flesh right at the top of her pussy.

So I focused my attention there, favoring the area with deep sucks and little nips, keeping my eyes fixed on her reaction. Her shaking knees and clenched jaw were an indicator she was getting close. I wet two fingers in my mouth before sliding them into her tight core. She whimpered.

"That's what you like, isn't it?"

She just panted her assent, an unspoken plea on her lips, trembling so violently I had to pin her down.

"*Stop!*" She moaned.

I paused, pulling up to look her in the eye. Did I do something wrong? Hurt her again?

She tugged on my arms, indicating she wanted me to move back up her body. I didn't have it in me to put up much of a fight. Of course, I wanted it too, to be back inside her, where I felt like I belonged.

The position was awkward in this later stage of pregnancy. I had to shift back to allow enough room but angled my hips forward in a way that still allowed us to be deeply connected.

I leaned down enough to lay a kiss over her open mouth and intertwined my fingers with hers, then I buried my face in her throat and started moving, thrusting deeply, giving myself over to her.

Again, I knew I would last long, although for entirely different reasons. She felt good, but the knowledge she was close spurred me onwards more than the stirrings of my own impending release.

She urged me on with indistinct whispers, words that I

couldn't quite hear but distinguished the meaning of. She reached down between us, fingers working over her slick, over-sensitive nerves and let out a low-pitched, keening breath.

I squeezed my eyes shut I as I surrendered to the inner battle between myself and my body.

The arrhythmic movements reached a fevered intensity before she convulsed around me. For a few heartbeats, I was immobilized as I resisted against the straining tendons and tautened muscles, before the impending tidal wave of pleasure crashed down around me as well. I came, hard, in unrelenting pulses that left me both hoarse and breathless.

Marie pulled my face up to meet hers, and laid a soft, wet kiss on my lips. She brushed her thumbs over my cheeks, whispering things I'd thought I'd never hear anyone say to me. I pulled her against my chest as tightly as I dared, tucking her head under my chin. We stayed like that for a time, while outside the sky darkened and sleet began fall. It beat a steady cadence against the thick redwood cedar of the cabin, which muffled the sound into a continuous, soothing undertone, lulling us into sleep.

"How many tours did you do?"

"Eight."

"Did you see a lot of combat?"

I could only nod through the thick feeling in my throat

growing larger. It wasn't something I wanted to remember.

"Afghanistan 2001 to 2003. Iraq, 2003. We were only there twenty-six days. The worst by far."

Early morning sunrise over the desert was so peaceful. Deceptive.

The permanent layer dust that coated every surface, no matter static or mobile. The repeated sound of gunfire that carried over the vast expanse and stayed with you long after the last shot had been fired. The men that were gunned down dead right in front of your eyes and even worse, the ones who suffered.

"So, Iraq was where you…"

"Yeah," I filled her in on the details.

"They discharged you for saving those boys?"

"The enemy, apparently, don't deserve to be saved."

"But they were children."

I nodded, "I'd also had previous warnings, not getting on with others in the team. Fighting with them. *'Difficult personality*." I finished with air quotes.

"I doubt you would have started anything the other guys didn't deserve."

I shrugged, "I guess I just didn't believe in the cause anymore…"

What the cause was specifically, I was never sure on. It

seemed wherever we were they wanted us gone, no matter what we were trying to gain, what side we were fighting for. The other men fought for immeasurable reasons; for honor, for their country, for their families to be proud of them. Some wanted to find a purpose. Some plainly for bragging rights, and the darker side no one talked about; for personal, financial gain.

There were also those naive souls who were out looking for adventure and no other way of funding it. Those were the ones who usually got sent back home, either under self-imposed misconduct discharge or in a box.

Unlike the others, I didn't have anybody waiting back home for me, whether I arrived there alive or otherwise. I had no home.

Home happened to be wherever I'd laid my head that particular night. Now, with Marie, I'd seen a reason, found a myriad of things to be appreciative of. Being under the open sky with no boundaries, no restrictions. A bed that didn't leave me with an aching back come morning. Fresh coffee. Clean clothes. Someone waiting for me.

Without realizing, my hand had come to rest over Marie's belly. A strong little nudge against my palm brought me back from my contemplation.

"The fuck was *that*?"

"His foot, I think?"

I withdrew my hand, pulling up the hem of her shirt. A small lump protruded out of Marie's rounded stomach, then just as quickly as it appeared, it retreated back then lurched forward again in little jabbing movements.

"Jesus, looks like he's pummeling you from the inside out. Be careful, kiddo. that's my girl you're picking on!"

Marie laughed softly, "He's been kicking loads recently. Haven't seen anything until now though."

"Does that hurt? It looks pretty violent."

"No, not at all. It feels weird though, like there is an octopus in my belly or something."

I bent down, placing my lips over her skin, "Hey there, little octopus, settle down." The jabbing stopped and the little bump pushed gently against his confines, right against my mouth. I placed a kiss on it and looked up at Marie, who had a tear resting in the corner of her eye.

"I love you both so much," I told her, drawing up to kiss her too.

"We love you too, Daddy." She whispered back.

Chapter Twenty-Four

MARIE

The third trimester brought with it an inner feeling of rightness. I'd already gone through what the book called the "nesting phase" where I'd found myself re-washing and re-sorting baby clothes at strange hours, organizing the already tidy kitchen cupboards and deep-cleaning the bathroom until it shone.

Jack got a little worried when he found me on my hands and knees trying to clear non-existent dust bunnies out from under the couch at three in the morning.

I was becoming increasingly exhausted now I was approaching the due date, although it was still weeks away, but the earlier sickness, and later nausea, I'd been experiencing had all but vanished.

This was replaced by sudden cravings in the middle of the night, particularly Cheez-It's with peanut butter, terrible mood swings and underneath it all, a constant yearning for something that I couldn't quite put my finger on. I could hardly eat half a sandwich in one go, or tie my shoelaces myself, or roll over in bed without considerable effort, but I was strangely enjoying my last few weeks of pregnancy.

"Well, aren't you getting big now," Dina mentioned one morning as I was placing the coffee pot back on the hot plate at the diner.

I smiled at her, "Don't I know it. My back is killing me!"

"Have as many breaks as you need, okay hun. We're not busy."

She was right, there was only one customer; a vaguely familiar, grey-bearded man tucked into the far booth, who hadn't required much attention. In the hour or so he'd been sitting there, he'd only indicated a refill on coffee once, and seemingly hadn't much appetite for anything more. But he kept to himself, filling in the crossword in the paper and occasionally checking his phone.

"Thanks, Dina. But I'm fine at the moment."

"Just let us know," She patted my shoulder and shuffled off in the direction of the back room.

Lisa, who turned out to be Dina's great-niece, was also on shift and was wiping down the counter absently while immersed in a news report running on the TV in the corner.

"In other news, Nicholas Hayes, founder of Hayes Enterprises, has released a statement this morning announcing his resignation from the board of directors. This comes after allegations of systematic fraud amidst senior management. Among those under investigation include Chuck Blake, former CFO, and Jean Thibodeaux, former General Counsel. Both have been missing since October."

Images of them filled the screen; Chuck's close-up looked like it could have been a mug shot whereas Jean's was hazy, as if taken from a great distance.

Lisa, no longer under the pretense of cleaning, slid onto one of the stools and slipped a straw into her can of cola.

"These new developments follow the disappearance of Hayes's wife, Marie, whose whereabouts have been unknown since September. Law enforcement are not treating her disappearance as suspicious." Another picture flashed over the screen, showing Nicholas with his hand draped around the back of my neck at an event.

"You know, that girl kinda looks like you, Layla..." Lisa commented, chewing thoughtfully on her straw.

I forced out a laugh, hoping it sounded disbelieving.

"I wish I was as pretty as that!"

She looked at me like I was crazy. "Are you kidding! You two could be twins."

I just rolled my eyes and headed over to refill the salt shakers, praying that she wouldn't figure out who I really was and call into CCN's tip line.

I'd finally managed to find a comfortable sleeping position on my side and drift off when the arm that was wrapped around me jerked, pulling me out of my relaxed state. I turned my head and tried to make out his expression through the darkness. He shuddered again and ground out a few indistinct words.

"Huh?" I whispered, reaching around to run my fingers through his hair.

It was then I felt his need pressing into the small of my

back.

"Let me," he rumbled again with more conviction, half-conscious, half-immersed in the unearthly confusion of an erotic dream. His hips surged forwards blindly, seeking acceptance.

I knew if he was fully awake, fully aware of the situation, he would never ask to use my body in this way. He was the most unselfish lover I'd ever known. I smiled to myself at the need in his movements, in the desire that painted his words and the promise that both would bring complete satisfaction.

I murmured my consent as I shuffled my sleep shorts down over my butt and angled myself toward him. The arm around my middle slipped down and his hand cupped my crotch possessively.

I moaned and rolled over onto my back with some difficulty. The maneuver jolted him out of his semi-conscious state and he whipped his hand away. The next second he'd leaned over and switched the bedside lamp on.

Stunned by the quick change in light, I blinked dazedly and tried to focus on Jack's face. His eyes were trained on mine, the conflict very apparent, desire dwindling away, leaving trepidation in its place.

I'd come to understand that protecting me was his top priority, and in some distorted sense of morality, he'd categorized himself as the biggest, meanest bastard around. He was terrified that what he wanted would push me away, that in wanting what he did, he would fuck it all up. And he didn't realize that was the one thing I needed from him most. His honesty.

I didn't want his restraint, or silence. I didn't want what he thought was good for me. I wanted all of him, however he came.

I reached over him, cradling his bewhiskered cheek in my palm.

"Let me do something for you, this time."

Then I slid down, as gracefully as I could manage, coming to rest between his already bare thighs. His manhood stood conspicuously, virile and weeping with need.

I leant down, brushing the head of his thick cock over my tingling lips, and tasting the wetness that gathered there.

"*Sweetjesus!*" He breathed.

A large hand reached down and cupped the back of my head, fingers twisting up into my hair. His hips bucked instinctively, unable to express his need in any other way.

As I took him into my mouth, his breathing all but stopped. Eyes flicking shut, grunting softly with each intake, letting out a coarse groan, shuddering every time the tip hit the back of my throat. The hand in my hair tightened, short nails scraping against my scalp.

With another rough spasm, he swore and then pushed me away.

I only had a few moments confusion before the room whirled around and my back came into contact with the mattress. Jack's weight pressed down over me, both comforting and exhilarating. He leaned down to press his lips over mine, before joining us together with a shared groan of relief. With every thrust, he touched that sweet spot inside me. His hands found and enclosed my own, weaving his fingers between mine.

He buried his face in my neck, increasing the speed of his movements, chasing his passion with increasing intensity. My breath came in short, sharp pants of need, reaching closer, higher with every shift of his powerful body.

And then he stilled, pushed into me so deeply I could barely breathe and shuddered. Unable to keep back the guttural moan that accompanied each wet pulse.

I watched his eyes as he came, which unexpectedly and unabashedly never left my own. The openness of it stunned me into silence, sharing in that moment of pure vulnerability that most people could search for their entire lives and never find.

Once he'd ridden out the last of the violent surges, his forehead slumped to mine, nothing but a thin sheen of perspiration between us.

"If I ever lose you…" it came out in more than a whisper, his throat tightened with emotion.

Just when I thought I was beginning to know this man, there was another barrier to break through, a thousand invisible walls separating us. Someday, I hoped I'd be lucky enough to understand him without the need for intervention, but for now, we still needed to exchange a few words.

I could barely breathe myself, but managed to force out a

reply, "You won't."

But the beads of moisture that dropped onto my forehead and ran down to hide in my hairline told me that he didn't believe me.

So he said I couldn't cook, huh? Well, he'd be saying something different when he got home and had a mouthful of the pineapple upside-down cake cooling on the counter. Old-fashioned, I know, but I'd found a promotional leaflet from the seventies wedged between the back of the cupboard and a broken food processor. The delicious aroma that floated through the air as the cake cooked reminded me of the old housekeeper from my childhood, Betty. She would bake a different cake every Thursday afternoon and I would sit on the worktop and lick the mixing bowl clean while she told me stories about growing up in New Orleans.

I was washing up the cake pans when I heard Jack come in. Strange, I normally heard the truck first, although perhaps I wasn't listening out for it yet. It was still light out and I didn't expect him home until the sun had almost completely disappeared over the crest of the nearby mountain peaks.

"Hey, baby," I called without turning my head, "You're home early?" Jack put something heavy down by the front door before locking it.

"I've just finished packing up our clothes. I'll need your help with the rest of the stuff tomorrow."

Jack still didn't reply. I knew he was a man of little words but he would have at least greeted me by now. Wondering if something had happened, I turned and gasped, dropping the glass bowl I was drying to the floor. The shattered pieces flew off in all directions.

It was Nicholas. Nicholas was standing in the middle of my living room.

His smile was solely predatory, twisted into mock surprise, "Hello, doll."

I was standing behind the kitchen island in the open plan space, shielding my rounded belly from view. I didn't want him to know about this baby at all. What if he figured out it could be his? Then I would never be able to escape him.

"H...how did you find me?"

"I have my ways," Came his offhand reply.

"You've been having me followed, haven't you?"

"Naturally, babe. I had to make sure you were safe."

I swallowed audibly, "Well, I'm fine."

"Are you going to come back home now? Stop all this bullshit?"

"No, Nic. It's over. I want a divorce."

He eyed me, his hungry gaze made me uneasy.

"It's not over till I say it is. Don't think I don't know what you did?" I could see the calm façade crumbling away, the hairline cracks formed before deepening.

"What?" I replied trying to make my feigned confusion sound genuine but I could feel the flush building in my cheeks. All around the cabin were pointers of mine and Jack's life together; a row of shoes by the front door, washing drying by the fire, Jack's belt draped over the arm of a chair.

"You and him! You *fucking* my BROTHER!" He shouted the last word, his rage getting the better of him.

"You know what?" His tone changed to one of bitter contemplation in a second, "I thought it was Jean for the longest time. I didn't figure it out until you were gone."

I worked to push back the tears I felt were going to overwhelm me at any second. I was heavily pregnant and alone; this was the last thing I needed. Nic wasn't supposed to find me! He wasn't supposed to find out about us!

I sneaked a look over to the back door, which which closed but thankfully unlocked, trying to figure out if I could make it out before Nicholas caught up with me. Although the broken bowl would be a problem; My feet were bare and would be shredded by the glass.

He shook his head groggily, like a dog trying to rid its ears of water.

"Please, Nic. You have to leave!"

"The only way I'm leaving is if you're coming with me."

Nic ignored me and came over to where I stood. "Just as I

suspected," He raised his hands to hold my belly and I jerked away from him the best I could without moving my feet.

"Reckon you are almost ready to pop. When is the little fucker due?"

"About three month's time," I answered all too quickly.

Nicholas shook his head a little as he gave me a sad smile, leaning in so he could whisper in my ear. I smelt the all too familiar liquor on his stale breath as he breathed out the single word, *"Liar!"*

It was then I tried to make a run for it. I turned and bolted to the back door, the jagged shards of glass cut into my feet making me cry out but not slowing me down. I wrenched the door open and bolted into the snow-blanketed garden, leaving a blotchy red trail behind me.

I didn't know where I was going but I had to get as far away from that monster as I could. I couldn't even think about what he was going to do to me. All those months of nightmares converged into one terrifying montage as I fled for my life.

What would he do to the baby? In the wild, male predators killed any offspring of its mate sired with another to be sure they wouldn't be a threat. When angered, Nicholas could be far more feral than any wild animal.

I got as far as the tree line when I twisted my ankle in a shallow, snow-covered ditch, landing heavily on my hip. Sickening pain radiated through my side but I continued struggling through the thick bank of powdery snow with all my strength until I felt his fingers close around my leg. I screamed and kicked out but he had a tight grip on my ankle, yanking me back toward him.

"You can't get away from me, babe. No matter where you run."

I begged him to let me go, not to hurt my baby. Something must have gotten through to him because he sobered a little and loosened his grasp.

"Come back into the house. You'll freeze to death out here."

I disentangled myself from the bottom branches of a fir tree with some difficulty before allowing Nicholas to carry me back inside, the soles of my feet stinging from the glass shards embedded in them. He deposited me none too gently on the couch before falling down beside me.

I placed a shaky hand on my belly to check the damage. I held my breath until I felt the reassuring nudges I had been experiencing since the start of the last trimester against my palm.

"Here's the thing with you," he started, "You seem don't understand that I'm in charge! See, we married when you were barely seventeen. Your daddy had to consent to your marriage which technically placed you under my guardianship."

"Nic, I'm sure that's not legally corr..." He brought a thick finger to my lips to hush me before starting on a different tangent.

"The day you left me tore me up. I need you back in my life, doll," He brought his hand down from my mouth to hold my belly. I felt sick.

"I promise I'll be a better husband. I'll spend more time with you. I want to be there for you and my baby. I'll go to counseling, therapy, whatever you need."

"It's too late for that…" I tried to reason with him.

"Please, baby. *Please!*" He pleaded, trying to snuggle into my neck. I was utterly repulsed by him. After having my eyes opened by Jack, I couldn't believe I was so blinded by this man's bullshit. That I could have gone on struggling to understand why he did what he did to me, and in turn made me believe I wasn't worth a dime.

He kissed my cheeks and caressed my body, rubbing places I didn't feel comfortable with him touching anymore.

"Nic, get off me…" I moaned, trying to push him off. When he didn't comply and his unwelcome touches became more urgent, I tried slapping him off.

In desperate attempt, I grasped the nearest object to hand, a hardwood photo frame resting on the side table, and bashed him in the head with it, hoping it was hard enough to knock him out.

He howled in pain and rolled off, cursing, "*The fuck?*" he looked back at me, an angry glint in his eye. I saw him spy Jack's belt on the end of the chair and he made a dive for it.

"Okay, *okay!*" I held an arm up to protect myself and one around my stomach. I still had a scar on my hip from the last time he held a belt when I was in the room.

"Put your arms and legs together," He leered, "Do it, Marie. Do it or I'll make you sorry." I was shaking uncontrollably as he bound my limbs together.

After making sure I was secure, Nicholas walked slowly around the cabin surveying things he didn't get a good look at the first time. He paused to review things, like the small pile of baby clothes I'd washed and folded in preparation to be packed. He half snorted, half sighed as he picked up a tiny knitted bootie, "Nice place you got here."

He pulled an unopened bottle of whisky from a bag near the door and slugged it down in large, greedy gulps, "*That* makes it so much more bearable." He opened another drawer and grinned back up at me. He'd found the cable ties.

"Now, I'm going to bind your hands with these," he held up the cable ties. They were made of thick, tough plastic, "And you are going to walk into the bedroom with me."

Nicholas let out a sob of pain. A chilling, primitive sound. I'd never seen him cry before and the realization stunned me. He wiped his eyes with the back of a trembling hand. The liquor he'd consumed hadn't been enough to overcome the shakes but enough to render his dick useless. Whatever he'd planned for me wasn't going to work unless his right-hand man complied. I'd never been gladder in my life.

I had watched him devour at least a third of the bottle

while he continued to poke around in every corner of the house, as if searching for physical evidence against me. Once he'd come up with nothing, he sat across the bedroom, intermittently swigging, and I watched as his vision slid more and more out of focus.

"You... *betrayed* me," he whispered, and I could hear how broken he was from his disjointed words.

"Did you ever think of what I've *done* for you? All my responsibilities? I gave you EVERYTHING!"

"Not everything. I was *never* enough for you!"

Nicholas rubbed at his red eyes, scouring away the wetness with the heel of his hand. He reminded me of a child who'd fallen over and skinned his knee.

"Your thing is control," I continued, "You need to control people. You need to have control over yourself, every element of your life needs to be calculated. I can't live like that, Nic. No one can."

"You think I don't hate myself in the morning? When I wake up and look in the mirror, do you think I feel nothing? Believe me, if I could stop just like that I would have done a long time ago."

He paused, glaring at the bottle of amber liquid in his hands, like he was examining the way the light reflected through the glass.

I winced, wishing I'd asked him to untie me. The way my hands were restrained were digging into my back, and the fall I'd had earlier was now making it ache something fierce. Not to mention the state of my feet, which were pulsating with pain. I was also dying to use the bathroom.

"You never loved me, did you?" the words fell from his mouth as he slumped back against the wall in defeat.

I could only blink at him. I did, once. A long time ago.

"I just..." Nicholas stopped to clear his throat. It wasn't like him to have trouble finding the right words. The man never explained himself nor did he find the need to.

My chest filled with icy comprehension. He was going to do something he couldn't entirely justify.

He pulled out a thick roll of gaffer tape from the bag he'd brought in, and a hypodermic syringe, the needle of which was visible through the pale green plastic of the cap. It was wicked-looking, two inches long, and filled with a clear liquid.

"What's that for?" I tried to swallow my panic but my mouth was too dry and the terror sounded in my voice. My vision started to warp and grow dim around the edges.

"Just try and relax, babe. It'll be better for you if you do."

The last thing I saw before I passed out was Nic approaching me with the needle un-capped.

Chapter Twenty-Five

JACK

It had been another long day and I couldn't wait to get home to Marie. The due date was only four weeks away, so we needed to move closer to a hospital. I was taking no chances this time.

Hoping to get back to a warm house, I climbed into the rusted Nissan Navara that had served us well for the last few months, and gratefully turned on the heater.

Although in bad shape, the pick-up was spacious, with seats in back and front, and had a generous, covered truck bed that met our needs. I'd already fitted the baby seat in the front, rear facing with the airbag deactivated, as the back was reserved for all of the things we'd need to pack into it that weekend.

Piled onto the middle seat next to me were a small heap of clothes for Marie. Her belly had gotten so big that she couldn't fit into her maternity clothes anymore. I assured her I didn't mind if she wanted to wear mine, but she pointed out she couldn't go around wearing jeans that were twelve inches too long, and she had a point.

I couldn't help smiling to myself as I recalled the way she'd looked when I'd left her this morning, sprawled over my side of the bed in nothing but one of my flannel shirts unbuttoned to the waist, a pink nipple peeping out, one bare leg slung across a pillow. She had a hand curled underneath her chin and was snoring ever so slightly, which I found endearing more than anything else. I kissed her between the eyebrows, gently so I wouldn't wake her, and backed out of the bedroom.

There are words to describe love, but none of them seemed to convey the magnitude, the depth of something I wouldn't even be able to begin to explain. Imperfect yet profound. Untamable. That's how it felt inside the confines of my own heart. There just weren't words big enough to articulate the feelings I held for her. The woman carrying my child. The woman who brought joy into my life like sunshine after eternal night. The woman I loved. The woman who loved me back.

The days were crisp, almost but not quite biting cold now it was nearing the end of March, although It still got dark much too early for my liking. The journey home was long; roads that twisted through frozen trails and forested ridges. Despite the journey's tedious length, the landscape was still beautiful. Tranquil and undisturbed by man. The lingering scent of wilderness fresh on the air, promising freedom and a simpler way of life. I cracked the window to feel the flow of it against my skin, sharp and pure.

Eventually, I turned in and pulled up in the clearing. All we had was a bit of dirt and some wood. It wasn't much, not by half, but it was home.

I sniffed the air, hopeful, wondering if there was something good for dinner. The house was in shadow, which was unusual; Marie hated the dark and usually left the porch light on for me. The first indicator something was wrong.

Then I felt it. A sudden, implicit hostility that raised the hairs on my arms and the back of my neck. With an uneasy weight in the pit of my stomach, I approached the door and grasped the handle. Unlocked. Something definitely wasn't right. All the doors and windows would usually be shut and bolted at the first hint of sundown.

"M're?" I called out.

No reply. I shut the door behind me and flicked on the light. The power must have been out, the switch was useless. My heart pounded against my chest as I took a few hesitant steps forward.

"Well well, Jackie. What a surprise seeing you here," The voice was calm, yet grave. He struck a match and lit a cigar, Cuban by the familiar smell.

Nicholas' face came faintly into view, illuminated by the small flame. He used it to light a candle next to him. His face, twisted in a dark mask of anger, seemed to be disfigured in the half-light. I took a step forward.

"Where is she?"

"You've been a busy boy, haven't you, Jack! Stealing my wife away, impregnating her and playing house with the little *slut*!" A bottle of something sloshed around as he twisted his wrist in slow methodical movements.

I stepped forward a few more steps, "Where. Is. she?" I repeated, enunciating each smoldering word.

"I wouldn't do anything rash, brother," Nic raised his other hand slightly and I froze. Resting on his leg was a compact pistol. The one taken from under his mattress. The one I'd armed Marie with to keep her safe.

"This whole time I thought you were someone I could trust. You saved my life once and I felt I would be forever in your debt," Nic was glowering at me, the raw pain in his eyes in the dimness made them look utterly black. He took a large slug from the bottle. The three remaining fingers of liquid shone like copper in the candlelight.

He let out a chilling, primitive laugh.

"I brought you into my house, my world. I opened up my heart to you when you had nowhere else to go. I gave you a job when nobody in their right mind would. I *trusted* you!" He got to his feet with surprising speed.

"Then you take my FUCKING WIFE!!" He screamed, spit flying from his mouth. The fallen cigar's hot bud glowed in its resting place against the rug before being extinguished by Nicholas' left shoe.

"Nic, take it easy, okay? Let me explain."

"*Explain*? How can you *explain* that! She left me a note saying she needed time to think about our marriage. She didn't mention you! She didn't mention *a baby*!"

"You were pressuring her. She wasn't ready for that," I spoke in a low voice, hands raised in the universally recognized gesture of compliance.

"How come she is pregnant now, then? You can't tell me she was ready for that with *you*?" The way his tone twisted the word '*you*' made it sound like wet shit hitting a wall. Like I was an inferior being, not a contender, not even in his league. Like I was nothing.

I let it slide only because of the gun staring me in the face at point-blank range.

I closed my eyes and let out a breath, "She was pregnant when we left."

"So the baby *is* mine?" There was a malicious glint in Nicholas' eye.

"Well, there's half a chance..."

"So you *were* fucking her in my house! I asked you to watch her not fuckin' take her away from me!"

He sobered for a second, "You know, I was switching her birth control. A few months before you even arrived I was giving her sugar pills instead of the regular ones."

I couldn't believe what he was saying. What he had done was unspeakable. If it wasn't enough to act the way he did, tormenting her, he'd forced Marie into making his choices too.

"You...*what*?"

"She's my wife. If I tell her we're having a kid, we're having a kid."

Apart from this backward way of thinking being completely mid-century, it was also an invasion of privacy, inarguably coercion, and worse, it broke one of the most meaningful sanctities of marriage.

There were no words to describe how disgusted I was with him. The man I had once called brother. The man who had raised me. I was nothing like him. Our core values were worlds apart. The minimal slither of respect I still had left for him died in that moment.

"Where is Marie?" I ground out through my teeth.

Nicholas smiled then, a volatile, wholly black smile.

"She's sleeping in the other room."

"If you fuckin' hurt her, I swear to God..."

"Why would I hurt my own wife?"

"Because you're a bastard!" I spat at him. Why spare him the details now.

Nicholas smirked at me again, his canines reared out wickedly in the semi-darkness. He looked truly monstrous, an incarnation of the beast who lived inside him. My own brother standing before me with a gun aimed at my head, inhuman, his eyes shining madly.

"You first, big man," Giving him a wide berth, I made my way to the bedroom. The fireplace had burnt out long ago and the room was uninvitingly cold. It was so dark I couldn't see. Nicholas poked me in the small of my back with something hard and heavy. A flash light.

I clicked it on. What I saw knocked all the air from my lungs. Numbness washed over me like I'd been plunged into freezing water. Water that paralyzes, consumes you entirely, until you can't think about anything else. You can't even draw breath because when you do the numbness turns to sharp, stabbing agony.

Marie's limp form was huddled in the center of the mattress, facing toward me, pale and bloodless. Her eyes were half open and unmoving, fragile wrists bound together so tightly her hands were deathly white.

442

"*Marie!!*" I rushed to her and put my fingers to her neck, checking for a pulse. For what felt like entity, I held my breath. Then I felt something. It was weak but steady. A heartbeat.

There was a pink-tinged stain beneath her, the mattress sodden, and flecked with darker splotches which were unmistakably blood. Her water had broken.

I turned and advanced on Nic. His arm was steady and his eyes were boring into mine.

"What have you done!" I growled. My mind was blank. All I could think about was protecting my girl, my child. I'd let him harm them. He could have killed them both. I may have been able to examine Marie but there was no way to determine the baby's condition without medical intervention, but that discolored wet patch on the bed was anything to go by, things didn't look good.

The rage inside me took control, rearing. Swelling. Filling me with an all-consuming, wild thirst for vengeance.

I continued prowling toward him until my forehead was resting squarely on the muzzle of the gun.

"Shoot me. Go on!" I didn't blink, staring into my brother's eyes, challenging him. Begging for another reason, the final provocation.

"FUCKIN' SHOOT ME!!" I yelled. But he didn't. Even in his irrational, hateful state, he didn't want me dead.

I took advantage of his hesitation, slamming my forearm into him and knocking the weapon to the floor. My years of being in the armed forces were going to help me now. I wanted Nicholas to feel the pain he had put her through. I wanted him to hurt like I did. I wanted him to *bleed*.

The first blow to his midsection knocked the wind out of him, the second and third came in quick succession, heavy jabs to the face. As the last made contact with his nose, it gave a sickening crunch as the cartilage broke. He fell to the floor, disorientated.

Blood trickled down over Nic's mouth, coloring his teeth crimson. He held his hand out, spat a mouthful of blood. Then in a sneak move, he swiped his leg out and took me down with him. The back of my head cracked against something solid, making white shots of lightning burst across my vision and bile rise in my throat.

He took that opportunity to roll on top me, hitting with more force than I would have expected. He got a few good shots in before I managed to knock him off.

We both made it to our feet at the same time, Nicolas swaying, a sneer fixed on his face, "Give me all you got."

He fought well, although without skill, but after a while, skill didn't come into the count. Even for me, a trained fighter. There was too much at stake and Nicholas fought dirty. No finesse, just pure, brutal force.

The blows came in feverish waves. I gave only a few more than I took, the knock to the head still ringing through me. I welcomed it, wanting to feel them. Wanting to suffer, I could take it. I'd taken a lot worse in my time. The pain wasn't as bad as the suffering I'd endured, and even that would fade into insignificance with what would happen if I couldn't save her.

He managed to get to the kitchen and pull a long serrated knife from the block standing on the counter. Like hell that was going to stop me! It was brighter here, the moon was full and gleaming in all its blazing glory.

I advanced on Nic fast, blocking his stabs. Although his movements were well slowed by alcohol, the knife still managed to slash through my shoulder. My arm should have been burning from the damaged sinew and muscle but I couldn't feel a damn thing.

That final action pushed me past breaking point. He was never going to leave us, leave Marie, alone. He was too jealous, too possessive to let us live in peace. I wished it could have ended in some other way, *any* other way, but I knew that I would be deluding myself. I needed to keep him away from my family for good.

So I grasped hold of the knife with my good arm and pulled it from Nicholas' grip and in one strike, I plunged it deep into his abdomen.

He made no sound. I watched his eyes widen, disbelieving. He fell to his knees, shaking hands scrambling at the handle. The knife was edgy but dulled from decades of use, barely sharp enough to cut through bread let alone flesh.

Nicholas pulled it out jerkily. He looked up at me, in his eyes a different kind of pain. Pure physical pain.

"Now GET OUT!" I screamed in his face.

The wound *might* not kill him if he put pressure on it and sought medical attention. By that time, I would have taken

Marie somewhere far *far* away.

Marie!! The adrenaline poured out of my veins as if they'd been sliced open. I rushed to her, checked her pulse again, beating, and shone the flashlight in her eyes. Her pupils dilated quickly. A good sign. I carefully scooped her up, draping the blanket from the couch over her on the way out to the truck.

Nicholas was nowhere in sight. There were small pools of scarlet in places where he'd fled, hot blood melting the snow. I didn't care where he went. I half hoped he would bleed to death but I didn't want my own brother dead by my hand, no matter how destructive he was. No matter how much I hated him. All I could keep telling myself was; it was the only way.

Running back inside to grab a few essentials, I found a palm-sized glass vial on the floor and quickly pocketed it. Pain was coursing through my body now, a dull throbbing starting in my shoulder and radiating through me. I slung a hastily packed duffle bag across my good shoulder and rushed back to the car.

"Mmm, Jaacc…"

"Yeah, baby? I'm here. You're safe."

Her chest rose and fell in shallow pants, and there was a crescent-shaped cut still bleeding around her left eye.

"Can you feel the baby? Is he still moving?" Her eyes rolled in their sockets, she wasn't with me yet. I gave her belly a gentle rub, climbed in the front seat and threw the car into reverse. The car spun around and we pelted off into the darkness.

The roads were clear of traffic, not even a patrol car in sight. Not that that would have stopped me. I sped down the highway at ninety, keeping my gaze firmly on the road.

By the time we'd hit the interstate, it had started snowing heavily. Snowflakes as large as dollar coins were spiraling toward the windscreen as I drove, obscuring the view.

Every thirty seconds or so, I would glance at Marie in the rearview. I'd placed her lying down across the back seats, all the seat belts done up around her. I didn't want her sliding around in my haste to get her to the hospital but I also didn't want to risk the pressure of the belt on her belly.

As we came to the town limits leaving Bertrner, flashing lights came into few and I slowed as much as I dared. On the opposite side of the road, an articulated truck lay on its side, along with other pieces of debris from another less fortunate vehicle.

What remained of the car was burning, the tall flames throwing long, writhing shadows over the backdrop of the trees, bringing the little that remained into sharp relief and sending billowing clouds of smoke into the dark sky.

As soon as the wreckage was out of sight, I sped away.

St Christopher's Hospital was an ugly structure. The outside a chalky red brick, angular and awkward in the flat landscape. It was technically US territory but it wasn't hard to see why they'd disowned it. The land was sparse and unforgiving, cold wind whipping around the corners of the building.

I wasn't allowed in the waiting room. I'd kicked up one hell of a fuss when they told me I wasn't allowed to be with Marie, yelled at a nurse when she couldn't give me an update, and almost hit the doctor when he said he'd call security if I didn't leave.

My shoulder wasn't bleeding anymore thanks to the truck's emergency kit but it probably needed stitches and proper dressing. I huffed the cold air once more before deciding to swallow my pride and apologize.

As I walked into reception, the girl at the desk looked up at me fearfully, having witnessed my previous outburst, "Sir, I think you should go back outside."

"Listen, I'm sorry about earlier but this probably needs attention…" I pulled the edge of the collar down to show the stained wadding and vest. She swallowed audibly and pressed a call button on the desk.

"I've called a nurse down. Please, wait over there," She pointed to a spot as far from the reception desk as possible, right near the entranceway.

"Thanks," I tried to smile at her but she recoiled from me. Catching sight of my reflection in the polished sliding door, I could see why. My face was swollen and gruesome looking, mottled with purpling bruises, eyes scarlet from burst capillaries. There were streaks of blood in my beard and over the scars on my cheek where any nose had bled and dried.

"Sir?"

I turned to see a young male nurse. He looked at me apprehensively at first, but seemed to relax once he saw the tension leave my body.

"You're not going to cause any more trouble, am I right?"

"I didn't wanna cause trouble in the first place..." I was just worried about Marie. He seemed to understand.

"Come with me," He beckoned me to follow into a private examination room.

"I'm Jack," I offered. He nodded. I took off my shirt and dressings as he doused a large cotton pad in rubbing alcohol. His name tag said Carl.

"This might sting a bit."

"Whatever," I replied. It did sting but nothing I couldn't take.

"Don't bother numbing it for the stitches either," I growled through my teeth. Carl ignored my comment and injected me with some morphine. Turns out they stapled skin back together now.

I was lucky, it seemed. The knife had missed my subclavian artery by inches, and although I'd bled a lot, it wasn't as bad as it could have been. I was spared the details, although I knew a few men who'd either bled out or drowned in their own arterial blood from shoulder injuries of similar severity.

"Looks like you have been through the wars tonight, Jack." Carl offered in way of conversation.

"Yeah, thanks for fixing up my arm Doc, but I gotta get back to my girl. D'ya know where she is?"

"Sorry, I don't know who you are talking about?" Carl looked genuinely confused which irritated me. I needed to keep my cool in case I got sent out again.

"Small woman, dark hair? *Pregnant*? She's in labour! They… *took her*… away from me…" Jesus fucking Christ! I was shaking again, my head spinning in dizzying circles.

"Calm down, Jack. Let me take you to the maternity unit. She may be in surgery."

Surgery?! My vision swayed as the morphine took a more dominant role. Dazed, I stumbled after Carl down the hallway. All I could see was a swirl of pale, sickly green walls. Was she okay? Where was she? *Marie?*

Two pairs of strong hands pushed me down into a seat. I heard people conversing in hushed tones not far away but I couldn't see where they were coming from. I only caught snippets. *Fetus. Breech. High-risk. Fatality.*

"*Please?*" I called out to no one in particular, "*Please?*" Carl bent down to my eye level; his face swam half into focus.

"Jack, listen to me. Marie and baby are in critical condition. The baby's heartbeat is weak, and Marie is in surgery right now!" The rest of his words were downed out by panic. *All they can. Best place. Save them.*

"I... I don't understand?" I managed to slur, or I thought I did. Please don't let her die. My world only kept on turning because she was in it.

"You need to wait here until we have some news for you, okay? Can you do that for me, Jack?"

I slumped down against the wall at the far end of the corridor. The doors to my future were ahead of me. Facing my density. The gates to heaven.

Next to me was a hospital bag Marie had prepared, I must have brought it in from the car. The corner of a blue fleecy blanket poked out of a partially zipped compartment. I pulled it out slowly, the fuzzy softness comforting, the only thing I could focus on.

My legs came up to my chest and buried my face in the blanket, letting the darkness swarm up and allow the consuming thoughts to finally cause my brain tick over. Why could I never be better, try harder? It was like it was hard-wired into me to fail. Programmed to be broken.

All I could focus on was the hurt. Despite what had been drilled into me as a kid, the space behind my eyes was burning. This was something I didn't know how to deal with.

There was pain and then there was *hurt*. Pain was a fist to the temple, the nasty aching in your head. Pain was a well-aimed bullet ripping through your flesh. Pain was temporary. Hurt was a whole other kind of ball game. It stayed with you. Lived inside you. Twisting with your soul in a maddening dance. It wouldn't ever let you forget that it's there.

Life gave me another chance at everything I'd ever wanted. And I still managed to fuck it up.

If anyone were to ask, I'd say this. There *were* times I'd wanted to end my life. It was a cowardly way out, I know, but there were days where the darkness stretched on into meaningless oblivion and the temporary warmth of a woman's arms couldn't keep the unrelenting cold at bay. Sleep never brought peace; I envied those who used sleep as a means of escape. I stared back at the reflection of a face I hated only through association with the disfigured soul that burned behind it.

If somebody cared enough to ask now, the answer would have only changed slightly. I'd ask for you, Marie, and then permission to die.

———————————————————————

At some point later in time, those doors opened, and from within shone a pure, transcendental white light. I was led through them, guided beyond. Was this it?

"Jack," you say. Tears fill your eyes, "It's your baby girl."

Slowly, more things came into focus. The glow around you dissipates. The strong, steady bleep bleep of a heart monitor. A half-moon cut around your eye, crusted with dried blood but streaked with sweat.

"Jack?" She said again. Then she smiled weakly, but with joy I'd not seen in such a long time. Joy I thought I'd never see again. She was pale, her lips grey. A nurse beside her helps support a tiny bundle in her frail arms.

A single sob escaped my throat and I almost choked on it. Overcome with emotion, I kissed her head. Then her cheeks. Then all over her face as she chuckled lightly.

"Want to say hello to Daddy?" she whispered to the swaddle in her arms.

Marie gave me the best smile she could manage, "Don't look so scared."

I sat in a chair across from the bed and the little bundle was placed in my arms. I was so afraid of hurting such a tiny, delicate thing, I didn't dare move an inch.

"You want to see her face?" the nurse asked. I nodded once, hesitant.

I carefully looked down at the alien face of the baby. It was actually kinda cute in a way I wasn't expecting. Her eyes opened for me, dark brown and captivating. Her nose was a little dimple of a button. She had a fluffy light down on the very top of her head, soft as cotton candy, curling around a tiny translucent seashell of an ear. I felt a smile work its way across my lips and bent over to kiss her forehead.

Loss is a thing that fades but is never forgotten. One person cannot fill the void left by the absence of another, not woman or child. But over time, the lacerated surface begins to mend itself. The barbed contours of hurt are blunted and start to slowly dissolve. The wounds on my heart healed over but the scars are still there, shining silvery white on the still beating tissue.

Holding my daughter in my arms I realized something. Through all the turmoil, all the shitty cards life has dealt me. I am a lucky man.

Outside the sun was rising on a new day, shell pink and pretty. Appropriate I think, given the circumstances. The first golden rays of light beam in through the high window, illumining her peaceful little face and for the first time in a long while, I am thankful I'm alive.

"What d'you want to call her?" I heard Marie say somewhere far off.

I gently lifted her up and laid a soft kiss on her tiny open mouth.

"Noah," I said, not taking my eyes off the little girl. My little girl.

Epilogue

MARIE
3 years later – Connecticut

Our daughter, Noah Amelia Hayes was born two thirty-two am March second, weighing only five pounds and two ounces. Luckily she was a fighter, just like her father.

It snowed twelve inches that night.

That was also the night Nicholas died.

Jack had filled me in. After I had blacked out, he came home and fought Nicholas off. He stabbed him deep in the stomach and let him drive away because he couldn't bring himself to kill his brother outright. Nic crashed his car when he passed out from either pain or blood loss.

I grieved for him in my own way, but ultimately I knew we were probably all better off without him. I *was* sorry for the way things turned out, hoped maybe one day we might have reconciled. I cried once, for the man I used to know, the first man I had fallen in love with, and the man who'd been controlled by his inability to resist temptation.

As fate would have it, we'd found out sometime later that the cabin we'd called home for nine months had burned down the same night, eliminating all evidence of our time there.

When I went back to the house in Cali, it felt like a museum I'd visited before. It was eerie; the empty husk of the place I'd once lived.

We inherited all of his money, sold everything, even the shares for the company and after I'd paid all of the shareholders back, there was just enough money left for us to buy a modest three-bedroom home in New England. I'm never going back to California, it brings too many memories. Besides I like the cold, it reminds me of Jack.

Standing at the sink, with the smell of maple pecan cookies baking in the air, I watch Jack in the garden with our daughter. They are in the grass with daisies littered all around them. Noah sits in Jacks's lap, chattering away, while he lovingly caresses her tawny curls.

Noah is lining up the tiny flowers in front of her, pink tongue poking from the corner of her mouth in concentration. Jack picked one to add to the line-up and Noah slapped his hand away lightly. Jack chuckles. Our little girl has a sweet but bossy nature, very clever and serious for her age. And she has her daddy wrapped around her pinky.

I smile as I watch Noah's chocolate-colored eyes widen in fascinated delight as some sort of small beetle lands on her wrist and starts to crawl up her arm.

"Look Daddy, a bug! What is it?" she yells, effectively scaring the creature away.

I laugh quietly to myself and look back down at the letter in my hands. It's a small brown envelope with long, scratchy cursive stating my name and address. I've had it for a week but I'm too anxious to open it. I know where, and whom, it's from but I wanted to read it alone before sharing.

Jack came inside, Noah hanging off the crook of his arm. Fatherhood had not changed Jack's appearance in the slightest. He was still hunky; bronzed and heavily muscled, thanks to his preference for manual labor and outdoor lifestyle. In the few years since we'd moved away, Jack had decided to become a carpenter, favoring to craft furniture from single pieces of natural wood. He ran the business from our backyard, despite my protests he didn't need to work anymore. That inexhaustible nature is ingrained in him, and I guess he'd be lost with it. Restless. Devoid of purpose.

He pauses to kiss me softly on the lips as he sweeps past the sink, swinging Noah up by the arms, her tinkling laughter filling the kitchen.

"Would Mademoiselle like to do some coloring?" Jack asks Noah as he lowers her onto a chair at the table. I quietly slide the envelope back into the drawer behind me.

"Yes!" she squeals in delight. Noah was very careful when it came to coloring. It took her hours and she always colored within the lines, much to my amazement. Jack picked up a crayon and began helping.

"No Daddy, like this!" she cries, showing him how it was done.

"Oh yeah, baby girl? You are doing a much better job than me."

"I know," She replies with a sassy flick of her eyes.

Jack glances up at me with an amused expression, eyebrow raised. We both know where she got that attitude from.

I didn't think Jack could love anything more than he loved Noah. He would have ten more children if he had it his way. She is his daughter even if she wasn't. We decided not to find out because it didn't matter.

I don't know if there will be any more babies, but that doesn't stop him trying at every opportunity he gets. Later on, once Noah has had a story and is asleep, Jack comes to lie on his side of our bed and lets out a contented sigh, staring at the ceiling with a slight grin on his face.

"What are you so happy about?" I ask, putting my book down on my stomach.

"Just thinking about the little rugrat... she's the best thing."

"She is pretty wonderful." I agree, rolling over to snuggle into Jack's side. He looks down at me, still with that little grin on his face. I push myself up so I can kiss him, "I have you to thank for that."

He smiles then, widely, with a hint of mischief in his eye, and rolls me onto my back, pinning me beneath him and settling a delicious amount of weight over me, "Let's have another one."

I shot him a half-quizzical, half-amused look. In return, he gives me a longing stare and pouts out his bottom lip, just like Noah does when she wants something.

"Oh no! No, *no*! Don't you look at me like that!" Jack doesn't reply, he just leans down and starts kissing my neck.

"Oh, *God!*" I moan and he ground against me through the bed sheets. He leans up to pull his t-shirt off and pry away the bedcovers that separate our bodies. He kisses down my neck, naked chest and belly, stopping at my cotton underwear. He licks the skin there where there's a long, white scar.

"This is my favorite part of you," He whispers against my belly.

I fight not to roll my eyes at this mushy display of affection, only because I knew it came from a place of deep love. Jack had become better at voicing his feelings to me, and for that I would be forever grateful.

I ran a hand through his hair, flighting down the impatience growing inside me with every passing second. Then I caught the wicked smile that curled one side of his lips. He *knew*. I huff in indignation and his low, dirty chuckle reverberated through me, igniting tendrils of desire burning low in my stomach.

He moves unhurriedly back up my body, pausing on seemingly obsolete areas, like my ribs and collarbone, while I wiggle, impatient. I was not in the mood to be kept waiting!

I began to push at him, I trying to roll him back over so I could get what I wanted, which I knew he would enjoy equally. He shook his head against me and continued taking his sweet-ass time. Something enigmatic flared to life in me then, dark and untamed.

"Either fuck me, or get off, Jack!" I snap.

Unaware if Jack knew, or if he was doing this purposely to draw this reaction, the intensity of my response seemed to surprise him. He recovered just as fast.

"Be more fun to get *you* off, kid!" He smirks but complies, reaching down to tug off my underwear. He lays back down to kiss me but I pull away, trying again to establish dominance. Only then did he begin to register the depth of my need for him.

His caresses became more urgent as I struggled against him, desperate for him to fit his body to mine in the way I knew he could give himself to me.

All of a sudden, he flips me over onto my stomach and settles heavily over me. My heart pounds in response, sending blood to my extremities, my body thrumming with adrenaline, readying itself for what was about to come.

Then I feel him pressing against me with determined vigor, rubbing over slick hypersensitive flesh.

"This whatcha want?" He rasps in my ear.

I can only whimper in reply.

He twists his hand into my hair so he can turn my face toward him. I arch into him, begging to be filled. His hand wound around my middle so his fingers could graze over my clit. The sound this elicits from me is almost inhuman, thick with urgent longing.

He fills me with a guttural cry, burying himself so deeply inside me I lost the ability to draw breath for a few seconds. Then he took up a steady, unyielding rhythm.

But it still wasn't enough to push me over the edge. I needed more.

"I *can't*...I ...need... *I*..." I pant breathlessly.

Jack shifts, and as his hand drew away I almost cry from the loss. The next second my hips are forced higher and he pushes back into me, snapping his hips to mine. At this more acute angle, the pressure is more intense, and with every thrust, I could feel myself reaching closer and *closer* until...

"*No*... I wanna see you!"

He flips me back over as easily as if I were a rag doll, and fell back into me with a groan so anguished it was like it pained him not to be inside me for those precious few seconds.

I jolt with each powerful stroke, my body quivering on the edge of agonizing release. And in turn, he is helpless to deny my demand, pushing, harder, deeper. Pain and bliss melding together in perfect ecstasy.

And then he said something that caught me completely off guard. In sharp contrast to his actions, his voice is quiet. Tender. Almost like he's afraid of the answer. He asks if I'd come for him. The words are husky, lost within the confines of his pleasure, but still clear, spoken into my throat. Imbued with so much raw emotion that my vision blurs over.

I wasn't sure if he needed to make me come out of some sort of masculine pride, or because he wanted me to give myself over to him. Or maybe being alone in such an exposed intimacy made him feel too vulnerable in that moment. Whatever it was, I'd gladly surrender everything to him.

He only lasts a few more strokes after me before his rhythm falters, and he spent himself in long, wet sustained pulses, eyes squeezed tightly shut as he shudders through his own violent release.

He's beautiful in his pleasure. I watch as he comes back to me in slow degrees of awareness, his wild green eyes refocusing on me, an expression I could only liken to shame present there.

"You okay, kid?" And the foolish man was wondering if *I* was okay, as if I hadn't experienced those beautiful few moments in the same paradise as he. I know he's overprotective, and what we'd done didn't come within the boundaries of gentle, not by a long shot. But it was still perfect. In fact, it was exactly what I needed.

I smiled at him before leaning up and capturing his lips in a tender kiss.

"More than okay."

He relaxes at that, letting his own smile appear, and leans back down for another kiss.

"And don't call me kid!" I add in a teasing voice.

———————————————

The next day I finally open the letter. I've been hunting down Jack's mother. From what he'd told me, she had left Jack in the care of his stepfather when he was just six years old.

It sounded to me like she had been deported and couldn't get back into the country. Jack's mom is half-Mexican but only had family in Mexico. She left Jack behind where she thought he would have a better life. She wasn't trying to be selfish; she did what she thought was best for her son. I've spent the last year looking for her. This letter would hold the answer.

"Dearest Marie,

I thank you most kindly for your letter. I cannot believe you have managed to get in contact. I would very much like to meet you and be reunited with my lost son. Please visit as soon as you can at this address.

Many kind wishes,

Josefina Rodriguez"

That word she used; lost. It made my heart ache to think of the pain she went through. I couldn't imagine having to leave my baby girl behind, even if it was what was best for her. Josefina was a strong woman.

There was a worn photograph enclosed, the corners folded and tatty. The grainy image showed a child with his mother's arms wrapped tight around him. He was grinning mischievously, a tooth missing in the top row. A grin that was purely Jack. There was a note scribbled on the back in the same handwriting as the letter. "Mi hermoso chico, 1983." My beautiful boy.

"Momma, why are you sad? Do you have a boo-boo?" Noah comes running from outside, stopping when she saw me. Her cheeks have that telltale flush she got from laughing.

"No baby, I'm just happy," I smile at her and hold out my arms. She comes over to sit in my lap.

"Then why are you crying?" She asks, touching her small hand to my cheek.

Jack came stalking into the house then, hunting for Noah like he was a tiger. They are obviously in the middle of a good game.

"Marie?" he asks, dropping his hands back to his sides. I hold the letter and photo out for him. He took them looking confused, and then his mouth falls open, fingers tracing the people in the photograph.

"She enclosed a phone number."

He looks up at me, still lost for words. Then he comes over to us, his girls, and wraps us in his arms.

His words come out in more than a whisper, rough and broken, but filled with unmistakable joy.

"*Thank you*," he sniffs into my hair.

———

JACK

Another few shingles and the roof would be repaired. A recent storm had blown some of the tiles loose, and once

I'd had a peak through I saw one of the beams had started to rot, I knew I had to do something about it quick.

I'd managed to repair it with little trouble, and only had to finish off nailing the slates in place now before the next downpour, which seemed imminent.

I didn't mind the work, in fact, I found it quite peaceful. Up on the roof, I could see the landscape for miles around. Burnished trees in all their autumn glory, red, orange and brown. Bronze and gold. One of the best parts about living in New England was the seasonal variations. Woodsmoke carried on the breeze, bringing with it cooler air and much-anticipated change.

I pick up another heavy sack of shingles to carry up the ladder when the droning of a new report came through the open window.

"According to the governing body, an internal investigation at Hayes Enterprises concluded that there "have been errors made in the past, but there are no issues with systematic fraud at Hayes Enterprises."

"Earlier this year, the SEC began an investigation after an externally based auditor dug up some unexplained numbers. All was not as it seemed though as the investigation uncovered questionable practices, among which are unethical accounting, where company earnings were underreported in order to increase share value."

"Additionally, the SEC discovered that over fifty million dollars of the company's turnover had been siphoned off during the last few years under the late CEO Nicholas Hayes's leadership, seemly with no trace. This has now been linked back to former CFO Chuck Blake, who is still evading the authorities."

So now we knew.

I stand in the shallows of the lake watching Jude show Noah how to kick warily. I'd reluctantly agreed for Marie to teach me how to swim, after being bullied into it by the whole family for weeks on end.

"It's cold!" I answer Marie's questioning glance.

She just arches one delicate eyebrow.

"You'll get used to it. Come on, if Noah can do it, you can too."

"Come on, Daddy!" Noah shouts from a few meters away, each kick splashing too much water to be effective.

I take another few steps into the freezing lake until it reaches just above my knees, "How long does it take to get used to it?" I grumble.

Marie rolls her eyes in an exaggerated way, and turned back to continue her conversation with Jude's mom, Elise. She seems pretty decent, and she's very grateful to Marie for taking care of Jude that summer a few years ago.

They'd come to visit for a few weeks over the summer while Jude was off school, and then stayed a bit longer, enjoying the milder climate. It seems they have no immediate plans to return. I also found an application form for a school in Vermont. Not that we'd mind in the slightest, it was nice having them around.

Jean also made a surprise appearance. He filled us in on some details. Like how Nic had accused him of sleeping with Marie pushed him down a flight of stairs. Now he had his spine fused in three places and enough metal pins in his body to avoid air travel for the rest of his life. It seemed Jean doesn't have any plans to move on either.

And Marie, she finally got to finish her education. As for what she wanted to do, her whole life is stretched before her, she has the time to decide.

After the trauma of everything; Nicolas' death and all the emotions that came with it, Marie sought out a counselor to help her deal with things. The woman suggested Marie keep a diary of everything that happened, as a homage to her previous life and as a way to let it go. Once she started, she found she couldn't stop. And what turned loosely into an autobiography, minus the intimate deals, was picked up by a major publisher. The book is due to hit the shelves by Christmas. I've never been prouder of my girl.

They say the grass is always greener on the other side. It's all a matter of perspective; an outsider looking in doesn't get the full scale of things.

If my goal was to seek absolution, then the only standards I had to judge myself on were my own. I had the power to forgive myself all along, I just needed some guidance along the way.

Marie was the only one I needed to help me get there. She told me that It wasn't what I had done, but what I do now that would matter. With her by my side, sitting beneath stars was as close to peace as I'd come in all the years I could remember.

So when they say the grass is greener, they haven't a clue what they are talking about. Because love is knowing that someone else is there for you. Love doesn't have to have words but it can be spoken for in great magnitudes. Love is everything you pour into your children; the only nourishment they need to grow.

Love isn't restricted by borders. It's acceptance. It's unconditional.

It's like coming home.

Gratitude

Thanks to all the friends and professionals who helped make this first book of mine a reality. Firstly my amazing beta readers; Sogol Abedin, Aishling Williamson, Lorraine Brown, Zoe Collins, and Tasha Windham.

Extra special thanks to Mike Z, a friend I have never actually met, nor knew his last name until recently. Mike, thank you for believing in me when no one else would, for reading my many (many!) revisions, putting up with my type-A-ness. For everything. Without you, this book wouldn't be what it is today. I am forever grateful.

Thanks to freelance editors Becky Sweeny and Tiffany Laflur, for helping me corral the story into place, and without whose support, this project would probably still be hiding under a literary rock.

Thanks to Matt Resta, for the beautiful cover design.

And thank you to my wonderful partner, Steve, who listened (however grudgingly) and supported me throughout the five long years it took to finally get it finished. You inspire me with your determination. I love you.

About the Author

Laura Brown is a writer from Hertfordshire, England, where she lives with her family. She likes all things chocolate and reading FanFiction on rainy Sunday afternoons.

*photographed by Joe Burgess